An Illusion of Thieves

AN
ILLUSION
of
THIEVES

Cate Glass

TOR

A TOM DOHERTY ASSOCIATES BOOK

NEW YORK

AN ILLUSION OF THIEVES

Copyright © 2019 by Carol Berg

All rights reserved.

Map by Rhys Davies

A Tor Book
Published by Tom Doherty Associates
175 Fifth Avenue
New York, NY 10010

www.tor-forge.com

Tor® is a registered trademark of Macmillan Publishing Group, LLC.

Library of Congress Cataloging-in-Publication Data

Names: Glass, Cate, author.
Title: An illusion of thieves / Cate Glass.
Description: First edition. | New York : Tor, 2019. | "A Tom Doherty Associates Book."
Identifiers: LCCN 2019006646| ISBN 9781250311009 (trade pbk.) | ISBN 9781250310996 (ebook)
Subjects: | GSAFD: Fantasy fiction.
Classification: LCC PS3607.L3645 I44 2019 | DDC 813/.6—dc23
LC record available at https://lccn.loc.gov/2019006646

Our books may be purchased in bulk for promotional, educational, or business use. Please contact your local bookseller or the Macmillan Corporate and Premium Sales Department at 1-800-221-7945, extension 5442, or by email at MacmillanSpecialMarkets@macmillan.com.

First Edition: May 2019

Printed in the United States of America

0 9 8 7 6 5 4 3 2 1

For Irl Bradford Glass Neilon (1918–2017),
who gave me the gifts of books and words.

For Laura Besze Ramirez (1966–2018),
a bright spirit who reminds me every day of joy.

to Eide

To Empyria, Lhampur, and Paolin

Invidia

Argento

Il Corsia

Kairys

Riccia-by-the-sea

Cantagna

Mare di Ossa

Cuarona

Tibernia

Varela

Hylides

Mercediare

Mare di Lacrime

Isles of Lesh

Rhys Davies

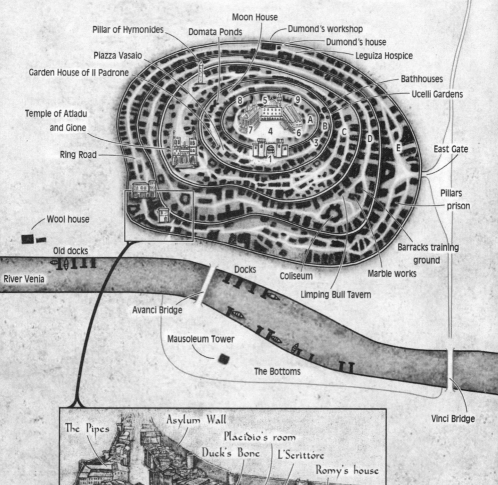

City of CANTAGNA

A. The Heights
B. Merchant Ring
C. Market Ring
D. Asylum Ring
E. Beggars Ring

1. Cambio Gate
2. Piazza Cambio
3. Via Mortua
4. Piazza Livello and
   Statue of Atladu's Leviathan

5. Palazzo Segnori
6. Gallanos bank
7. Philosophic Academie
8. Palazzo Fermi
9. Palazzo Ignazio

Moon House
Pillar of Hymonides
Domata Ponds
Dumond's workshop
Dumond's house
Leguiza Hospice
Piazza Vasaio
Garden House of Il Padrone
Bathhouses
Ucelli Gardens
Temple of Atladu and Gione
Ring Road
East Gate
Pillars prison
Wool house
Old docks
River Venia
Barracks training ground
Docks
Coliseum
Marble works
Limping Bull Tavern
Avanci Bridge
Mausoleum Tower
The Bottoms
Vinci Bridge

The Pipes
Asylum Wall
Placidio's room
Duck's Bone
L'Scrittóre
Romy's house
Ring Road
Outer Wall
South Gate
Lisard's Alley

Rhys Davies

An Illusion of Thieves

CHIMERA:

1. a mythical creature, a fire-breathing female with face,
body, and limbs of three different beasts

2. something that exists only in the imagination and is not
possible in reality

I have never believed in fate or destiny or any other concept that invests the courses of our lives with portentous meaning. Most people in our godless world believe we are born into random circumstance, and it is solely our own deeds and choices that determine whether we find ourselves in a palace or prison when we die. I'd not disagree.

Yet we of the Costa Drago still swear by Lady Virtue and Lady Fortune—the two abandoned children of our lost divinities—as if their hands are equal, and we behave ourselves and beg them for gifts that never seem to arrive in the guise we wish. Indeed, the peculiar events that gave me both the preparation and the opportunity to alter the streams of human history, while glimpsing truths of a world beyond my imagining, could not have been better chosen had they been mapped out at the beginning of the world—before the fear of magic condemned a portion of the world's population to extermination.

The particular random circumstances of my birth and up-bringing arrived at this life-altering confluence on a day that began in settled happiness and common intrigue . . .

I

The Shadow Lord's face gleamed bronze in the lamplight, serene in his strength. Such demeanor befit a man whose quiet word could fulfill a petitioner's deepest wishes or leave his gutted carcass hanging on Cantagna's gates.

We have no kings in the lands of the Costa Drago. Our nine great independencies are ruled by men or women whose power stems from family wealth, strength of arms, or brutish arousal of the rabble. Not one of those men or women could match the ruthless wisdom of Alessandro di Gallanos, known as *il Padroné*—the Master—Cantagna's Shadow Lord.

Peering through slits in the painted screen, I observed the Shadow Lord's first petitioner of the day. Boscetti, the antiquities merchant, leaned earnestly across the table between them.

"*Padroné*," he said, "my son has taken over my trading partnership with Argento, as you in your wisdom suggested. But bandits have looted his caravans three times in a month because

Captain di Lucci's condottieri refuse to honor their contract with me. If you could just speak to di Lucci . . ."

As the merchant wisely ignored the cup of good wine on the table and answered a few incisive questions from the man seated across from him, I watched and listened carefully, as always. I relished my privilege to sit hidden behind the painted screen, laughing at the fools folk could make of themselves when confronting true power, while at the same time adding the minutiae of names, family connections, desires, loyalties, and vanities to my treasury of such matters. The man others addressed as *il Padroné* and I called Sandro took pleasure in discussing the complexities of his world with a companion who could comprehend them. Even better, so he'd told me, that I could offer observations and ideas of my own.

My education had been extensive—history, music, languages. Dancing and logic. Enough blade-work to defend my owner or myself. Even now, I pursued art and philosophy, the divine study. Sandro called me his chimera—the impossible made flesh—a fantastical creature who mirrored every part of his own soul.

The two voices beyond the screen changed tenor. The conversation had become negotiation. The merchant desired *il Padroné* to force the mercenary captain, di Lucci, to honor their old contract, since the new owner of his trade route was a member of the merchant's own family.

Boscetti was a fool. Sandro was too wise to squeeze condottieri for a merchant's favor. Besides the ever-present threat from old enemies like the southern independency of Mercediare, a stirring discontent among Cantagna's older families had him worried. These families had been staunch allies of Sandro's father and grandfather. But their resentment of House Gallanos's stranglehold on power, most especially Sandro's determination to spend the city's wealth on public works instead of channeling it into their own purses, lurked amid the present peace like deadly nightshade in a garden.

One incident, one misstep, and the poison could foment an armed rebellion. Civil war. Sandro would need Captain di Lucci and every other soldier he could hire. It was no false concern that induced Sandro to keep ten armed men about him wherever he walked—even through the modest neighborhood where his family had lived and granted favor and assistance to all comers for almost a century.

"What of the commission you undertook for me, Boscetti?" Sandro deftly changed the subject of the conversation without agreeing to anything. "Have you had any success with that?"

"Ah, *Padroné*, my agents believe they might have found the artwork you seek—the Antigonean bronze—buried deep in a vault in Mercediare. Extremely difficult to retrieve. Dangerous. Expensive. The rumors of its Sysaline origins and the bad luck that brings. I doubt I have sufficient resources to retrieve it. Such an unusual portrayal of Dragonis and Atladu, unique in all the known world. Perhaps something more accessible would suit your pleasure just as well?"

"My requirement has not changed."

Only one who could read the subtle silence between *il Padroné's* clipped words would recognize his mounting fury. Boscetti, a purveyor of antiquities, was trying to manipulate a man who hated to be played.

I sat up straighter. This was a matter of much more interest. For five years *il Padroné* had searched for a particular ancient representation of the monster Dragonis and Atladu, lost God of

Sea and Sky. Supposedly Antigoneas, divine Atladu's own smith, had cast the small bronze statue at his forge in Sysaline— the city drowned in the Creation Wars—imbuing it with sanctity unknown in our godless world.

Sandro believed that if he could gift the statue to his most powerful ally, a most pious grand duc, it would create a true friendship, fixing their alliance against any challenge from his friends turned rivals. But this particular merchant . . . Boscetti . . .

I didn't know Sandro had commissioned *Boscetti* to find the statue. Had he heard the gossip that Boscetti's wife hailed from Triesa, one of Mercediare's two hundred tribute islands?

The brutish Protector Vizio, tyrant ruler of the sprawling independency of Mercediare, coveted Cantagna's wealth. Every spring she demanded a share of it, and threatened to seize it by force if Cantagna failed to pay. Someday her legions would march north to challenge us. Thus, Boscetti's petition, together with his suspect wife, could signify a great deal more than a contract dispute with Lucci's mercenaries. The Costa Drago bred conspiracies in the same abundance as it did mosquitoes.

"Expense is of no consequence," said *il Padroné*. "I shall instruct my bursar to record an increase in your finder's fee. I'm sure double would be acceptable. Once I have the artifact in hand, you will reap additional rewards."

The easy capitulation surprised me. Had Sandro some new intelligence to make his purpose more urgent or was he testing Boscetti? I couldn't wait for evening when he would tell me all and I could warn him about the merchant's possible entanglement with Cantagna's old enemy.

A wafting scent of soap drew my attention from the parlay beyond the screen.

Stupid girl! My gangly maidservant Micola had crept into my hiding place. Round cheeks of burnished copper, dark eyes glazed with terror, she did not so much as breathe as she tugged on my sleeve, drawing me to the open door behind me.

Well should she be terrified! If *il Padroné* detected the least noise behind the screen, he might forbid me sit there when he received petitioners. Micola knew I'd never forgive her for such a deprivation. Far worse would result if the *merchant* detected us. Micola would be whipped to death as a spy, and I would be exiled at best, for *il Padroné* and the Shadow Lord were one and the same, and discretion was a pillar of the Shadow Lord's power.

We slipped out on bare feet, my silken gown but a whisper, Micola's hand clutching her skirt to keep it silent. As soon as we passed through the closet passage and my dressing room into my own rooms, I closed the door carefully behind me and then whirled on her. "Are you entirely mad?"

She fell to her knees, breathless and shaking. "Please, mistress, the villain said you'd die did I fail to deliver his message to you right away. Certain, I'd only dare set foot beyond that door for mortal need."

"What villain?"

"A young ruffian startled me whilst I tended your sheets, and how he got past the guards 'tis the world's own mystery. The youth swore he knew you from childhood, and I'd never have believed that, ragged as he were. But he showed me a luck charm exactly like one in your jewel case—that'n graved in bronze with the squiggles and coiled whip—and said tell you 'twas *Iren* brought you the message."

The world's own mystery . . . Surely my own eyes glazed with fear. "What message?"

"He said—please, mistress, I'd never speak such crude words to you, but for the luck charm so like yours, and you're ever so kind to me."

It required every scrap of control I could muster not to choke the words out of her. *Iren* could be none but my brother Neri. We had once believed backward spelling our impregnable secret cipher.

"He said, 'The rutting tyrant is for the chop,' which means a terrible, wicked cruelty, and I told him that no fine lady as you . . . none so educated, so elegant and beautiful . . . would even know about lowborn punishments. But he claimed you'd know exactly what he meant. I was dread fearful he were an assassin, as some folk use *tyrant* to name—"

She paled, knowing how close she was to treason.

But her panic could not touch mine. As if the brilliant colors of the muraled wall had sloughed away, leaving only gray plaster, so did the false and foolish illusion of my life vanish. Left in its place was appalled confusion.

Only Neri ever called our father a *rutting tyrant*. Only Neri could walk through impossible barriers by use of true magic, forbidden since the dawn of the world. Yet his message wasn't about unmentionable skills that could get both of us executed, but the horrifically mundane. *For the chop.* My father was to lose a hand for thieving? *That* was impossible.

I halted the girl's terrified babbling. "Did he say when?"

She gaped at me, disbelieving.

"Tell me, Micola."

"Dawn tomorrow."

My father was dull and stiff-necked beyond reason. He was a law scribe, and every word he copied in service of Cantagna's law was his life's accumulated treasure. Never in the world would he risk losing a hand. Indeed, the self-righteous fool would let his family starve before breaking his precious moral code. Multiple times he'd refused to accept so much as a copper solet from his eldest daughter, the Shadow Lord's whore. Such an impossible risk—and my fool of a brother's message—hinted at dangers I dared not ignore.

"Give me your gown and cloak," I said. "Now. I have to go out." Fortunately the rangy Micola and I were of a size.

She squirmed out of her garments. "But, mistress, *il Padroné*—"

"He will be at least another hour with petitioners. More likely two. Do as I tell you."

In moments she was left in her chemise, while I wore her old-fashioned blue overdress and narrow black sleeves.

I laid hands on her quivering shoulders. "If *il Padroné* sends for me or comes to my chambers in search of me, you *must* speak only truth. That way, his annoyance will be for me alone."

"But mistress . . ."

Even fools and children knew that the wrath of powerful men fell on those who spoke truth as well as those who told lies. But there were certain things she must not speak at all.

"Sweet child, just tell him this . . ."

With strength swollen by fury—at Neri, at my father, at necessity and circumstance and the vile Lady Fortune—I backhanded the girl. She stumbled backward and slumped to the thick Lhampuri rugs *il Padroné* had imported for me. As she moaned, groggy and confused, I brushed a thumb across her forehead. Naught but dread necessity could force me to what I had to do.

With a skill rusty from disuse, my will touched the blighted piece of my soul I had walled away since childhood. Only a moment's touch. Cold, viscous otherness squirmed like maggots in my bones and slithered through my veins, chilling, nauseating, as it had been since the first hour I understood the evil I could do. Magic—this single form of magic my body knew—allowed me to do one impossible thing.

I considered the words the girl must not say and whispered her a story to replace them: *Mistress Cataline received a message that her father is gravely ill; for honor's sake, she had to go to him. I, Micola, delayed a whole day relaying the message.*

The girl would forget the truth and remember only what I'd told her. How despicable to alter a person's mind without consent. I hated living with the ever-present fear of discovery, but even more I hated the taint itself, lurking inside my soul like rot at the heart of a tree, waiting to corrupt me as it did all of my kind. But the consequences of Neri's actions could endanger more lives than my father's.

Shivering and sick, I fled through the palace, grieving for the bruises I'd left on sweet Micola's face, as well as the chaotic knot inside her where a few simple words had replaced a name, a face, and a message. I'd no time and no skill to tie off every thread of memory.

· · ·

Cantagna sprawls across the golden hills of the Costa Drago's heart in a pleasing pattern of concentric rings. Radial boulevards lead from the airy, sunlit Heights, where the oldest families of the city live alongside the Palazzo Segnori and the Philosophic Academie, through a wall to the Merchant Ring, home to merchants, bankers, guildhalls, elegant bathhouses, and the rambling family home of *il Padroné* and his uncles, cousins, and friends.

Narrower streets feed through gates in the second wall down to the bustling Market Ring, where cobblers, tailors; glovers, spice merchants, and the like sell their wares, before plunging downward again to the Asylum Ring that comprises artisan workshops, cheap lodgings, and respectable brothels, intermingled with hospices, houses of confinement, and the seedy shops of alchemists, fortune-tellers, and charm-sellers. Squeezed between the fourth wall, the River Venia, and the outer defenses is the crowded, noisome Beggars Ring and Lizard's Alley, my childhood home.

Shoving a path through the smoke-filled streets in the sweltering afternoon felt like plunging into the Great Abyss, where the *demoni Discordia* awaited the unvirtuous. The Beggars Ring housed thieves, laborers, pigs, thugs, beggars, pimps, whores, and damaged people of all kinds. Included was one stiff-necked man who refused any work that failed to meet his exacting standards, produced more healthy children than his labors could support, and protected a secret it was death to expose—that two of his living children bore the taint of magic. My father.

I had never decided whether Da truly cared for Neri and me, or whether he was just too weak-livered to do as every other parent in the Beggars Ring would have done upon discovering their child was cursed—drown us in the nearest body of water. The weak-livered theory had been ascendant for many years.

At the only wide spot in Lizard's Alley someone in decades past had built a dirt-floored stone hovel, probably to shelter their pigs or a mule. I'd spent most of my ten years of childhood there.

I flipped aside the tattered rug hung across the doorway, stepped across the iron sleugh—a trough of oily water that supposedly warded the household against demons—and yelled, "Neri! Dolce!"

The dim interior was no less filthy than the alley or the streets beyond it, but the thick walls shut out the noise and most of the light. Neither Neri nor my sister Dolce were in evidence. Rather, the scene was exactly the same I'd witnessed on my last visit, some three years past. A crone sat on a stack of folded blankets in the corner, her sagging breast suckling a ruddy babe. The infant would be my mother's tenth child yet living, as far as I knew, out of thirteen live born. She was not yet forty. At four-and-twenty, I was her eldest.

I crouched in front of her. "Hey, Mam. Neri sent a message about Da."

Dark eyes, sharp and hateful, rose to meet mine. Nostrils flared, mouth twisted into ugliness, she averted her gaze as her thumb traced a demon ward on the babe's forehead.

"Romy the harlot."

My mother's disgust no longer devastated me. She had loathed me since discovering I was born tainted with magic. When I was ten years old and my brothers and sisters were crying for bread, Mam had rented me for a night to a man in the street. The following morning my *suitor* returned with a bag of coins and told her I was never coming home. He was a procurer for the Moon House, where anonymous, unblemished girls and boys were transformed into courtesans to serve the old *Padroné*—Sandro's uncle—and his wealthy friends.

The procurer had told me Mam laughed and kissed the silver, so he passed along her word that I was a troublemaker who would need strict discipline. She hadn't mentioned my true evil.

Three years later, when I dared risk a beating to visit my family, I told my parents what they made me do at the Moon House. Da had averted his eyes and staggered out to the alley to be sick. Mam had spat on me.

I'd never understood what she'd thought would happen—that men would simply pat me on my pretty head or gaze at my naked body without touching? Or that I would kill myself rather than yield my virtue, while allowing her to keep enough silver to feed the rest of her brood for a year?

"Mam, talk to me. What's happened? Where's Da? Where's Neri?"

But my mother said nothing beyond that initial expectoration of my birth name, abandoned when I became Cataline of the Moon House. Exasperated, I sat back on my heels.

"Fortune's dam! You came!" A tall, bony girl had shoved the hanging rug aside. Rough, rouged cheeks confused her age, which should be something like fourteen.

"Dolce?"

Three grimy faces, all girls with black curls and great dark eyes, peered around my sister's skirts. Outside this room, naught could have told me they were my kin.

"Neri's hid, soiling his netherstocks," said Dolce. "Da's in the Pillars, awaiting the axe. Can your devil lord fix that?"

"*Never* call him that," I said, reflexively. The wrong partisan, hearing the insult to *il Padroné*, would cut her throat. "What's Da accused of?"

She folded her arms across her greasy tunic. "He were writing for a lawyer called Dontello up the Market Ring. Dontello shares chambers with a 'luminator, and Da made the mistake of admiring the book the woman was inking—one that had three rubies set in its cover. By next morning the rubies were dug out of the leather and vanished, no matter the chamber was locked up tight as a pimp's purse. Either Da took them or a thief *walked through the wall.* Constable was going to bring in a sniffer till Da confessed to the snatch."

Liquid fury scorched my veins. Dolce's spare account made the awful situation very clear.

"Da told *Neri* about the book," I snapped. Neri, whose magic could take him anywhere his imagination had an object to latch onto. Neri, fool enough to believe he could steal rubies from a locked room without someone bringing in a sniffer to determine if magic had been used in the crime. And what was Neri's idea of saving my father, who had evidently chosen to sacrifice his hand . . . his livelihood, his life . . . to protect him? Fetch his despised and disowned sister Romy, *il Padroné's* harlot, and lay the impossible, intractable dilemma in her lap.

Ready to tear my hair from its roots, I yelled at Dolce and Mam, at Da and stupid, stupid Neri, wherever he was. "Idiots! All of you! You should be out of the city by now."

"Wherever would we go?" said Dolce. "On the road we've got nothing, lest I or Sofi here go hoorin like you, which Da forbids. Cino and Neri's been up to the Asylum Ring digging for the new coliseum now and again. But, of course, if Da gets chopped, we'll lose their coin, too, as the devil—excuse me, *Il Padroné* the Generous—made it clear he mislikes his citizens thieving, so no city project will hire a thief or those kin to one. Yet Da don't dare plead he's innocent, now does he?"

Dolce smirked, as if she thought a situation that could leave us all wrapped in chains at the bottom of the sea was naught but a players' comedy.

"Did Neri admit using"—I didn't know if the younger ones understood Neri's forbidden talents as yet—"his *particular* skills? There's no doubt?"

"Told you he was shitting his nethers, din't I? Think he would have come begging to you elsewise? The 'luminator had only fetched the book that very day. Not another soul but Da even knew she had it."

Magic was demonfire, so it was said, remnants of the gloriously beautiful monster Dragonis who had fractured our land at the dawn of the world. The monster had ravished both men and women, implanting its evil in them and their children. Supposedly the Unseeable Gods had battled Dragonis for a thousand years, until at last they imprisoned the monster under the earth. But the fight had depleted them so terribly that they vanished into the Night Eternal, leaving only the twin sisters Virtue and Fortune to see to the world of their creation. Sorcerers— anyone born with a talent for magic—were the monster's descendants. No tribe, kingdom, clan, or city in the Costa Drago had ever permitted sorcerers to live, lest they raise their monstrous ancestor to terrorize a world with no gods left to defend it.

I wasn't sure what I believed about the gods. And I didn't know if it was an imprisoned monster who made the earth shake, leveling cities, or caused our mountains to spew fire and ash, swallowing whole provinces or changing the course of rivers. Certain there was some truth buried in the stories. No land but ours birthed sorcerers. No one could say how many of us were left in the world, but I'd learned early that anyone proved to be a sorcerer or a sorcerer's kin must die.

"Where are the rubies?" A glance about the hovel's pitiful furnishing of chests, stools, and heaped rags gave no hint.

Dolce snorted. "Good and he didn't hide 'em here! Constables rousted the house when they came for Da. But the goods was already dumped in the river, so Neri says. Weighed with a rock."

Spirits, was she stretched out on mysenthe to snigger at such peril?

No one had ever explained to me why magic infected some of a sorcerer's kin, but not all. Certainly Dolce demonstrated none, nor did Cino. Nor did either of my parents. But nullifiers— those who owned and ran the sniffers—took no chances. Let Da lose his hand and his family would likely starve. Let a sniffer identify Neri as a sorcerer, and his family was certainly dead.

I was not exempt. The Moon House kept no records of their courtesans' family origins. But someone around here would re- member me. A neighbor. A cousin. Some friend of Neri's, Dolce's, or Cino's, or a comrade of my three brothers who had died in a riot years ago. Someone would have heard a whisper that the law scribe's eldest girl—what was her name?—had been bought by the Moon House, had been washed, educated, and trained to please men or women of wealth in both seemly and unseemly ways. Eventually they would connect Romy of the Beggars Ring to Cataline, courtesan of the Moon House, the Shadow Lord's mistress. So I would die, too, and forever taint Sandro with my corruption . . .

"I'll speak to *il Padroné*," I said, smothering the ache in my breast. Only he could stop this.

2

I was back in *il Padroné's* residence by the Hour of Contemplation. Sandro had shown me his secret ways in and out, tunnels and passages that allowed him to walk amongst the people
in disguise to hear what they would not say when he walked
amongst them as himself. He took a measure of pride that he
heard little to contradict the image he had chosen for himself:
an intelligent, generous, fair-minded, and very dangerous
man, who would hear a poor widow's petition as equably as a
wealthy merchant's, even as he shaped every aspect of Cantagnan life. For our city's greatness, he said, and for his family's
honor.

I crept into my chambers to ensure that none but Micola
waited there. The girl sat on the velvet stool at the foot of my bed,
wearing a clean dress and apron, the match for the filthy ones
I wore. "Sssst!"

She spun around, and I winced to see her poor bruised face
brighten. "Mistress! Where—?"

"I need a sponge bath as quick as can be," I whispered. "And my brush. The dark green gown, I think. It's a favorite." And modest. I would not have Sandro think I offered some tawdry bargain for the favor I must beg. Everything of me was already his.

My well-trained Micola did not question. She always had hot water at the ready, so it took but a short time to clean the stink and grime of the Beggars Ring away. As she finished perfuming my hair, I took her hand and drew her around in front of me. She sank to her knees, to keep her head below mine, though I had no rank to demand such. Her gaze fixed to my slippers.

"Well done, as always." I brushed her soft curls away from her swollen cheek.

She flinched when I touched the purpling flesh.

"Forgive my fit of temper, sweet one. You did right to fetch me. My father is very ill and I needs must speak to *il Padroné* about the matter. But I want to make sure you are all right. And to ask your pardon."

Micola's head popped up, her expression—her whole posture— opening like shutters in spring. "I—I was in a muddle about it, shamed I had passed you the news about your father's sickness so late, but I couldn't recall why I would delay a whole day. It was so strange." Her bruised brow wrinkled. "Whyever would I choose to fetch you from the secret closet? You always warned me not to. When Gigo came to fetch you, I was so confused."

Fear clogged my throat. "I'm so sorry."

Most tales of magic spoke of horrors, like houses ablaze, limbs rotting away, or infestations of rats or spiders or demons. At best, my magic created confusion. But at worst, it could surely break my victim's mind.

"I was sent for while I was gone?"

"Aye, mistress."

I breathed away panic. Sandro had not dispatched searchers, else I would have been intercepted in his secret tunnels. He trusted me, and indeed I had never lied to him. But there were certain questions he had never asked. And now . . . Whatever happened, nothing could ever be the same.

"What did you tell Gigo?"

Her fair complexion bloomed rose, and she giggled. "I blubbered. A fit you might call it. Told him I had displeased you and didn't know where you'd gone—which was true. You told me to speak only truth."

"Yes, good. And what did he say?" Sandro's bodyguard was no fool.

"Naught. He examined . . . this." Her shoulder lifted toward her swollen cheek. "Never came back."

"All right then. Well done." Detestable as were the blow and my theft of her mind's truth, the lie had likely saved her life as well as mine.

As Micola straightened up the clutter from my toilet, I wandered over to the garden doors. This hour was a part of *il Padroné*'s day that did not belong to me. He would be drinking a tisane or milked coffee with his wife as he did every evening before retiring.

Marriage, for Cantagnans of position and wealth, was a negotiation of business, family, and politics. Sandro's negotiations had allied him with a silver merchant's daughter—a fourteen-year-old budding rose with the mind of a walnut. He had not bedded her, nor did he intend to do so until she was of decent age. But he treated her with all courtesy and respect, and held hopes that their life together would be satisfactory for both. My path and hers did not cross.

How best to proceed? Likely he already knew I'd returned. And he would be curious; I never struck the servants.

All my habits of fear and secrecy, so ingrained these nine years that I never had to think about them, were jarred into terrible life. If I did nothing, he might decide I wished to be alone and not send for me until morning. Worse, he might believe I didn't want him to know what caused my unusual behavior. He might come to think I had secrets, a danger I meticulously avoided. Yet I needed to see him. My father had only hours until he was mutilated—or dead from the shock of the axe.

The problem was that I could not approach the Shadow Lord on my own. To the world I did not exist as a person. I was a rare and beautiful object in his house, like the illuminated codex of Endogian poetry chained to a stand in his library, or the ancient marble statue of the lost god Atladu that graced his foyer, so gloriously lifelike it was believed to be a relic of the vanished sea kingdom of Sysaline. I could no more choose to spend an hour with *il Padroné* than his silver spoons could choose to feed him supper. Thus, I ever awaited his attention as did they. Though Sandro viewed me very differently, he knew that accepting the world's expectations helped keep me safe from his myriad enemies.

Once, on a cool moonlit evening after feasting with the twelve oldest families in Cantagna, we had strolled the gravel paths of my private garden, talking of one guest and then another, of which might prove an ally when the unrest among them showed its true face, and which a betrayer. I remarked that it must be difficult to anticipate betrayal from lifetime friends.

"It is as it has always been," he said. "From boyhood, I've had to assume that every person at my table, friend or stranger, carries a knife ready to let my blood or wears a pocket ring primed to drop poison into my wine. It is a not-so-nice consequence of Lady Fortune's abundant blessings. Certain, the habit has saved my life more than once."

He had stopped abruptly and spun me around to face him. "Then you came into my world and opened your heart to one you had every reason to despise. In these few years you have gifted me in ways no other ever has. Tonight's gathering reminded me that I've wanted to bring you some small token in kind."

From his cloak he pulled a small bundle, two gifts wrapped in silk and tied together with a gold ribbon. One was a slim gold ring set with emeralds that hid a tiny poison pocket. The other was the very same pearl-handled dagger my tutors had presented me on my departure from the Moon House—and Sandro's bodyguards had taken from me upon my arrival at House Gallanos.

"To keep you in the height of fashion," he said, teasing, as he strapped the soft leather sheath to my thigh. A thrill chased up my spine. "But truly, so my ferocious chimera can protect me."

The gifts left me speechless, overwhelmed by the enormity of their meaning. For those weapons had nothing at all to do with fighting off assassins, but everything to do with trust.

Now, on this terrible day, I had to challenge that trust.

"Micola," I said, drawing her from her tasks. "Go to Gigo. Tell him I inquired how his new mare is working out. Mention that I've just returned to the house and bathed." That should be enough to let *il Padroné* know I wished to see him.

Micola dipped her knee and hurried for the door.

*   *   *

Not an hour later, the dressing room door swung open.

I did not raise my eyes or rise from First Pose, a posture of graceful, dignified submission, the first a future courtesan was taught. You sat on one heel, the other leg forward, slightly bent, toes pointed, gown or draperies arranged to best advantage. *Spread the arms*, they'd told us, *cup the hands, lower the eyes. Always present yourself as beautiful, open, available, ready.* From First Pose, I could rise in one flowing movement, slip smoothly into complete obeisance, or remain still for hours. Nine years had gone since I'd last used it.

He smelled of coffee and wine, of clean skin and pine bark. The air embraced his approach—or so I always imagined. I had spent so many hours observing every muscle and sinew beneath that bronze skin that I knew how every part of him interacted with his surroundings, like an eternal dance with sun or starlight, moon or fire, whether in the company of strangers or between the two of us alone.

The knot of apprehension beneath my breastbone grew into a mortal ache as his long finger lifted my chin with the tenderness that had replaced the ugly linkage of master and bound servant with ties of the heart.

"Ah, my glorious chimera, what troubles you?"

I dared not look at him, lest I crumble. From the night I was led into his presence expecting horror, and he had, instead, offered me protection, education, and the power of consent, I had promised myself never to ask him for anything.

Eyes closed, I began as did every petitioner who came to this house. "*Padroné*, with honor and humility I lay my needs before you, trusting your wisdom to show me a path forward, pledging you my gratitude and loyalty in whatever service I might provide for you in turn."

Silent, he moved away, and I feared I might already be undone. He had spies everywhere.

But he had simply fetched a chair, and now sat it square in front of me and himself in it. I looked on his fine boots and longed to remove them as prelude to an evening of conversation, laughter, wine, and pleasure. Instead, I shifted my cupped hands to my lap, still open to receive whatever he might grant. A courtesan's discipline matched that of any soldier.

"Tell me your need, Mistress Cataline." Sober, unruffled, as ever with his petitioners. Nothing left of the caring lover, only the concerned *Padroné*.

"My father is a law scribe, a man of reverence for Lady Virtue and respect for his useful work. A man Lady Fortune has blessed with an overabundance of hungry children."

Sandro had never asked about the people who had sold me to the Moon House or anything of my life before I was taken there. Neither did I speak to him about his dead uncle, the old *Padroné*, who was known to blind and flay anyone who crossed him, but only after he had raped their sons and daughters, making that horror the last thing they looked on before their torment. Not even those who most resented Sandro's outsized influence over Cantagnan life would deny that many, many things had changed for the better since he had become the House Gallanos segnoré.

I told Sandro of the ruby-studded book and the locked room and of the constable's conclusion that none but my father could have stolen the gems. "On my life, he could not have done the crime, *Padroné,* not even to feed his children. It was my mother, not he, who sold me."

Child-selling had not been a crime, of course. Not then. Sandro had made it so because of what was done to me.

"My father's work, helping to implement the law to keep this city prosperous, strong, and noble, is his life's honor. To lose his hand would kill his soul, and his family would starve . . ."

When my telling was done, I begged Lady Fortune keep Sandro silent. He knew me. Trusted me. Loved me, so he said and I believed. He would know this pleading was as hard a thing as I had done since the night I was brought to him from the Moon House—a gift from his degenerate uncle—and I asked him please not to peel off my skin once he had taken his plea- sure with me. He had not forced me that night or ever. So let him gift me this without questioning. Did I attempt a lie, he would surely know. Omissions—like the matter of my father's *confession* to this crime—were not lies. And the truth . . .

"Did they find the rubies in your father's possession or in his house?"

My heart died a little. "No, *Padroné.*"

A long silence. Then, "Did they discover evidence that he had paid his debts or did they question others who might have done the crime?"

"No and no." I had watched him trip up petitioners who answered one query of a pair and not the other, believing it a way to avoid a lie.

Another silence. I held still.

"Did they bring in a sniffer to seek evidence of perverse practices?"

My eyes remained fixed to his boots. The butter-soft leather was lovely. The feet within were fine, as well. Those elegant bones . . . "No, *Padroné*."

I near shed my skin when his hand touched my face, gentle first and then firm, forcing my head up.

"By Reason's bright center," he said, quietly insistent, eyes dark and unyielding as smoked steel, "why did you strike Micola?"

And that significant question I could not answer fully without condemning myself and Neri, and every person who shared our blood. So I closed my eyes and shut him out. "I was afraid. More than that I cannot say, *Padroné*. Forgive me, I cannot say."

He took his hand away and retreated toward my dressing room. His withdrawal left me cold and shivering. From the distant stillness, he said, "Remain here, Mistress Cataline. In one hour I shall return and render judgment."

Years had gone since I'd experienced such an hour. I dared not think, which meant I had to move. But everything in my chamber, from the porcelain cups that waited on the low table beside an atlas of the world, to my bed pillows, to the terrace overlooking a flower garden, spoke only of the Shadow Lord. Since that first night, he had given me everything I could ever want and more. And in return, I was begging him to ignore the First Law of Creation, infused into every man and woman in the Costa Drago from the first drop of mother's milk, and sworn to at one's coming of age, included in wedding vows and contracts and every public celebration: sorcery is the certain taint of Dragonis and must be obliterated.

After the small eternity, the dressing room door opened again, and I sank to one knee. He did not raise me up. Did not touch me at all. My bones hardened to ice.

"This is the judgment of *il Padroné.*" His voice was empty. No anger. No accusation. No anguish. "Your father has confessed to the crime. That cannot be undone. He will lose his hand at dawn. Because he cannot return the gems to their rightful owner, he must also forfeit his house and his possessions with the exception of one blanket for every member of his household, two pots, ten spoons, and two flasks. At the moment he is released, he will take his wife and eight youngest children and leave Cantagna, never to return."

"You cannot—"

"Do *not* presume to tell me what I can and cannot do." Hard-edged now. "You do *not* wish me to reopen this investigation, mistress. I am no fool. I have had your brother under observation for several years. He is rash and stupid, and my man has saved him more than once from the consequences of certain unexplainable actions."

Neri under observation . . . Lords of Night!

He walked away for the moment, leashing the temper he worked so hard to control. The air shifted when he turned back to me.

"Your concern for the family who did you such ill does you credit, but I cannot and will not allow this incident to pass. Everything I have accomplished in this city, everything I have yet to accomplish, takes its root in the rule of law. If I am complicit in lawbreaking—if I interfere and exonerate a *confessed* felon because of my personal preferences—then I am no better than my uncle you once named monster. Have you not preached to me how the victim of a crime deserves justice, too? So if I say, 'This man did not steal because a voice I trust says it,' then I must permit and encourage *every* avenue of investigation, including magic-sniffers. Do you wish me to do that?"

I could not answer. Nor breathe through rushing fear. His hard, hot gaze speared me to the marrow.

On the floor in front of me, he dropped two canvas bags, one the size of my fist, one the size of my two fists together.

"You will take these and do exactly as I say. Speak of them to no one. The smaller purse goes to your father, to feed his brood until he can heal and find work, but solely on the condition that he, your mother, and the eight youngest children leave Cantagna as I've said. My condottieri will publicly expel them from the city gates, and if they so much as look back, I will reclaim the purse and take his alter hand."

His arrogance that usually so pleased me began to rankle. And *eight youngest* . . .

"What of Neri and me?" I said. "Are we to be hostage or made an example of or turned over to—?" I couldn't speak it. The tenor of his voice, the very air between us spoke his anger and . . . ah divinities . . . his horror. By the graces and spirits, did he suspect me of sorcery, too?

"Your brother has a foul tongue and has been heard repeatedly reviling his betters, myself in particular. It's what called my attention to him in the first place. I cannot allow the Gallanos name—my father's and grandfather's name—to be sullied in such fashion. Our peace is too tenuous. As he is underage, I shall request a Sestorale parole to allow him to mend his behavior. *You*, mistress, are now responsible for his every action and will bring him to the parole administrator every Quarter Day to report on his progress. Whatever punishment he earns from this day forward will be yours as well. It is not fair. It is not righteous. It is not what I would choose for you had I the freedom to shape the world as I do this city. But for now, it is all I can see to do. You must hammer this understanding into him, or bring him to me and I'll do it. I would not have you dead. Thus, the larger purse is for you, to keep you, to—to—allow you to make a life of your choosing, and to ensure your future should your brother allow you to have one."

The moment's stumble tore at my heart. But it did not last.

"None of this bag's contents will be shared with your parents, your brother, or any other person, else I will have your brother arrested by a nullifier and tested by his sniffer. From that day, I could and would do nothing more on your behalf."

"Sandro—"

"Silence! It is no longer your privilege to address me by that or any other name. You will leave this house by midnight, taking only these purses, garments sufficient to cover you, and whatever possessions you brought with you when you came to my house. From that hour, this house is closed to you. My protection, my notice, and my interest in you and yours is ended. Cataline of the Moon House is dead."

The doors between his rooms and mine slammed shut, one and then the other. Bolts, long unused, clattered.

My head sank to the carpet.

On my first night in the Moon House so long ago, once the attendants had stripped me, shaved off my dirty, knotted hair, scrubbed and oiled my skin, and scraped my teeth with willow sticks, they shoved me naked into a windowless closet to sleep alone for the first time in my life. As she locked the door, one of the women said to scream and cry all I wanted, for beginning on the next day every tear or whimper would earn me a beating. She said the child I had been was dead.

Indeed, I had screamed and wept all that night, clawed at the door, banged my shoulder and head on it. And certain, tears had made no difference at all. I'd felt as if I'd fallen into a well of tar. Looking upward, I had seen my familiar life as a tiny circle of color, receding faster than I could climb after it.

This night was very like, save that the colors of the receding circle were so very much brighter, and the pain of the impossible distance so much sharper. I had shed no tears since that night and I was not going to start. But, divine graces, the hurt . . .

• • •

The world did not end. When the passing hour proved I would not die, either, I climbed to my feet, exchanged my green silks and brocades for Micola's soiled blue overdress that I had worn earlier, and stuffed the two purses into the linen apron. I had brought the pearl-handled dagger from the Moon House, so it remained strapped to my thigh. My necklace, bracelets, earrings, and finger rings I dropped into the overflowing jewel box that would stay behind. But as I closed the lid, the thumbnail-sized bronze disk tucked into the corner caught my eye. The luck charm. That, too, was mine.

On my first stolen visit home when I was thirteen, five-year-old Neri had given it to me. He'd said a metalsmith in a market stall gave him one of the disks, saying that anyone with *skills like his* should carry a luck charm every hour of every day. When Neri told the old man that his lost sister Romy had strange skills, too, the man gave him a second charm like to the first, just in case his lost sister was ever found.

Strange skills. Magic. My sole talent was this ability to steal a fragment of someone's memory by instilling a lie in its place. A perverse skill. And paltry. My courtesan's training could make a man forget his own name and the events of half his life, so Sandro had told me.

A coal in my belly heated as I thought of it. Even my paltry magic could not make *il Padroné* forget the great lie I had lived. Yet neither could I forget that he had known of my danger for as long as his man had watched Neri. He had never asked, yet neither had he warned me. I could have sent Neri away . . . done something that would not involve mutilation of an innocent man.

How could I grieve for a mother who had sold my childhood into degradation or a father who had left me there? How could I grieve for sisters who begged Lady Fortune every day to strike me dead? But it was not righteous that a law scribe should lose a hand to protect a foolish son born with abilities he did not ask for.

I snatched up the luck charm and left my chambers by way of the garden doors. Halfway across the fragrant beds of fruit trees and flowers, a dark shape darted through the trees. My rogue heart leapt, naming it Sandro pining for me already.

Reason crushed that idiocy instantly. Yet someone trespassed upon the Shadow Lord's private garden, and habit raised my defenses. So I raced after and grabbed an ankle, just as the intruder started up the stone wall. A body thudded to the turf facedown, and I straddled the slender frame, knees on the gloved wrists, my knife in hand.

Certainly not Sandro. And not Neri—my second suspect. This one wasn't even as tall as I.

"Any night is a dangerous night to be sneaking about the

Shadow Lord's garden," I said, growling, ensuring the hooded villain could see my dagger in the flare of distant torchlight. "But my blood rages this particular eve, so speak quickly or die."

"I expected you would slice my throat long before. But your papa's gone to the axe, and you—the concubine who blinds *il Padroné* to his duty—are banished from his presence. I dare you cut me now."

So small a voice, so young a soul to express such hatred and defiance and ugly enjoyment. Sandro's little wife!

I leapt up and stepped back, gripping my knife hard.

"Silly child. Never . . . never would I harm you." No matter how I might wish to. "He chose you to marry. To bear his children."

"He chose my father's treasure."

That was true. Gilliette de Manvile's father had no noble blood, nor was he even the most powerful man in Argento, the northernmost and smallest independency of the Costa Drago. But the silver scraped from the mountainous demesne had made her father very rich indeed. Her dowry had provided the funds for Cantagna's new coliseum that had drawn architects, builders, artists, and artisans to Cantagna from all over the Costa Drago. It provided good work for our own citizens as it rose from the rubble of hovels and stews, and would do so in the future. When completed it would be a wonder of the world.

Gilliette scrambled to sitting, a dark tight bundle backed to the wall.

"Alessandro plays only tea party with me." The deepening night masked the pouting face, but not her petulance. "I have my blood already, but he comes *never* to my bed."

I walked away.

She called after me. "Every night I watch from this garden and you are so much talk, talk, talk, until he . . . feels needs . . . and does those things with you to make babies. But now"—triumph threaded the bitterness—"now he will *have* to turn to me."

Why did her smirking triumph make me feel so ancient?

"You are his honored wife," I said, reversing my path until I stood over her. "You bear his name, and the dignity, privileges, and respect that name brings with it. You, not I, accompany him on official occasions. You will be mother to his children. This means more to him than any pleasure he and I shared, because the honor of his family name and his family's great works for Cantagna are so important to him. Women like me don't bear a great man's children."

Sandro's own beloved grandfather had seen to that when shaping Cantagna's laws about sanctioned marriages and inheritance. Not even the Shadow Lord could ever convince the Sestorale to sanction his marriage to a Moon House whore. Not that I ever would have allowed his or any man's seed to catch in any case. No one knew how a child became tainted with magic.

"He discards you like the offal you are."

"As you say, lady. And he will surely come to your bed as you wish, just not until you're old enough he won't hurt you, and old enough to carry a child should Lady Fortune bless you so."

"But he will *love* me. I am darker, prettier, younger. I can tat lace and sing. My hands are small."

Suddenly weary, I sank to the ground beside her. The warm garden earth smelled of crushed thyme. "Do you know how to read, little wife?"

"Some, but—"

"Here is my advice: Ask him for books. Ask for a tutor. *That* will please him and you will find great enjoyment for yourself as well. Learn stories. Learn to draw or paint, for he loves to talk about images and what they mean and how they can be used to further his aims. Learn to listen. Listen to everything spoken in your house and remember it, for the least bit of gossip can be useful. Learn history. *Il Padroné* does not care for singing or lace. But he loves history. He wants historians and philosophers to write about his family and the glorious city of Cantagna and the justice, law, and art that are its foundation."

"He said I would stand at his side in a history book, but I thought—I can do these things, watch and listen."

She was too young to hate. For now, Sandro valued Gigo more than her. But he would need his wife's ears . . . her mind . . . assuming the little walnut could be cracked open.

"*Il Padroné* is not always a good man," I said. "He will do things you might find terrible. If you choose to become his trustworthy partner, you could help him see the right. I did that for a long time, but in the end I failed him. Never lie to him. If you are fortunate—and learn these things—then perhaps, someday, love may blossom between you alongside honor and respect."

She was so quiet for the moment, I thought she'd stolen away. But then she whispered, "*You* love him."

"Just now, I loathe him. But I do believe in him. Here"—I dug into my apron pocket and pulled out Neri's luck charm—"if you ever need someone to talk to—because you can never, *ever* speak of *il Padroné* to anyone else, not your mama or your nurse or your

sister or your maid—send a servant to the Beggars Ring to find
Romy of Lizard's Alley. I'll come."

Perhaps I would kill her then.

"He has cast you off. We will *never* have need of you."

"Likely so."

3

Surely I had been foolish to give the little wife my luck charm. It had served me well. I was a sorceress who had lived with the Shadow Lord nine years, and I was not dead. If Moon House training had done anything, it had made me practical.

At dawn Neri and I stood at the back of the jeering crowd outside the Pillars prison as the lopsman cut off my father's hand. I'd no desire to witness butchery, but a respectful presence seemed a small thing to offer a man who suffered such a horror to keep his family alive. Of course, Da was ultimately responsible for our danger. He had not allowed Mam to drown Neri or me when they discovered we bore the demonfire. Most days I was grateful for the life he'd saved. Certain, he did not deserve this.

More important than such dry sentiment—all I could summon after a sleepless night choked with guilt and helpless grief—Neri needed to witness the full horror of his stupidity. When I'd delivered Sandro's judgment and his purse, Neri had immediately started babbling his perennial defense: "We needed the coin from those rubies, Romy. Wallowing in your jewels and fineries, you couldn't know—"

"Don't you dare blame me," I snapped. "*You* chose your actions. *You* failed to think. And it's only by Da's grit and sheerest luck you haven't murdered us all."

"They'd never have known it was me." The fool preened like Sandro's little wife. "None can follow me where I go with magic. And I wear a rat's hide under my shirt and lead pellets in my boots. Digo and Fivelli down the Duck's Bone claim that's the way sorcerers hide from sniffers."

I would have laughed save for the danger of his ignorance. "Alas, your drunkard oracles are incorrect . . ."

When I informed him that the Shadow Lord's men had marked his indiscretions for years, he near swallowed his tongue.

". . . but he's *reported* only that you've insulted your betters, and he's made you my responsibility from this day forward. I've no choice but to do it, because I heard what he did not say. You step out of line in any fashion, and he'll send a sniffer after us both. So until you prove yourself trustworthy, you will stay at my side. At the first hint of disobedience, I swear I'll haul you to *il Padroné*'s dungeons myself for a beating."

I had no confidence that words or threats would contain the banty rooster. And so I forced him to watch every moment of Da's ordeal. Trembling, his face the green-yellow hue of soured milk, Neri stood at my side in the sweltering sunlight as the axe fell, and as Da remained bound to a post, woozy, moaning, and unsuccored until midday. Flies buzzed around his seared stump.

I had ever deemed my father complicit in my childhood debasement. A hundred lawyers in the city were in his debt because he found errors in their writs as he copied them, but he had never prevailed on any of them for a favor. Not when his children starved. Not when his ten-year-old daughter was thrown away for a few silver coins. Yet he had chosen mutilation to protect us all. Perhaps his liver was not entirely weak.

When the noon bell tolled, Da was unbound and shoved toward the road where Mam and the younger ones waited. He stumbled and fell. His cry was that of a wounded animal.

Neri twitched as if to run.

I gripped his wrist and held him at my side. "Watch and learn. Remember."

Da staggered to his feet. Condottieri in plumed helmets slapped whips and staves on the road behind him, driving him and Mam and their gaggle of eight toward the city gates. Thirteen-year-old Cino dragged a sled holding blankets and two wailing urchins, while a defiant Dolce carried a bulky, clanking bag—the allotted pots, flasks, and spoons. A wrapped shawl bound the infant to my mother's chest and three more weeping children clung to her skirt.

A hellish cacophony roared from the crowd. Rotted fruit and clots of dried mud and dung pelted the family from every side. Gritting my teeth, I dragged Neri through the streets behind the dismal processional.

Two scrawny butcher's boys carrying armloads of rubble dodged into the street from an alley and were soon launching one missile after another toward Da and the others. When a rock hit Cino in the back and sent him sprawling, dumping sled, supplies, and wailing children onto the filthy roadway, Neri wrenched his arm away and hurled himself at one of the youths. They crashed to the ground. Growling and cursing—sobbing, too, I suspected—Neri wrestled the youth onto his back and smashed the bawling boy's nose to pulp with one of his own rocks.

"Stop it!" I tugged at Neri's arm.

Two more blows split the boy's cheek before the second youth and I dragged Neri off him.

"Get out of here, you stupid twits," I yelled at the two, who were arming for revenge. "They'll arrest you for interfering with the judgment. Hey, Captain!"

I waved at the nearest plumed helmet, though my yell was not near loud enough to be heard over the general noise. The rock-throwers didn't know that, and scuttered back into the alley.

"You are on parole, fool," I snapped through clenched teeth. "Did I not make it clear? You get arrested, we're dead."

"Let me loose," snarled Neri, on his feet now, his own cheek scratched and bloody. "I'm getting out of here."

"No! We see it through. They are our blood, and they suffer because of *us*."

Maybe watching would make him think.

"Up there." I shoved him toward a broken brick wall. A short climb and we had a clear view of the city gates and the pitiful procession passing through. Da trudged along slowly beside Mam, hugging his damaged arm to his chest. The pain must be dreadful. From time to time he nudged one of the little ones to face forward. He remembered they were not allowed to look behind. *Oh spirits, Da . . .*

No matter hurt and bitterness, my heart ached for them all. What was Da to do? What future did Dolce and Cino and the others have as children of a marked thief? I could not interfere.

Il Padroné's conditions bound the purse that might save their lives.

Was Sandro observing from one of the gate towers or some other spot above the crowd? Had he ever considered the kind of punishment he meted out so casually to children?

I hated him in that moment. What kind of *enlightened city* treated its citizens this way—even a confessed thief—even in a case where magic might be suspected but not proved?

Of course he had considered these questions. If ever a man embodied two souls, it was Alessandro di Gallanos. He was *il Padroné*, who worked quietly and generously to move the city forward, strengthening the rule of law while bringing it peace and prosperity, beauty and enlightenment. He was also the Shadow Lord, who did what he believed necessary no matter how difficult.

Neri didn't run. Neither did he look away. His scraped and bloody face hardened to stone as he watched the cloud of dust swallow them. Certain, they were more his family than mine.

Once the dust settled on the empty road, the rowdy throng melted away. Time to turn our minds to practical matters. The Shadow Lord had forced Neri and me to stay here for a reason he'd not chosen to reveal. After this spectacle, I could not believe it was any lingering care for me. Far more likely he wished to keep the danger we posed close. Easier to arrest us later, when people had forgotten his mistress. He had gambled that keeping Neri under the law's scrutiny would ensure my own good behavior. Until he revealed his purpose, I had to learn to live on my own. With Neri.

"Come," I said, exchanging my grip for a hand on his shoulder.

"It's time for us to start over. Your parole binds us together and to this city, no matter how much we both hate it."

Bruised and sullen, Neri wrenched his shoulder out from under my hand. But he followed. His stomach was growling.

With a coin from Sandro's purse I bought sausage, olives, and bread, and we sat on an upended trough to share it out. Neri devoured his portion in moments. A single bite of the fatty sausage sat in my gut like a ball of lead, banishing any thought of a second. The afternoon shimmered with damp heat, casting a yellow glow over splintered houses, shabby stalls, and the pigs, geese, and occasional mule sharing the crowded market street with even shabbier humans.

We might have been sitting in the docks ourselves awaiting a magistrate's sentencing. Neri sat silent, but he quivered like water just before it erupted into a boil. I fixed my gaze on the greasy meat in my hand. It felt as if every passerby stared at us, gawking at the scribe's son left behind, wondering if I was the one they'd heard rumors of, wondering if the boy's tavern blathering about his sister the whore had been true.

We needed to move forward.

"Dolce said you've been digging at the coliseum site," I said. "Are they expecting you this afternoon?"

"Went up there yesterday. They told me not to come back. No thief's kin allowed to work there."

Just as Dolce had warned.

Sandro's purse was generous and no fool's pride would prevent me using it. But it was not bottomless. I was only twenty-four. Neri was almost sixteen and uneducated; I wasn't even sure he could read. We needed a place to sleep and we needed work.

"Maybe someone around here has some other work you could—"

"Wouldna been sharing a pallet with Cino if I'd a choice, would I? No work to be had in the Ring. Tried for a year before the coliseum started hiring. Sweeping, digging, ratting, hauling . . . fifty others were waiting for anything I could do." He eyed the sausage in my hand. "I s'pose you've got work enough lined up, but Moon House didn't come calling for me."

I ignored the bitter jab and gave him my sausage.

There was no returning to the Moon House, not after Sandro had declared Mistress Cataline dead. Moon House courtesans could be gifted or sold to new owners, but were allowed to return to the House only when honorably retired, not when they were deemed unsatisfactory, as I had been. Not that I would have gone back anyway. I would submit to a lunatic asylum before selling myself anywhere—in a brothel, on the streets, or from the Moon House. Beyond that resolution, the future stood ahead of me like a city wall, its gates hidden. But we couldn't stay here in the street.

"Who put Mam out of the house last night?" I said.

"Two magistrate's men came and hauled everything off, save spoons and blankets. Posted a paper on the wall and said to go and not come back. What do you care?"

When I'd returned to the Beggars Ring, Mam and the others had already been sitting in the Ring Road. They'd been told to report to the prison yard before dawn to wait for Da's punishment and release. I'd given Mam the purse and told them of the Shadow Lord's conditions. While Dolce used some of their coin to buy food and ale, Neri and Cino got them moved. They'd wanted no help from me.

I stood. "Come on. I want to read that paper they left."

• • •

Twenty-three silver solets from Sandro's purse bought the hovel in Lizard's Alley from the local bondsman, whose name had been on the notice nailed to the house. From the way he was grinning as we left his market stall, I'd paid far too much for one empty, dirt-floored room closed off from the alley by a hanging rug. But he wouldn't take less, and I didn't know what it might cost us to rent a room or where might be too dangerous to stay. The neighborhood around Lizard's Alley was familiar at the least.

Neri and I spent the rest of the day scrubbing the stone walls and the single shelf and acquiring a few furnishings—pallets, blankets, a lamp and oil for it, a table and two stools, a water cask, two cups, two spoons, a tin pot, and a clay brazier to replace the old cracked one that had been stripped out with everything else. Every time we thought we'd bought enough to get by, we had to return to the market for something else—a shovel of charcoal for the brazier, flint and steel to light it, a few candles, apples and cheese for supper, clean rags for wrapping our cheese and washing ourselves. I refused to live without soap. Neri insisted on mounting ghiris—spiky knots of pomegranate twigs—over our one window and doorway to snag bad luck before it came inside. I deemed it too late for that.

The Beggars Ring seemed dirtier, shabbier, and more crowded than in the years I'd lived there. Perhaps that was just a child's perspective, for the scattered market stalls had more variety and better goods than I remembered, and more people seemed able to buy.

Neri's sole comment of the afternoon was, "So we're not to be drinking anything but river water?" Thus, another trip for a flask of wine, a jug of ale, and a few sorry-looking herbs for tea.

When Sandro had stretched the system of water pipes, wells, and conduits from the upper Rings to the Market and Asylum Rings—one of his first acts after assuming his uncle's role as *il Padroné*—even the Beggars Ring had benefited. Water had been diverted from the river through troughs and conduits, and the spill from the conduits flowed into a public cistern. For the first time Beggars Ring citizens didn't have to haul water all the way from the river. Sadly, that hadn't made the river water any healthier. Da had forbade us to drink water unless it had been purified by soaking herbs in it.

Neri showed me the way to the cistern and the diversion conduit, now called The Pipes, and we filled our water cask. I'd never understood why my parents kept such a small water supply for so many of us. I believed they just didn't care that we were always dirty. But after Neri and I lugged our small cask from The Pipes, not even half the distance it would have been from the river itself, their choice made more sense.

The evening bells had long fallen silent by the time we ate our apples and cheese. It didn't take long to demolish most of it. While Neri rewrapped what was left of the cheese, I lit the lamp and pulled out the loose foundation stone Da used to safeguard his coins. Before stowing my silver, I poured it out in my skirt to count. To my horror, the hoard that was to ensure our future was almost a quarter spent.

Stupid Romy!

I was accustomed to friendly bargaining for whatever I wanted in the cleaner, more luxurious Merchant Ring markets, sometimes with Sandro at my side, sometimes with Micola, a bodyguard, and an embroidered silk waist pocket that *il Padroné* never allowed to be empty. But I found it impossible to bargain with the Beggars Ring potter whose thin, bony children hawked his cups and braziers, or the toothless old woman who wove decent blankets when she could scarce see. I was ashamed to be stingy when I had a fat bag of silver—and I had no idea what price was fair for anything. Neri, resentful when I insisted he stay with me instead of wandering off on his own, had sneered and offered no help.

We'd bought no luxuries to my mind, but demons . . . I had to do better. I dropped the bag in the hole and shoved the stone in on top of it.

Exhaustion weighed on my shoulders like a leaden mantle. My mind refused to hold back the sounds and sights of these two horrible days. Da's bleeding stump. Wiry little Cino's bent back. Dolce's hopeless defiance. Sandro's bitter dismissal, each word an icy blade carving out a hollow where I'd once had a heart: *do not presume . . . no longer your privilege . . . closed to you . . . interest ended . . . dead.*

"Are we done here? Have I played your slavey long enough?"

Neri's insolence roused my blood. All of this was his doing. "Go to bed."

He edged toward the doorway rug that swayed in the stinking night breeze. "Too early. I'll just be down to the Duck's Bone."

I stepped between my brother and the doorway. "No. You won't. As I've said three times already, you will not go anywhere on your own until you show me you comprehend our predica- ment. One slip, a fight, an ill-timed word, pilfering a fig from the market—yes, I saw you do that—could get us dead. Be sure our suffering would be far worse than what Da endured today. Tomorrow we have to find work, find something to cover this damnable dirt under our feet, and something besides that filthy rug to keep drunks from wandering inside our house to piss. Now sleep. I'll sit on you if I have to."

Clearly, every muscle in his body wanted to fight me. To run. But he retreated to his pallet and hunched against the wall, his eyes never leaving my clenched fist. Only as I reached to douse the lamp did I realize my pearl-handled dagger had found its way to my hand.

Spirits, Romy, get hold of yourself!

Blood pounding, I retreated to my own pallet and laid the knife close by. Impossible to sleep now. Deploying my fury like a shield to hold visions and grief at bay, I sat in the dark fretting over what kind of work I might do that did not involve lustful men, libidinous women, haggling at the market, or incessant stares from strangers. After four-and-twenty years of haphazard education, I ought to have a few useful skills besides the obvious.

As often happens, the answer came with the morning.

4

Law scribe? You? A fancy tart, taught at that Moon place to do things a man . . . can't even imagine . . . is gonna write words for hire? You know how to do that?"

Neri's astonishment was so profound and so jaw-droppingly innocent, I forgave him the insult.

"With Da gone, there's surely writing work to be had. I recall the names of many of his clients. And no, I've not forgotten how to read and write despite my *former* profession. In fact, my skills have improved amazingly. My hand was required to be strong, elegant, and clear . . . writing-wise as well as in other endeavors."

As with every skill a courtesan's master or mistress might require, elegance of phrasing, proper forms of address, and perfection in form whether composing poetry, keeping estate accounts, or recording shopping lists had been taught with a willow switch. My knuckles stung at the recollection.

"I've actually been known to read and write for pleasure, so why not get paid for it? But before I can begin, we need to go back to the market."

Three hours hunting told me the Beggars Ring could provide no decent parchment, pens, or ink. Much to the delight of Fedig the pen seller in the Asylum Ring, I brought home a goodly supply of his. I also bought a lightweight blue mantle—expensive, but necessary to cover my soiled servant's dress if I was to present myself as a sober, reliable citizen. A leather jerkin that someone's boy had outgrown would serve to mask Neri's filthy shirt. I was not ready to leave him alone.

Over the next few days, we carried my letters of application to twenty lawyers and notaries who had been Da's longtime employers, offering the services of a scribe who had wide familiarity with Cantagna's law. After Neri's experience, I did not mention Da's name.

On the third day, I won my first client, a wizened notary named Renzo, who was willing to take a chance on a scribe with no references as long as she charged no more than two copper solets a page. As I carried home a stack of deeds and marriage contracts, I was excited to think of replenishing the rapidly shrinking bag of silver so easily.

Two days later as I climbed the tight, steep staircase to Renzo's chamber, shoulders aching, ink-stained fingers cramped from hour after tedious hour of writing, eyes burning from squinting at his crabbed, endlessly annotated script, I was not quite so sanguine.

Notary Renzo resided in a hot cramped room above a bakery. Sadly only the heat of the baking ovens rather than the sweet smells they produced made their way up the stair. He had likely not washed himself or his food-splattered gown since I was born.

"Ah, *l'scrittóre!*" he said cheerfully as I set the stack of copies on his writing desk. "Finished already?"

Not caring to sit on his extra stool that looked as if owls had roosted on it, I stood as Renzo carefully licked his finger, turned each page, and examined it carefully. He set aside two where I had failed to sharpen my pen soon enough to avoid blots.

"These two need to be redone. But fine work overall. No errors. I'll be pleased to give you more. Bring these two when you return the new pages." He shoved another stack of parchment across the desk in my direction and then hopped off his tall stool and crouched down where I couldn't see him.

A metal box appeared on the writing desk, followed by the reappearance of his wispy hair and smiling face. Renzo counted out fifty copper coins—exactly half of a silver solet—and his finger most exactly moved four aside to hold until I replaced the blotted pages. Once I'd reduced the remainder by the one copper I had paid for each raw sheet at the pen seller's, two more for the blotted sheets I would have to replace, as well as the two for the entire bottle of ink I'd used, I almost wept. For two exhausting days with almost no sleep, I had earned exactly seventeen coppers. Enough for a quarter shovel of coal, so I had learned. Or a quarter of a day-old roasted duck. Or one loaf of bread, one sausage, and a wedge of cheese that Neri could devour in an afternoon.

"Thank you, Notary Renzo. I'll have these back as soon as I can."

"Two days, if you please. No later. Fortune's benefice, *l'scrittóre virginé.*"

"And Virtue's grace."

A despairing humor accompanied me down the stair. It had

been long years since anyone had called me virginal. But indeed I was a virgin scribe. If we were to survive, I needed to learn my business. Unfortunately my brother could be no help. As I suspected, he had successfully evaded Da's teaching, and remained illiterate as well as ignorant.

I'd left Neri downstairs to wait, but he was nowhere in sight when I emerged from the stair. I scanned the bustling lane, started up toward the Market Ring wall a few steps, then back downhill the way we'd come. A chill shuddered my bones as if an overhanging roof had sluiced frigid water down my back. *Fortune's dam, Neri, where have you got off to?*

I pushed through the crowd at the noodle vendor's stall across the lane. A mother with four children picked out supper. Three draymen were grabbing a cup while their mules brayed in annoyance and their carts blocked the lane. A beggar and a grimy urchin of undeterminable sex eyed each other as they waited for someone to drop a cup or a spoonful.

Another frigid shudder. I spun around. Deep in the alley between the bakery and a barber's stall, a dark shape moved. I arrowed across the lane and into the alley.

Neri slouched against the wall, licking his fingers. He dropped his hand quickly when he noticed me.

"What have you done?"

He shrugged. "Waited for you out of the street. Thought you were going to be quick."

"You've been eating." Which wasn't a crime, except that he'd not a coin of any kind, so he had whined for two days.

He pointed his chin at the shop. "Baker's a *kind* woman. Gave me a biscuit."

I might have believed it, save for the way his guilty gaze

flicked between me and the bakery's doorless alley wall. From inside the shop I could hear a child wailing. "I never did, gammy! Wouldn't never!"

"Did you lightfinger your biscuit or, demon spirits, did you *walk* to it?" Walk through that wall into the kitchen while no one was watching. Use his damnable magic. "Shall I go inside and ask what the child did to get a scolding?"

"Had naught to eat all day. And there's none of *those creatures* around here." Sniffers, he meant.

"And you're certain enough to wager your life and your soul's corruption on that? For a biscuit?" I pointed at the pavement. "Wait right here, if you want to eat again this month."

"You just— I'll never—"

"Wait. Here."

The baker's shop was clean and tidy, and my stomach near caved in at the smell of butter, honey, and cinnamon. A small, flour-dusted girl sobbed quietly in the corner.

I held out two coppers to the flustered woman. "Whatever I can get for this," I said, my skin surely as hot as her ovens.

"Four biscuits or a half a butter loaf."

Spirits . . . so expensive. I was learning fast.

"The biscuits," I said, donning Mistress Cataline's self-assurance and her most gracious smile, "but keep two. For the sad little one. Missing my own mite, left with her nan."

"But you don't need—"

"'Tis my delight."

As I hurried out of the door with the two biscuits in my pocket, she dipped a knee, as if I actually inhabited my old self. Made no sense at all when the baker was dressed better than I.

• • •

From that day, I forbade Neri to be out of my sight. When he accompanied me to Notary Renzo's, he had to wait at the door where I could see him. He stood behind me as I delivered more applications to potential clients or revisited houses where I'd left one before.

When he chafed at my restriction, I reminded him how the Shadow Lord had offered to beat some sense into him if he failed to understand the terms of his parole.

"You'd never take me to him," he jibed. "He threw you out of his house in the middle of the night."

And certain that was true. But I needed to frighten the fool enough to make him behave. If he wasn't afraid of sniffers, why would he fear his sister?

"You're right, I can't take you in for a beating myself, but it's dead easy to have someone else do it," I said, making a story on the fly. "All I have to do is raise a finger to a Gardia warden or a constable. Do you think that after nine years, every one of them doesn't know my face? Do you think the Shadow Lord didn't mean what he said? If I tell them you called *il Padroné* a prick, they'll see to what's needed. You even think about magic or running away or doing anything that could get us arrested, I'll do it."

He wasn't sure he believed me, but every once in a while I would let him see me walk up to a warden or a constable out of his hearing. I'd been well trained to charm a laugh out of a stranger, but Neri didn't have to know that.

After a while I didn't even need to remind him. I simply wriggled a finger at a nearby warden and Neri blanched.

While I worked, Neri fidgeted or slept. Threats forced him to stay, but I'd no idea how to make him to do anything useful.

Meanwhile the silver that would ensure our future continued to dwindle like dew in sunlight. Neri, thin as a winter-stripped willow, was forever hungry, and Renzo's coppers could scarce pay for the expense to earn them.

I added a second client. A lawyer advocate in the Market Ring lamented his inability to find anyone who could match his former scribe's precise work. When I swallowed hard and named myself as Da's writing student, he hired me right away. Garibaldi paid better than Renzo, but required better parchment, so I earned scarce more than I did for Renzo.

Neri grumbled that I should take one of the coppers I'd earned and display it on our window sill wrapped in laurel leaves. That way Lady Virtue would see how industrious I was and grant us her favor. "Same way folk hang up likenesses of themselves and their brats or hang up the tail after they trap a rabbit. I told Mam they ought to get someone to do a drawing of them and all the thirteen of us, as birthing seemed the thing they was best at. Maybe if she'd done it, none of this would have happened."

"I think I have a more useful plan," I said. "I'll visit one prospective client every day."

Maybe Lady Virtue would appreciate the effort and whisper a good reference to one of my prospects. Without another client our silver would vanish before winter.

• • •

Lawyer Cinnetti, an advisor to an Asylum Ring builder, had set up a table and comfortable chairs in the small forecourt of his house, so he could sit with clients in full view of passersby. His broad-brimmed hat and padded doublet swelled an already imposing presence, and you couldn't see the soiled inner layers of his stiff neck ruff until you were a bit closer. Garibaldi had referred me, saying he knew little about Cinnetti, save that he "seemed a decent fellow" and supposedly paid well for scribes who wrote with a fine hand.

"Four coppers a page, increased to five if the script is as perfectly formed as that on your application, damizella." Cinnetti's grand moustaches seemed to expand with his wide smile. "Would that suit you?"

I proudly maintained my businesslike sobriety instead of spinning for joy at the offer. Visions of a proper bodice and kirtle, a spare chemise, planking to cover our dirt floor, or perhaps a roasted goose every once in a while raced through my head. And silver to refill the bag. The silver was the key.

"Acceptable, good sir."

"Excellent. Step ta my hall, right through here, and I'll show ya my needs." His open hand invited me through the open doorway.

I signaled to Neri, who was leaning against the painted column that marked the lawyer's yard. Sour and bored, his annoyance was palpable. I'd told him to come as far as the door if I went inside.

"I've very particular requirements as to form," said Cinnetti, as I moved past him, across the threshold sleugh that was caked with muck, instead of the oil-and-water barrier to demons.

My feet slowed. The dim hall stank of boiled fish and mold. The frescos that had once adorned its walls had darkened and peeled. A glimpse through an open door to the right revealed

a long table burdened with jumbled stacks of parchment, leath-
erbound ledgers and journals, along with mugs and at least
three wine flasks.

"In there?" I said, not quite so elated as in the courtyard.

"No need to go farther." The big man grabbed my shoulder,
spun me around, and slammed my back to the wall, his big body
pinning me tight. One huge hand threatened to rip my hair from
my scalp, while the other lifted my skirt and fumbled with his
codpiece. "I can show you what work I need done right here."

"Boy! Fetch . . . constable!" I screamed as the lawyer's fleshy
lips mauled my face. He reeked of sour wine.

The mere clatter of Neri's boots distracted Cinnetti enough for
me to draw my knife and threaten to remove what he thought to
use on me. The Moon House had taught us to defend our valuable
selves, as well as our owners.

As I backed toward Neri and the door, Cinnetti laughed and
flattened his own back to the wall in mock helplessness. "Told
you I'd show you my needs, pretty Romy. And certain you fulfill
all my requirements of *form*. Just want to see more of it, and *feel*
your hand as well as see it. Come back when you're tired of
scribing. I pay better for . . ."

I shoved Neri out the door ahead of me as the man chattered
filth that followed us across his courtyard. He finished his
unseemly litany by breaking into verse:

> *"Romy, Romy, Scribe Romy,*
> *Come back and give me a lick!*
> *I'll ruffle your feathers, and give you a kiss,*
> *And you'll feel the plunge of my—*

"Oh, here you are, sweetling! Come back to me already?"

Cinnetti had slid to the floor. Bellowing a laugh, he raised a bota in offer.

I kicked him in the balls. While he caught his breath, I knelt and laid a thumb on his forehead. With a completeness I'd never attempted, I considered his every mention of my name and sight of my face. Then I invited the magical vipers inside me to spew their venom through my blood and replace that story with something new: *I interviewed a scribe named Faustio today, a stunted, ugly fellow. My foul tongue insulted him terribly, and he's promised to return one night very soon and cut off my prized possession. His brother is a constable and he swears that no one will ever believe my complaint. They're coming after me . . .*

Snatching up my application that lay on the filthy floor, I raced out the door and collided with a frowning Neri.

"C-come. Hurry," I said, my teeth chattering.

Once we were far enough away we could no long hear Cinnetti's pained cursing, I propped myself on a post and inhaled deep breaths to keep from vomiting. My limbs would not stop shaking.

"Did you put a knife in him? Or cut his face? That would show him." Neri was near jumping out of his skin.

"No." I swallowed over and over, trying to abate the sickness. Even after so long, the crude fumbling and cocky assurance of one who presumed to control me left me feeling dirty and angry. And frightened—he could have had a rope or a knife to assert his will. And stupid—did I think the world had changed so much since I was fifteen?

"Demons, Romy, did you kill him?"

"Worse." For certain it was the magic that had me trembling

and sick, more than the attack. To use it here in the middle of the city . . . because I was angry and scared . . . when a sniffer could have been in the street . . .

Neri's heated belligerence went as cold as winter in the northlands. "You didn't really want me to fetch a constable, did you?"

"Of course not. What happens when a reputable lawyer complains to a magistrate that he was bloodied by a Beggars Ring scribe who wears a maidservant's castoffs? What if he discovered I really had been a whore? I knew you'd come to look first. Distract him. You saved—"

"You used your *magic*." Fortunately he'd lowered his voice.

"I had no choice. I couldn't let him remember my name or what we looked like."

I squeezed my eyes shut, as the truth of my future settled in. I didn't want to look on the teeming stew of the Asylum Ring. No one was going to come to my rescue, and replenishing the bag of silver was never going to buy back what was lost.

"You flirt with wardens and constables, but they don't know you. All this time you've played me for stupid. Made me think it was only me was the evil one 'cause my magic feels like I'm supposed to use it, like it could make life better. You made me think there was something wrong with me that needed beating out. But first time you need it, you jump right in."

"But you were careless. Rash. You wouldn't listen. I don't want you dead." But he had already walked away.

• • •

I sat in our hovel that afternoon, alone, cursing my stupidity. I'd worked magic after forbidding him the same. I couldn't regret that. I was protecting us, not stealing a biscuit. But then, it had been many years since I'd gone hungry. Certain he was right about the lies.

Night fell. Three pages for Garibaldi and Renzo lay blotted and ruined before I gave up work and chewed my fingers.

It was past midnight when Neri finally came home. Staggering drunk. I dared not ask how he, who had no money, could buy wine. I was terrified he'd tell me it was the same way he'd got the sweet biscuit from the baker's. The same way I'd made sure Lawyer Cinnetti could not find me and try again to get what he wanted.

I didn't yell at Neri, just helped him to bed. "I'm sorry I lied to you. I was wrong to do it. You're not evil, not stupid, and I shouldn't have said it. But we've things we have to get straight."

"Tomorrow," he said. "Certain we'll get things straight."

Deep in the darkest hours of that night, a scraping noise woke me. A moment's listening, a moment's peering into the dark to pick out the crouched figure in the corner. Neri was wriggling the foundation stone that hid Sandro's purse.

"You sneaking, thieving weasel!" I batted him under the chin with a club I kept by my pallet and shoved him to the floor. "I should throw you in the river and be done with you."

I lit a candle from embers in the brazier, so I could make sure he'd not already taken the silver.

"Wanted to buy you summat," he said through blood and spit and a slur of wine. "That's all. A present. Some good wine. Cheer you up."

Even had I been idiot enough to believe his claims, the rope-tied bundle on his bare pallet belied them.

"So you planned to steal what's left of our future and run away? That would cheer me up considerably."

"Wasn't going to take it all. You're just so angry all the time. I just want to live like a normal man."

"Did it never occur to you that *il Padroné* granted you a *parole*—not your freedom? He forbade you leave the city with Da and Mam. Your name was on the latest parole list posted in the markets—so everyone in the Beggars Ring understands you have to remain here. He *knows* about us, Neri. No, I can't twitch my finger and summon him to punish you. And yes, I did what I've forbidden you to do; it was dangerous and I hate it, but I saw no other way to keep that brute lawyer from coming after us. But the Shadow Lord's spies watched you for years. *That* was no lie. They could still be watching."

Though I questioned even that. Sandro had said his interest in me was ended, his protection withdrawn. He'd said the same to a man named Maso, one of his oldest friends, who had embezzled funds from one of his banks. Within days the man was found floating in the Venia with six distinct knife holes in him. Without Sandro's protection, the man's other dissatisfied business partners had taken him down.

The memory echoed in the emptiness inside me, raising old doubts . . .

I brushed them off and spoke certainties to my ignorant brother. "*Il Padroné* does not make idle threats. He made me responsible for you. If you should just happen to vanish—with or without this purse—you will be in violation of his judgment. You *will* be hunted down, and I *will* share in your punishment. I refuse to die like that."

Before Neri could start again with his excuses, I ordered him to bed. I didn't sleep. Somewhere in the dark hours, I took the scrap of rope from his bundle and tied his right wrist and left ankle together, the best I could do with the short length. He could likely get the knot undone, but it would take him a while. I knew what I had to do.

5

At dawn, while Neri yet wallowed in his drunken stupor, I slipped the bag of silver into my pocket and hurried to the ironmonger down the Ring Road and bought a longer, thicker piece of rope, one braided with wire to strengthen it. I also bought an iron staple and borrowed a hammer on the promise to write out the next contract the ironmonger wished committed to paper.

Gossip . . . tales . . . claimed wire-threaded rope could bind a sorcerer, causing burns if the sorcerer tried to use magic. The few times I had seen accused sorcerers marched through the streets, they were always bound with wire rope. But I had no idea if those prisoners were ever proved to be sorcerers or if the wire rope truly kept them from escaping or even how a sorcerer might be able to escape from any rope. Snap it with a wish? Set it afire with a word? But it was true that sniffers were kept on chain leashes and the Executioner of the Demon Tainted bound convicted sorcerers in chains before they dropped them into the sea. So maybe there was something to the antagonism between iron and sorcery. Whatever the truth of such stories, Neri likely believed them.

He was halfway through our last loaf of bread when I got back.

"Left me trussed like a randy bull," he said through a mouthful. "What was that about?"

"You were drunk. Didn't want you wandering off and falling in the river. Or stealing my silver."

I hammered the iron staple to the foundation stones that divided our house from the tenement behind it and left the wire rope coiled beside it.

Neri stared at it, but must have thought better of asking. Certain, he was thinking of the stories. A shiver ran through him.

"I'm sorry I lied to you, and I'll not do it again. I swear. But I'm not going to apologize for keeping you safe. You can't run away, Neri. Not if you want to stay living."

"Can't just sit idle," he said. "Makes me think about things I . . . don't want to think on. It's just, I don't—"

He chewed on some idea along with his bread. "All right. Maybe I could go out today, look again for work so's you won't have to do all this."

My surprise at his civility was unfeigned. This was not the tack I'd have guessed he'd try next.

"That's a fine notion. And if you're going to act responsibly, you can bring home supplies for tonight and tomorrow. You're likely better at bargaining than I am."

I gave him twenty coppers. My blackened fingers twinged at the thought of the hours I'd spent to earn them. But I owed him another chance.

When he'd finished off his breakfast, he donned his leather jerkin, swiped a hand through his shaggy black curls, and left.

Concentrating on copying an elderly tinker's will for each of his five brothers, two sisters, and six nieces and nephews as well as a copy for the city archives occupied the day. But always at the back of my mind worry nagged. Night fell. I lit the lamp. I made tea with the last of the herbs, but could not eat.

What if Sandro's spies were watching Neri after all? There had been a night when wine and lovemaking had emboldened me to ask if he had truly ordered his boyhood friend Maso, the embezzler, killed as rumor had whispered. He had drawn his finger down my cheek, jaw, and shoulder in his delicious, dangerous way, devouring me with a smoldering gaze.

"When I was very small," he said, "my grandfather would take me walking through Cantagna's streets every morning, showing me his favorite places—the prospect from the Ucelli Gardens, the vineyard where our oldest grapevine yet blooms, the sweet, crumbling courtyard off the Via Rosa where a group of twenty-one men and women argued Cantagna's charter as a citizen-ruled independency into existence.

"'Inhale this dust, Alessandro,' he would say, "inhale the stink of Cantagna's stews, the fragrance of its lemon blossoms, the hungers of its beggars, the golden gleam of its stone, the extraordinary energies of life that stir behind its walls every dawn. I shall gift you the means to shape this city into something sublime, as Vandini the sculptor does with Portian marble. Honor, will, and the rule of law are the proper tools for your sculpting. Your father, the son I cherish, holds his honor dear, but his will fails when difficult choices must be made. Your uncle Lodovico, the son I mourn, has will enough to rival Dragonis itself, but he sells his honor for corrupt pleasures. Neither of them comprehends the beauty of the law. You, though, Alessandro, the grandson of my mind and heart, shall create a light to awaken the soul of the world.'"

Sandro had returned to his own bedchamber, then, leaving me with only a kiss on the top of my head and a few parting words. Whether it was a warning or a reprimand I'd never decided. "That you need ask about Maso tells me you don't know me as well as you think."

Which was no answer at all, save that pearlescent Portian marble is one of the most precious substances in the world, yet our visits to the sculptors' workshops had taught me that one must chip away bits of it, grind some of it to dust, and risk mistakes that ruin large pieces in order to create something sublime. Sandro was the Shadow Lord, who would do what he believed had to be done. Even to me.

Not long after the half-even anthem had rung, marking three hours until midnight, Neri burst through our rug door, dropped two loaves, one half-eaten sausage, and a packet of herbs on his pallet, and then hurried back to the alley to heave.

Twenty coppers. Ten hours of writing. When he staggered back inside, I held out my hand. "Where's the rest of my money? Even a novice like me could have spent no more than five for this lot."

"I owed Fesci down to the Duck's Bone," he slurred. "The she-wolf wouldn't give me nothing more to wet my mouth less'n I paid her."

"Naturally, you'd not earned a copper on your own through a whole day."

"Tried. Those I asked wouldn't even talk to me. Called me *poison* and *thief's spawn* and *maligner*."

The parole list accusing Neri of *slandering the name of a prominent citizen* had been posted all over the Beggars Ring. Everyone knew who *prominent citizen* meant, and who would hire an unskilled boy who was crossways with the Shadow Lord?

Furious, I snatched up the pitiful foodstuffs before he collapsed on his bed. "So you hurried back to the Duck's Bone and the taverner let you go back into debt?"

"She din't need to. I din't need to use magic neither." He rolled onto his back and burst out in drunken hilarity. "Fesci's partial to girls, so I offered her a go with my sister. Listed all the things you was good at—all those things that lawyer said you could do to him. Fesci said no, but five fellows give me a copper each to 'tell Romy' their names. I din't have to magic me the night's refreshment after that."

"Idiot child! I *trusted* you."

I snatched up the wire rope, and before he could get his sagging lids open to see what I was doing, his wrists were bound.

"Don't use that, Romy," he said through clenched teeth as I tied off the wrist binding to the staple. "It's too stiff. It hurts. Demonfire can't get me out of *plain* rope neither, nor even cotton cord. I have to *walk* to wherever I want the cursed magic to take me, and I have to know exactly what the thing's like that's waiting there, like that book with the rubies. I have to want it so bad, it spins my head. You don't under—"

"Things like a *biscuit*? Spirits, Neri! Magic blights the soul and corrupts your mind until you don't know right from wrong, until you go mad and do dreadful things."

For generations no burnt town, poisoned well, or building collapse had tormented the Costa Drago, but that sorcerers were proved to have caused it. It didn't matter if there was truly a monster under the earth, when the devastation sorcerers wrought was so terrible.

Neri tried to kick my hand away as I started wrapping his ankles. "Daren't try nothing anyways. Not if your devil cocksman's got sniffers about and you won't let me wear rat's hide—"

I boxed his ears and shoved him to the dirt.

"Plague it all, Romy, how's a whore learn to fight like you do? Never saw an ordinary person so quick with a knife."

"I don't want to hear your excuses. Close your mouth and think about what it means to be a man—a person who takes responsibility for what he does. Think about Da, and Dolce, and Cino, and the others, and what their life must be like now, because you didn't think before you thieved. Think about how you and I are to stay alive."

• • •

I took no chances. For a sevenday, I kept Neri bound from the moment he fell asleep until dawn. For the other hours I never let him out of my sight. When I released him on the eighth morning, he didn't start whining or babbling excuses. I considered that a victory. But I gave him fair warning: "You go nowhere without telling me. Let me catch the slightest whisper of drunkenness or magic, loose talk or thieving, and you'll be back in the wire ropes the whole day around if necessary."

All those years, Sandro's men could have slit Neri's throat and dropped him in the river and I'd never have known. I had to believe he'd kept Neri alive thinking I might care about him. But

I couldn't count on that forbearance anymore, and to my eternal astonishment, I did care.

Neri was rash and foolish like any ignorant, frustrated human person who had been forbidden to use the single incredible skill Lady Fortune had given him. But of my myriad siblings, he was the only one who'd thrown his arms around me on that first stolen visit from the Moon House and begged me not to leave again. He had given me the bronze luck charm to keep me safe. On my most recent visit, three years previous, we had wept together when he told me how Guero, Leni, and Primo, the three good-hearted brothers born between the two of us, had died in a riot when the Shadow Lord burned an entire quarter of the Asylum Ring to open up a new marble works for the coliseum. Perhaps Neri had laid Da's terrible dilemma in my lap, not because he was stupid, but because he knew his own recklessness could kill me, too.

"Just want a breath of air that isn't this house," he spat as I coiled the wire rope and laid it aside.

"I don't blame you for that. But you *must* learn to think."

He glared at me, but said nothing and turned away, rubbing his wrists—red and raw from the ropes.

• • •

Over the next days, Neri behaved himself, but rarely spoke. He moved his stool into the alley in front of the house to do useful tasks like whittling us new spoons and a piercing fork, or grinding the herbs I liked to keep for cleaning my teeth and combating chills or fevers. I allowed him to make trips to the market; they were quick and efficient. He agreed to fetch or deliver documents for Renzo and Garibaldi, so I gave him twenty coppers and sent him to Ghita the sewing woman to get himself a better shirt, as his was ragged from wear, and to get me a wrapping cloth to keep the documents clean, as his fingers were forever greasy. He came home with a decent brick-red tunic and a bag made of cloth scraps. He also, very pointedly, laid two coppers on the table.

Some might have rejoiced in his behavior, but I couldn't. His resentment had hardened into a silent barricade between us, and I'd no idea how to breach it.

One afternoon, as the two of us hurried past the Duck's Bone on the way to leave another application, a pock-faced boy with a slack lip called after us, "Hey, Neri, is that the witch? Looks awful pinchy for a high-class doxy."

The boy's brawny companion snorted with piggish laughter. "Ripe and tasty though. Very tasty. Likely she just needs a roll with a real Beggars Ring man."

Neri's color deepened and his feet slowed. "I'll speak to them."

"Leave it," I said. "Words are nothing. I can defend myself."

After that I piled my hair into a frowsy knot, bought a decent but ugly russet overgown to wear instead of the blue mantle, and scowled a great deal. Life no longer required me to display myself as beautiful, open, available, and ready at all times.

That afternoon a third client, Lawyer Aventia, legal advisor to an orphaned shipping heiress, gave me work—only two pages, but she promised better as she established trust with her young client. Aventia struck me as a sensible, intelligent person, and bold to pursue a profession where few women had ventured.

As I rose to leave, I pointed to a distinctive blue stone jar that sat on her writing table. "Dama Ciosa's teriaca," I said. "Do you find it helpful? I've heard many opinions."

Dama Ciosa claimed her *very* expensive physic, if ingested every day, could protect a person from every poison known, head off terrible diseases such as falling sickness and consumption, and improve the complexion. Tiny amounts of the poisons themselves were supposedly used to formulate the secret mixture, along with enough detestable ingredients to make dipping a cup in a Ring Road mud puddle seem a desirable alternative.

Aventia looked up, surprised. "I can say, unequivocally, that I have neither fallen ill nor died from poisoning in the years since my aunt persuaded me to take a daily dose of teriaca. Considering the many threats, warnings, promises, and ill wishes thrown at me from every side as I read law and served as a magistrate's aide, I would offer that as a strong recommendation."

The spark in her eye permitted my laughter. She joined in.

"Fortune's benefice, segna," I said, "and may Dama Ciosa's miraculous physic maintain its efficacy."

"Virtue's grace, Damizella Romy."

•   •   •

Despite my certainties, I kept an eye out for Sandro's spies over the next days, peering around corners or darting into alleys or shadows to expose any follower, frequenting little-used byways, and familiarizing myself with the other residents of our district. Never did I see a face from Sandro's household nor catch even a suspicion of observation. Just as I'd thought. I professed myself pleased.

A halfmonth of the silent war between Neri and me brought us to Summer Quarter Day and our first required visit to the parole administrator. We climbed all the way to the Palazzo Segnori in the Heights at noonday, so that we could wait four tedious hours in the afternoon heat for the sweating clerk to make two small checkmarks on his roster. Though I recognized a few men and women who'd come to the bustling center of Cantagna's governance on this day of transfers and settlements—legal, contractual, office-taking, marriage registration, and the like—no one looked twice at me. Well and good. I did not die of shame or regret when walking a district where I had once wielded influence of a kind. Neri simmered, but controlled himself.

As we left the parole office and descended to the Beggars Ring, a certain satisfaction settled my mind. My brother and I could make a decent life. He wouldn't maintain this coldness forever; we shared much more than blood. When we got home, I sent him out with fifty coppers to fetch new supplies of wine, ink, and cheese from evening market, while I wrote and copied the pages for Lawyer Aventia.

Whenever I visited Aventia, one or the other of us commented on the fact that she had still not succumbed to poison or consumption, thus proving the virtue of Dama Ciosa's teriaca. It was pleasant to laugh with another person, to speak of something that was not dire or secret. I nurtured a hope that we might share tea sometime . . . have a conversation about the news of the world . . . about history or what new artists had joined Cantagna's flourishing community of talent. My mind craved nourishment beyond wills and contracts; my spirit craved an acquaintance who was not my brother.

When I next looked up, night had fallen and Neri had not returned.

My dagger felt solid in my thigh sheath. Sandro's sorely depleted purse sat in its hole and tallied exactly. Neri's leather jerkin hung on its nail. A brief panicked search led me to the

Duck's Bone, where Neri hunched over a corner table with the slack-lipped boy and the piggish one, all three of them awash in ale. Neri was spewing some foul-mouthed diatribe about his "she-devil trull of a sister" who was afraid of his "slippery fingers."

Alarmed beyond my fury, I paused behind the roof post nearest them.

"But the she-devil won't know about this job. And Scandi's so cranked on mysenthe, he'll never notice a few of his silvers missing come morning. Maybe I'll buy a cask of my own and share it with you two. If Scandi says anything, I'll tell him the man what owned my whore sister will gut him. You can't rat me about this job, nor blab about neither of them ever, cause the devil lord's got spies. Got assassins. 'Tis a danger even to mention, as he's the—"

"Enough." I kicked the stool out from under the damnable fool. He fell on his backside and I dragged him home by his hair. Slobbering drunk, he wriggled and swore as I tightened the wire rope around his waist.

"It was just talk. They was ragging me, cause you tie me up. Wasn't truly gonna do magic. Wasn't truly gonna say his name. I'm not daft."

I gripped his hair, forcing him to look at me. "You think my master wouldn't gut *you*? Let me tell you about the time I accompanied him to Andalussi to oversee the questioning of a suspected sorcerer. The local alchemist had drunk a single cup of mead and got into an alehouse fight, bragging that the Unseeable Gods themselves had given him *skills* that made his brews and tonics more efficacious than any other throughout the Costa Drago. The nullifier started with his cods . . ."

The memory was one I had banished for years. Sandro's face had been as bleak as the windswept barrens outside the Invidian tribute town. An earthquake had collapsed one of the Gallanos quarries, burying a hundred and twenty workers. The people of Andalussi believed that the arrogant alchemist had waked Dragonis to kill their husbands, fathers, and sons, and after hours of torment, the man had confessed to the act. Half dead already, he was dispatched in chains to join the death ship that would deliver him to the Executioner of the Demon Tainted, who would throw him into the sea.

Whether Sandro truly believed the alchemist was a sorcerer or that he had actually caused the earth to tremble, I never knew and did not ask. It was the first year after his uncle's assassination and the whispers had already started that the new young segnoré of the Gallanos family had taken up the mantle of the Shadow Lord as well as that of *il Padroné*. I, his besotted courtesan, heeded those whispers and buried all thought of magic and fiery monsters very deep indeed.

Once Neri had emptied his stomach in a bucket, I stretched his time of restriction another month and tethered him every night and every daylight hour I had to be out. His wall of silence had shattered into untamable rage. Not once did he submit voluntarily. The constant arguing, the repeated wrestling, and the need to watch him every moment drove me near out of my mind.

Two days before his restriction was to end, I caught him sawing at his tether in the middle of the night with my own pearl-handled knife. Anger near shattered my skull. I heated the blade in a candle flame, put it in Neri's hand, and bared my wrist. The law drowned sorcerers, but Mam had said the only sure way for one sorcerer to slay another was with fire—a conflagration or boiling oil or a heated blade.

"This is the end, Neri," I whispered, hoarse from yelling. "If you want me dead, just do it. Once I'm a corpse, you're free. Go out and work your magic. Steal, get drunk, and curse *il Padroné* and your hard life. Let the Executioner of the Demon Tainted throw you from a cliff into the sea. But I'll not watch it happen, and I'll not drown with you. You are my brother and I dearly want you alive. Yes, we are damned. It isn't fair and will never be fair. But I'm tired and I want to sleep a whole night and not worry that I'll wake dressed in chains designed to sink me to the bottom of Night's Ocean. So do it."

"I'll do it, you cursed witch!"

My brother's rage filled the room, beautiful in its passion and monstrous in its torment—like Dragonis itself. When the heated blade touched my wrist, it took everything in me not to move. But I held still and silent and expressionless. Moon House mistresses had beaten me for days on end to teach me that skill.

Neri's hand did not shake . . . but neither did it press any harder. "Romy," he said hoarsely, "you've never had to—"

"Don't you dare make excuses," I said. My rage matched his. "Don't you dare speak. Cut me or drop the knife."

When the blade plummeted to the dirt floor, I snatched it up. That was when he started trembling like leaves in a storm wind. As did I.

I sliced through the rest of his bindings and waved the knife at him. "Lie down and go to sleep."

Eyes dark as charcoal pits, he scrunched his lanky body on his pallet as if to make himself one with it. I sat on my own blankets, back to the wall, and doused the lamp.

After a long while, his tight, short breaths grew long and even. Yet another night passed without sleep.

• • •

Morning light sneaked through the shutters and poked Neri awake. Nothing moved but his eyes, watching me heat water over our brazier and wash my face, neck, and hands—a small inviolate moment I stole every morning to remind myself there were other ways of living.

"I can heat the knife again or we can talk," I said, hanging my washing rag on a peg. "Which will it be?"

"Talk." His eyes were smudged with despair, not anger. "I don't want you dead, Romy."

His croaking whisper prompted me to start a brew of hawthorn seed tea, a poor man's nasty substitute for coffee.

"Go on."

"Every night I dream about Da's bloody stump." Neri's knuckle hammered on the table as if to jar out each word. "And I can't forget how Mam sold you when you was naught but Lina's age. Last spring, the little ones couldn't even cry, they was so empty. And then I think of those rubies—of the fine things I saw in that house where you were—of other goods out there for the taking, things rich folk mightn't miss. With this cursed magic, I could fetch them."

One would think I'd opened an aqueduct.

"I've stole bread with my magic. A duck once from the polter. Oil when Mam couldn't buy none. And yeah, a biscuit and a fig and wine and such, but it weren't never enough to make me feel anywise but a coward. And I'm so stupid, I didn't even know what to do with those rubies. Who buys 'em? Do they bring in sniffers if the one selling jewels is like me? I'm so scared of gettin' sliced up, burnt, drowned—all what you told me—and just *wanting* so hard, I can't think straight. But I swear I never told no one what I can do, nor what you can do . . . magic, that is. Nor who it was owned you." He glanced up, cheeks ablaze. "Didn't mean to make things so bad."

Neri's rushing confession trailed away. Maybe he'd opened a part of himself he hadn't intended. For certain his story had raised my own long-dismissed guilt. No matter what I'd told myself all these years, no matter logic, even at the Moon House I'd never starved.

"Coming to fetch me at the Shadow Lord's house, to warn me, was as brave a thing as anyone ever did," I said. "Even what Da sacrificed for us—he didn't have any choice. You did."

I poured the hawthorn seed tea and we drank in silence. When the cups were emptied, it felt as if a peace had settled over the house.

"An idea came to me last night," I said. "You held my knife all cockfisted. I think you need to learn proper fighting techniques. You're almost sixteen and your sister can take you down as if you were three. It's not just because I've eaten better than you for fourteen years. It's because my Moon House tutors taught me to kill a man as efficiently as to rouse him."

Neri's mouth moved but nothing came out of it, and his narrow cheeks flamed like the sun at its birth. To witness such total embarrassed stupefaction was almost worth three exhausting months. Ever cautious, I did not laugh, but by Lady Virtue's hand, I wanted to.

I didn't want to believe Neri hopeless. To survive, he needed discipline. That, along with some tricks with knives, I could teach him. Other subjects, too, if he would allow it, but first, I thought, give him the teaching he would value most.

Neri had seen enough over the past months to admit I knew things about combat that he didn't. His alleyway flailing had never gotten him anything but bruised and humiliated. So we set aside an hour every evening to work. I began as the Moon House tutor had, teaching Neri ways to break the hold of a bigger and stronger attacker. From body positions and unexpected moves, we went on to strikes to nose, eyes, or side of the knees, where to plant elbows, and how to use the fist and fingers like a knife. I made him repeat each technique over and over every day until it was perfect before we moved on to the next. Discipline.

"Such things were never to be used on one's own master or mistress, of course," I told him, when he marveled that a whore had been taught such things. "And never on their master's friends who'd been given permission to use such prize possessions as Moon House courtesans are."

Neri—still a boy in so many ways—blushed when I added such scraps of information, no matter he spoke worse with his tavern friends. I pretended not to notice. I'd sworn to be honest with him, hoping he would be honest with me in return.

"None of this will make you a soldier or a duelist. It might be enough to get you out of a scrape, but only if you're quick enough and smart enough to run away once you've done it. I was groomed to become a complete servant who could pour coffee with grace, read my mistress poetry, or hold an assassin at bay long enough for my master to escape and summon his soldiers. We'll work on the holding an assassin at bay before manners or sonnets."

"You're thinkin' to sell me to the Moon House?" Neri snickered, but with enough of an edge to tell me the jest had sober roots.

"Oh, I see how girls look at you," I said, nudging him a bit as he gulped a cup of ale. "But the Moon House wants children young enough that they can beat them down to nothing and start over. You're far too old and stubborn for that."

"Demonshit, Romy!"

Exactly so.

• • •

Ten days into our truce, Neri and I were making progress. It was the knife work he wanted, of course. He had no idea you could kill a man with a knife to the back of his neck or pierce a man's heart from under his breastbone. I said I would teach him those things only when I could trust him not to use them unless in extremity. ". . . and before we go further, you have to start paying for the lessons."

"Told you none'll hire me. I tried. Wasn't lyin'."

"I believe you. So you're going to work for me. Your pay will be your keep and more teaching."

I hoped to solve several problems at once. The larger problem was that the only skill Neri had was magic; to avoid the temptation to use it, he needed a way to earn his own money and to defend himself.

The lesser, but still critical problem was that it was near impossible to keep the damp and dirt from sullying my clients' pages. My father had taken only clients who supplied a place for him to work, but I dared not leave Neri on his own for so many hours. Our little hovel still needed a real door to block the wind and a real floor to minimize the damp.

With the stifling discomfort that I was throwing away a good proportion of our remaining coin, I laid seven precious silver pieces in Neri's hand. "Starting today, I need you to make us a door—something better than this scrap to keep out wind and rain. I also need you to cover this damnable dirt with wood."

"Me? But I don't—"

"Yes, you. *I* certainly don't know how to do either task. Talk to people about it, watch, ask. Start with the ironmonger on the corner. He can likely tell you who to speak with and where to get the materials. We can't afford to hire it done, and we cannot spend a copper more than's necessary, certainly no more than this I'm giving you. If you need an extra hand for something, I'll help, but you have to do the job. That's how you earn more lessons."

He glared at the coins with such spite, I thought he would throw them in my face. Then without a word, he stormed out. I hoped I hadn't ruined our peace. I hoped he would come back.

It was a very long morning. But shortly after midday, he dragged in a few planks, a rusty chisel, and a wooden hammer. In less than an hour, I had to move my writing work to the Duck's Bone, as his clumsy attempts to fit the splintered pieces together stirred up a maelstrom of dust, dirt, and unending streams of invective.

Every evening he had to show me his progress and tell me what he'd learned. Most days he also vowed to quit, swearing I'd only given him the task to make him look the fool. The toolmaker refused to make a wedge for *a thief's spawn*. A beggar woman stole the auger the ironmonger had given him. He cut his thumb trying to shape pegs with his eating knife.

I helped bind the wound, but did not relent. If he showed me progress, I taught him something new, reminding him again of the consequences of brawling, thieving, or even thinking about magic.

One of his excursions ended with a split lip and an eye swollen shut. His only explanation: "It was nothing. Didn't scrap. Didn't use magic. Didn't spill secrets."

I had to trust him. That was the hardest work I'd ever done.

By the end of a month, Neri declared his project complete. He pulled me into the alley to admire the newly hung door.

No one would hire Neri to build a house any more than they would hire him to protect their children. Not yet. The splintery floorboards were more crooked and uneven than the course of a river, and the lightest spring breeze was going to whistle through the gaps in and around the plank door. But a well-fitted band of metal held the door planks together, the hinges didn't screech, and the latch was solid, and when I sat on my pallet, I smelled clean pine beneath me, not piss-infused dirt. He'd even scooped the filthy oil and water from our sleugh and replaced it with new. Maybe it would keep our own demons at bay.

"Decently done. A fitting day to move forward," I said. "Did you know this is your birthing day?"

"Today?" Was I imagining that he stood a bit taller? "Knew it was close—summer and all—but never knew exactly . . ."

I showed him a page I'd been working on, pointing out the words he couldn't read. "First day of the Month of Vines. Sixteen years ago today. On the night you came squalling into the world, I asked Da how I could remember the new baby's birthing day and he showed me the date on a page he was copying."

"Da was a fool. Should've drowned us."

I couldn't chastise him for a sentiment I'd voiced so often.

To celebrate the completion of Neri's task, I coiled the wire rope and hung it on the wall. At the night market we bought him a dagger of his own. Once home again, I taught him how to kill a man with a single thrust.

That was as far as I could take him. On the next day, I went looking for the best swordmaster the Beggars Ring had to offer.

6

*T*hat is a listed duelist?"
I couldn't believe the bedraggled bulk huddled in the mud behind the Duck's Bone could lift a sword, much less earn his living fighting other people's contests of honor. He didn't even lift his head as he spewed half a cask of wine into the fetid swamp of a horse yard.

"The name Placidio di Vasil moved from unknown to second on the duelists' list in Tibernia in less than half a year, when he was not even three-and-twenty," said Fesci, the granite-boned, gravel-voiced woman who marshaled the Duck's Bone. "My brother lives in Tibernia, in the shadow of the conte's palazzo, and swears the story true."

"What happened?" The wine stench likely told the story. Drunkards' tremors would ruin a swordsman.

The taverner's boot nudged the man's hind end and elicited no response but a groan.

"One match happened. Placidio was standing for the conte's

own cousin, who was also his chancellor, who had challenged the conte's birthright. The duelist Gaetano di Brun, first on Tibernia's dueling list for seventeen years and still in his prime, carried the honor of the conte himself. My brother witnessed the match, and says Placidio had Gaetano well in hand, toying with him to please the crowd before dealing the final blow. But the conte's supporters near rioted, shouting that the upstart chancellor must have bribed Gaetano to fix the outcome in his favor, and the fight was stopped. The referees conferred and concluded that all was legitimate, especially as Gaetano was red-faced, sweating, and swilling wine as he waited, while Placidio stood cool and sober at the edge of the dueling ground."

"Then how . . . this?"

"Placidio lost the bout. Some said he yielded because he feared reprisals from the Tibernian conte, whose fiefdom includes his own village of Vasil. Some said it was only luck he'd got so far up the list and Gaetano's mastery won out. My brother believes that Placidio judged Gaetano too drunk or too ill to fight, and backed away from the win out of respect. Whatever the reason, Gaetano laid such a beating on Placidio as will never be forgot. The disgraced chancellor was banished forever from Tibernia and his children disinherited, no matter that the conte himself was childless, and that most believed the chancellor's claim was righteous. Placidio fled. Eventually he came to Cantagna and started from the bottom again. Never made it more than halfway up our list. On occasion, you can glimpse the fighter he was. The rest of the time . . ."

Some unintelligible mumbling shifted the muck by the duelist's face.

"What's that, old man?" Fesci pulled a bucket from the rain

barrel by the Duck's Bone's back door and doused the swords-man's head.

"Win more'n lose. Poor folk need champ'ns, too."

This was delivered with a sloshy resignation that did not bode well for clients relying on Placidio de Vasil's prowess. You might stay alive by hiring a listed duelist to fight your battles. But if your champion lost the match, you still had to pay the fine, yield the land, suffer the marriage, or lose whatever honor you had submitted to the adjudication of Lady Fortune and the sword.

"And he teaches swordsmanship?"

"If you don't mind he's drunk more than not. None who's put up with his teaching for more'n a month failed to learn summat, no matter they can't say a rapier from a shepherd's crook to start. You said you needed cheap . . ."

"Life mus' balance. Fast, slow. Win, lose. Drunk, sober. Live, die."

The big man rolled to his back, filthy beard, threadbare finery, and overpowering stink entirely at odds with a position even halfway up a list of fighters who relied on skill and wit to keep them alive to collect their pay. But the price the taverner had quoted was much less than every other swordmaster I'd queried, and perhaps a tutor whose wits were frequently clouded might remain unaware of the dangers associated with Neri and me.

"Where does he teach?"

"Uses the old barracks yard up to the Asylum Ring like all the others."

"That won't do." Condottieri, the mercenary soldiers hired by merchants and wealthy men like Sandro, often trained there. So did nullifiers. "I'll find a place."

Grudging, I showed the duelist two silver solets, then dropped them in Fesci's hand to hold for him. "The month's retainer. Report to Romy in Lizard's Alley at half-morn tomorrow. Sober. Bring variant arms suitable for a novice youth."

A grunt served for acknowledgment.

I argued with myself all the way home. Neri needed this. But only fifty silver coins remained from Sandro's purse of some hundred and fifty. I'd thought the purse could last us five years. My belly hollowed at the thought of living on my writing fees. I wasn't yet earning enough to feed us.

•   •   •

"Humph." The grunting swordsman stood in our open doorway. "Your place here—unexpected for the neighborhood."

But for the accuracy of his sentiment, one might easily doubt that Placidio di Vasil's swollen, seeping eyes could take in the details of my household. The rest of him was no more promising. He reeked of wine and urine. An angry scar creased his face from the left eye to a square chin buried in a clotted rats' nest of black hair. Grime and grease disguised the colors of his limp shirt and threadbare doublet. Yet my expectations were not entirely correct, either. I'd thought him run to fat, but the buff jerkin and leather breeches hugged a big frame layered with muscle and sinew, and though the taverner Fesci had called him *old man*, not even his unhealthy skin would mark the duelist past five-and-thirty.

"Fortune's benefice, swordmaster. Be welcome." I motioned him to step inside.

"You're no lawyer, are you, Romy of Lizard's Alley?" he asked, lip curled enough to twist the ugly scar. He dropped a large bag

of scuffed leather as his glance scoured the table and my shelf of
pen cases, ink flasks, and stacked parchment.

"Why do you care what I am?" I said, more curious than
annoyed.

"'Tis unsafe to have me waving a blade near vermin."

Truly, many citizens had reasons to be wary of lawyers. "Be
at ease. I'm but a lowly scribe," I said. "And it's my brother Neri
will be your student."

"Student?"

My brother had arrived in the doorway as if his name had
summoned him. He scowled at the slovenly man whose height
topped his by the length of his forearm and whose shoulders
made a solid wall the bedraggled garments could not disguise.

"I know how to swill wine well enough." He set a stack of
clean parchment on the table.

I'd hoped Neri's errand to Fedig the pen seller would keep
him away while I interviewed the swordsman. Fearing I'd be
unable to find a teacher we could afford, I'd not told him of my
search.

"Segno di Vasil is a swordmaster and comes recommended.
Supposedly he teaches better than he washes. We'll hope."

My jab slid off the man, whose bleared eyes took Neri's measure in turn. Neri fretted that he'd not yet reached my height.

"A scrapper, are you, boy? Mostly fists and feet, and lose
more'n you win, I'm guessing. But a new blade at your belt." The
swordmaster extended a scarred hand that could enclose an
infant's head entire. "Let me see it."

"I do all right." Neri clamped his hand on the metal bound
sheath and glared at me. "Don't need a new teacher, Romy. This'n

looks more like to steal the blade than to know what's to do with it."

I jerked my head sharply in the direction of the duelist. "Show him."

Only an idiot would leave her fool of a brother at the mercy of a drunkard swordmaster half again his size and infinitely more skilled, but I also had hours of copying to do before the next morning. I needed to get a sense of the swordsman quickly and, if he seemed promising, see their first lesson done.

Grudging, Neri passed over the dagger. Placidio examined the grip, quillions, edge, and point as a physician explores skulls, tongues, and urine.

"Well chosen," he conceded. "A good length. But what need has a Beggars Ring boy for a new blade and finer skills? Have you acquired a new enemy? 'Twould likely be cheaper to hire me to fight than pay me to train a hothead to skewer a dunderwit."

"You don't look a man who could teach anything *fine*," snapped Neri, his forehead scarlet.

The duelist rolled his eyes at me as if to say, *You see?* So, the fellow's perceptions were not entirely dulled.

"He has no particular enemy," I said, as Neri smoldered. "But the world is hard and dangerous. We've recently lost our father, and my brother approaches his majority. Experience has taught me great appreciation of the sword's discipline. I thought perhaps a swordmaster could impart something of that discipline to my brother, though doubts gather about you along with the flies."

Ebullient laughter burst from him like crisp new wine from a new-opened cask, only to be swallowed so quickly, I doubted my own memory of it.

"Can't argue that, now can I?" he said, harsh and low. "So where shall we retire to give this a try? I understand you're not keen on the barracks yard, and I'd hate to splatter blood on your parchment, lady scribe of Lizard's Alley."

"The old wool guild storehouse," I said. "Beggars sleep there in winter, and no one's sickened from it or been hauled to the Abyss by demons."

Placidio shrugged and hefted his armaments bag. "'Tisn't the dead bother me."

We trooped out our new door and through the crowded lanes toward the River Gate and the Venia—Cantagna's lifeblood.

A century before I was born, the Sestorale had co-opted the wool guild's dockside storehouse to house victims of the plague. Thousands of Cantagnans died there. Even after that horrific storm had passed, neither the wool guild nor anyone else would use the place. No one even wanted its individual building stones or timbers, for fear of reawakening the horror. Thus the wool guild's fine stone building sat empty save for birds, cats, and seasonal beggars.

We emerged from the narrow gate in the city's outermost wall well upriver of the new docks Sandro's father had built two decades past when fire destroyed the old ones. The wool house stood stark in the distance, lone amid the burnt and crumbled ruination at a bend in the river. The duelist moved ahead of us, leaping between rocks, mounded river wrack, and rotted remains of other structures with a lightness that belied his size.

"*Stronzo*," spat Neri, glaring after him. "Filthy sot. There must be someone better. Set a pitcher of wine on a rock anywhere close and I could take him down with my boot."

"That might be so," I said, "but I doubt it. Watch how he moves. And I'd guess he could describe every detail of our house as accurately as he assessed you."

"But I'm not—"

"Certain, you're a hothead." I bumped his shoulder with mine. "Isn't that why you spent three months tied to an iron hook? You can't take me down yet—not if I'm awake—but if you practice what I've taught you and whatever he can teach, you'll be able to do that and more. If and when you've emptied this Placidio's well, and if we can afford the fee, we'll try for someone better. Besides, I've paid for a month already."

Neri halted for a moment, then quickly caught up with me again. "That's his name . . . Placidio?"

"Aye."

Whatever curiosity the name roused in Neri was quickly lost in aggravation, as the swordmaster insisted we use fallen timbers to scrape out a sandy arena in the center of the old storehouse, a task which took us a sweat-soaked hour. But after a few brief tests with a rapier and a long sword that seemed to wield Neri rather than the reverse, Neri was glad of our efforts. Every trial ended with his face plowed into damp sand rather than rubble, spiders, broken shells, rusted nails, splintered wood, dung, and a wide variety of dead things.

Placidio traded a short sword for the long sword in Neri's hand. "All right, boy, come at me again. This time low."

A growling Neri charged and swung the short sword like an axe at a tree trunk. Placidio stepped aside and whacked the side of his head with the flat of his blade. The short sword went flying. Neri stayed upright, but bent over, hands propped on his knees, breathing hard.

Placidio offered him a bright green flask with a stopper shaped like a frog. "Drink. It helps with the dizziness and gut churn."

Neri stared at the flask for a long moment, then shook his head and straightened, watching Placidio intently as the man returned the flask to his bag.

Placidio extracted another quick victory, scarce twitching his hand before Neri crashed into the wall. I moved to call a halt. This was getting nowhere. The brute had long proved his prowess over a boy who'd never held a blade longer than his hand. But the man waved me off.

"All right," he said to Neri, "'tis clear you've no instincts with swords. But you've this fine new dagger, so you must have some belief you can use it. Get it out."

Neri drew his dagger and took a close starting position in front of Placidio, settling his grip as I'd shown him. The duelist had not yet drawn his own weapon. Rather he rubbed his eyes and gave a great yawn, as if he'd rather be anywhere else.

In an eyeblink, Neri's hand thrust forward and up toward Placidio's breastbone.

"Neri!" I screamed, paralyzed as the duelist jerked . . .

Only he didn't fall. Impossibly, Placidio's great paw gripped my brother's wrist. A round sweep of that powerful arm and a quick sliding boot, and Neri's back slammed to the earthen floor. The unbloodied dagger went flying.

His gaze wintery, Placidio stared down at my brother.

Horror paralyzed me as Neri lay still, then inhaled with a great gasp, rolled to his chest, and scrabbled on all fours toward his fallen dagger. The man strolled after him.

"Neri, wait! Segno di Vasil, please—!"

Placidio's boot stomped Neri's backside. Boot and earthen floor squeezed out another groan.

"You have a move, pup," said the duelist, nodding in affirmation, calm as death's aftermath. He lifted his boot. "Shall we try it again?"

"He didn't mean—"

"Don't tell him what he means, lady scribe. It's his task to figure that out. Then he can learn how to focus that intent in body and weapon, not in dithering the air around him. That's the discipline of the blade. It's not knowing the Santorini Thrust."

As he bellowed this last, Placidio's toe nudged Neri's ribs, eliciting a muffled hiss.

"Stand up, boy, and fetch your weapon. A few more knife trials to see what other moves I need watch for, then I'll let you at me with bare fists. I'm guessing you'll like that better."

A few more taunts got Neri moving. He snatched up the knife and bounced to his feet. The heat of his shame and fury pulsed halfway across the wool house.

My own heart yet galloped; my skin was clammy. Neri's move had been meant to kill. Was Placidio truly going to let such an attempt pass unpunished? And if so . . . Fortune's holy dam, what kind of fool was I to give my brother skills that made his smoldering rage mortally dangerous? A lesser tutor would be dead. I'd never seen a hand so quick. My master at the Moon House had sworn that no one in the world could stop the Santorini Thrust at close range.

Placidio goaded Neri into test after test. To my relief, my brother attempted no more killing attacks. At first he flinched at Placidio's every twitch, and shifted stiffly at the man's direction. But as the hour moved on, he allowed Placidio to touch his shoulder and arm, shaping and directing his awkward movements. No longer sullen. No longer resisting. I didn't understand either one of them.

After a few rounds with bare fists, including one shining moment where Neri's flurry of blows did manage to cause the duelist a moment's irritation—perhaps akin to a gnat in his ear—Placidio again offered Neri his green flask.

Neri accepted it. Without looking his tormentor in the face, he gulped and then violently spat out the mouthful.

"Nasty," he croaked, as he shoved the flask back into Placidio's huge hand. "Like you."

That Neri would dare such insolence astonished me. He had to be terrified. I certainly was. My body ached as if I'd suffered every humiliating blow.

"As you please. Bring your own replenishment from now on, then." The duelist drained the flask and wiped his mouth on his filthy sleeve. "But ginger tea, salt, and lemon works well for what we'll be doing. What you'll be doing."

Placidio nodded at the jumble of discarded blades, clubs, bucklers, and canvas wrappings. "Student packs the armaments and carries them back to town."

Stone-faced, Neri bent to the work. He could not hide his aches, but he wrapped each weapon carefully, packed it away, and hefted the scuffed leather bag.

With a cheerful—mocking?—bow, Placidio invited me to lead us out of the wool house.

The warm midday smelled of the river and the rotting wasteland. I felt as if I'd spent an eternity in another world. But I kept my eye on the duelist and Neri. Something had happened between them, and I hated that I didn't understand it.

"You've a few decent moves." Placidio motioned Neri to stay beside him, even while striding onward at a pace that soon had my brother huffing again. "More than I expected, truth be told. But you've no endurance, no quickness, nor much of any speed save what nature plants in a boy of—what?—seventeen?"

"Near enough."

"Before you pick up a blade again, we'll work on those three skills. You won't like it. I didn't. No one does. But there's no use to any weapons training until you can get out of an opponent's way, avoid his blows, outlast, or outrun him."

"Won't run away. Not never." Neri grunted as we climbed the steps to the open gate.

"Which says nothing good about your wit. Doubt I can improve that. But pigheadedness will do for now. Give me a month of work to earn your sister's silver, and you'll see a change. Are you game? Or can I wallow in my bed later tomorrow? Doesn't matter to me, you know." He cast a baleful glance over his shoulder in my direction. "Coin doesn't pass but one direction between us."

Years of caution insisted I cancel the whole business, but I liked what I'd seen of Placidio's teaching overall, and I liked how Neri had responded to the man's forbearance. Perhaps he had at last realized the dangers of his temper. I would let him decide.

We were halfway back to Lizard's Alley before Neri made his answer. "I'll work. Don't want to hurt this bad ever again."

Placidio bellowed a laugh. "You won't. 'Twill be worse. Every day worse."

He turned to me and bowed. "Scribe Romy of Lizard's Alley, Fortune's benefice for the rest of your day. I'll fetch him same time tomorrow. No need for you to accompany us, unless you want. Though he may wish it, I won't kill him. It would spoil my reputation and drop me straight off the dueling list. And you can rest easy. If he kills me, there's none'll seek vengeance."

"Virtue's grace," I said. And meant it.

The duelist grabbed the heavy armaments bag, threw it over his shoulder as if it were a wet towel, and vanished into the crowded street.

Neri stayed silent as a post as we trudged the rest of the way home, stopping long enough to buy two loaves of bread, a spiced sausage, and a flask of weak ale. The day had turned out hot and sticky. Once back to Lizard's Alley I seized a wedge of one loaf before Neri devoured the entire rest of it and a good portion of the cheese from our shelf.

Only as I cut an old apple to share did I attempt a word. "What in Lady Fortune's true name did you think you were doing?"

"Guess I wanted to prove I weren't no coward nor my sister's suckling."

Several deep breaths were required before I was calm enough to answer. "I'm proud that you stood back up and faced the consequences of what you did. But, spirits . . . the Santorini Thrust! All that proved was that you're an idiot. I told you only one man in thousands could defend it. You were very lucky."

"Not *lucky.*"

Neri jumped up, latched our new door, and closed the thick shutters on our single window. Then he returned to the table and spoke softly. "This Placidio . . . the name struck me when you first said it. But I didn't imagine it could be the same Placidio as the *duelist*. It was that green flask with the frog's head what told me for sure. He carries it with him when he fights. I've watched lots of fighting over the years—down here and up to the Asylum

Ring. Tovi and I go up there oftimes, sit on the wall, and watch the dueling."

He stopped here and bit his lip, eyeing me closely. I stayed quiet lest I stem the tide, curious when he leaned forward again.

"That story you got from Fesci over't the Duck's Bone? It weren't none of those reasons—respect or weakness or bad skills—lost Placidio that match in Tibernia. I've seen the man with the frog flask lollop through a bout with some fighters, doing all but offering the win to the other on a spoon. Sometimes he'll take it for himself. Sometimes he'll let the other get in a strike to take him down, even wound him pretty wicked. But I'd swear it is *ever his own choice* as to whether he wins or not. A few times I watched him fight a man high on the list. The better they were, the better he fought, and I saw him—Romy, I got to where I could see him start his defense move when the other had scarce begun an attack, like he knew what was coming. And so today . . ."

Horror near overwhelmed me. "You used a killing move on purpose, believing he could *anticipate* it?"

Neri grinned as I'd not seen since he was four years old. "And he did, didn't he? He knew what I was going to do at the very moment I started it. Maybe before that! And when he grabbed my wrist, I felt it."

Appalled and confused, I shook my head. "Felt *what*?"

He leaned closer. "His *magic*, Romy. Placidio di Vasil is a sorcerer."

"No, no, no. That's impossible. A sorcerer would never live . . . use his magic . . . so publicly."

"That's why he can't win too often," said Neri. "That's why he had to lose the Tibernian match. That's why he lives in the

Beggars Ring. Certain, better dueling fees could get him lodgings in the Asylum Ring. Move up the list, and he could live as high as he wanted. But he daren't."

I refused to believe it. To my knowledge I had never met another sorcerer, yet I could not imagine anyone less likely than a slovenly, drunken duelist.

"You said you felt his magic. How is that possible?"

"When he held my wrist, I felt the surge . . . the fire in the blood, same as mine. But magic doesn't fire my blood unless I'm working at it apurpose. It had to be his."

If this were true . . . how could I let Placidio teach Neri if he might recognize what we were?

Neri's excitement blazed through the hot dead air in the stifling house. "I could show you. Where's your luck charm?"

"Left it behind. I hadn't much time . . ." I didn't want to tell him I'd left his charm with a spoiled little chit who had likely discarded it.

"We'll use mine then." Fervor undimmed, he untied a bit of rag from up his sleeve and shook the bronze charm onto the table. "Hide it in the alley. When I use magic to seek it, you can hold my wrist. I'll swear you'll feel it."

"Are you mad? We're not working magic here or anywhere. Not ever. The traces linger and sniffers can detect them. Follow them." Everyone knew that.

"But, Romy, if I'm right about Placidio, we might learn more from him than swordwork. Tales say sorcerers can make light without fire or cast people to sleep or turn iron to gold. How fine would it be to do such things?"

No matter his enticing projects—and who knew if sorcerers could actually do such fantastical things?—the memory of using the wormlike power that crept through my body disgusted me. That was the truth of sorcery—the corruption that drove a person to slaughter children or set a village afire. I'd seen the results of those things.

"Consider," I said, "a sorcerer also might turn us in to divert attention from himself. Perhaps he kills the people who know his secret or forces them to deeds against their will."

I'd seen what powerful men did when threatened. And if Placidio was a sorcerer who could anticipate an opponent's moves, he was powerful, no matter where and how he lived. "He must not know we're demon tainted, whether he is or not."

"Aye. I s'pose." Neri's enthusiasm waned only slightly. "If touching someone while we're using magic could reveal us . . . maybe that's how sniffers identify us. Touching people."

"Maybe." I shook my head to erase the image of the fearsome creatures.

"So I go ahead with Placidio? He's not going to know about me as long as I don't use any magic. And I didn't do naught to let him know I was onto him."

"Except attack him with a kill move."

"He would have said something. Given a sign. He thinks I'm a dullwit."

"We'll see if he shows up tomorrow. Maybe he runs away when anyone finds out . . ."

That's what I wanted us to do—run. But Placidio might be no threat at all, whereas violating Sandro's parole was certain danger.

". . . or then again, maybe he kills us tonight."

"I'm for sleep." Neri's grin turned to a grimace as he stretched his shoulders.

"Wash first," I said. "You stink like he does."

Despite my anxieties, Neri's eagerness pleased me, as did his discomfort from his lesson.

As Neri slept, though, worries crept back. Surely our own danger was multiplied if Placidio di Vasil was a sorcerer. Was it even possible a person could use magic so often as Neri thought the swordsman could? He didn't seem on the verge of madness.

Neri needed tools and discipline to stay alive, and where better to learn what was necessary than with a man who had to live with the same risks? If Neri behaved himself, his parole would not last forever; the law said an underage parole would expire at age twenty. Once free of it, we could leave Cantagna forever, and instead of mere survival, we could turn our minds to living.

7

My wakeful night went for naught. Placidio did not arrive for Neri's lesson as promised.

"Maybe we should go find him." Neri poked his head out the door for the tenth time since the city bells had rung half-morn.

"Maybe we should find a different swordmaster." I forced my eyes to focus on the page of cramped writing in front of me.

The long night had left me bleary-eyed, nervous, and irritable. Not even the wine that sat beside my ink bottle had improved my state.

How foolish was I to allow a sot of a swordsman to know where we lived or to let Neri show off knife moves an uneducated Beggars Ring boy wouldn't know.

For so many years, I'd considered myself a woman of the world, educated, sophisticated, experienced in intrigue. Ambassadors, aristocrats, and the wealthiest merchants had paid court to *il Padroné's* mistress, knowing she had his ear. But all that had been illusion. Indeed my opinions had swayed Sandro's judgments and my questions illuminated his thinking, but I had never had to face the consequences of my choices. Shielded by the Shadow Lord's power, I had been playing games, not living. Living was dirty, scary, and complicated.

I'd no idea what to do about Placidio, and misjudgment could cost us our lives.

"He took your silver, Romy. A listed duelist can't afford to be known as a cheat."

"A youth and a whore born with a price on their heads daren't challenge anyone."

"But he's one of us. I'm sure of it."

"There is no *us*, Neri. No guild of demon-born sorcerers. No anyone. You can't expect benevolence or fraternity. Of all people, you should recognize that. Likely Placidio ran after all—thinking you discovered his secret."

Neri yanked open the door yet again as the city bells rang midday. "Well, you can hide here forever and mourn your fine life with the devil lord. I'm going to the Duck's Bone and find the man who owes us either service or silver."

I drained the wine flask and threw it after him, which did naught but splatter our new wooden door and stain the oily water in the sleugh. What a stupid custom—the threshold sleugh. Demons had roosted inside this house for very long time.

It was impossible to work. I stoppered my ink and took out down the alley after Neri. Lady Fortune's macabre humor likely had a sniffer lurking at the Duck's Bone waiting for him.

By the time I arrived, Neri had found Placidio facedown in the horse yard, just as I'd seen him the first time. Fesci the taverner was washing her hands at her rain barrel. "He lost a duel last night. Always makes for a bad morning."

"Is he wounded?"

"'Taint bleeding, if that's your question."

"Then tell him he shows up at our house tomorrow half-morn or we pass the word he's a cheat as well as a drunkard."

Clients would hire duelists who were drunkards, as the referees wouldn't allow them to fight if they were besotted. But no one would hire a duelist who cheated his employers. The matters involved in duels were too serious to entrust to someone without honor.

On the next morning Placidio stood in our doorway promptly as the bells rang half-morn. He was neither clean nor humble.

"Forgot to mention my regular business must come first," he said, stomping his boots as he entered, ensuring muck fouled the sleugh, not my new floor. "Whether the event itself, the preparation, or the aftermath."

"So a month's lessons are not quite the number I believed." The pinch of the purse had become an ever-present worry. I'd need to double my client list to support the swordmaster's fee without emptying our purse.

Placidio shook his shaggy head. "We'll do extra hours most days. Certain, you'll get your full month's tally."

Though he did not carry his armaments bag, the green flask with the frog stopper hung from his belt.

"I'll have him back by noontide," he said, as Neri swallowed the last of the stale bread I'd soaked in wine and oil. "Likely won't be worth much. But after a rest, he'll still have work to do, so if he sits idle, you'll know he's not serious as to what you want of our arrangement."

"You'll be at the wool house?" I was not entirely reconciled to letting Neri go off with him alone.

"Aye, there. And maybe up and down the river for today. Maybe a climb up the Boar's Teeth. Come along if you're feared I'll bruise the laddie."

Neri's resentment billowed like steam from a kettle. "Don't need a wet nurse."

"I'll stay behind," I said before Neri blurted anything stupid. "I've work to do."

Placidio motioned Neri into the alley. As he pulled the door closed, the duelist stuck his head back inside. "Won't kill him."

The door slammed shut.

∙ ∙ ∙

And so it went almost every day. Placidio arrived at half-morn and led Neri away with a promise not to kill him. From time to time, I tagged along to watch—from a discreet distance. He had Neri running up and down the riverbank, picking his footing through rocks, ruins, mud, and sand. He chased him up the steep rocks of the scarp known as the Boar's Teeth, slapping a whip on the track behind him. One day he threw my brother in the Demon's Washtub, a bottomless spring in the hills east of the city. He had to jump in after him. Neri had never bothered to learn to swim.

Never did the duelist reveal a hint of magic. Never did he ask where Neri had learned Santorini's Thrust or the other moves I'd taught him. From what Neri said, he never spoke of anything but their work. And whenever Neri swore to quit, Placidio invited him to wrestle or fight him with his dagger—telling him to use any move he wanted, taunting him until he could not possibly walk away.

One day as I watched, Placidio bound his own left hand to his belt. I was proud when Neri refused to attack him until Placidio unbound himself, though I reminded him later how stupid it would be to give advantage to an enemy. Inevitably, Neri received a drubbing with a full measure of taunts. But each time I saw him beaten, he had improved.

The rest of the time Neri was too tired to give me any trouble, and he learned quickly that Placidio could tell whether or not he had done the running, swimming, or other exercise he assigned for evenings. Evidently, the consequences for slacking were awful enough that he did what he was told. After a while, he didn't have to be told. Discipline. I approved.

At the end of our month, I had put aside enough to renew Placidio's services without emptying the purse. By the end of the second month, my brother ran, jumped, swam, and did acrobatics as if he were a jongleur in a wedding processional. My greatest difficulty was keeping him fed.

Every few days Fesci at the Duck's Bone would send a message that Placidio's regular business must take priority for the morning. Neri would groan in pleasure and go back to bed. And then, early in their third month, we received no message and Placidio still didn't arrive.

YEAR 987: AUTUMN

"Maybe a match cropped up unexpectedly," I said, as Neri glared down the alley. The hour was already near noontide. A chill drizzle warned that winter would soon be on us.

"I'm going to ask after him," said Neri. "We were going to start real blade work today."

"I'll come along," I said. "I told Fesci I'd write a letter for her mam." Few in the Beggars Ring could read or write, and it was often more worth my while to charge a small amount to fill a poor man's need, than more for a lawyer's work. Finer law required finer parchment, better inks, and hours of walking and waiting for clarifications.

Neri didn't wait for me to assemble my writing case. By the time I arrived at the Duck's Bone, he had searched the tavern and the horse yard behind it.

"He's not in the yard nor the alley. Fesci says he staggered in just after dawn to warm up, saying he'd fought a duel early, but he didn't intend to cancel my lesson. Already drunk, though. Fesci says if he's not wallowing out the back, maybe he's gone to The Pipes to get the blood off him. Guess it's bad for dueling business if he wears too much."

Placidio wasn't at The Pipes. The poor citizen's laundry and bathing pool flowed cleaner than usual today, thanks to the rain. A toothless codger washing his shirt told us where the duelist slept.

The dim, damp, rat-infested stair beside a butcher's stall brewed a primal urge to bathe. No sound came from inside the unpainted door at the top of the stair, but my knock swung it inward a little. "Segno Placidio? Are you in?"

I nudged the door fully open. Though no one would call the low-ceilinged chamber clean or pleasant, not with the stench of rotting meat from the butchery below, it was reasonably tidy. A rolled pallet filled the corner, soiled linen heaped beside it. A carved chest sat under a grimy window, and a battered, plainer chest, long, flat, and bound with leather straps, hugged the end wall. Two shields hung on the wall, one a very old round war shield of leather, wood, and iron, the other a beautifully tooled and lacquered leather buckler of deep red, such as men carried in processionals and ceremonials. A dueling prize perhaps? A spear and a poleax hung beside them, amid various empty hooks and nails. There was no sign of the duelist's leather bag.

"You said he never took two challenges in a day, so it wasn't that another job interfered," I said, as we descended to the street. "And it certainly sounds as if he was planning to fetch you. Elsewise, he would have told Fesci. So maybe he was drunker than he thought. Collapsed on the way to Lizard's Alley."

"We would have seen him on the Ring Road," said Neri.

The matter had become a puzzle I wanted solved. For those who live condemned, an abrupt change in settled routine could not but rouse anxiety.

"So perhaps he comes to Lizard's Alley by some back way instead of the Ring Road," I said. A mediocre duelist could have many reasons to stay out of the common eye. Especially a duelist who was demon tainted.

Neri knew every alley and byway in the Beggars Ring. It was on our third try, a circuitous route along the riverside, through the stinking vats and colorful, soggy, flapping pennons of a dyer's yard, and into a deserted alley behind it, that we found him. Placidio's big body was slumped under the stair that led to the rooms above the dye shop. Had the torch by the shop's back door not been lit against the gloomy afternoon, we'd never have spotted him. A pool of vomit helped as well.

"Segno di Vasil, it's Romy and Neri of Lizard's Alley."

I touched his shoulder. He slumped sideways.

"So drunk, he can't breathe." Disgusted, Neri squatted beside him and shoved the duelist's chest. "Segno Placidio, wake up.

You could have sent us a message. Guess you lied: you said you never picked up a blade while you were drunk."

"I don't think he's drunk," I said. The man reeked of sweat, blood, and vomit, not wine. His complexion was gray, his skin dripping with sweat, not just rain.

"Placidio," I spoke directly into the man's face, "are you ill? Or wounded?"

He shuddered an agonized breath. His trembling hand pawed weakly at his left arm, then dropped back to his lap.

I tugged the duelist's sodden cloak aside. His ripped left sleeve exposed only a short, bloody gash on his upper arm. Pressing the clammy flesh beside the wound yielded little new blood, but his hands were cold and the beat of life in his wrist near undetectable. His heart . . .

I laid my cheek on his breast. Had I been impatient, I'd have thought that shuddering breath his last. But his heart spasmed weakly.

"Have you other wounds?" I said, eyes and hands searching for more blood. "Sisters, what's wrong with you?"

Shivering and struggling for breath, Placidio grimaced and pressed the heel of his hand onto his forehead. "Woolfffs— bn"—harsh, forced gasps punctuated his syllables—"bag—need blue—and fiiiiiire. . . ." The last word dissolved into a labored exhalation.

"Wolfsbane?" whispered Neri, appalled. "He's a dead man."

Poison lore had been a part of my education, just as knife skills were. Wealthy citizens of the Costa Drago used poisons and potions as freely as they used spices and lace. But my dismay echoed Neri's. Wolfsbane had no proven antidote.

"Have you nightshade?" Though my tutors had been skeptical, some of the herbals we studied claimed the wicked belladonna—itself a poison—could combat the horrors of wolfsbane.

"Bag. Blue. Packet."

A quick survey showed no sign of the leather armaments bag. "Spirits! Where's his bag? Neri . . ."

Neri's magic could surely find the thing. We couldn't let a man die.

But a quick search had Neri hauling a dark mass out of the deepest shadow of the stair.

Relief flooded my skin. "A packet, he says, but it's more likely a vial or flask. Careful with it."

I put my face in Placidio's; his vision would be blurred, but his mind clear. "Open your eyes, segno. Look at me. Is it night-shade you have? Must I *heat* it? How much should I give you?" Even mixed in wine not more than a droplet or two else the remedy would kill him.

His only answer was a labored, "Blue. Fire. Please."

Neri scrabbled through the armaments bag, scattering sharpening stones, oil flasks, the green drinking flask, and an oilskin pouch containing several paper packets. He examined them all. "There's only this that's blue."

I held the packet of bluish dust in front of the duelist's nose. "This powder? In wine? Then . . . ?"

"On wound. Then flame. Hur—" Placidio choked, halting both words and breath. He slumped further sidewise in the wavering light.

I shook him, pounded his chest. Yelled at him. When I detected a hiccup that might have been a breath, I sprinkled a little powder on the innocent-looking slash, and then sat back helpless as the blood soaked it up. That couldn't possibly be enough to do anything.

"He said flame." Neri had fetched the torch from the dye-shop door. "Maybe that's why he stopped here."

"But what do we do with it?" I said.

"Srrrr"—it sounded like another exhalation—"it."

"*Sear* it? You can't mean that." The memory of the lopsman cauterizing my father's bleeding stump raised bile in my throat.

Divine graces . . . I couldn't use the torch. It would mutilate, if not kill him. So I emptied the rest of the powder on the wound, twisted the thin paper into a palm-length taper, and stuck it in the torch flame.

It smoked. Charred. *Curse it, take fire!* A gleeful flame singed my knuckle then winked out.

I was likely wrong about what he intended, but knew nothing else to do. He had spewed prodigiously, but if the poison had come directly through the wound, emptying his belly wasn't likely to eliminate it.

Hand shaking, I tried again. This time the twisted paper caught fire. Cupping my fingers about the weakling flame, I moved it close to the wound. Orange light streaked Placidio's dying eyes. A slow racking breath, then he exhaled, "Now."

I gripped the duelist's hand so he couldn't flail. Neri sat on Placidio's legs, clamping his knees tight, and grabbed his other arm.

The wound gaped at me like a red mouth. *Cleanse this foulness,* I said with all my will, *keep him alive.* I touched the tiny yellow flame to the wound.

"Aaagh!" Placidio bit off a scream. Blood and blue powder boiled in the gash.

"More," he gasped, when my hand yanked the blazing twist away.

Again I touched the blue flame to the smoking center of the wound.

My fingers stung with the heat, yet not so much as I expected, for the blaze did not consume the paper. It should have been ash in moments. His skin should be blistered, scorched, cracked, but was not. *Magic* . . .

"Spirits, Romy, do you feel that?" A thunder in my head almost drowned out Neri's murmur.

The flame flared brilliant blue—or was it Placidio's eyes that blazed sapphire, tinting the twisted paper? Scorching heat raced up my arm, as if the burning taper stretched itself and wrapped around my limb, infusing vein and sinew with a power that cleared rain and fear and fog from my head.

A deep breath calmed my racing heart. Surely the heat in my veins flowed from both hands—from the blue flame and from Placidio himself. Incomprehensibly, as the moments passed, my fingers that gripped his wrist told me when his heart picked up a normal pace, when the writhing agony in his gut eased, when the torturous labor of his lungs smoothed.

The blue flame faded to yellow.

I dropped the flaring taper as it disintegrated into ash.

"He did it." Neri, his face pale and suffused with awe that must surely reflect my own, scrambled off Placidio's legs.

"Scribe Romy . . . you should go. Get out of the rain." The whisper drew my gaze back to the duelist's unshaven visage, which was screwed into a grimy knotwork of pain, exhaustion, and wary questioning.

With the thunderous fire inside me damped, the sodden bustle of the Beggars Ring afternoon returned in a terrifying rush. How close must a sniffer be to detect magic? Could Placidio somehow detect that we felt his magic and knew what it was? Such an education life had granted me, and not a scrap of it could help in matters of true importance.

My confusion provided no answer to his questioning glance but the commonplace.

"We can't leave you here. I've a honey salve for the burn"— which was scarce more than a red-and-black roughness about the wound—"and I've been taught how to stitch a wound, though I've no practice." Yet he wasn't bleeding. "We could help you to your lodging or ours . . ."

He heaved his big body into a semblance of sitting. "No. I'll just rest here a while. Needs must postpone today's lesson."

"Tomorrow will be soon enough." I heaved a breath. "Placidio—"

His hot, blood-streaked hand settled firmly on my arm, silencing me. His dark gaze spoke no threat, but serious intent. "I *must* ask you not to speak of this. It's my old granny's remedy. Wouldn't dare try it on anyone else."

"I've a notion what this was," I said, without averting my gaze. I could not let him mistake me, though I prayed the rain and gloom could mask the danger I spoke. "But I'm no surgeon or alchemist, and thank Lady Fortune, I've little experience of healing practices. Never in the world would I *consider* speaking of this incident, trying to explain it, or attempting such a thing on my own. But someday . . . Perhaps we can talk more next time you fetch Neri."

His returned gaze might have left gashes on my own skin. "Best not."

Slowly, he turned his attention to Neri, peering close as if seeing him for the first time. "What of you, lad?"

Neri scowled at the ugly wound. "I'm thinking you did that just to scare me off or make me look stupid. If I mentioned it to anyone, they'd laugh. I won't scare. I want to learn blade work."

If a man who had just smelled the odors of death's halls and used a skill damned since the founding of the world to remedy it could possibly laugh, I'd name di Vasil's coughing grunt just that. His head sagged to the wall at his back. "Believe me, boy, I've far better ways to scare you. Until tomorrow then."

I rose. "Come, Neri. I've work to do. The graces be with you, Segno Placidio."

I thought I heard a quiet "in your debt" as we hurried away. But when I glanced back Placidio di Vasil had vanished. He'd not just faded into the shadows. He was gone. We needed more lessons from him than blade work.

• • •

To my frustration, the astonishing incident behind the dyer's yard did not birth any kind of intimacy with the swordmaster. Neri reported that Placidio was all business during their sessions and would permit no other conversation. When I invited the man to share a meal with us or to sit and rest a while, he always had an excuse. He needed to focus on Neri's training, he said. He professed that he didn't like to become too familiar with his students or their families, lest it taint his teaching. When I asked if his shoulder was healed, he said duelists believed it was bad luck to speak of injuries.

I didn't want to force it. A man who lived in constant danger had a right to make his own rules.

Thus we moved forward. My days were spent writing. Wills and letters, leases and agreements. Writs of eviction. Records of debts and payments. Boring, tedious work, it left too much space for unwanted thoughts. Of the irretrievable past. Of the unimaginable future. Of some monstrous, looming anxiety I could not name. I discovered that mixing wine into my hawthorn seed tea dulled those intrusive thoughts while still permitting the concentration needed to accomplish the work.

During the day I could pretend. That I was strong enough to build a life of my own. That I could convince Neri that if we worked at it, we could forget our curse and live without fear.

Nights were far more difficult. I could not dismiss imaginings of Cino racked with coughing like the potter's child down the road, or a starving Dolce allowing someone like Lawyer Cinnetti to have his way so she could eat. In the dark I ached for the sharp-edged brilliance of every hour I'd spent in Sandro's company and the secure comfort of each night spent enfolded in his arms. At night I felt my mind dulling like neglected silver, and the murky intelligence of superstition and rumor replacing the complexities of history, politics, and grand intrigues.

At night I saw the truth.

At night, I omitted the hawthorn tea and let wine drive me to oblivion.

Placidio's arrival in the mornings lit the only spark of curiosity in me. His magic was a mystery and a wonder. Such power. So

clear, so clean, so ... huge, it had felt. It reminded me of an evening a few years previous, when Micola and I shopped in the
Market Ring. We'd seen a man hauled away in wire rope, accused
of sorcery. Bystanders said he had run around the night market
creating music from fire—each torch, lantern, or cookfire
sounding like a different instrument.

When red-robed investigators of the Philosophic Confraternity
questioned the witnesses, most said the sound was like the
screeching of wounded animals or the wailing of demons. But a
few insisted it was a clear and glorious harmony that made them
forget they were tired or hungry or unhappy. The philosophists
ordered their praetorians to beat those few, and warned them to
come to the Academie for proper cleansing. I'd assumed the
demon sorcerer had mesmerized them and only those who spoke
of screeching heard true. What if I'd been wrong?

"Neri," I said one night as I sat in the dark with my wine flask,
"when you use magic, does it feel the way Placidio's did, like fire
and color and ... clarity?"

"Aye," he said, drowsy. "Something like. Not quite so grand,
but like."

"I didn't know it could be like that. Mine feels like a nest of
cold vipers deep inside. When I touch them they squeeze out
droplets of venom that infest blood and bone. And always I'm
left with chills and an aching head. I thought that's what everyone experienced—the evil of it."

"Never felt evil from the magic. The thieving ... I knew that
wasn't righteous, but I've never understood why everyone believes the magic itself's so wicked. Maybe when someone uses it
to burn a village or bury a quarry, it's the person who's evil, not
the magic."

My mother believed any person carrying the taint was evil.

We had lived near the sea when I was small. While Mam nursed my brother Primo, Da would sit me in his lap and tell me the gods-and-heroes tales he loved. I adored those hours. I felt safe and special, his voice booming in my chest as he held me. He prided himself on his excellent recall of every tale he'd ever heard, and he wasn't so burdened with worry then as later on when his work could not keep pace with the infants that kept coming. But young as I was, I wasn't fond of the stories themselves, much preferring birds and cats and small, adventurous girls to evil monsters and righteous bloodshed.

Sometimes Da would let me tell him a story. Delighted, I would solemnly pronounce that I would speak the *Lay of the Desperate Thief* or *The Mountebank's Journey to Leviathan's Lair*, only the desperate thief would be a hungry crow trying to steal a pie from Sallichi the baker's window, and the mountebank a clever fox who prowled a stream bank in search of a talking fish. Da would frown and tell me to speak the story correctly, pretending to be offended at my silliness. But his arms around me would say different and when he didn't think I saw, his lips would twitch and almost smile.

One stormy night though, Mam laid Primo in his basket and asked Da what was that idiot story he was telling me.

"*The Hunt of Karylis and Atladu,*" he said. "A sea storm at night requires a tale of the mighty Atladu."

"Atladu is not a cat!" she snapped. "And why would he be hunting a frog in company with a swan?"

"No, no, woman. That's one of Romy's tales, not mine."

It wasn't merely that Da was confused. He told three differ-ent stories that night, swearing he told them as he always did—

yet all turned out to be nonsense stories of cats and birds, of scorpions that sang and trees that walked. His horror, when he looked at me and realized that he could not recover the right words, no matter how he tried, had felt just like the earthshaking that had flattened half our village and collapsed our roof.

I couldn't recall what using the magic felt like as I stole my father's stories, but I well remembered him saying, "Virtue save us, 'tis only demon magic would do such a thing."

And I well remembered how my howling mother snatched me from his arms that night, dashed into the rain and sleet, down to the black, churning sea. I kicked and screamed as she held me down in the cold water. As the salt waves choked and blinded me, she screamed, "Demon, demon, demon," and squeezed my neck.

Da dragged me away from her. He carried me home mumbling, "Unrighteous woman. Unrighteous to slay your own blood."

Though a stiff-necked servant of the law, Da refused to slaughter his own child. Instead, he moved us to Cantagna lest someone else had noted my perversion. Hiding us in the crowded Beggars Ring, he taught me to read, and made sure I knew the thing I must never do—tell a falsehood while touching someone's flesh, lest my evil magic corrupt a mind. He and Mam seeded one child after another as if to make up for the flawed thing they had brought into the world. But he never told any of us another story, never held any of us in his lap. And he never remembered his god stories. Not that night; not ever.

How was it possible such evil as magic could heal a poisoned wound or save a decent man's life? It was as if the world I understood had reversed itself, as profoundly as it had on that night by the sea.

"Neri."

"Mmm." So not yet asleep.

"When Placidio lay there dying, before you spotted his bag, I was going to ask you to use your magic to find it. Could you have done that? Would you have?"

"Certain, I could and would have done. Whyever would I let him die if my magic could do aught to prevent it?"

It was easy for me to forgo magic in the name of safety, because my talent felt like a disease, and did nothing to balance the wickedness of corrupting a mind. But if Neri's magic was like Placidio's . . . if he could learn to be careful and use it only for important things when there was no alternative . . . do good with it . . . why shouldn't he? Why would it feel so marvelous to him if it was so dreadful? Maybe it was something broken in me that made my magic so awful.

"I have to deliver some eviction notices to Notary Renzo tomorrow afternoon," I said. "I'm thinking—just this once—we might try what you suggested. I could hide your luck charm and let you find it. Only I'll hide it somewhere you've never been. If we were ever to face something like Placidio's situation again, in a strange place, we ought to know if you could manage it."

The breathless dark told me he was still awake, though he didn't answer for a long while. "Romy, are you drunk again? Seems we're going through a barrel of wine every—"

"Maybe a *little* drunk," I said. "But I just . . . I need to know."

Where did the true evil lie? In the intent, or in the magic itself, or in the soul that made use of magic?

8

YEAR 987:

LATE AUTUMN

The city bells rang the evening anthem as Neri and I entered the Temple of Atladu and Gione, a towering ruin in a blighted area of the Market Ring. A rumble of distant thunder gave warning we oughtn't stay too long.

"Have you ever been here?"

Neri's nailed boots clicked on the faded mosaics of the rotunda. "Nah. Mam said it was cursed. Or haunted. She were always spooked about something."

"No ghosts here," I said. "It never housed the dying as the wool house did. This was built in a prosperous time."

I told the story in the words it had been told to me, back when I was eighteen and the mosaic of history, myth, and art had come alive for me. "In those peaceful days, some came to believe that the Unseeable Gods had returned at last and merely awaited our notice. The hopeful built temples like this one all over the Costa Drago, tall spare structures that shaped the light. They filled them with artworks that rejected the forms of common life in favor of the ethereal and sublime."

I pointed up to the astonishing dome, its soaring windows bereft of glass. Peeling frescoes revealed only bits of once-brilliant color.

"They added fountains and channels to carry Father Atladu's waters, and orchards and gardens to honor Mother Gione and her bounteous earth. They designed labyrinths to prevent demons from infesting the space. But just as the temples were completed, the plague struck. Wave after wave of disease scoured the world over a span of seventy years. By the time the last body was burnt, the Costa Drago had lost half of our people, and no one believed in benevolent gods anymore, seeable or unseeable."

Indeed, in the recovering world, merchants and bankers like Sandro's family had found more profitable concerns than myths and superstitions and gods who could not bother to make themselves known. The temples of the Unseeable Gods fell to ruin.

"I was brought here once to see the art," I said, pointing to a bronze relief that depicted a willowy Gione tending a forest, while the unnaturally tall and slender Atladu bathed her with rain. "The style is very different than that of modern artists, who imagine true muscle and bone beneath the skin. Both are beautiful, but—"

"*He* brought you here," said Neri, no more interested in the elegant sculpture than he was in the dust piled in the corners. "*Il Padroné.*"

"Yes."

Only with effort did my voice remain steady as I recalled the light in Sandro's eyes as I embraced the beauty and despair of this place. No image, certainly no structure, had ever so touched my heart. On that day, here amid failed hopes of the sublime, Sandro first shared with me his vision of a city renowned for justice, prosperity, and beauty. "Gods, how I loathe this noxious, unending contest for power," he'd said. "So much time wasted. Imagine a Cantagna invested with works as beautiful as this, but robust and real, something to inspire even those in the Beggars Ring to full humanity, as elegant abstractions never will."

He believed this fervently. Growing bold in our deepening intimacy, I had suggested that people—even Asylum Ring or Beggars Ring folk—were not children forever to be guided, and that they needed more than noble vision to replace their homes and businesses destroyed for his great projects. I could not but think of my three brothers who died trying to prevent the Shadow Lord's servants from burning tenements for the new marble works and coliseum. Even then he heeded my opinions. It was after that conversation Sandro began his *listening walks* around the town in disguise. That was when I began to believe in his vision, as well as the man himself.

"Will you ever tell me about him?"

"No."

"Romy, I—when I took the rubies, I didn't mean to ruin—to hurt you so."

I couldn't say it didn't matter. "There's naught to be done about it."

"He knows about me. For certain?"

"Yes." At the least he suspected. But he could not arrest Neri as a sorcerer without admitting that he himself stood in violation of the First Law of Creation—the single eternal, immutable, unifying law of the Costa Drago—by ignoring those suspicions.

Yet time could change that determination. Sandro was ever his own harshest judge—which did not mean he let the exactitudes of law or over-righteousness deter actions he deemed necessary or desirable.

"Does he know about *your* magic? Is he going to come after us someday?"

"Honestly, I don't know." The wishing dream that Sandro yet loved me and would fetch me back had long faded into wine-soaked despair. "He granted you a parole. For now, we should read that as a mercy."

Never in my hearing had Sandro questioned the extermination of magic users. He did not subscribe to the popular belief that every ill in the world could be laid at the feet of Dragonis's descendants. And indeed when we talked of history, I learned how fear of magic could fuel such accusations as easily as firm evidence. Yet our mountains still belched fire and ash or flowed with molten rock that could swallow cities, and the earth shook with fury that could destroy whole provinces or change the course of rivers, and no one could explain it. Sandro had come to the belief that the fear, jealousy, and corruption magic bred was a certain evil—and until someone could refute the beliefs that had driven us through millennia, the world was better off without sorcerers.

How long had he known about Neri? I had believed I knew all his secrets.

Only half a year since my exile, and Alessandro di Gallanos already felt as remote as Atladu and Gione. He seemed more like these fleshless myths than the man of muscle and sinew who had sat naked in my bed, hunched over parchment and pen, sketching his ideas for a theater where any citizen could hear poetry or plays or music. He had tossed his attempts aside that night. Laughing, he had kissed me and sworn me never to tell of his awkward scribblings, lest his detractors have him thrown off the Sestorale's Commission on Public Artworks.

Neri's parole ensured we had to remain in Cantagna. To imagine the Shadow Lord would leave two sorcerers loose in his city forever, risking his own downfall if his connection to them ever became known, was idiocy. Unless he loved me. But that, too, was idiocy. He had made it clear.

"So, are you ready to show me what you can do?" I snapped—harsher than I intended. "There are a hundred chapels, fountain rooms, vestibules, gardens, and labyrinths in this temple. Your charm is hidden in one of them. I brought it here this morning."

Neri held out his arm.

As my fingers circled his bony wrist, he closed his eyes. His sinews grew taut. But I detected nothing else, even when he started walking. If there was a path to the charm, his magic would lead him down it. If not, the magic would allow him to pass through obstacles like walls of solid brick. I'd seen it.

Neri and I had last played with magic together as children. The sister and three brothers born between us had shown no demonic taint. Da wasn't sure about Neri until a day Mam threatened me with a beating for stealing a packet of cherries from the chest that was our larder. A distraught three-year-old Neri had walked straight through one of our stone walls to fetch the pits from the alley where he'd hidden them.

Da protected Neri from Mam's wrath, just as he had saved me from drowning, but then he made me responsible for teaching Neri the dangers of what he was. I resented the responsibility. I was ten years old, and my father couldn't bear to look at me, my mother wanted me dead, and my other siblings were afraid of me. Now I had to spend all my days with a demon child.

But I didn't want Neri dead either, so I tried to do what Da had done with me. I took Neri out in the maze of Beggars Ring alleys and got him to show me his talent, so I could teach him not to use it.

Neri thought it was all good fun, giggling and playing chase-and-hide, and I couldn't convince him to stop. And he was so innocent, so loving, and so happy for my attention, I couldn't be angry with him either. I even came to think that being able to walk through walls like Neri did might make being a demon worthwhile. Then, of course, Mam heard us laughing in the alley and was sure we were plotting some demonic evil. In the matter of a day, she started beating Neri regularly to convince him of his wickedness, and she sold me to the Moon House. All concern about our tainted souls was buried as deep as any sin could be.

Now I was encouraging my young brother to use what he'd never wanted to stop. He strode through one chamber after another, through a desiccated garden and myriad turns of a winding labyrinth to a grand statuary hall. There at the heart of the temple, Chloni, the serene, sexless Creator of Stars, towered over us in marble majesty, slender arms spread wide in everlasting benevolence.

We ascended a tightly spiraled stair to a columned gallery overlooking the statuary hall. The gallery took us through a series of archways, opening into views of chamber after harmonious chamber.

No matter how marvelous the view, Neri didn't look around. His eyes were open, but fixed straight ahead. I still felt nothing in his wrist but his pulse. His luck charm lay in the marble palm of Veitan the Gateward, the knee-high guardian statue at the dry well at the lowest level of the temple. Nowhere near our path.

Beyond the fifth arch, the gallery walk dead-ended at a balcony. Below us was a dry fountain, its centerpiece a depiction of Virtue's children—Reason, Justice, Temperance, and Courage—though most of Courage lay in rubble. Above us rose one of the temple's many spires.

Neri pressed his fingertips to his eyes and shook his head. "Can't seem to call up the magic. Never had this trouble before."

I dropped his wrist, exasperated. "You started out the wrong direction."

"Makes no difference," he said. "When the magic's working, it tells me when I've strayed. It's like someone's pinching me all over till I get it right."

"You said you had to want the thing so bad it made your head spin. Maybe you fail because you're trying to find your own luck charm."

"Maybe it's because this is a dead place that—"

I hushed Neri with a touch on his arm. A faint chinking noise, regular as a heartbeat, echoed through the stone halls, seemingly from everywhere at once. Determined footsteps joined the metallic echo. More than one person.

"We should hide," whispered Neri, as the chinking footsteps, louder now, were joined by muffled voices. Urgent voices.

"There's nowhere up here to hide but the archways between the rooms," I said. But those were quite narrow, little better than the columns. "A look from the proper angle and someone below could spot us. Besides, it's not illegal to come here."

Yet indeed our intent to work magic left me guilt-ridden and inclined to hide, too. It was never wise to attract undue attention.

We should get back to ground level, the labyrinths. Even so, we'd hardly a chance of getting away undetected. We'd come too far in.

I drew Neri close and whispered, "If we meet anyone, just let me talk."

The click of Neri's boots grated my nerves as we headed back the way we'd come. My small relief at reaching the head of the stair without raising shouts reverted quickly to dismay. Quick, quiet steps were coming up. No chinking. No murmurs. This was someone else.

A round bald head was our first glimpse of a breathless, dusty man as short, thick, and solid as a bridge piling. His cheeks pulsed scarlet. Thick-fingered, dirty hands clutched at a leather satchel hung from his shoulder. He seemed as alarmed to see us as we were to see him. Brows like black scrub brushes sat above wide-set, obsidian eyes. "Who in the great wanderings of the universe are you?"

"We've come to visit the temple on our way to market. 'Tis odd, we've heard. Is it forbid to ordinary folk?" I added just a touch of grievance. While holding my head high, I slipped my fingers into my pocket—the one with the slit that allowed me to retrieve my knife.

His clean brown tunic and hose could mark him anything from a merchant's clerk to a guild craftsman. His small black eyes darted from Neri to me and back to Neri.

My heart skidded when he stepped closer to my brother, squinting.

Neri's eyes widened.

"You're Dumond the metalsmith!" Neri's astonishment raised

the name to uncomfortable volume. "It's so odd, your being here, as we were just using—"

My heel on his toe stopped him cold.

"I don't know you." The man cast a sharp glance back down the stair. The chinking steps were closer, faster, but not in sight as yet. "Get out of my way."

Neri shook off my hand as I tried to draw him aside. "Romy, this fellow made our luck charms. I think he knows about people like us."

Stupid Neri! My hands yearned to tumble him down the stairs.

Instead I said primly, "'Tis no fault of ours to be born to a thieving lout."

My feeble attempt at misdirection came too late. The man's face opened in recognition. "You're the Beggars Ring boy! And you had"—pale as sea foam, the man whipped his head around to me—"a sister with *skills*. Lady Virtue's bastard, we must get you out of here. It's a *sniffer* on my heels! They think sorcerers caused some explosion up to the Heights this afternoon. They're scouring the city for the likes of us."

A suffocating blanket shut out the world. My stomach hollowed. *A sniffer.* The chinking and footsteps . . . Sniffers were kept on chain leashes.

"There's no place to hide up here," I said, forcing calm. "It's a dead end."

"Can't go down." Dumond the metalsmith pointed back the way we'd just come from. "Follow me."

"I told you there's no way out that way."

"There's always a way," he said through his teeth. "Just have to make it. Trust me or take your chances with the sniffer."

Dumond jogged off down the gallery, swift and silent. Neri and I exchanged a terrified glance.

"Romy?" He was trembling.

"Your magic can get you home, yes?" I said. "Try it. Go."

He shook his head. "Sniffer would know magic was done. I can't leave you to that. It wasn't working in here anyways."

Trust had never come easy. Only Sandro had ever earned it; now even that faith was shaken. But I didn't know enough to get us past a sniffer, and the metalsmith, if that's what he was, seemed to believe he did.

"Come on." Neri and I joined hands and raced after the bald man.

When we reached the shadowed archway that opened onto the balcony, Dumond knelt on a square of canvas, pulling a flat crock from his leather case. His pudgy fingers unbuckled a strap and yanked a lid from the pot, filling the air with an acrid odor. Next he produced a wide brush from the bag and dipped it in the . . . paint pot? I'd thought he might have a rope in his case!

Speechless with dismay, I watched him slap long streaks of brown paint on the old stone of the alcove wall.

"Open one of the small pots, boy. Black or yellow. I need contrast. And hurry, if you please."

Neri knelt beside him.

Panic loosened my tongue. "What are you—?"

"Wait and see. You can't conjure fire by any chance?" Squinting, he painted a third strip that, with the floor as one side, formed a tall rectangle. He slathered paint in its interior.

"No."

"Always seems to work better when there's a flame to warm it."

So much for trust. A madman wasn't going to save us. But jumping from the gallery would kill us for certain. And a sniffer . . .

Neri's trembling hand set another flat pot—black paint—on the spread canvas.

"Now find the yellow, the ocher, the white, and narrower brushes."

Voices called to one another down below. "Not in here!"

"He were running, segnoré!"

"Search deeper in. One of them's here." This was the leader, booming his well-shaped words with authority. *Segnoré*, an honored gentleman. "Nothing from your creature?"

"Naught as yet, segnoré."

Unflustered by the cries so close, Dumond used a smaller brush to overlay his brown swathes with thin black strokes. With a natural artistry, Dumond coaxed the dabs and strokes of color from his pots and brushes into the image of a door. Metalsmith. Painter. Surely he didn't imagine . . . And yet Neri could transport himself through walls.

"You're working magic," I murmured.

"Not yet. Not till it's good enough," huffed Dumond as his hand sped through layer after layer of detail. "Soon as I reach for magic, they'll be on us. No sooner, I hope."

He threw down the black-stained brush and took the next one Neri offered. It swirled yellow and brown paint into brass hinges and a simple latch.

I had seen Placidio heal a wound that should have killed him. Neri had stolen rubies from a locked room. Was it so far-fetched to imagine a sorcerer could create his own doorway? Articulating such a thought stole my breath. Where would a magic-wrought doorway lead?

"Pack it all up, boy," Dumond whispered, his hand never stopping. "Try not to spill or smudge the paint. Damizella, if you would see where our pursuers are? The better I can make this, the more likely 'tis to work."

The image of a common oaken door centered one wall of the archway. While Neri fumbled with pots, lids, and buckles, I peered over the balcony rail. No one. But I could hear them.

"Get your creature in here, Ugo," the gentleman's voice commanded. "There's new footprints in the dust."

"That stair goes nowhere, Segnoré Bastianni."

"All the better."

Their words told me where they were. I didn't need to risk looking. But dread fascination drew me to the other side of the archway to peer down, and a blight fell upon my soul when a burly dun-haired man, armed with axe and bow, and wearing the bilious green tabard of a nullifier, strode into the statuary hall below. He joined a taller man wearing an elegant crimson toque and a matching cloak with a sheen of gold thread—a scholar of the Philosophic Confraternity, who was examining the spiral stair. Those who guided the studies of philosophy, mathematics, and astronomy in service to the twin divinities, Virtue and Fortune, were especially ardent in their pursuit of sorcerers.

But it was the one trailing behind the nullifier who caused my knees to weaken. An iron collar about his neck linked him to his master's belt by a chain that chinked as he walked. The sniffer.

From the crown of his head to the soles of his feet, his body was sheathed so tightly in dark green silk that he was all but naked. Though head, limbs, and torso testified otherwise, the eerie color and lack of fleshly characteristics left him more like to a giant worm than human. No openings for eyes, ears, or mouth were present, as a sniffer's ordinary senses were dulled to refine his ability to detect magic. How he was fed, I didn't know. Only two small breathing holes in the hood served to remind one that this obscenity was a living creature.

Sniffers were once sorcerers, humans born with extraordinary skills they never asked for. But when these sorcerers were captured, they accepted a terrible bargain—to trade cruel death for existence at the end of a chain. They were always male; females might birth more of our kind. And they were always gelded to ensure they could not force their tainted seed upon innocent women. To expiate the crime of their birth, they were allowed only a single purpose, exposing those of us who might yet walk free. How could they be anything more than animals who devoured their own kind?

The academician flicked his hand toward the gallery. "Take your creature up there, Ugo. I believe one of our assassins might be cornered."

Cold, trembling, I retreated to the flimsy shelter of the arch. Neri crammed paint pots into the bag, while Dumond's strokes gave depth to the timber frame of his door.

"They're on the stair," I whispered.

Dumond nodded, bit his lip, and detailed a highlight on the latch plate. The back of his hand swiped at his watering eyes. "I need more time."

Terror and hope shredded my nerves. Neri shook so hard he could scarce buckle Dumond's straps. Threatened with a cruel death, would he allow himself to be mutilated . . . sheathed in silk . . . turned into one of these hounds of death? He was just a boy.

I spun round and watched the gallery. When moving shapes

beyond the farthest arch told me our pursuers had arrived, I shifted position to block any view of Dumond and Neri.

"Stop right there, philosophist!" I cried. "How dare you bring this foulness to a holy temple?"

From behind me Dumond whispered approval. "A few moments only."

"I'll warn you, woman, do not interfere with my purposes." The taller figure emerged from the first arch, his robes billowing in hues of fire and blood.

I swept my pale blue mantle over my head and strode down the gallery toward him with all the hauteur of the Shadow Lord's favored courtesan passing his whispering subjects. One archway, two, and then I halted just outside the third. One wall and its short tunnel and sixty paces of empty gallery separated me from the pursuers.

"Intrude no farther, corrupter," I called to him. "I am Magdalena di Fortunato, priestess of the Unseeable Gods."

"A *priestess*? I believed your kind faded in another age." The tall, lean man paused in the dark arch, younger than most Confraternity academicians I had met. His toque dipped down and then up again as he examined me. "Oh, worthy lady, how I would delight in speaking with you—discerning what you believe and why. But, alas, I am in pursuit of abomination and cannot be detained. Step aside, please."

The spare planes of his face imparted an ascetic dignity to the philosophist. His voice was mellow, his earnest sincerity indisputable, yet his words grated like metal on glass.

"My order is sorely diminished," I said, attempting to show the same pride as a tribal holy woman from the Kewaine Straits who once visited Sandro's salon to demand tribute for his ships' passage. Dignity and righteous determination had left her tattered robes and blistered feet all but invisible.

"We have no resource to restore the glory of the Divine Ones' halls," I said, "but we travel the length and breadth of the Costa Drago to keep them free of profanation. You have brought your own abomination here."

His gaze followed my accusing finger to its target. "I can understand your distaste for sniffers, revered dama, and yet we've brought the creature here to pursue *your* own gods' mandate. This afternoon a terrible crime was committed in our city—a magical explosion aimed to assassinate prominent members of the Sestorale as they led a citizens' processional, honoring the hundredth birth anniversary of Giovanni di Gallanos, one of Cantagna's great men."

"Assassination! The Sestorale . . ." I faltered. *Gallanos*.

I slapped my numb fingers to my breast. Forced my numb lips and tongue to speak as a priestess must. "Magical explosion! Heinous murder."

Sandro preferred to work outside the glare of public attention, thus rarely attended public celebrations. But Giovanni di Gallanos was his beloved grandfather. He would have been at the head of the processional. An easy target.

"Yes. Another despicable crime from the hands of the demon tainted."

"Were there victims? How many?"

"Two of the dignitaries and perhaps a dozen common folk died in the horror. Many more were injured and will likely die as well. We summoned sniffers immediately and discovered traces of magic. *Il Padroné* himself granted us an open warrant to root out the murderous demons. This creature caught a scent in this neighborhood and followed it here. Evil lurking in the rubble of the divine."

Il Padroné's warrant . . . *Graceful spirits.* Relief engulfed me. He lived. But this Dumond, was he one of the attackers?

A shrill whistle from behind near burst my settling heart. Neri's poor imitation of a shrike.

"No sorcerers come here," I said, as my foot glided backward a long step. "Only faithful worshippers of Atladu and Gione."

Questions for Dumond would come later. Never would I turn any sorcerer over to a sniffer. I whipped around and bolted.

"After her!" The command pursued me along the gallery through the rooms and arches.

Chains clanked on marble. The thud of heavy boots shuddered the floor.

Dumond tossed the brush into his satchel, slung the bag over his shoulder, and spread his arms wide. Near invisible flames burst into light from his cupped palms.

"Zhaaaa." A nerve-stripping, wordless cry like the howl of a wolf shattered the air behind me. I glanced over my shoulder. The three hunters had emerged from the last arch before ours—not sixty steps away. The sniffer's green silk finger pointed straight at us.

"*Esse ancora, lo spirito maligno!*" The dun-haired nullifier nocked an arrow and raised his bow.

Hearing the damning curse directed at me might have frozen me with fear, but it was awe that halted my feet when I reached Dumond. A warm draft smelling of paint wafted through a rectangular opening in the archway wall. Neri stood beyond it holding open a heavy door—the one Dumond had painted.

"Come, damizella, hurry," snapped Dumond.

An arrow whizzed past my cheek.

The painter reached for my arm with his fiery palm. I backed away, but the fingers that clamped my wrist and dragged me toward the dark opening did not burn. No living blaze charred my sleeve, though fire ripped through my veins, inflamed my chest, seared my lungs, charged the world with color. The faded hues of the temple took on the sunlight's brilliance and washed together as if Dumond's paint pots had spilled over my head. Magic.

Glory! I felt invincible, enlightened, alive. Surely the secrets of the divine lay just beyond my seeing.

"Blink, woman. Breathe." The man spoke through clenched jaws and yanked my arm again. "Take another step. You'll get us snatched."

I staggered forward. Squeezed my eyes shut. Released a breath, then opened them again. A grim Dumond stood one step below me on a stair landing, his color-stained hand latched to my arm. His cheeks and brow were ash gray and furrowed, his black eyes a wasteland.

We had entered a square tower. Homely scenes of fountains, rivers, and ponds adorned the walls, seeming to glow of their own light. But between us and the opposite wall opened a fear-some plunge to unseen depths. The stair clung to the ancient walls, descending to a landing at each corner, like the one where we stood—a pause before resuming its downward path. Above us, bars of afternoon light fell on us from high, narrow windows and the sunny chamber where the stair had its origin. The Stair of the Well. We were still in the temple. Not three hours previous, I'd descended these very steps to hide the charm.

"Get out the way, Romy!"

Neri stood just behind me, holding open an oaken door that had no relationship to the stair landing.

I stepped back, twisting my neck. To left and right, like a phantasm superimposed on the tower wall behind me, stretched a ghostly columned gallery, the image of the place we'd just left behind, stained with a purplish light.

"Feeling his magic, eh?" My brother's grin spoke his wonder. "Get the canvas!"

Dumond's spattered canvas was just visible through the doorway. Neri reached through, snatched it, and flung it to the metalsmith, then gave the heavy slab of oak a great shove.

A purple shadow coalesced about the door and thick fingers plunged through the gap between door and jamb, transforming Neri's good cheer into panic.

Grunting with renewed effort, Neri shoved on the oaken slab. Dumond hissed and let go of my arm. Heat, color, enlightenment, and invincibility vanished. He squeezed around me and joined Neri, trying to push the intruding attackers back so the door could close.

I snatched my knife from its sheath and slashed at the intruding hand and broad forearm. Flesh and tendon ripped. The blade grated on bones. I wrenched it out and struck again. Curses bellowed as profuse as the flowing blood. The mangled arm jerked back.

With Neri's ferocious growl, the massive door thudded shut. He shot a bolt which looked entirely inadequate just as the door shuddered with a massive blow.

A second thud. The nullifier carried an axe.

A third blow splintered the wood, a crack seaming the oak from the latch to the top.

Dumond shoved Neri and me down the steps and slapped his hands on the door. "*Sigillaré!*"

As suddenly profound as a punch below the breastbone, so did the door, its frame, and the ghostly gallery vanish, their removal significant and complete. Only the tower wall and the stair remained.

"Come on," said Dumond, heading downward. "There's no going back."

"To leave the temple we must go up," I said, standing firm.

"But to retrieve the cause of all this, we go down," insisted Dumond. "If we hurry, we can get out the lower processional door before they have all exits blocked."

"What do you mean, the cause? Did you come here to set off another explosion?" No matter this astonishing escape, I could not partner with a murderer.

"I'm no assassin," said Dumond. "I was finishing a piece of work over to a guildhall. On my way home I noticed one of my luck charms was abandoned here and thought to stop in and fetch it. But the streets are crawling with the damnable philosophists and their damnable praetorians and their twice-damned nullifiers. They must have sniffed traces on me and followed me in. Hounded me up here instead of where I was headed."

He squinted up at us. Understanding dawned. "The luck charm is yours."

An angled bar of light illumined Neri's guilty face. "Mine," he said. "Romy hid it here."

"Told you to keep it with you, didn't I, boy? What good are luck charms when they're not on your person? *Bad* luck, that's what. If they're left about, there's a bit of the working tugs at me, so's I can retrieve it. But it's likely quicker if the lady—" He gestured for me to lead our party downward. "Move on. I swear I had naught to do with murderous explosions."

But I was still flummoxed by his admission. "You gave a child a *magical* charm? A charm that could attract a sniffer!" And I'd kept one in the Shadow Lord's house for nine years and left it with his wife! "Are you mad?"

"The charms *deflect* sniffers, lady witch. Mayhap that's how the *child* grew up this far." Dumond's patience seemed near an end. "I happened to unlock my storeroom one night and found a boy nicking a silver bracelet. Then he leads me a chase through places he should'na been able to get through. Being a spit more clever than a boy with no more years than fingers, I caught him anyways. A sniffer would have had him right there. A sniffer's not going to find any magic on the charm, even if it's in his gods-cursed paw. But I worry the *casting* of it might lead 'em to me. That's why we've got to fetch it. So . . . if you please."

He jerked his head to the downward stair.

Still uneasy, I sped downward. All Neri and I knew of magic was gossip and rumor from those as ignorant as we were. And those tales were the same whether the teller sat in a Beggars Ring tavern or the Shadow Lord's salon.

A quick visit to Veitan the Gateward's little statue and the charm was safely returned to Neri's pocket. Dumond led us through a lower entry, where temple servitors had once come and gone, and devotees had assembled to carry water from Atladu's spring up to the great hall.

We soon cleared the temple precincts and scuttered through side streets into the bustling heart of the Market Ring. The atmosphere was subdued this evening. The cheerful cries of barkers, the back-and-forth shouts of hagglers, the bustle and laughter of folk nearing the end of the day had been replaced by frowns, sharp words, and furtive glances.

The lamplighters were setting to their evening tasks. The twilit sky was clear. The thunder we'd heard in the afternoon must have been the explosion . . . magic.

In the thickest part of the crowd around the noodle vendors, Dumond pulled us close together and lowered his voice. "I'll make my own way from here. No need you being involved if someone does get the notion to follow me. Hold your power close. Whether these assassins were truly sorcerers or someone who wanted the deed blamed on sorcerers, the hunt is on tonight. People will die."

"So you're truly not one of them."

"Trying to explode the Shadow Lord? Demonshite, no! Life's troublesome enough."

"You said you were working at a guildhall . . . using magic?"

"I use a bit of my talent time to time when it serves my business. Likely more than's wise. But the surest way for one like us to get himself dispatched to the Executioner is to mess with the affairs of the mighty."

I was inclined to believe him. He'd seen what Neri could do years ago and not exposed him. I certainly wasn't going to accuse anyone of assassination without more evidence.

"Thank you, Segno Dumond," I said. "We were playing a dangerous game. If our ignorance has put you at further risk, I'm sorry."

"You provided the time I needed to get out," he said. "That was a brave thing."

"Didn't feel at all brave. Just desperate."

"Bravery results from desperation more often than we'd like

to think." Dumond's gaze flicked nervously from passersby to each dark doorway and alley only to fix on Neri and me again, as if to read our bones. "Stay away from me. I don't think they've a suspicion about who they were chasing. There's only one more of my charms separate from its owner, and it's in the same place it's been for years now—a house I daren't visit. But it's unlike to draw a sniffer there, unless one of you can tell me different . . ."

"Don't know nothing of that one," said Neri, quickly. Too quickly.

Dumond's eyebrows lifted ever so slightly. "Some day we'll talk. Until then, no more games. And wear your charms. They're charged with a drop of your blood. In your case, damizella, with your brother's blood. Sniffers can always detect the use of magic and the energies left behind after it's been done. But the power lives inside us even when we're not using it. Dormant, you might say. Not all sniffers can detect that dormant magic, but some might, and the charms are supposed to obscure your . . . scent . . . if you want to call it that."

"But *you* use your skills," I said, yearning to know more. First Placidio, and now this man—such magnificence at their beck. "This piece of work you were doing . . ."

". . . is none of your business."

"Then answer this at least. How many of us are there?" Meeting two sorcerers in the space of a few months after a lifetime without hinted that there were more than I believed.

"Not a notion about that. Met a few through the years. Most are hidden so deep you'll never find them, I believe. Some give themselves away—like they just can't hold it inside anymore. A few just can't hide what they are." He jerked his head at Neri. "If they're lucky they run into someone like me and learn better."

"We'll be careful," said Neri.

Dumond nodded and quickly vanished into the nervous throng.

The noise and stinks of the evening closed in around Neri and me as we hurried down the road to the Beggars Ring, every movement, every glance, every shadowed corner menacing. We didn't breathe free until we had turned into Lizard's Alley.

Once behind our own door, Neri pulled cheese and sausage from our shelf and threw it on the table. I lit the lamp and poured us wine, but in the end I could only stare at the food. The enormity of what Dumond had done and the horror of seeing the sniffer's finger pointed our way, like a carving knife ready to sever flesh from bone, churned my gut. Neri's, too, I guessed. His eating knife tapped on the link of sausage as we emptied our cups.

Only after a full hour had passed with no hammering at our door did we eat what we'd laid out. Even then, we didn't talk. Neri curled up on his pallet. Work beckoned, but instead I doused the lamp, drew my knife, and wrapped myself in cloak and blanket, keeping watch for a dusty metalsmith who might decide he didn't want a sixteen-year-old boy and his witchy sister to know his secrets.

"You tried to steal a bracelet when you were *six*?" I said from the sleepless dark. "Whyever that?"

"Wanted to have something pretty for you next time you came home. Thought it might make you stay."

For a moment, my composure fractured, threatening long abandoned tears. A good thing Neri couldn't see it. He was no longer that innocent child, but an incautious youth. So I reassembled my resolve, and sniped, "Now you're stuck with me."

"Aye," he mumbled. And after a long pause, "Could be worse."

9

N o sniffers showed at our door that night or those following. Even so, events at the Temple had frightened me. Neri, too, it seemed, for when I insisted we attempt no more magic, never mind curiosity or possibility, Neri didn't argue. Rather, he devoted all his energies to his work with Placidio and the tasks I set him to earn the lesson fees.

The swordmaster began actual sword training that month. Neri was much happier, though he confessed that the hated running, jumping, and climbing had helped him immensely. He kept it up between his lessons and the tasks he did for me. I hardly saw him. Over the month he must have grown a handspan and definitely put on muscle.

With Neri so busy, I had to make more of my own deliveries. One sunny morning, I tidied myself up more than usual, as I needed to deliver documents to Lawyer Aventia. I was doing more work for her, as her client list had grown well beyond the young shipping heiress. Our exchanges had never gone much beyond Dama Ciosa's teriaca, but I felt certain they could, if I could just take the first step.

"I'll have these back in three days," I said, taking the new stack of contracts she offered.

"Thank you, Romy. I appreciate your promptness as well as your fine work."

"Segna . . . it is such a lovely morning. I wondered if you might like to visit Kallinur's—an excellent tea-seller just a few streets away from here. Perhaps you know it already. He serves a most excellent brew. Brought from Lhampur itself, I've heard."

Her glance flicked from my mud-stained skirt to my ink-blackened fingers and back to the painted box where she kept her coins. She carefully counted out my thirty coppers before answering. "I've recently taken on a new client—a gentleman of good family. He occupies a great deal of my time nowadays. So sorry. Fortune's benefice, Mistress Romy."

A rime of frost stung my flesh. "And Virtue's grace, segna."

Telling myself her answer was exactly the truth and no judgment of me was useless. I had seen the same hesitation, the same slight withdrawal, when I misinterpreted the pleasant interchange with some lady or gentleman at one of Sandro's salons. Most of his friends and guests cared naught that I was his bound servant. But those others made their disapproval clear when I stepped beyond the unbreachable barrier between gentlefolk and whore—no matter how educated, how witty, or how beloved that whore might be.

I retreated to Lizard's Alley and drank a bit more wine before settling down to copy . . . something.

• • •

On Winter Quarter Day Neri and I set out early for our pilgrim-
age to Palazzo Segnori to fulfill Neri's parole. The trudge upward through the city was a misery. A dreary cold drizzle had
settled over Cantagna, the kind that made it impossible to keep
anything dry or warm for days on end. Black pennons hung in
sodden folds atop each gateway arch, as if the city were in
mourning for the sun. No gossip we heard among the thousand
others on their way to do quarterly business could explain the
pennons, save a rumor that had spread only this morning—that
this Quarter Day, even more than usual, was a *day of righteous
judgment*. What did that mean? No one knew.

The singularity of this rumor and the lack of competing gossip
suggested it was someone's very specific plan. The Shadow Lord
was expert at keeping close-held secrets, and unless things had
changed in half a year House Gallanos had an army of spies large
enough to spread a rumor quickly and pervasively.

Another possible source of a singular rumor was the Philosophic Confraternity. Since their founding, in the years before
the Costa Drago could boast of even one great city, it had been
the Confraternity's goal to shape the world's perceptions regarding magic and religious matters. They claimed to enforce
the divine mandate to exterminate sorcery. With Philosophic
Academies found in every independency of the Costa Drago,
offering advanced education in philosophy, mathematics, history, and astronomy, they had developed a widespread web of
agents adept in communications.

Yet, there was more to the overwhelming unease of the day
than weather, pennons, and rumor. Soldiers stood at each of the
Ring gates.

Lodovico di Gallanos, Sandro's wicked uncle, had kept the

eight inner gates—two on each of the four inner Ring walls—
closed and guarded to ensure that *citizens who had proper business* were the only ones allowed to visit the upper Rings without
special invitation. He claimed it would keep the *lower orders* in
their places, reducing thievery and murder amongst righteous
citizens.

When Sandro became the Gallanos segnoré after Lodovico's
assassination, his first public action was to appear before the
Sestorale and recommend that the gates be kept open to all
citizens at all hours. He argued that it would encourage healthy
commerce between artisans, laborers, shopkeepers, merchants,
and buyers. After generations of prosperity, his uncle's few years
as the House Gallanos segnoré had left Cantagna starving in all
ways, he'd said. Not only from too many hungry citizens, but in
business, art, and trade.

Much argument ensued about Sandro's youthful folly at rec-
ommending such an abrupt change, about Lodovico's crimes and
his murder and the possibility that open gates might encourage
more such violence, and about the possible ways the Sestorale
might wish to alter the workings of the city now Lodovico was
gone. After an hour of listening, Sandro requested a few moments' indulgence. He simply wished to remind the honored
members of the Sestorale that payments on all loans from the
House Gallanos bank would remain suspended for six months
to help settle the natural unrest after such an abrupt change in
the order of things. The Sestorale immediately agreed to his recommendation about the gates.

The aftermath of this incident had many aspects.

The people of Cantagna had rejoiced at the freedom to travel their own city as righteous men and women, and in the ten years since had come to think of free passage as their right.

To one and all Alessandro di Gallanos had asserted himself as *il Padroné*. It was clear that the young Segnoré di Gallanos would not only restore the generous patronage of his father and grandfather, but would make amends for the aberration that was Lodovico.

And among those who had thought to assume the mantle of *il Padroné* for themselves, deep-buried seeds of resentment burst and sent up tiny shoots.

In the month since the magical explosion had killed not fourteen, but fifty-seven people, the blue-gray livery of the Gardia Sestorale had reappeared at the Ring gates. Two or three wardens stood watch day and night. They created no impediment to free passage, and citizens seemed to think it a reasonable precaution until the sorcerers who'd done the murderous deed were caught. But on this Quarter Day when black pennons drooped from the gate arches, the wardens at each gateway bristled with swords and spears and numbered no less than twenty.

"What do they look for?" whispered Neri, as we threaded our way through the Merchant Ring toward Piazza Cambio, the grand apron fronting the gateway between the Merchant Ring and the Heights. "Sorcerers don't wear badges to say what they are. And none's going to confess to a Gardia warden that they've plans to kill the Shadow Lord if only he would just let them through a gate."

"I'm not sure," I said, my steps slowing.

The city bells rang noontide. At least a dozen praetorians— soldiers of the Philosophic Confraternity—had joined the Gardia wardens at the Piazza Cambio gate. Their yellow badges and tabards, trimmed in scarlet, were unmistakable.

"This is not just extra guards added because it's Quarter Day," I said. "I'm thinking they've found the murderers."

Neri exhaled long and slow. "A day of righteous judgment."

Before we could reach the gate, the praetorians and wardens surged forward, shouting for all to clear the center of the piazza and the boulevard that led down to the Market Ring.

"Quarter Day business will resume shortly!" shouted a Gardia warden to an elderly couple trying frantically to get through the gate. "Just got to make way for now."

To the shouted questions as to what was happening, their answers were "a judgment" or "don't know more'n that." Any who balked were forcibly moved.

The normal commotion of a city crowd grew to an ear-splitting uproar, everyone babbling questions and speculation as they shifted toward the periphery of the piazza. Fear wriggled in my head, demanding I see what transpired. I could not say fear of what. Thus as Neri and I shifted backward, we locked arms and yielded ground slowly, letting others flow past on either side of us. Though quickly subsumed by a press of wet shoulders, wet cloaks, wet leathers, and dripping hats, we ended up near enough the front of the crush to view whatever was to come.

Wardens and praetorians took up positions in front of the crowd, creating a warlike colonnade around the great oval. Clearly the judgment was to be carried out right here. Well calculated, I thought, as no other than Quarter Day would find such a large representation of citizens in one place. This judgment was to be rendered without prior announcement, and before this larger population instead of simply the mean-spirited who flocked to a prison yard to witness bloody spectacle as they'd done for Da. This was no common judgment—or perhaps the one to be judged was uncommon.

It was the sudden infusion of red into the scene that confirmed and increased my uneasiness. Soldiers in red tabards and bright helms flowed from the gate and every lane and alley that branched off Piazza Cambio, seeping into the spaces behind and between groups of onlookers like blood into murky water. They were Captain di Lucci's condottieri—the Shadow Lord's favored mercenaries.

"They're expecting trouble," I murmured, where only Neri could hear.

I glanced around the thickening crowd, searching for answers. There would likely be clumps of other liveries, retainers of the wealthy houses, here to protect their segnoré's or segnora's interests. My heart near seized when I caught the bilious green of nullifiers here and there behind the onlookers; only to be expected after the magical explosion that had killed so many. But no house liveries were to be seen, certainly not the dark green and mustard yellow of House Gallanos. What was one to make of that?

The condottieri did not challenge the Gardia or praetorians. Perhaps the city itself had paid di Lucci to be here . . .

The bells from the tower of the Palazzo Segnori began to toll. The somber cadence drew every soldier to attention and quieted the expectant crowd. The yellow-liveried praetorians, evenly spaced about the great piazza, raised their swords in a deadly salute, as eight of their fellows marched through the Cambio Gate. In the center of their rectangular formation a mule pulled a small farm cart hung with fronds of prickly juniper and dried lavender to ward against evil. Inside the cart stood a bent figure robed and hooded in the same putrid green as the sniffers and bound with same type of wire-threaded rope I'd used on Neri. A condemned sorcerer—a man, I guessed from his size, but it was impossible to be sure.

A young man and woman, clad in the white-and-red robes of Philosophic Confraternity initiates, marched behind the prisoner's party. They carried a huge banner painted with two words. *Mago. Magrillaio.* Sorcerer. Butcher.

From every side of me rose a hiss so huge, so spiteful, and so contemptuous, imagination named it the spew of Dragonis itself as the monster had gazed upon paltry humankind. No matter what I told myself, that Neri and I were good people who wished no evil upon anyone, and that at least a few sorcerers were not to be feared or despised simply for existing, hate seeped into my bones like a poison designed to dissolve them. I held tight to Neri's arm. He quivered, too.

The contemptuous hiss, accompanied by a few sobs and scattered whispers, persisted until the party of the condemned passed out of view, making its way down to the other ring gates to end at the docks . . . and a death ship.

The praetorians lowered their swords, but the dreadful processional was not over. A group of men and women clad in fur-lined gray robes marched slowly from the gate in two ranks of ten. I counted them three times to be sure.

This was the Sestorale itself. Only on the most solemn occasions did the titular governors of Cantagna appear in public together. Today, perhaps, to evidence the Sestorale's unity in this *righteous judgment*—rather an all-but-one unity, as there should be twenty-one of them.

The two ranks diverged, each forming a half circle on the left and right of the empty space in the center of the piazza. My eyes peered through the dismal mist for a well-known form. He would be near the end of the ranks, as he was a junior member; only two years ago had he allowed his name to be put forward for election. Several of the sestorali had similar moderate height and slender build, but it was impossible to be sure. Most of them had raised their hoods—either against the damp or against prying eyes. Sandro would be one of the latter, preferring to avoid attention . . . unless he was the missing one.

To the continued tolling of the bells a mule-drawn wagon rolled into the center of the Sestorale half circles. Grooms unhitched the mules and led them away, while others set the brakes and chocked the wagon wheels with wedges of wood and iron. A man clad in black leathers and hood had joined those at the wagon.

My stomach lurched at the sight of his axe. The city headsman. *Spirits!* Who was to die here?

Gardia pikemen with weapons at the ready escorted a second tip cart holding a single, standing passenger. The man's hands were bound at his back, making it difficult for him to maintain his balance as the cart jounced over the cobbles. This prisoner was a big man with thick white hair straggling over his shoulders, his elegant satin and brocade garments in filthy tatters. I would know him anywhere. A few years ago, after spending a particularly lively and entertaining evening with Sandro and me at one of *il Padroné's* salons, he had offered in great good humor to buy me. Sandro politely declined and offered to sell him a vineyard instead. The three of us had laughed about it.

Naldo di Savilli. His identity explained everything—the

secrecy, the precisely delivered rumor, this pageantry of armed might and political unity by the Sestorale. The man about to lose his head was a segnoré of Cantagna's old aristocracy, whose family owned thousands of hectares of vineyards, forests, and pastures, and he was the highest-ranking member of the Sestorale. And no wonder the condottieri had been brought in to supplement the Gardia and the praetorians. House Savilli had a highly trained family cohort of at least two hundred men.

Two soldiers followed the cart, carrying a banner that read, *Magrillaio. Tesure. Trattiere.* Butcher. Paymaster. Traitor.

Naldo di Savilli had paid the sorcerer who caused the explosion. It confirmed my suspicion that it had been intended to assassinate *il Padroné* as he marched in a processional to honor his beloved grandfather. Certain, Naldo had a deep and abiding dispute with House Gallanos—the upstart bankers, he called them. He believed he should be the grand duc of Cantagna, a title his sires had borne for two centuries.

For decades he had held his ambitions in abeyance, a strong ally of Sandro's father and grandfather as House Gallanos had transformed Cantagna from a pleasant town into a great and prosperous city. Like the other grand segnorés, Naldo had tolerated Lodovico, too. But unlike many of them, Naldo had maintained a sincere friendship with Sandro when he became the Gallanos segnoré. Sandro had hoped that Naldo would ultimately judge Cantagna's welfare more important than a moldy title.

Alas for hope and friendship. That Naldo was a charming, generous, and witty man could have no bearing in a case of fifty-seven murders.

The evidence against him must have been so glaring, so

obvious that even those on the Sestorale—Naldo's longtime friends, business partners, a cousin—had accepted his guilt. Had he been so confident of support from those who sympathized with his claim that he had moved on House Gallanos so baldly? If he had used his family cohort to waylay Sandro and assassinate him, as had been tried at least three times in ten years, the others might have looked the other way, secretly applauding the deed. But Naldo had dared to suborn sorcery in service of his ambition. That was likely what brought the Sestorale together to condemn him. Naldo's daring move boded very ill for Sandro's chances to avert open rebellion from his onetime allies, who saw his vision for Cantagna as theft of their long-held privileges. Danger loomed on the horizon. Civil war.

As the old man was dragged from the cart and shoved up wooden steps to the wagon that had become an executioner's platform, I murmured in Neri's ear. "Let's go. We don't need to see this."

"They're not letting no one leave," Neri whispered back. Indeed, the condottieri had blocked all the streets, preventing Savilli's men-at-arms from rushing in to save him—assuming any of them were still living and free.

The bell's steady toll gave way to a deafening clangor that drowned out Savilli's last words. As they shoved him to his knees, I buried my face in Neri's shoulder. I needed no more bloody visions. But I could not escape the dull thud of the blow rebounding from the buildings around the piazza. And Neri's bone-deep shudder confirmed the axe had accomplished its task.

An hour after cart and wagons had removed evidence of the righteous judgment, Neri and I stood in the sodden queues of those who still had Quarter Day business in the Heights. Some people were subdued. Most gossiped.

Rumors were already spreading about the identity of the hooded sorcerer—Savilli's bodyguard? his son? his barber?—about the evidence against him, about others among the Sestorale who might have joined him in rebellion against the Shadow Lord were they not cowards. Some voices sympathized with returning to the old order of things—before the Gallanos ascendency. Others shouted them down, saying Savilli and his kind wanted all to be slaves, not citizens. The execution had shocked words out of people that they would not dare say in other times. The only thing all agreed was that suborning sorcery pointed to Savilli's ultimate downfall. Evil would out.

"Step forward, damizella. They're almost ready for you." The stringy, black-bearded warden waved me toward one of his fellows, a stumpy soldier standing just inside the gateway arch alongside a solemn, square-faced praetorian. We were required to give our names and business before we were allowed through. No one ahead of us had been turned away.

We halted just outside the arch, where the rain funneling off the gate tower dripped and spattered over our already soaked shoes. Torches cast a wavering light from inside the gate tunnel, setting the runnels of water sparkling.

As the praetorian dismissed an earnest young couple come to register their marriage at the palazzo and waved them through the gate, a round-bellied man in a bilious green tabard and plumed hat strolled out of the archway. Grotesque, inhuman, his sniffer emerged from the arch behind him, gliding almost weightless at the end of his chain leash, stopping when his master stopped.

"Shite!" None could have heard Neri's panicked curse, but his grip on my arm near yanked it out of its socket. Dumond's luck charm sat in Neri's pocket. Now, I supposed, we'd know if the cursed thing worked. Mine still resided in Sandro's house. Meanwhile I had to come up with a story quickly. In no circumstance would I speak our true names within hearing of a sniffer.

"Now, *Iren*," I said, smiling up at Neri, as if we were but on a day's pleasure stroll. "After our business, should we find that noodle seller in the Market Ring again? I have a craving for her mussel broth we tasted yestereve."

Neri gaped at me as if I were mad. I just hoped he noted my use of his backward spelled name—the same childhood code he'd used on the day I was banished.

"Speak your names, district of residence, and business in the Heights," said the Gardia warden, a thick-necked soldier with a wide, flat nose.

"I am Damizella Ennitia di Varni of the Market Ring, come to bring my cousin Iren, born in Invidia, to register as a citizen of Cantagna. He's just come of age and will be the heir to my small property, as Lady Fortune has conspired with her divine Mother to leave me barren. So anxious am I to settle matters that I wished not to wait another quarter despite this miserable weather. I told Iren that Cantagna's winters are mild compared to those he's used to up the northlands of Invidia, but I'm not sure he's believing that today."

I laughed aloud and hugged my sodden cloak around me as my mind grasped at threads to weave this web of lies. I had to forge ahead before they could decide what to make of us.

"And certain, I do believe you've frighted the tongue out of this boy with a beheading. So dreadful and, of course, just and righteous, but awful to witness, and then that devil sorcerer who exploded things right here in our midst, and *other* dreadful creatures about"—I leaned toward the bewildered praetorian as if imparting a confidence—"some not so far away from us here. And while we wholly appreciate their divine mission, it is not so nice to actually *see* one. Quite shocking. But I've ever been so curious since childhood, so tell me, with its eyes covered so tight, how in the names of the Unseeable does the creature know when to halt without toppling over?"

The increasingly agitated warden glanced over my head as the queue piled up behind us.

"Does she speak true, boy?" snapped the praetorian, glaring round me at Neri.

"Aye . . . your honor . . . she d-do," Neri stammered. "I come from Invidia to learn to make cheese from cows, as it's my favorite and all we can make at my home is goats' cheese, which has a stink what won't leave you. But Ennitia says—"

"Move on." The praetorian and the warder spat the order at the same time.

I breathed. *Good work, little brother.*

Not daring to smile, frown, speak, or look at each other, we clasped hands and strolled into the gate arch as if we had no worries beyond cheese-making and inheritance.

A heavy hand fell on my shoulder. I wrenched away and spun around, pressing my back to Neri, my heart near exploding from my chest.

Bulbous eyes glittered under the nullifier's plumed hat. "It don't *see*, chattery lady. Don't need ta. It sniffs its master moving, and it sniffs when I stop."

Chortling, the nullifier rattled the chain leash in my face and turned back toward Piazza Cambio. For the instant the leash remained slack, the sniffer stood facing us in the wavering torchlight.

Spirits, he was shivering. The green silk that sheathed every part of him like a second skin was soaked, so that I imagined I saw through it to the bare flesh beneath. Certain he was freezing.

If he was shivering with the cold, was his stomach growling with hunger, too? Were his silk-clad bare feet bruised and aching from the old cobbles, as mine were, now the soles of my shoes were worn thin? Was he human, after all?

And if so . . . was he mad? If not, what did he think of as he was led about the city on a chain? His past life? A family? Vengeance? What had driven him to such a dreadful choice? I had always assumed that it was either cowardice or the natural corruption of a sorcerer's soul made a man choose to be a sniffer. Had he truly been *given* a choice? Stories . . . rumors. Whatever the answers, I would not see any sniffer the same as I had before this night. They were human. In the same moment that truth stung me, I came to doubt the nullifier's assertion. Beneath the wet silk, the sniffer's eyelids lifted. I believed he saw our faces.

I neither moved nor breathed until the rattling chain grew taut. His silken feet splashed an ice-skimmed puddle as he trailed after his master.

10

R umors, dour faces, marketplace bickering devolved to
fisticuffs, family cohorts strutting their colors in the
Market and Merchant Rings, as if asking for trouble . . .
Cantagna grew more restive as the Month of Winds brought
green hillsides, budding trees, and early blooms of madder
and bell-like bindweed. Placidio wouldn't let me pay him the
new month's retainer as he had missed so many days for his
other profession.

"Stupid spats over nothing," he said. "I'd sooner kick their
backsides than uphold their honor in dogfights. Everyone in
Cantagna has a spike up their ass." That was as much as he had
ever volunteered about his matches.

Perhaps everyone was having dreams like mine. Since the
events of Winter Quarter Day, I spent my nights running from
magical explosions, bloody axes, or hollow eyes that stared at me
through screens of green silk. In the day I told myself that the

sniffer had detected nothing about my magic. He had let us pass. In the nights he memorized my face.

To add to the general anxiety, my business stalled. Most of my work from lawyers and notaries comprised settlements, like contracts, wills, and eviction notices. Perhaps in such anxious times, people weren't in the mood to settle things. On the other hand my reputation had risen in the Beggars Ring. Some ordinary people brought me private business, sometimes just to hold a message for a friend or write a letter to a relative. But Beggars Ring folk could not afford decent fees, and I had to count on word of mouth for them to find me at all.

In an hour of desperate boldness, I gambled half of our remaining silver to buy a small, ramshackle storehouse on the Ring Road, a few houses down from the Duck's Bone tavern, and just around the corner from our house. Neri cleaned it, shored up the roof, and moved my shelves and a new writing desk in. Now people could find me. Perhaps even a few shopkeepers or artisans from the Asylum Ring, those who would never venture down a Beggars Ring alley, would patronize a reputable scribe in a respectable shop on the main thoroughfare.

To earn another month of sword training from Placidio, Neri built a shelf of ten locking boxes that people could rent from us, using them to exchange private messages or parcels with family or business partners. He cut a hole in the front wall for the boxes and built their own little roof to keep the rain off, so they could be accessed when I was not in the shop. We promised discretion and security with Neri to guard the boxes, and I no longer had to host writing clients in my bedchamber. The boxes were so popular, he added a second shelf of ten more.

I carved a small lettered plaque that read:

L'SCRITTÓRE

COPYING, LETTERS,

CONFIDENTIAL MESSAGE EXCHANGE

My father had used the old designation for a scribe. It seemed fitting I do it, too, leaving off the appellation *virgine* that Notary Renzo had given me so many months ago. I knew my business now.

I hoped. Copper solets seemed to flow through our fingers and vanish before they could join the fourteen orphaned silver coins remaining in Sandro's purse.

• • •

One morning Neri burst through the door only an hour after he'd left. He planted himself in front of my writing desk like a lawyer before a magistrate. "Placidio had a last-minute summons, so no lessons today."

"Mmm." I was in the middle of a rare contract from Lawyer Garibaldi, trying to unravel the mysteries of his scratched notes, crossed-out phrases, and arrowed lines. The more the man trusted me, the less finished the documents he gave me to copy, and in thin times I wasn't going to complain.

After a moment, I glanced up. Neri hadn't moved. His expression was solemn, but his flushed cheeks said he'd either run all the way from the wool house, or something more exciting than canceled lessons had happened. Unworthy visions of stolen rubies or one of his feminine admirers announcing that we would have a new mouth to feed pummeled my aching head.

"What have you done, Neri?"

A grin of purest joy illuminated Neri's face. One would think the sun had rolled into the door to visit. "I got work."

Though I could scarce believe the news, I could not but share his delight. "Doing what? Where?"

"Fesci wants me to keep order at the Duck's Bone."

Now I was truly astounded. "Throw the drunks out, you mean? Stop the fights?"

"Aye. She says she'd heard I was working hard at getting stronger and faster. She'd asked Placidio if that was true . . ."

"Placidio recommended you!"

Neri rolled his eyes. "He told her I could likely wrestle a small dog to the ground on my best day. But then she said he'd never spoke so much for anyone else, so it must be high praise. And as I'd not been slobbering drunk nor in a scrap for a few months now, I didn't have any lingering enemies among her customers, so I could be fair if needed. I'm to go in every morning so's she can tell me if she needs me that night or not, and she's going to pay me *two coppers* for a night's work—evening bells to midnight. Is that good pay?"

There was no way to express the relief his news gave me. Two coppers a night wasn't going to refill our purse or even pay my bill at Fedig the pen seller's, but certain it would help. And the value to Neri was incalculable. I walked round the table and squeezed his shoulder. "That is fine pay to start. And you'll do very well at it."

"I just—Romy, I want to—" His color deepened.

I didn't make him say what was stumbling around his tongue. Just ruffled his hair and returned to my stool. "I knew you'd find your way. Maybe we'll survive after all."

Spring Quarter Day could hardly have been more different than our last trek to the Palazzo Segnori. Blue skies. No condemned sorcerers. No beheadings. Nullifiers, though, and their sniffers gliding along behind. We saw them frequently nowadays. It was difficult to refrain from running the opposite direction or darting into an alley. Always I wondered if one of them might be the sniffer who'd seen our faces—the shivering man imprisoned in green silk. Had Neri's luck charm prevented him detecting the magic inside us? I wanted to believe that. More likely he just wanted to get out of the cold.

While we were inside the Palazzo Segnori, I applied to be the official scribe for the Beggars Ring. Our district had never had one, which meant Beggars Ring citizens were always at risk for violating laws they didn't know about. My application stated that my service would enhance the good order of the city as its governors wished. Notary Renzo and Lawyer Garibaldi had written statements vouching for my skills.

Though the clerk laughed at me, opining that even if someone in the Beggars Ring could read, none would ever abide by the law, she approved my application. It would earn me a copper a page. Poor pay, but steady and much less complicated and precise— thus less time consuming—than law writing.

Thus in addition to my normal work, I wrote innumerable copies of the REGULATION OF WEIGHTS AND MEASURES decree to post in Beggars Ring shops on the first day of every month, just as they were posted in every other shop and marketplace in Cantagna and its tributary towns. Whenever one of *il Padroné's* REGULATIONS FOR GOOD ORDER regarding sewage or pigs or the use of public wells was released, I made copies of that, too. Those who could read would spread word of the rules.

For the first time in almost a year, I added a silver solet to our purse.

Even as I read his words and accepted his city's coin, I stopped hearing Sandro's voice asking what I thought of his rules, or why the Flax Guild so despised his limits on shipments to Kairys, or what I thought might be the best way to deal with men who beat their wives. I told myself it was time and work that muted the hurt, but in truth it was the wine.

The amount of wine needed to numb the memories of that other life seemed to grow by the day. With Neri working at the tavern every evening, there was no reason to moderate it. Once I was done with writing for the day, wine filled the void of company, of conversation, of curiosity and study. I knew it was stupid and wasteful of the education Fortune had granted me. Some nights, instead of sitting alone with the wine flask, I would try wandering through the night market to find some conversation. But after three nights running fending off lusty bargemen wandered over from the docks, I retreated back to my own company.

Then came a night when Neri found me collapsed in the alley, unable to get up. I lied to him that I had a fever.

On the next morning, Placidio stood in our doorway waiting for Neri to finish choking down a cold meat pie. Neither of us had waked until Placidio thumped on the door. Neri never woke until I shook him, and it had taken me a great deal of wine to fill the caverns of the previous night. Which was why I'd gone out to the alley to heave and collapsed instead. Something had to change.

"I want you to train me in sword work, too," I blurted. "I know some prudish masters don't like training women or think it might somehow damage our delicate bones. But I don't break."

"Guessed that."

"I had a few lessons when I was younger."

"Guessed that, too. Not many Beggars Ring lads—or their sisters—are born knowing the Santorini Thrust."

I wished the swordmaster's head to pound as dreadfully as mine did.

The duelist registered no surprise, but no eagerness either. "Had some threats, have you, lady scribe? Maybe Beggars Ring folk are not so fond of the law as you seem to be. Or maybe it's would-be suitors?"

"None of that. Well, some of that. But I just—I like to take care of myself. And I won't get anything to eat around here if I can't defend my share."

My attempt at humorous riposte drew guffaws from both Neri and Placidio. Which just made my head hurt worse.

Placidio swallowed his humor quickly as always.

"I won't go easy because you're the one pays me," he said. "And I won't go easy if you wake feeling poorly." His boot nudged the three emptied wine flasks waiting by the door to be refilled. "I'd advise you come clear-headed."

I wanted to frame a proper retort to the man I'd met swimming in his own vomit, but the pain in my skull dulled my wit. Besides, Neri might be tempted to mention that I'd done the same.

"Every third day," I said. "I've no more time than that to spare."

"We'll start tomorrow. After your brother's lesson. Half his fee; pay in advance."

Placidio started me running and jumping, and I hated it as virulently as Neri had, especially as spring brought rain and sultry heat. The toll of the wine shortened those early lessons, as I spent the second half of the hour spewing whatever I'd eaten the day before.

I felt awful all the time and came very near quitting. Nausea did not help my concentration when I returned to my writing work. But I had told Placidio I didn't break. He seemed to believe me. Just as he'd warned, he gave me no quarter.

So I didn't quit. As the days moved toward summer, tiredness often drowned my worries faster than the wine. On those nights, I slept without dreams and woke with my mind clearer the next morning.

Training to fight was no magical balm to heal the hollows grief had carved out inside me. But I liked the clearer head. Our sessions were the only time in any day I felt alive.

• • •

And then, one steamy night in late spring, just past a year from my banishment, I was sitting at our table, finishing a bit of writing work I'd brought home from the shop. An insistent knock on our door popped me to my feet.

I dropped my pen and drew my dagger. Neri, already drowsing on his pallet, was instantly on his feet, sword in hand.

My clients never sent for me in the night hours, and those who rented the message boxes would never look for me at home. Which meant our minds could not but turn to the demonfire in our veins. I had never shaken the sense that the sniffer had seen our faces on Winter Quarter Day.

"Who's there?"

No one answered. Hand on my dagger, I pulled open the door.

A ragged, red-haired boy stood waiting. "Please, dama, I need work," he said. "Haul ashes. Haul water. Sweep. Empty slops. Don't matter what."

"We've no work to give," I said.

"This is Lizard's Alley, right?"

"Aye."

"And you're the one called Romy?"

"And if I am?"

"I was told that Romy of Lizard's Alley has help to give those in need."

My name was no secret, yet hearing it sent spider feet crawing up my arms.

"It depends on the need and who's asking," I said. "Who told you that?"

He cocked his head, like a curious bird. "Folk higher'n me passed it on. So are you the one?"

"I am Romy."

"Well, all right then." He didn't even twitch, though I suddenly got the sense that he was no street urchin, but an experienced messenger.

He held out his fist. "I was told to give this to no one but Romy of Lizard's Alley and to say, 'Midnight on the Avanci Bridge. Alone.'"

He dropped a small bronze disk in my hand. Its fine engraving depicting three intersecting arcs—one concave, one convex, one sinuous—bracketing a tightly coiled spiral. My luck charm.

"Is that all?" I yearned to ask whose hand had passed it on. Whose voice had spoken my name. But even an experienced young messenger would know nothing of importance. A chain of anonymous go-betweens would link him and *il Padroné*'s little wife.

"I was told to say, 'He needs your help.' "

Warmth flowed through my veins that had naught to do with wine. Color charged the woven blankets I'd hung on our walls and cleared the stench of the Beggars Ring from my nostrils.

"I'll be there."

II

A sultry breeze blew down the Venia, bearing scents of river wrack laced with the heavy sweetness of wisteria and lemon blossoms. The midnight anthem would ring at any moment, the clangor confusing my dithering anticipation even further than it was already.

For an hour, hidden in the shadow of the cityside abutment of the Avanci Bridge, I had revisited every choice I'd made since the red-haired boy vanished into the night. To stand exposed or remain hidden. To carry my knife or forgo it. How to greet her. How to greet *him*, did my mad, unbidden, impossible imagining prove true. How to summon enough cold reason to judge whatever was asked of me. How to face a nullifier and his sniffer if the Shadow Lord had chosen that to be my fate; the luck charm in my pocket would hardly divert their attention if Sandro sent them to greet me.

Neri, horrified by my tale of the foolish Gilliette and my rash promise to her, had begged me not to go. I had silenced his protests with assurances of safety I could not fully support.

But as the first tones of the anthem struck, a mortal clarity settled me. I knew Sandro better than anyone in the world. The person awaiting me would surely be Ettore, Sandro's favored assassin, dispatched to make a quiet ending to the Shadow Lord's sentimental mistake. Gilliette had most likely yielded Sandro the luck charm in the first hours of her girlish triumph. My satisfaction must be that it had taken him a year to use it.

I could not regret the year, nor even the inevitability of its end. Neri, stronger, more mature, more settled, could now take care of himself. He knew how men with gifts like his had to live in order to survive. Wherever they were, my family was as safe as I could make them. And I had proved to myself that I could survive on my own. Yet I could not envision growing old writing other people's words, and no other course had presented itself. Lady Fortune would see me dead of boredom, drunk and alone.

I climbed over a false buttress and found the plain door in the mold-blackened undercarriage of the bridge. My fingers had not forgotten how to release the tricky lock that allowed Sandro or his favored associates access to the stair hidden in the massive abutment.

The first time he'd brought me here I was near paralyzed with fear, thinking he'd discovered my secret and planned to throw me into the river. But all he'd wanted was to show me the wonders of the full moon on the one night a year that it rose exactly along the course of the Venia. He'd asked me if I would like to take a boat down that golden path someday and did I think it would sail down to the sea or into the moon itself. I was but fifteen and still in awe of him. A month it had been, and he had not so much as touched me.

A quick climb, another hidden lock released, and I strolled onto the narrow bridge that connected the city walls to the Mausoleum Tower across the Venia. Archers used the Avanci Bridge and its downriver twin, the Vinci, to defend Cantagna's docks from river-borne marauders.

The damp wind teased my hair from its braid as I reached the center of the span. When a dark-cloaked figure appeared on the Tower side and two more on the city side, I commended my soul to the Night Eternal. No use running, even if I'd somewhere to go. If what I feared was true, postponing it would make no difference. Either way, I had to know.

Only one of the three walked out. It was difficult to judge size in the mottled gleam of the lanterns hung on the bridge, but Ettore was not so large as his fearsome reputation suggested. Nonetheless, he would need no assistance to deal with me. I gazed out on the powerful surge of the water below, already half dizzy, when words, not a knife blade, touched me.

"I was afraid you wouldn't come, Cataline."

I spun toward the woman's voice so quickly, I had to grip the parapet to keep my balance.

Gilliette, sober, earnest, stood beneath one of the bridge lamps. "I'm in such terrible, wicked trouble and had nowhere else to turn. If Alessandro learns what I've done, he'll kill me."

Her hood was lowered, else I'd never have recognized her. In the year she'd grown a handspan taller and matured in many ways. Her childish cheeks were now slender, yielding dominance to eyes of lustrous midnight. Her thick black hair was bound with jewels, womanly, graceful. I wondered if her spirit had matured as impressively.

"What sin could you possibly commit to offend him so deeply, segna?" I spoke politely, but did not bow or bend. Certain it was curiosity and no concern for the girl prompted my question.

"You gave me fair warning," she said. "But I acted stupidly, thinking to please him. And before I could tell him what I'd done, he had pledged his own and his family's honor to the matter. I dare not tell him he pledged a lie to one of his enemies!"

"Divine graces, lady!"

Her desperation was not that of a child, but of a woman who perfectly understood her danger. I could not even rejoice in such a disaster, for she was right that she had likely found the single offense for which Sandro might kill her with his own hand. The foremost truth people spoke of *il Padroné*—whether friends, enemies, or those who could not decide which they were—was that Alessandro di Gallanos was a man of his word. Should reports of his compromised oath be proved and circulated in Cantagna and beyond, the foundation of his power would crumble, without sound or dignity, without recourse.

"What in Night Eternal did you do?"

"I listened and learned as you told me." Her glance at my ink-blackened nails prompted a careful examination of her own slender, jeweled fingers. "He does not yet confide in me as he did with you, but when I ask him serious questions, he answers. It pleases him, just as you said, which pleases me. And it is not too boring."

Memories burgeoned like smoke from wet wood. I denied them and crushed the yearnings they bred, leashing my desire to shake the story out of her faster. Clearly, she wanted to preen as well as beg. "Go on."

"Last evening, as we drank coffee, a messenger arrived from a merchant named Boscetti. Alessandro had the fellow brought immediately, not even bothering to send me away, so I knew it was something terribly important."

The name provoked wariness. Boscetti was the devious antiquities merchant who'd visited Sandro on the day Neri's idiocy broke our lives.

"The messenger reported that 'the Antigonean bronze had arrived in the city,' and that Segno Boscetti awaited *il Padroné*'s word as to the delivery and settlement. Until such time, the item would be kept safe in the house of Rodrigo di Fermi, as Palazzo Fermi was better defended than Boscetti's own house."

Fermi? Sandro would be livid.

Like the murderous Naldo di Savilli, House Fermi had harbored the festering discontent of old privilege since the days of the dissolute Lodovico. Like the other old families they worried that Lodovico's young nephew and heir, Alessandro, would either be too weak, so that Cantagna would fall to her enemies, or too strong, and think to expand on the frivolous notions of his father and grandfather. Certain, Sandro's first play as Gallanos segnoré—free passage throughout the city for all—had proved that second worry justified.

Gilliette rattled on. "Alessandro thanked the messenger, saying he would send a reply to Merchant Boscetti."

"But he was not happy about the news," I said. "The terms of payment and delivery would have been addressed in their original agreement."

Sandro was meticulous about such things. So the mention of

awaiting settlement implied some change. Boscetti had already raised the price once, on that day a year ago. He and Fermi must think to use the statue to gain something from Sandro—tax or trade concessions, perhaps a new estate.

"Not happy at all," said Gilliette, "though he was very polite. When we were alone again, I asked what was this Antigonean bronze they spoke of. He told me it was a depiction of Dragonis and the god Atladu, a small thing, scarce bigger than a wine flask, and not exceptionally beautiful. But it was very old, he said, and his good friend, the grand duc of Riccia, had long desired it. He had hoped to give it to the duc for his birthday."

"You understand that the grand duc of Riccia is the most powerful lord in all the Costa Drago," I said. Careful. Respectful. Something in this tangle of alliances, friendships, favors, and betrayals had brought her to me. "His alliance with *il Padroné* brings a security that no other treaty can."

Riccia-by-the-sea was neither the largest nor the wealthiest of the Costa Drago's nine independencies. But Lady Fortune had graced its mountains with precious ores and gemstones; its coastline with exceptional harbors and easy access to the riches of the east; and its people with a temperate clime and fertile fields that produced more food than they could eat. All this grace needed defending, which led to the salient point. The grand duc of Riccia, undisputed heir of the oldest noble bloodline in the Costa Drago, commanded the largest standing army in the Costa Drago or its neighboring countries. For independencies like Cantagna that relied on a small city guard supplemented by mercenaries, Riccia was an indispensible ally.

"My father said something like before I was married," said Gilliette, "but now it makes sense. What I didn't understand was

why Alessandro was so angry when told *Fermi* had the statue.
Indeed he could have bitten off iron nails!"

"Old grievances from Lodovico's time," I said. Because behind
layers of manners, sworn allegiance, and fraternal entertainments,
House Fermi had quietly tried to undermine every Gallanos
endeavor since Sandro's ascension, using their favored methods
of rumor, nuisance lawsuits, abduction, and poison.

Gilliette chattered onward, never getting quite to the point. "I
said that surely Rodrigo and this merchant, Boscetti, would give
him the statue, as the Fermi are his close friends and petitioners.
Alessandro always does favors for them. Then I asked when he
would get the statue, as I would very much like to see a thing he
viewed as so important."

"And he told you it was merely a matter of time and business."
Sandro had been similarly dismissive with my first tentative
questioning. I came to understand that he was trying not to
concern me with the crueler dangers of his position. At fifteen, I
believed everyone must admire and love so fine and generous a
gentleman.

"Yes! That is always his answer. I find it intolerable to be put
off that way. The grand duc's birthday is only three days hence
and his lordship arrives in Cantagna for a visitation on that same
afternoon. Alessandro wants so very much to give the duc this
special gift."

I waited without comment as she admired and adjusted her
jeweled bracelets.

With a dismissive huff, she continued. "So as it happened, I
was invited for coffee with Lucrezia di Fermi this morning. She
is a most disagreeable woman, and I'd been of a mind to beg off,
saying I had a headache. She forever teases me that Alessandro

has not bedded me, and that he likely never will, as his Moon House harl—mistress"—Gilliette could not hide a spiteful glare—"drove him out of his mind. But I determined to go, thinking I might be able to help speed the negotiations for the statue."

Oh, you stupid girl; interfering in the Shadow Lord's business? You had no idea of the wickedness involved; Fermi, ally of a man who was beheaded for murdering fifty-seven souls while attempting to assassinate your husband . . . Merchant Boscetti, who tried to drive a wedge between the Shadow Lord and his favored condottieri . . . Boscetti, whose wife was born in Mercediare, Cantagna's eternal enemy . . . Lost in my own problems on the day of my downfall, I'd never had time to ask Sandro if he knew about Boscetti's wife.

This time it was Gilliette's parti-colored satin skirts that required her attention. It was all I could do to hold rein on my impatience. She wanted me to beg her for the story. "And so what happened?"

"Lucrezia showed me the statue before I could ask about it!" she said. "I pretended not to know what it was. Lucrezia bragged that it was a gift for a noble lord, who would shower his favor on her brother Rodrigo. And Paola di Boscetti laughed with her and said her husband had already written to the grand duc to tell him where he'd found it. They plan to present it to him at the great feast Alessandro is hosting for the grand duc's birthday."

The implications came clear. "So Fermi and Boscetti are not just using the statue to squeeze concessions from *il Padroné*," I said. "They intend to seduce Riccia's *loyalty*."

Sandro had hoped the gift of the bronze would transform his pleasant acquaintance with the shy, reclusive grand duc into a true friendship that might give him breathing room to work his reforms. If Fermi were to bind the Riccian alliance to himself instead, the move would surely anoint House Fermi as the leader of those in opposition to House Gallanos. Such a significant alliance would embolden the aristocratic malcontents to challenge *il Padroné*, stirring the embers of rebellion.

"And you, segna, what did you say to these women?"

She smirked like the child she was. "I admired the statue, pretending to be in awe of their men's cleverness, saying that Alessandro would be so pleased that such friends would be in the grand duc's favor . . . and lamenting that I could not tell him, as he refused to speak to me of serious matters. I even asked their advice as to how to make him trust me with his business, as he had trusted you."

"What did they say to this?"

"I gave them no time! The silly bags could only watch as my sorrow threw me into a fit of fear and grief that Alessandro would never love me. I screamed and vomited and fainted, and when they scattered to call for servants, I snatched the bronze and stuffed it between two cushions. They brought in my escorts— Gigo, Alessandro's odd-looking bodyguard, and the maidservant Micola, whom you trained very well, though she detests me and talks of nothing but you when she thinks I can't hear her—and they called in Lucrezia's own physician and all sorts of other servants. I fooled them all! Indeed I frightened everyone so terribly that they bundled me home straightaway with that fusty statue hidden under my skirts."

"You stole it!" My shock elicited a radiant smile that shrank quickly to petulance.

"I just took what was rightfully my husband's! Unfortunately, I had no chance to tell Alessandro of my triumph. When he brought his own physician to see to me this afternoon, other visitors were in my bedchamber. Certainly, I could say nothing to him in front of anyone, as I had feigned such illness and distress; I am very good at that. Then, before I could get rid of them all, constables arrived to arrest Gigo and Micola, who'd never even seen the statue the Fermi reported stolen. Alessandro was so angry, and the only way he could prevent them being taken—"

"—was to give his most sacred oath that the statue was not in his house." Not imagining his silly little wife was the thief.

Gilliette had given Fermi exactly what he needed to undercut Riccia's support for *il Padroné*. The statue would give Fermi a hearing. And alongside examples from the vile Lodovico's time in power, and Fermi's own long-nurtured tales of grievance, new evidence of Sandro's dishonor might well persuade the honorable grand duc to House Fermi's view of the world. Even a rumor of Riccia's legions at Fermi's back could fan the embers of rebellion into a holocaust.

"Ah, segna, what in the name of every Unseeable God do you think I can do about this?"

Her air of clever triumph twisted quickly to venomous malice.

"Very simple." She fumbled under her cloak, and then thrust a heavy bundle into my hands. "People in your family are thieves so accomplished they can steal rubies from a locked room. Have them put this cursed relic back where I got it before the grand duc's birthday feast, three days hence. Better his lordship receive the gift from Fermi, than Alessandro's sworn word be proved false, don't you think?"

"Yes, but—"

"If you refuse—or if this statue mysteriously vanishes before it is back where it came from—Alessandro will hear that his jilted harlot was lurking about the Fermi palazzo in the same hour his prize went missing."

Horror left me voiceless, as my mind painted a scenario as detailed as Dumond's magical door in the Temple.

A dismissed whore with intimate knowledge of city politics plotting a hated master's downfall.

A family of thieves to teach her their tricks.

The whore's treacherous maidservant present at Palazzo Fermi at the right time to open a side door to let her inside.

I would be arrested. Neri, too, because he was on parole and the son of a thief, and everyone would assume he'd helped me. We'd both lose a hand. And if the story of stolen rubies and a locked room was revived . . . *Gracious spirits!*

No one would doubt lovely, innocent, wronged Gilliette di Manvile's claim that she'd seen the tainted Cataline sneaking about the Fermi residence on the day the statue was stolen. All these months *il Padroné* had acted as if the Moon House mistress was dead. But people knew how those things worked; his wife would certainly know the truth.

No matter what he knew or believed of Gilliette's story, Sandro would be able to do nothing to stem the damage. He would be couched either as a weakling fool, played by a harlot and a thief, or as a liar who set his whore to steal for him. And as wolves relishing the kill, those like Savilli the butcher and Fermi the weasel would use the Riccian alliance to wage their war. Generations of noble accomplishments, and all those Sandro might yet bring to our future, would be dragged down with him. Enemies would come ravaging from every side of the Costa Drago to pick at Cantagna's bones.

What could I possibly do to prevent such consequences?

Take the statue to Sandro and tell him the whole story? If he would agree to see me—not at all a certainty—I believed he would accept my word over Gilliette's. I wanted to think so. But whether I gave him the statue along with the truth or sent him the statue anonymously, *possessing* it would only make his dishonor more brazen; he had sworn before witnesses that the artifact was not in his house. None would believe Gilliette had stolen it on her own. He could neither return it to Fermi and Boscetti nor present it to the grand duc without proclaiming his sworn word meant nothing.

No choice at all. The statue had to go back to Palazzo Fermi.

I choked out my answer. "I'll see it done."

Gilliette smirked, raised her hood, and strolled away.

If I failed at the task, I would be the instrument of Sandro's downfall and the chaos that followed. Not least among the tragedies of that chaos, I feared, would be Sandro himself. He would never abandon Cantagna to the wolves. Bereft of choices, he would cling to his position of power with brute strength alone, destroying *il Padroné* and becoming solely the Shadow Lord.

· · ·

I remained at the center of the bridge until the dark figures at either end had vanished. Even then my feet would not move, as if I could avoid choosing a course of action as long as I remained there. Beneath me, the dark water flowed inevitably seaward. Fortune, events, and necessity were drawing me forward with the same inexorable power.

I should have shoved the little vixen off the bridge when I had the chance.

My fingers knotted about the bridge parapet as if it were her scrawny neck. The very thought of acquiescing to her scheme gnawed at my soul.

Yet the Shadow Lord himself had taught me of balancing justice and judgment, crime and responsibility. You could not avoid the difficult things, the awful things. You had to think harder, search deeper, find the twisting path around them to make the world better than when you started.

A single clang of sonorous bronze marked the first hour of the new day. As the shivering tone faded, leaving only the surge of the river below to weave the silence, my rage hardened to a certain determination. Neither Boscetti nor Fermi nor even wicked, foolish Gilliette must be allowed to reap triumph from their devious doings.

Rodrigo di Fermi could not be allowed to undercut Sandro's relationship with the lord of Riccia. Boscetti could not be allowed to grow rich from the road to Cantagna's misery. Gilliette could not be allowed to think she could dally with *il Padroné*'s honor— and all the lives dependent on it—without consequence. And like the cream atop a pile of succulent strawberries to finish this conspiratorial banquet, the grand duc of Riccia must receive the Antigonean bronze for his birthday, courtesy of *il Padroné*.

Events move ever forward, yet a single rock could change a river's course. If I could accomplish such an unimaginably lunatic thing as returning a stolen item to such a well-guarded fortress as Palazzo Fermi, then perhaps I could find a rock to toss into the stream that would change how Fermi's scheme played out. I had nine years' schooling in intrigue from the Shadow Lord himself. I had a little magic. And I had a brother who could walk through walls. Surely I could come up with a plan.

12

I'm glad to find you awake," I said, as I arrived home from my midnight encounter with Gilliette. Neri sat on a rickety bench outside our door, honing the old sword Placidio had found for him.

"Came awfully near chasing after you."

"I told you to stay away, and I was right." I dragged him into the house after me and closed the door solidly. "She had at least two bodyguards with her. And she's playing a wicked game . . ."

Once I'd poured us each a cup of wine, we pulled our stools close where we could talk without risk of being overheard from the alley. I told him everything Gilliette had said, and led him through the impossible alternatives.

". . . so I'm left with only the one choice. I've got to give the statue back. Fermi and Boscetti must have no suspicion it was ever stolen."

Neri popped up from his seat as if I'd slapped him. "Are you balmy? Give it to *il Padroné*! Leave it on his doorstep. It's *his* wife. *His* mess. He can figure out how to make it right."

"No." Grabbing his hand, I pulled him back to the stool. "I can't give it to *him*. There's no explanation he could give that proves him anything but a liar who's gifting the grand duc a *stolen* artifact. The lord might not even believe it's the one the merchant dug up. Boscetti certainly won't tell the truth. It has to be put back where it was."

"No. No. No." Neri shook his head violently. "You'll die for this, Romy. And I will too. If they catch you, we're done for. What says this little wife won't set you up to get caught right when you're taking it back?"

"That's a certain risk." More likely from devious Gilliette than he even knew. "But she can't know when I'll do it. I just can't allow Fermi's scheme to succeed. I've told you why. Thousands of people could die if Fermi feels confident he can rid the world of House Gallanos."

"But you don't want this Fermi using it. How can you stop that if you just sneak it back to him."

"Once it's back, somehow I'll . . ."

And here did the late hour take its toll. I'd come up with all sorts of grand schemes as I raced home from the Avanci Bridge. Not a one survived the translation into words.

"I suppose I'll need to get hold of it again and make sure *il Padroné* gets it—but with the big difference that neither he nor Gilliette nor I will be implicated in his having it."

Certain, I'd not a glimmer of an idea how to make such a thing happen. Steal it back and then what? Post a bounty for anyone who stole it back for me? Get one of my lawyer clients to file a writ against Boscetti for breaking a contract?

I drained my cup of wine. "Maybe I'll just solicit bids for the cursed thing like a barker at a pig auction."

"Pfft." Neri's skepticism gave me the reaction I deserved. "Find another statue. Give 'em each one, so's they can both give the duc a toy for his birthing day."

"Two statues." The words blinded me like an errant sunbeam. So simple. So obvious.

As the pieces of the puzzles spun in my head, some connecting, some colliding and bouncing off each other, my fingers unsnarled the knotted twine that bound the heavy bundle Gilliette had given me. Layers of canvas and silk wrappings fell away and I stood the cast bronze statue upright on its base.

The dull green-gold bronze stood no taller than my forearm, elbow to wrist. The sculpted metal was wrought with more angular sweeps and curves than lifelike details of god or monster, but there was certainly no difficulty in identifying its subjects. The naked male was Atladu, for he wore earrings shaped like the coil of a wave and his sigil-marked hand carried a barbed spear. The sleek, faceless suggestion of a winged creature that loomed over the god was surely Dragonis, whose spiked tail had carved out our twisting ragged coastlines to the south and shattered the tip of the Costa Drago into the islands of Mercediare.

It was the depiction of the two that was unusual. Every image of Atladu and Dragonis, whether drawn, painted, carved, sculpted, or assembled in mosaics so ancient the sun had leached their color away, recreated the ferocious duel that purportedly lasted a millennium. But this sculptor artist had depicted the two figures side by side, facing the same direction, the god's muscular shoulder touching the beast's extended haunch, the monster's wings fully spread, as if the two were hunting partners chasing down the wind. A powerful image. Enthralling in its peaceful energy.

Every story I'd heard or read claimed Dragonis had hated the gods from the moment of its creation, jealous because its beauty and brilliance was so far superior to humankind and yet somehow not enough to make it one of the gods. Why did this artist see something different in the story? Likely *not* because he was *Antigoneas, the gods' own smith, who cast it in his mighty forge in Sysaline under the sea,* as my father's lost tales had told.

More important to me just now—why did the grand duc of Riccia want it so badly? Sandro had never told me. So there was no undoing Fermi's plot from that end. But if there were two statues . . .

"If we could come up with a good copy of this," I said, "we could do exactly as you said. We could return the copy to Boscetti and Fermi, and they could present it to the grand duc. We give the real statue to *il Padroné* and he can make his gift as well. It would be up to the grand duc to decide which was the one he wanted. At worst it would leave a stalemate."

I dragged my gaze from the bronze to my brother. "I would need your help to make it happen."

Neri's eyes widened, as if he knew what I was hinting at.

"Can you do it for me? You know . . . walk into Palazzo Fermi and leave something like this behind?"

"Certain." He didn't even blink. "And I would. Gladly."

"I know I've said we can never—"

"Describe something inside the house well enough, and I can get there, put the thing down, walk right back out."

"But what about the *wanting*? You said you had to want some object so badly your head spins."

He leaned back against the wall and crowed. "Well, since I stole those cherries, I've wanted to do magic so bad it makes my head spin." Happily he'd lowered his voice again. "And I prefer to keep both my hands. And I want you to keep yours. I think that's enough *wanting* to make it work."

"Can you focus on a place, instead of some particular object?"

"You just have to tell me about it exact enough I can see it in my head."

I would have to think about that. I'd visited Palazzo Fermi and could describe many of the rooms and artworks, but the right placement for the statue was critical; somewhere it could have been mislaid and overlooked . . . somewhere they could find it. But first we must deal with the question that could end the attempt before we began. Neri was sixteen. He believed he could do anything he set his mind to.

"I suppose we need to make sure you can really do the magic whenever you want. Last time you tried, in the Temple . . ."

His grimy, scarred fingers, witness to months of rough learning, twisted his wine cup, which seemed to have drawn his intense interest. "Won't be a problem. That was a poxy case . . . the luck charm. Evidently, the charm is made to stay hid. Magic don't work on it." He glanced up from under his eyebrows. "Dumond told me."

"Dumond! You've *spoken* with him?"

"Had to know why it didn't work. Had to be sure I'd not lost the skill. And I haven't."

Shock yielded to a rising fury. "By the Sisters, Neri, you worked magic behind my back."

"I have." Damn Placidio and his training; my anger no longer intimidated Neri in the least.

Of course anger was wholly illogical, given what I was asking of him, but I couldn't let this pass. "You put us at risk after we agreed we—"

"*I* didn't agree!" The lamplight sculpted his narrow face with unflinching determination. "I just didn't argue the point. But I wasn't stupid about what I did. Only tried enough times to be sure. I was careful, Romy, and I put back everything I took. But someday I'm going to do more. Learn more. You felt the magic when Placidio healed his wound and when Dumond opened that door. That is *not* a demon thing, or if it is, then I'm a demon and glad of it. You were glad of it, too, when you stole our names and faces from that raping lawyer. Looks like you're going to be glad of it again, now it could serve that person you won't talk about. That person who had Da chopped. That person who *owned* you. Will it make him take you back to your rich life?"

My hands pressed my temples, trying to crush the conflicting urgencies that threatened to crack my skull. "This isn't about pleasing *il Padroné* or going back to him. It's about stopping a war. It's about a vision of the future. About Cantagna. About justice."

But how could he understand, a boy—a young man—who had never seen beauty or justice or imagined a future past the next day?

I lowered my clenched hands to the table and forced them open. "Twelve families, Savilli and Fermi and their ilk, want to go back to Cantagna's old ways. Before *il Padroné's* grandfather stopped it, these families could arrest anyone with whom they had a grievance and try him before their own family courts. Their segnorés or segnoras could require the marriage of any girl or boy from a tribute town with someone in their family, or someone who held their debts, or anyone at all. If you stole from the Fermi, they could execute you. There was a custom called *boons*— exorbitant fees above your rent or taxes. If you wanted to build a warehouse you had to yield House Gavonti a boon amounting to a quarter of everything you stored in it. In his Cantagna— Fermi's Cantagna—the half-blind weaver who sold us our blankets would have to pay a boon amounting to half of every solet she earns to House Malavesi, as they own all the market land in the Beggars Ring. Traders would have to pay a boon to House Longello every time they wished to have the city gates opened for their caravans. These ordinary citizens, and all those like us who benefit from their work, would be driven further into poverty to enrich these dozen families who believe it is their right to do as they please. Only last year was *il Padroné* able to rid Cantagna of the last of those monstrous boons, because he believes all citizens will prosper if merchants and artisans, laborers and shopkeepers are allowed to flourish. He will fight any attempt to overturn our laws. This means war. And who suffers most if powerful families go to war?"

"Everyone else but them." Neri sighed heavily. "I just don't see how a statue is going to stop it."

"Nor do I. I've no idea what might prompt a devout and scholarly grand duc to switch his support to Fermi. You'd think it would have to be more than this statue, no matter how rare it is. But Fermi's not a stupid man—and he's younger and more patient than Savilli. And now he's risked putting himself in direct confrontation with the Shadow Lord, so I have to assume he believes he's going to reap what he wants from the duc's gift."

"And you really think the Shadow Lord's better, even though

some call *him* the tyrant?" Neri wasn't convinced, but was no longer angry. That had to do for now.

"I do. Someday I'll tell you more of him. But we've only three days to get this done. And yes, it's good you're sure of your magic, but above all things, we have to trust each other, be honest with each other. Every day. Every hour. Our danger is real—and everything either of us does affects the other."

"Should have told you," he said, drumming his fingers on our table. "Knew it. Just . . . didn't want you all blistered about it. So I'm to take this thing into Palazzo Fermi where they can find it and think it was lost, not stole . . ."

So easily Neri left our rupture aside—as he had when he was a child. Why could I not let things go?

". . . but you don't want the statue I leave to be this one." He touched the ancient metal.

"That's right," I said. "While you place a false statue in Palazzo Fermi, I get the real one to *il Padroné.* There will need to be witnesses who can vouch that *il Padroné* has obtained it from a reputable source *other* than Boscetti. When Fermi's statue is revealed to be a counterfeit, Fermi will be proved a fool, and *il Padroné* will have a chance to strengthen his friendship with Riccia."

"So we need the second statue." Neri frowned at the bronze. "Where do we find something like?"

"To copy a bronze casting is not so difficult." Memory took me to the myriad artisans' workshops Sandro and I had visited, even as my hand touched the bit of bronze in my pocket—the luck charm brought to my door this very night.

Another piece of the flying puzzle settled into a tentative position. We knew someone who might be able to help us.

"When you met Dumond to ask about the charms, was it at his workshop?"

Neri's cheeks flushed copper. "Aye. I didn't tell him anything else about us, names or such."

"He's proved himself trustworthy. And it's useful to know about the charms." I laid my charm on the table. Dumond could paint magical portals, but more importantly for this scheme, he could cast identical bronze luck charms.

"Did you see any bronze castings at his shop? Objects like statues, cups, or bowls? Anything large or complicated?"

"Certain he sells metalwork," said Neri, creasing his brow. "Small things like the charms, some silver like the bracelet I tried to steal for you. Some tinwork. Not sure about the rest. Mostly it's cups and oil flasks and bowls. He has a shelf of those little statues as folk use for grave remembrances like Mam got for Primo, Guero, and Leni. And alongside were some of the Twins, like the ones shopkeepers put above their lintels for luck. None shaped anything like this, though."

"Good." Natalés—the grave remembrance figures—were almost always bronze so they wouldn't rust. More importantly, their casting told me Dumond knew how to make complex molds.

To make a mold from the statue, cast the copy, and do proper finishing to make the two almost indistinguishable would be difficult enough to manage in three days. One of the assistants from the city's art workshops would surely have the skills we needed. But Dumond was a Beggars Ring man, someone we knew, and skilled at keeping secrets.

"If Dumond can cast and finish a good copy, we can make my plan work. Do you think he'd do it for us?"

"Pay enough and I guess he would. Says he's got four daughters, none married as yet."

"So where do we find him?"

DAY 1—FIRST LIGHT

We were on our way well before first light, ready to set our plan in motion. The Beggars Ring had no central marketplace. It was too crowded and had seen too many fires. Shops and tradesmen's stalls were stuffed into alleyways and odd corners all the way around the ring; sometimes a few shops were clumped together for efficiency—like Potters' Lane or Bakers' Corner. We had to hike halfway around the city to find Dumond's foundry. Surprising that a metalsmith would set up his foundry so far from the river.

Dumond's lack of concern for fire risk was made clear when we arrived. His shop was naught but a three-sided stall built with wooden crates, tucked in between a small stone building marked as a chandlery and a cooper's yard sheltered by a broad wooden roof. There was no evidence of a foundry at all. Not even a lingering smell.

A sleepy girl in a smudged apron sat up straight and brightened her lantern as we approached. "Fair morning, dama, young sir. We're well stocked this morning."

She waved her hand at a few pieces of gaudy jewelry that only a boy of six could admire and some charms stamped in tin—none bearing the image of arcs and tightly coiled spiral as our bronze ones did. But, indeed, there was bronzework, too.

Some workmanlike bowls and cups sat beside six ugly candle-sticks shaped like irises. The natalés, though, the finger-high statuettes that parents placed in the graves of their dead children to distract demons from tender souls, were very well done. From infants to older youths of both sexes, the details of faces and garments were replicated exactly in cast bronze. But lacking a foundry, did Dumond even produce them?

"Are you looking for something particular, dama?" asked the girl. "I could fetch more from our storeroom." Though she spoke to me, her smoky gaze rested appreciatively on Neri's faint bristle of sprouting beard and his broadening shoulders. She was something near his age.

"We're looking for Dumond," said Neri. "Might have some work for him."

"Da'll be out soon." Her fingers twined ebony braids. "Sure you'll wait, yes? I'm Cittina."

I fingered the natalé of a straight-backed, youthful soldier who might have been modeled on my dead brother Primo. "Did your father design these himself?"

"Aye, dama. He designs all our wares. Tin, bronze, copper, and silverwork, hammered and cast. Have you lost a child, then? Sorry, if."

"A brother," I said. "Could you *fetch* your da? Our business . . . our grief . . . is urgent."

She sighed and tilted her head, widening her eyes at Neri, who was assuredly returning her appreciation. The fringe of hair on her brow shone like polished ebony, and slender cheekbones highlighted a smooth, caramel-hued complexion. "Guess I could, if you really want."

"We need to get back to our mother," said Neri, trying very hard to keep his voice from cracking as it still did from time to time.

"Certain, I'll help you, segno."

The girl leaped from her stool with the willowy grace of a young doe, retreated exactly two steps behind the stall, and bellowed, "Da! Customer!" at the volume of a legion's trumpet.

Quick as a hawk moth, the girl darted straight back to Neri's side, her long lashes fluttering in pained sympathy. "We lost my only brother as a babe. I wept for an entire year after. A friend's comfort can help."

Neri looked as if he might combust. I suppressed a smile that wanted very much to show itself.

Thankfully, we did not have to wait long for the balding, dusty Dumond. One look at us and he dispatched a sulky Cittina to help her mam with the morning's chores. Evidently the metalsmith's home and workshop lay somewhere behind the chandlery.

"Told you to keep scarce, lad," said Dumond as soon as we were alone.

"We've a piece of bronzework we need duplicated in a hurry," I said. "My brother seemed to think you might be able to do such work. The bronze charms . . . these natalés. But of course we would need a mold made . . . and a foundry, which it seems . . ." My hand gestured the rest.

"I share a foundry up to the Asylum Ring, if that's your question," he said, cautious in word and expression. "Have to use it at night, when the bigger shops are shut, but it keeps my expense down. So I could certainly do what you want. Whether I *will* or no depends on the job and the pay. I'm a busy man. And careful, as you know."

I pulled the wrapped statue from a bag strapped to my shoulder and passed the heavy bundle over.

Dumond unhooked the lantern hung on a post over his shelves and set the bronze atop the stacked crates to get better light on it. His hands turned the piece slowly, fingers tracing the curves and details of the god and the monster. I imagined I heard the clicking of his mind, assessing the likely composition of the metal and the difficulties of making a piece mold that would replicate the details of the figure without trapping its protrusions inside the rigid clay. He had to plan the tubular openings that would allow air to be pushed out of the mold while molten bronze was poured in, and decide what supplies he might need to replicate coloration and age.

"It's had a piece broke off," he said. "Just here."

He showed me a rough edge along the back of Dragonis, as if another being had raced alongside the god and the monster. Time and age had dulled the sharp edge and colored it the same as the rest.

"Looks as if it was done long ago," I said. "I don't think it's a worry."

A jerk of his head acknowledged my judgment.

From his belt pouch he drew a soft brush and went over the whole thing again, examining the details, including its flat bottom. I'd looked there, too; no maker's mark was visible.

My throat tightened, for as he worked, the furrows in his brow deepened from dispassionate evaluation to curiosity. By the time he looked up at me, suspicion had cast deep shadows in those creases.

"Where did you get this?"

"A gift," I said. "Why does it matter?"

"It's unusual. The composition of the metal's not been common for centuries. And the artwork's old, too; it's not the Temple revival period, nor even the classic that came before. Never saw anything quite like. There's something more to it. Can't say exactly what. This is the kind of thing can be prized by some."

"Its age makes the finishing more difficult, I know—the alloy, the patina, the wear you can see on the monster's scales, the spear where it appears one barb has broken off. But I'll pay well to have an exact copy, with the exception of one detail."

"So you know a bit about these matters." His gaze held me fixed. "What detail?"

"I was hoping you might tell me. Something that would prove which was the copy, which was the original. I'd not wish to be deceitful and pass off the copy as authentic."

His scowl dissolved into a wry skepticism. "Except perhaps to someone who didn't know enough to notice? Like its rightful owner? Perhaps you think to use what secrets you know of me, counting your silence as payment for some nefarious scheme. That won't work."

He shoved the statue toward me. "I know enough to keep our secrets balanced, Romy of Lizard's Alley."

I raised my palm to stay him.

"You saved our lives, Segno Dumond. Never will I presume on the extraordinary circumstance of that rescue. And I'll never betray your confidence, never set foot in this lane again, if you say. But before you refuse, know that I offer silver as payment. I'm familiar with what the Nicosi or Padinino workshops would charge for such a copy, but I prefer to keep this more private— and benefit an artisan who has proved himself *discreet.*"

I raised a finger to my lips to postpone his response.

"I swear that our intent is to return the original to its rightful owner—as near as we can tell—and deliver the copy to those who most deceitfully deprived its rightful owner of his possession. A scheme, yes, but not so nefarious. And I offer quick payment."

After a long, silent assessment of both Neri and me, Dumond glanced at the statue in his hand. "When would you need it done?"

My relief set my knees quivering, even as I braced for his next reaction.

"Day after tomorrow by the Hour of Contemplation." The eve of the duc of Riccia's birthday. Most of three days and two nights.

The deadline was brutal for such complex work. But I had to get the original to Sandro in a public fashion no later than the birthday morning. Neri had to get the finished copy in place so it could be found before the birthday feast, and he needed night's cover for his venture to Palazzo Fermi. And Dumond could not release either the true or false statue before he'd completed the finishing details, which took fine chisels, chemicals, heat, exacting care, and time.

He blew a long, thoughtful exhale. "That, damizella, will cost extra."

13

A s the city came to life with the graying sky, Neri and I joined the flow of servants and tradesmen heading up through the rings. We had left Dumond with the statue and six silver coins—half of his payment plus enough for a bribe to get him daytime access to one of his Asylum Ring workshops. We had also set an evening appointment to decide on the flaw we would introduce to expose Boscetti's statue as a counterfeit when the time came.

I felt almost naked as we walked out. Worry hollowed my stomach, well beyond the risks of our plan. Only five silver solets remained in Sandro's purse—exactly enough to pay Dumond. Until Neri or I got paid again, the coppers in our pockets had to feed us. Unless I found more clients or Fesci gave Neri more hours of work, we'd not be able to pay Placidio for the next month.

But of course, if we didn't make this plan work, we wouldn't be needing any more sword training or meals either one. Thus, for the moment, we needed to reconnoiter Neri's route to place the false statue.

"This way." I hurried through the bustling spice market, where cooks and householders already crowded around colorful, aromatic displays of mounded powders, pods, and leaves. Neri's feet slowed as we threaded the noodle market, where a copper solet could buy a fistful of fresh noodles ready to dunk in one of the bubbling kettles of sweet fish sauce, lemon thyme broth, or thick garlic tomato soup.

"After," I said. "We need to get in and out of the Via Mortua in the Merchant Ring before the coffinmakers open their shops."

Neri halted and glanced uneasily at the charcoal sky. "Coffinmakers? Why? It's bad luck to—"

"You need a good route in and out of Palazzo Fermi," I said, speaking low as I dragged him through the Market Ring's upper gates. "There are still wardens on the alert at the Cambio Gate. If someone spots you inside Palazzo Fermi and raises an alarm, you won't get through. Not with traces of magic on you. And you certainly don't want anyone to see you vanish through a city wall."

"Yeah, yeah. Too many sniffers about town already."

"So I'm showing you a less public way between the Merchant Ring and the Heights."

We sped through the Merchant Ring, across the Piazza Cambio where Naldo di Savilli had paid for his treachery, past guildhalls, townhouses, and prosperous shopkeepers washing their stoops or drinking tiny cups of coffee with neighboring tradesmen. Well around the eastern side of the Ring we rounded a corner into a dim, quiet, clean alley called Via Mortua.

"You're not the only one who thinks it bad luck to visit a

coffinmaker when the sun is low. So the shops here don't open before half-morn and they close by midafternoon, which means this lane . . ."

". . . is deserted early and late."

"Via Mortua also happens to end at the Merchant Ring's upper wall"—the high wall that separated all of the lower city from the Heights.

Neri's shoulders hunched as we traversed the pocket of silence in the midst of the city noise. Past the last closed shop, we trod a narrow path through a maze of old brick and stone rubble. When the mortared stones of the massive wall barred our way, we pulled away a flimsy sheet of rotted planking, exposing a solid rectangle of blackened oak.

"Certain people wish to move between the Merchant Ring and the Heights without notice on occasion," I said. "One of those people showed me a number of private doorways with tricky mechanical locks that only those who've been shown how can open."

"The Shadow Lord," he murmured. "You walked out with him like—"

"Like ordinary friends," I said. "I was neither chained to his bed nor kept in a cage, and he was never ashamed to be seen in my company. Nor I in his."

Even after he married. He could not compromise the standing of his future children, thus it became necessary for the little wife to accompany him to formal family gatherings and official functions of the Sestorale. But I had been his chosen companion whenever custom allowed choosing.

The lock had not been changed. The door opened to a short, dim tunnel through the thick wall. We pulled the door closed behind us, using a thin rope to pull the sheet of planking up behind it. Twenty steps took us to another lock, this time on a grate at the upper end of the tunnel, and we soon walked out of an alley into the quiet immensity of the Piazza Livello—the heart of Cantagna.

Before us and on every side, the grandeur of Cantagna's wealth rose in a magnificence of towers and spires, sculpted facades, and sprawling palaces. A gushing fountain centered the piazza, a monumental bronze of Atladu's Leviathan drowning the kingdom of Sysaline on the day it washed Dragonis out of the sky.

Behind the fountain stood the Palazzo Segnori—the same venue Neri and I visited for his Quarter Day parole reports. The palazzo's pillared loggia stretched left and right, and above it the harmonious rows of windows, like bright eyes ever open to the world. The loggia was mostly deserted so early of a morning, only a few sleepy clerks making their way through the great doors.

A Gardia warden rode by slowly, eyeing us. Neri ducked his head and I dipped a knee, then we scurried across the piazza, rousing waves of annoyed pigeons. Around a corner we entered the network of alleys that serviced the great houses of the district. Three turns and we arrived at Palazzo Fermi.

Unlike Sandro's family, who had grown their modest home in the Merchant Ring to magnificence by absorbing those nearby, the Fermi had torn down five elegant houses in the southeast quarter of the Heights a few years ago, and built themselves a sprawling new palace, appointed with every luxury wealth could commandeer. Neri and I crouched in an ancient olive grove that stood awkwardly in the middle of the lane behind the newest wing; it was considered bad luck to cut down Lady Virtue's favored tree.

"The receiving room where Gilliette threw her fainting fit is on the third level of this wing." I pointed to a row of dark windows that ended at a rounded tower. "It's something like the fifth window past that tower toward the front of the house; its balcony overlooks a small garden. An alcove opens off of the inner corner of the receiving chamber. They use it for a flower room—creating bouquets to decorate Lucrezia di Fermi's chambers. The last time I was there, a life-sized marble sculpture depicting the Five Graces screened the flower room door. That's where the statue needs to go, as if someone picked the thing up and set it aside while they were tending Gilliette. Leave it sticking out a bit. They have urns of flowers around the sculpture, so you could tip one over as if someone bumped it to reveal the bronze. Does that make sense?"

"Aye. As long as I can imagine the place well enough to get there."

"I can certainly describe the receiving room, but will that be enough? Between here and there are the stable yard, a guarded wall, the courtyard beyond, and a long passage flanked by butteries and candle and linen rooms. A servant's stair can take you up. Do you need me to describe them all? I've walked the way, but I'm not sure I can remember everything."

Neri blew a long exhale. "I've never done such a big place," he said softly. "Going through one wall is easy. But each one after takes a bit more out of me, just having to think about it so hard and want it so hard. I've never tried breaching more'n three or four for a fetch, so the further I can just walk or climb or sneak without magic, the better. It'll leave me some to get out with."

No fear trembled his words. How did he come to be so brave?

"Good. When we get home, I'll draw the best map I can and describe the reception chamber for you. The sculpture of Five Graces, I recall exactly." Sandro had called it *dross*, and I had memorized its appearance so I might recognize dross next time I saw it.

Neri nodded. "That ought to do me."

We retraced our route through the alleys and across the awakening Piazza Livello to the gate and the tunnel to the Via Mortua. I had just finished drilling Neri on the latch—the order of undoing and resetting was critical—when we heard voices in the lane.

Neri quietly replaced the rotted planking against the door, and we crept through the rubble. The city bells rang the Hour of Business. Though Via Mortua itself yet lay in shadow, the angled sunbeams had already reached the street beyond its end. The arriving coffinmakers would be suspicious of anyone sneaking out of their ill-favored street before the shadows had dispersed, and we could not afford to be stopped, questioned, noted. Nor did I want the passage through the wall discovered. The Gardia would seal it were they told.

I turned the frayed lining of my cloak outwards, wrenched away the ribbon that tied my braid, and mussed my hair into a tangled cloud. As when I walked out with Sandro, I donned the skin of the person I wanted to be. I needed to do it well.

Neri whispered, "What are you d—?"

"Shhh," I said, gushing as noisily as the Piazza Livello fountain. "They're sleeping now."

Reliving the wine-soaked blur of my worst hours of the past

year, I hung my arm around Neri's neck and urged him toward the three men who looked our way as they opened the shutters on their shops.

"There's naught like bedding with ghosties to set me right, Cousin Bertie," I slurred. "None to paw under me skirts; none to steal my sweet little bota."

I pulled out the wineskin that lived in my inner pocket— emptied less often since I'd been working with Placidio—and dangled it in my brother's shocked face. My fingers pinched his chin to be alert.

"Love's lorn lordly, heart's trembled thornly," I warbled, thick-tongued. "'Twas kindly you've come to drag me home, love, though it's a deal too early. Too bright out there. Erf . . . me gut's churning like Mam's butter paddle."

The boy's grip firmed and dragged me, staggering, toward the street. "Come on, then, you sotted cow. Puke on me and next time yer mam tells me fetch you, I'm dumping ye in the river." He tipped his hat to the coffinmakers. "Lady Fortune preserve ye gentlefolk from drunkard cousins!"

Disgusted murmurs and a blur of sober grays and blacks from the corner of my eye marked the pinchy gawkers. Two females had joined the men. Clever Bertie shoved me into the sunlit street and around the corner.

"Keep her out!" a woman yelled after us. "Don't like swillpots nesting here!"

"I'll drown 'er sure," Bertie bellowed sourly over his shoulder.

I stumbled onward, retching, singing, moaning, throwing myself on Cousin Bertie, trusting his hand on my collar to guide me through the waking streets. He tried to steer me around passersby, but a man shoved me to the cobbles when my flailing arm touched him. Cursing broadly, Bertie dragged me up and shoved me forward before taking hold again. I kept on singing.

"None's followed," he whispered after a while. "And none's looking at you."

I rubbed my arm, bruised on the cobbles. Kept walking. Words to the song wouldn't come no more. Couldn't think of the next verse.

He gave my cheek a light slap. "Romy, are you all right?"

"Stop that!" I batted his hand away and straightened up. "Of course I'm all right."

Though indeed dropping the playacting felt something like crawling out of a hole. I tied my hair into a tail as we walked, flipped my cloak to hide the ragged lining, and bundled it about me to quiet a shiver of nerves. "You took up my ruse very well."

"Thought you'd cracked your head or something," said Neri as we stopped at a Market Ring stall and splurged on a deliciously warm hollowed bun, filled with buttered noodles and garlic. "You didn't even look—swear to the Unseeable, if I'd been the one standing there, I wouldn't have recognized you."

"Good. I didn't want anyone prowling around to see what a respectable law scribe and a tavern doorward were doing in the back of that alley. Didn't think the person who showed me the passage would appreciate that. No one will remember another drunk."

Neri devoured his portion without taking a breath. I let the steam warm my chilly hands and the savory noodles soothe my unsettled stomach as we headed homeward, talking of what to do next. So many pieces had to fit to make this plan work.

"Should I even go with Placidio today?" Neri asked. The swordmaster would be at our house at the half-morn anthem.

"Go ahead. I'll make a sketch of the palazzo receiving room, and we'll go over it later until you have all you need. But first I've got to figure out how I'm to get the real statue into Sand—*il Padroné's*—hands in front of witnesses. I've an idea, but there are difficulties—"

"*You* can't do it. He'll know you, less'n maybe you went as a drunk." Neri glanced at me doubtfully. "I suppose I could learn enough to pretend I was a messenger from the one who has the statue."

"Neither would do much to make anyone believe the messenger is a reputable purveyor of antiquities. The witnesses must be able to attest that *il Padroné* didn't steal it from Boscetti. Besides, you'll need to be about your own mission, so I've got to do it. I know a bit about disguises."

Changing hair, bleaching or blackening it and using Moon House powders and potions, kohl, rouge, or henna could alter a woman's appearance dramatically. Enough, surely.

Neri, still skeptical, wiped his fingers on his tunic. "If you're the one who delivers the statue, then who's to be the reliable witness?"

"*Il Padroné* sits on the Sestorale Commission on Public Artworks. I'm thinking that one Vincenzio di Guelfi, an adventurer of modest family from . . . let us say . . . the Independency of Varela, will send a letter to the commission today informing them of a new cache of antiquities he's found. He has heard of the commission's interest in pre-classical bronzes—*il Padroné* sent inquiries to a variety of knowledgeable people last year—and will be in Cantagna on the day after tomorrow in the evening with several samples of his find, including one extraordinary bronze.

He is seeking a stipend to further his exploration and would be happy to appear before an evening session of the commission. Certain, he can provide references from reliable historians."

"But who—? Oh. *You* think to play this Guelfi."

Neri halted just past the Beggars Ring gate and raked me with an appraising glance. "Romy, aren't you a bit . . . womanly . . . to play a man? Unless your disguise can flatten your chest and give you a beard. And what reliable historians would write *you* a recommendation?"

A fraught mix of panic and laughter bade me shove him aside and hurry on down the lane through a mob of desperate men and women waving their arms to get the attention of barkers hiring laborers for the day. Neri elbowed through the press and caught up with me. "'Twasn't an insult, Romy."

"None taken. I was thinking more of playing Vincenzio's wife or partner . . . sister, I think. I've more experience at sistering. I'll say he's sick and sent me in his stead. So, yes, the disguise is troublesome, but I can't involve anyone else. And I'll write the references, of course. I know what names they'll believe."

But what disguise could hide me from Sandro's scrutiny if I was the one doing all the talking? That was the problem that would require extra thinking.

"The statue will distract *il Padroné*, fascinate him," I said, reassuring myself. "The members of the commission will be excellent witnesses. Several of them will be able to recognize the design of the bronze and its true antiquity."

The historians Piero and Beatrice di Mesca headed the commission. They were loyal to the Gallanos family, but not beholden to Sandro, and they had impeccable credentials when it came to antiquities.

"Sandro will accept their judgment. He doesn't trust Boscetti or Fermi; he'll see the attempt to blame a *theft* on his bodyguard and my former maidservant as their attempt to discredit him. When they show up to the duc's birthday feast with the counterfeit, he'll have them in his fist."

Assuming I could persuade the commission to meet Vincenzio di Guelfi.

Assuming I could carry off the disguise.

Assuming Dumond could make a competent duplicate in time.

Assuming Neri could get the counterfeit in place.

Then, perhaps, we could win out and live another day.

14

P lacidio will do it."

Neri's blurted pronouncement shattered my concentration. I glanced up from the mess of ink and parchment on my writing table, my head spinning with words—polite words, precise words, words clever enough to intrigue the eight members of the commission, deferent enough to keep them at ease, strong enough to ensure respect and hearing. Trials and scraps of messages lay everywhere, dusted with scrapings from cleaning parchment to retest my phrasing and sand from drying two completed letters. I'd locked my shop door and missed out on three clients as I wrestled with it.

"Do *what*?" I snapped.

Neri seemed taken aback by my annoyance, but his abrupt arrival had jolted a last perfect phrase from my head.

"He'll play the adventurer—Vincenzio. He'll go with you to the Artworks Commission."

The whirling puzzle pieces in my head settled into a new arrangement. *"Placidio? Is he mad? Does he have any idea how dangerous—?"*

"I told him that we were working a scheme to save your life and prevent a war and that we needed some playacting done in front of *il Padroné*. He asked if there was silver involved. I said it was possible, but not sure—not wanting to give your word to it. He said it wasn't necessary, but that he would need some clothes, as his only decent suit is his dueling rig and that wouldn't hardly do. I guess he drinks up most of his fees."

"Placidio?"

The terrifying thing was that it made good sense. A man so robust would certainly be more convincing as an adventurer than the best disguise I could imagine for an adventurer's sister. Cleaned up, in good leather and velvet. The duelist was no fool. His whole life was dangerous playacting.

"But why, Neri? Why would he? He doesn't need the risk. He's shown no particular loyalty to Cantagna. He has no family here that we know of. I've seen no signs of attachment to any of his clients. If war came and he didn't care to fight for one side or the other, he could just move on to somewhere else. How can we trust him?"

Neri downed a flask of weak ale and two aged apples in the span of a heartbeat, and then cut a length of sausage that had cost two days' writing fees.

"He said he couldn't afford to lose two paying students. But I think he decided to do it when I mentioned the scheme was about a very important man's birthday gift for the grand duc of Riccia. He said, 'Certain I owe Eduardo a favor.' But it was mumble and I don't think he meant for me to hear it—or even knew I had. For certain he never told me who Eduardo was or even mentioned him again."

The name made everything clear and added questions at the same time.

"In the match Placidio lost on purpose to prevent people noticing his magic," I said, "the one that knocked him off the dueling list in Tibernia, he lost to the conte of Tibernia's champion, which enabled the conte to retain his title. The conte then banished his cousin the chancellor. The sister of that banished, disgraced cousin who believed he had legitimate claim to the title is Eduardo di Corradini's wife."

Understandably, Neri's confusion was not yet satisfied. "But who is Edu—?"

"Eduardo di Corradini is the grand duc of Riccia." But who was Placidio di Vasil to be calling the grand duc of Riccia by his personal name?

"I'll have to speak to Placidio before we go forward." Though I would be hard-pressed to find a reason to avoid so fine a solution.

"He's fighting today midafternoon. But he says he'll not take any more challenges for three days, if you decide to have him. And he says he'll not get drunk for three days neither, if you should be worried about that. I'm to leave a message with Fesci at the Duck's Bone as to when you want to meet with him."

"Evening bells at the Duck's Bone. Three hours should give time enough for his fight and whatever he does after." We would see if the man stayed sober. "Then we go to Dumond at half-even to decide what flaw he's going to mold into the false statue."

"I'll tell Fesci the time." Neri drained another mug of ale.

"And find Fesci's boy Aldo," I said, as he wiped his eating

knife. "Tell him I've a delivery needs to be made. He should wash his face and clean his nails, put on a clean shirt, and be here when the next hour bell rings."

"Right."

"And Neri . . ."

He looked back from the open doorway, confident, handsome, clever, generous, trusting, a man now, and worthy of a destiny so much more than he was likely to find. My heart ached for his promise and for his danger.

". . . go with care."

His grin flashed bright and he slammed the door.

As I finished the message to the Arts Commission, the image of my brother's face would not leave me. Few people in the Costa Drago prayed. Those who did so were hopeless optimists who believed the Unseeable Gods were yet capable of influencing human affairs if you just spoke to them often enough with rituals of fire or water, pain or lovemaking—anything that might breach the boundaries of the Night Eternal. But no matter how they tried, we yet suffered plagues and wars and the earth yet shook and the mountains yet fumed.

Supposedly Lady Fortune and Lady Virtue, merely the daughters of gods, could not change the ordering of human events, but offered guidance to those who heeded the workings of the world. Fortune revealed her secrets through augury, though finding diviners who could truly hear Fortune's true whispers and not just their own venal hearts was ever a challenge. But Virtue bestowed her gifts of wisdom, generosity, and courage randomly on worthy souls—thus we painted tributes or erected statues or held processionals to honor virtuous men and women to show our appreciation and keep the Lady's bounty coming. We also devised story after story of how we might influence the direction of Lady Virtue's gifting.

When the message to the Arts Commision was sent, I grabbed a loaf of bread and hurried down to the riverside. Sitting on a lonely rock, I scattered crumbs until I was surrounded by a legion of warblers and swifts, buntings and martins—Lady Virtue's favored creatures—and I whispered my petition in hopes they would carry it to through the blue skies to their beloved mistress.

"Please, any divinity who will listen, let me not be foolish in pursuing this enterprise. It is not for me. It is not for my onetime friend of the heart Sandro, who declared me dead. This is for Alessandro di Gallanos's vision that a city of enlightenment might live long after us. And this is for Neri, that he might live."

DAY 1—EVENING

"When will we get the commission's answer?" Neri kept his voice low, though the twirling pipes, clattering tabor, and inharmonious chatter of the tavern's patrons left no risk of us being overheard. "I don't understand why you didn't send the letter to *him* direct."

Neri always bulged his eyes and bobbed his head when he referred to Sandro, as if I might miss his meaning elsewise.

The corner table where I sometimes met clients was situated far enough from the hearth to be out of the way when patrons helped themselves to a mug of Fesci's mysterious bone-and-scrap soup, while near enough to be warm in the winter—certainly warmer than my shop which had only a tiny brazier. Neri had joined me from time to time through the last hour, as he roamed the common room, the alley, and the horse yard behind, making sure no patron overstepped Fesci the taverner's rules.

"It will take the head of the commission awhile to contact the other members," I said. "I hope to get an answer by midday tomorrow. And my sending the application to anyone else—no matter how powerful that person is—instead of those officially in charge, would be seen as terribly rude and cast a venal light on Vincenzio di Guelfi's motives. But if Placidio doesn't get here soon, we'll have to rethink the whole scheme."

The evening anthem bells had rung a half hour since with no sign of the duelist. I kept envisioning him slumped in an alley spewing vomit or gouting blood. His willingness to join us had relieved me of a huge burden, and now . . .

"Don't fret," said Neri. "He'll come."

Two boys' jostling devolved into a grapple as they sniped at each other in the usual dialect of ancestry, cowardice, and male appendages. Neri moved off to drag them outside. The chilly draft from the open door flickered the smoky lamp and swirled sparks from the hearth.

Giggles from several customers distracted my attention from all the ways I could murder Placidio di Vasil. Someone had come in as Neri hauled his charges out.

Yet another curse on Placidio's head rose to my tongue when I saw the newcomer was just a tall, awkward, clerkish sort of man, whose deep-set eyes roamed the common room uncertainly. His short hair and out-of-fashion gray cloak and doublet marked him above the common for the Beggars Ring. Sure as nightfall, two girls descended on him like ants to honey.

Pipes and tabor rattled into a new tune, inviting all to the dance. I returned attention to my cider; no use giving Placidio an excuse to inebriate himself if the damnable sot ever showed up. And if he didn't? Curse it all. I had written of Professoré di Guelfi's sister-assistant in his application, but had dropped my notion to mention a recent bout of illness that might excuse the man himself from appearing.

Someone smelling faintly of lavender water cleared his throat. I glanced up. The clerkish newcomer towered over me . . . a man whose hands could enclose an infant's head entire and who sported a scar that reached from his left eyebrow to his square chin.

"Placidio?" Even with such distinctive evidence, I wasn't entirely sure.

"The scar ruins it, yes? Didn't think it would stand out so awfully after that barbarian barbering." He dropped heavily onto the stool Neri had vacated. "Maybe a hat would help?"

My hand flew to my mouth. No one so genuinely despondent deserved laughter.

Only when composure returned did I venture, "I know a salve to mask . . . skin blemishes. It might be of use to lessen if not hide the scar. I suppose an adventurer like Vincenzio di Guelfi might be expected to have experienced some rough encounters in his life."

"Indeed so!" The duelist's face brightened, then immediately clouded again. "Though I didn't think to ask who might be at this commissionary sitting. It's not only merchants or guildsmen who've hired me. A few nobs like a duel on the cheap from time to time."

"Certain I can tell you who's likely to be there: Beatrice and

Piero di Mesca, Hue di Santorini . . ." I rattled off the eight
commission members, ending, naturally, with ". . . Alessandro di
Gallanos, otherwise known as—"

"—*il Padroné*. Neri told me. Good. None of them ever hired me.
But the lad says you've met Gallanos and that he might even
recognize you. He wasn't stretching the story to intrigue me?"

"No." I fixed on his cinder-gray eyes and dropped my voice
even lower. "And it does pose a risk. I have to be there. To watch
him, to listen, to discover what I can of his belief, to know whether
to let Neri risk his part of our venture. But if you're willing to
risk partnering with me, you deserve to know all . . ."

He bobbed his head, understanding my pause. "You can trust
me, lady scribe, as I've trusted you."

"For nine years I was companion to the Shadow Lord, his
favored . . . courtesan."

"Fortune's dam." The words dropped like stones in a still
pond. But to his credit, Placidio did not gape, sneer, blanch, crow,
take a fresh inventory of my body, or run away. He did blink,
swallow hard, and signal to one of the disappointed tap girls to
bring him a mug of ale, not speaking again until she had withdrawn.

"Never imagined. I mean I knew you were intelligent and
educated, experienced in ways no Beggars Ring woman likely
ever was, but such never crossed my mind."

"I appreciate that," I said. "I'm not ashamed of it. It was not a
life I chose for myself, nor would I have done even if I'd known
those years would be as good as such a life can possibly be. But
our relationship is a year dead and that will not change. I swear
to you that this venture is not some scheme to reclaim his favor.
I would as soon he never know I was involved."

The words flowed easily, jolting me with the certain truth they expressed.

"Thus—thus you can see my difficulty, as well as the additional dangers of joining me." I told him of Gilliette and the luck charm, of the stolen statue and her threat to my safety, and of the risk of civil war if Riccia's favor supported *il Padroné*'s enemies. The only thing I withheld was how we had come to know Dumond or any hint that our forger shared our demonic taint.

In honest turn, Placidio revealed that he had wondered about Neri's boldness at trying the Santorini Thrust at his first lesson, as well as his knowledge of a sophisticated technique. But he had only come to believe Neri was demon born on the night we'd saved his life, when he'd heard Neri ask me if I'd felt Placidio's magic.

"We helped you save your own life," I interrupted. "The power you wielded that night . . . it made me think the taint not such an evil as I've always believed. It's certainly a divine curse that can destroy lives so easily, but—"

"It is our human curse, not divine," he said, harsh as I'd ever heard him. "History corrupts our gift, twists it, forcing us to corrupt and twist ourselves. You are bold indeed, lady scribe, to enlist your brother's skill in a righteous cause. To enlist your *own* skill, as well, I think, for if you perceived my power that night, you're one of us as well."

Bile scalded my throat. "I wasn't trying to hide it from you; you just need to know it's so minor as to be irrelevant. When touching someone's skin, I can make that person forget a bit of truth and recall something different in its stead. But that replacement memory usually raises more questions than it quiets. I could make the Shadow Lord believe that a false statue was the real one, but unless I touched every member of the commission, as well as the grand duc of Riccia himself, and told them the same, it wouldn't solve anything."

"Hmph."

Silent, he rested his arms on the table, his fingers touching the droplets on his mug's smooth side as if they were pearls. Then his gaze flicked to me, sharp, as if he'd worked out a puzzle.

"I was not born a duelist. As a boy, I was considered to have exceptional eyesight, because I could tell my parents how my young brother had unlocked the wine store with a bit of wire or set fire to the stable by tormenting my father's horse into kicking over a lantern, even though I was found far from the scene of each crime. But of course I had run away when I saw these things happening—not even understanding that I *saw* them in time to stop the events before they actually occurred."

"As you do when you're dueling. You must use your gift sparingly, lest someone take notice."

"Aye, that." His scarred fingers flexed and twined themselves into a tight knot. "It was a hard road to understand what I could do, and a great deal of work to harness it to be of any use—'tis only a moment's advantage, not an hour's. But my meaning is, if you've not had a chance to explore your gift, then you might be surprised at how it shapes." His lips took on a bitter twist. "I might even volunteer to be your subject. There's a number of things I'd like to forget."

I raised my mug in mock salute. "Like yours, my gift offers only a limited advantage. I can erase the memory of a woman you talked with this morning. But I don't know how to erase the memory of why you were talking to her in the first place, or who she reminded you of, or where you had seen her before, or the thousand other things associated with that conversation. I would leave so many disconnected fragments, it would drive you mad trying to connect them."

"Ah. Too bad." He sipped at his ale and shook his head like a hound shaking off a dousing.

But I couldn't let our confessions rest quite yet. "So—you must understand I have to ask, because we've no way to know how this may all play out—has any one of those things you'd like to forget something to do with Eduardo di Corradini?"

Blackness deadened Placidio's eyes, and his body tensed as if on the verge of flight. For certain the easy part of our conversation was finished. He lowered his gaze to the dregs of cider swirling in his cup. "Yes and no."

He glanced up as if to judge if he'd said enough. Then he blew a soft sigh. "Don't know how you've come to know whatever it is prompts you speak about him and me. That frights me a bit. But I'll tell you I bear the man no ill will. Rather the other way round. I believe him to be a good man on the inside as well as the out, deserving all the honor rumor speaks. The circumstances of that understanding I will keep to myself, despite your having shared your own privacy so frankly. I will *not* bend in this. But please believe my withholding is not, in any fashion, a matter of my trust in you, nor should it affect this plan of yours in any way for good or ill. Does that suffice?"

In other circumstances, it might not. But the more I considered my plan, the more convinced I was that I dared not go alone into a room with Sandro. The duelist was a private man, but we had worked with him for a year. He had kept Neri's secret and his suspicions about mine, and we had kept his. The results of our bargain—the results of his good teaching—had been more than satisfactory, and I'd seen nothing to concern me about his trust-worthiness. Almost nothing.

"Sober until it's over?" I said.

"On my mother's womb."

"Then I'll accept your boundaries for now. And I welcome your help," I said. The words did not seem enough. I extended my hand and we clasped wrists as is done for the most solemn contracts.

15

Extraordinary, Segno Dumond!" I said. "I never expected to see it so soon. But of course with our short deadline, you had to be quick."

On a large littered worktable in a stone shed behind the cooper's yard stood the Antigonean bronze in all the power of its shaping, and beside it stood a wax model without a flaw that I could see, from the sigils on Atladu's hand to the silken curves of Dragonis's wings.

Neri would have been amazed, too, but he had stayed behind; Fesci worried that the full moon was addling her patrons. Neri would also watch for anyone hunting message box number six at the writing shop down the road from the Duck's Bone. No answer had yet come from the Commission on Public Artworks.

"My head's true wearied with this mold," said Dumond, nodding at the small, odd blocks of hardened clay stacked on the table, each carefully numbered. Expertly placed protrusions and matching divots on each mating face would have fit the pieced mold together for the pouring of the wax. "The rippled wings. The god's shoulder and the beast's haunch twined and undercut as they are. Took three tries to get it right. Fortunate I had extra clay, and some . . . special techniques . . . for setting the clay quick." He glanced up.

Magic . . . for so mundane a thing as drying clay molds. "You are a brave man, Dumond."

"I've taken more risk for less worth. Decided long ago to live as I want."

His hard fingers rearranged some lengths of wax rod for no purpose I could see. "I've worked the wax a bit to take off the parting lines and correct some details to match the original. Soon as I fix these sprue rods onto the model, I'll be ready to set the final pouring mold. Then we pour."

"Tonight then."

"Aye. A friend at the foundry up to the Asylum Ring started the bronze melt a couple of hours ago, soon as his master shut down for the night; he thinks I'm making more bronze birds for an impatient client." He nodded to another mold fitted together in a block. "I should have the pour done by dawn. That'll give me most of two days for the finish work. Not much cushion for mistakes."

"And the flaw that will expose it as a counterfeit? What do you suggest?"

A false ease enveloped him as he settled his backside to the stone wall and folded his arms. If I so much as blinked out of time, he would notice. What might so powerful a sorcerer do if he was frightened? Recalling the flame in his hands as he opened his painted doorway prompted caution.

"Who's going to be inspecting our two bronzes to decide which is true?" he said.

I breathed away a sudden chill. I'd no mind to deceive him. "The one who must be convinced the false statue is the original is a procurer of antiquities, holding whatever knowledge that implies," I said. "He's not the brightest fellow, but he could surely recognize something too obvious, like an extra finger or misplaced foot or a variation in the patina."

"This would be the person who *most deceitfully deprived* the true owner of his artwork?"

"Yes, along with his partner who is perhaps less experienced in artworks, but assuredly more experienced in deception. The ones who must expose it as a counterfeit are prominent historians who know their business, and some men and women who know a great deal about art and antiquities, including the true owner."

"Any chance of a sniffer in either group?"

"A sniff—?" The question caught me up short. "The Antigonean bronze carries *magic*?"

"Not magic as I experience it." He moved back to the table and brushed his finger along the beast's rippled wing. "But it has a strangeness that's something like. Hold it long enough and reach, as you do for magic, and you will touch something beyond . . . beyond this life. Not at all sure what it is. If any one of your inspectors can—and will—do that, then there's no reason to introduce any common flaw."

Breathless with astonishment, I said, "I can't imagine there would be a sorcerer in either party. And certainly none who would confess to it before witnesses."

But certain, this made me wonder not only about the bronze, but about the man who wanted it so intensely—the grand duc of Riccia, who claimed it was of *divine* origin.

"Even if I'm present at the moment of revelation," I said, "which is in no way assured, I wouldn't dare suggest that sort of test."

"I'd not say sorcery is the only way to experience what I did." Dumond retracted his hand and shook his head. "It might be only one pathway. But I must tell you, damizella, I'm not sure anyone in this city should possess this statue. Had I come across it on my own, I would pack it away in a cave somewhere until I had scoured this world for the wisdom necessary to make sense of it."

"Why? You must not think it evil, else *wisdom* would not unlock it. That would violate the most basic tenets of philosophy."

"I make no claim of good or evil. Try it yourself and judge."

I retreated a step, as if he'd pushed me closer.

"It wreaks no hurt or harm that I can see." He flung his arms open, then tapped his chest with his fingertips. "My heart yet beats. My gift yet answers my call. Not even my wife has noticed an alteration in me save a strange new desire to study myth, and she is an exceptionally perceptive person."

This was no time for mysteries. Yet if this demonic taint Neri and I bore was a *gift*, as Dumond and Placidio both named it, and if it could reveal some danger in this bit of metal that should not be in powerful men's hands . . .

Reach, he'd said. He'd used the same word in the Temple when invoking his magic. I had never reached for magic but rather *touched*, like opening the stopcock on an ale cask and shutting it again after the first droplet. Closing my eyes, I tried to imagine what reaching must be like. Instead of cask and stopcock, I envisioned an open barrel and dipped my hand . . .

Warmth flowed over and through me. I allowed it—the forbidden, the terrifying—much like the first night I told Sandro he could do as he wished with me, the first night I meant it and wanted it. All he'd done was touch, gentle, but firm and sure, everywhere, waking me to something new. As on that night, my heart beat faster, my breath came quick and shallow, my muscles melted. So it was with magic there in Dumond's workshop. Whenever fear threatened, I imagined Sandro's hand slowing, his voice soothing me until I let go.

So the infusion of magic continued until my whole body must surely be swollen with warmth and life. There I held. As on that night so long ago, this was not to be a consummation, but an introduction. A test.

Alive with magic, I opened my eyes and laid a hand on the mottled green-gold statue. So solid. Cooler than the heavy night breeze leaking through the door and shuttered windows of the stone workshop. And as if the earth opened beneath my feet, I fell breathless, fearless, into another place . . .

Filmy veils of gray, white, and palest green, and others of soft colors that had no name wafted in a liquid breeze, cool on my heated skin. Beyond the veils a circle of tall torchieres in the guise of gleaming gold lilies centered a vast, domed hall. Their flames wavered in sinuous light, as if I viewed them through flawed glass. The arched ceiling rose far higher than the torch flames could reach, yet a pearlescent glow illumined figures, faces, beasts, plants, symbols carved on slender arcs of pure white stone.

The breeze, the firm stone under my shoes, the snap of the

flames and their scented smoke testified that I stood in this other place. But as I moved past the veils, the better to see the hall, my feet glided, dreamlike. Not so much walking as floating.

Supporting the dome was a circle of pillars of polished stone, finely mottled in rose, green, and ivory. The dome itself was not a solid shell as I expected, but a maze created from the white arches—bridges they might be, though scarce wide enough for two feet. Each one arced higher or lower than the next, originating at some points around the circular base in a pattern I could not guess, and ending at points masked by other arches. Above the seven or nine whose origin points I saw, more of the graceful arcs sprang from higher points—a wonder matching any I had ever seen. Here and there behind the harmonious maze, I spotted wedges of midnight black. I could not tell whether these were merely areas of black paint or openings to a sky empty of stars.

Some of the arches were carved with figures and beasts. Others were incised with words and symbols. I could neither read the words nor identify the figures at such heights, even if they were words or images I might understand. But everything in my spirit said the words were meant to be read and the figures and symbols to be studied. Indeed—I spun around, slow, my eyes on the maze, the fluid air suspending my hair—for every carved arch there was a partner arch positioned exactly so that an observer standing on the partner could get a close-on view of the first. If one knew the point to begin, one could traverse every arc of the maze. What story would the journey tell?

This place was no imagining, for nothing in me could have devised such a structure. It instilled a certainty of truth, though it was not the truth I had lived in my five-and-twenty years. Such clever artistry. Such serenity. Such . . . I could not name the swelling emotion that flowed into me alongside wonder. I hungered to know more.

The place where I had entered the rotunda was no longer distinguishable, the veils vanished behind the pillars. The only break in the supporting colonnade was a vaulted opening that welcomed me to travel onward to some new mystery. Above the archway were incised three glyphs in a symbology that felt familiar, though undecipherable.

Yearning for understanding, I moved past the ring of torchieres and through the arch into a passage—or perhaps it was the torchieres and pillars that moved past me for I had no consciousness of walking. On either side of the passage, for as far as I could see, niches large and small were inset into the walls, each with a stone tablet hung beside or below it. No lanterns or torches, but the same ivory glow from the stone itself illuminated the passage, revealing that each held a sculpture of gleaming bronze. One niche, though—

Rippling unease flooded through the vision, through me and around me. The air began to quiver with heat. One gleaming bronze toppled slowly—impossibly slowly—from its niche. Then another and another. Cracks appeared in the glowing stone, streaking and forking like summer lightning, and the currents that bathed me grew hotter, scalding. I screamed and ran, but the great white arches were cracking—

"Damizella! Romy!" A hand tapped my cheek, only to leave off as quickly as it had begun, in a burst of epithets. "Shite, shite, shite!"

"No! Wait!" My eyes yet strained to peer into the stone passage, but the vision was broken.

My hand had fallen away from the statue, and I was sitting on a stool beside the wall. A grimacing Dumond fanned my overheated face with a kerchief while pressing his other fist to his chest with a ferocity that bespoke pain.

"By the Sisters, woman, I thought you were going to burst into flame. Scorched my hand you did. What did you see?"

"A great rotunda, domed with narrow bridges . . . carvings of figures and words, torches shaped like lilies, cold flames that cast no light and walls that glowed of their own. And a passage of knowledge . . . revelation . . ."

Dumond transferred the kerchief to his own round face, blotting his brow. "Evil? Dangerous?"

"Not at all. It was all about knowledge, truth." And something else. "Sadness, perhaps. The hall was so empty of life. And I think"—I touched the bronze carefully, experiencing no sensation save its chill solidity—"it is the place where this belongs." One of the niches along that vaulted passage had been empty.

"But there at the end everything changed. The structure was breaking; the bronzes were falling, and these waves of heat . . ."

"Come, let's get you tea. You'll find yourself cold soon enough."

"I'm not—" But I was already shivering, not sick and horrible as before when I touched magic, but deeply chilled as on those rare nights that snow dusted the hills of Cantagna. "Yes, please." Arrows of ice shot through my bones as I stood.

Dumond threw his own thin wool cloak over my shoulders and led me from the stone workshop. We hurried down a dark alley that skirted the back of the cooper's store and the uphill wall that separated the Beggars Ring from the Asylum Ring. Enough warm light leaked around wood shutters to reveal a wood door with dark metal strips embedded in its length, but no latch or knob or hole to grip.

The door swung open silently at Dumond's touch. Between the clattering of my teeth and rattling of my ice bones, a guess manifested itself: Not just anyone could push that door open. Was that magic or smithing?

"Vashti! We need the jasmine tea!"

I followed him inside and, had I not been shivering so hard as to keep me awake, would have believed I had again fallen into a vision, this time of perfumed warmth and riotous color packed into a tiny box of dust and stone.

"Sit." Dumond steered me to a pile of cushions, worn and misshapen, but still blazing with brilliant-hued designs worked in silk thread. Hangings from the distant lands of the east softened the grimed walls. Some depicted homely life in field and garden; some were worked with no design beyond the sheerest exuberance of color. A threadbare carpet centered the cracked stone floor, and everywhere stood lamps of brass and bronze, copper plates, bronze-cast running children, ball players, and a lark on the wing, shaped with such truth of flight I could almost sense the rush of air.

"Your work, D-Dumond?" I said amazed. Such sculptures would take a place of honor in any of Sandro's homes. "This lark is m-magnificent." My frosted bones rattled.

"The bronzes are mine," he said. "But the truest artistry here is the needlework, don't you think?"

"Truly b-beautiful," I said. "Such harmony of c-color."

From behind one of the fringed hangings emerged someone draped in green and orange carrying a tray. The ebony sheen of braided hair and willowy stature suggested Dumond's flirtatious daughter Cittina. But she glanced up as she set the tray on a low table. The web of creases beside her beaming eyes put her at an age with the middling Dumond, though her smooth skin, the hue of deep, rich sand at eventide, glowed as fresh as the girl's.

"Basha deems I feel no worth if someone admires his bronze bird," she said, with a lilting accent. "I say him there is worth enough in the world for both of us."

"Romy of Lizard's Alley, meet the truest treasure in my home. My wife, Vashti Saryali of Paolin. Vashti, this is my most unusual customer who will provide our Cittina with a dowry."

"P-Paolin!"

Far beyond the rocky hills and harbors of Empyria, where our traders had found markets rich with spices, strange and delicious fruits, colorful tapestries, and fine needlework, lay the kingdom of Lhampur. In Lhampur giant horned beasts brought silk through ranges of mountains that touched the vault of the sky from lands even farther east . . . from Paolin, the Land of Smoke and Silk.

"Here, Romy-zha, jasmine and ginger will warm you." The woman's smile laid another blanket around me. "Basha is often cold after magic work."

The painted porcelain cup seemed fragile as a rose petal. A small crack seamed its lip. But I thought no more of the vessel as I inhaled the rich fragrance, sipped, and let heat and spice thread its way through vein and sinew. One cup stilled my teeth. A second quieted my limbs. The third eased the rigor in chest and back. I felt almost human again.

Dumond had dug into a bowl of noodles that smelled of ginger and pepper and other things I couldn't name. Vashti offered me the same. With apologies, I stayed with the tisane. It banished the cold, but not the vision.

"What did you see when you touched it?" I asked, when I could speak without stammering. Clearly Vashti and Dumond had no secrets.

"A city of domes and spires crumbled to ruin," he said, laying down his spoon. "I stood atop a strange mount made of living creatures of every color, and there it was below me in a deep ravine. Sad, as you said. Dusty white with growths of lichen everywhere—and quiet, as if color and music had been lost even before its dwellers abandoned it. In the cliffs behind the city were caves, and like you, I was certain as sunrise that if I could enter them, I would learn something important."

He blotted his mouth with a tatter of embroidered linen.

"Soon as I thought it, I stood in one of the caves that was stacked in every crevice with chests of books and scrolls. The end wall was carved with figures three times my height, but I can't recall them—only that great cracks in the wall had broken them. There was an enchantment about the place. Magic? Maybe, maybe not. But when I think of it too much, 'tis all I can do to stay at my work and not try again." Creases seamed his broad face until he shook his head as if to clear the remembrance.

Marvelous and terrifying. Would Neri see a third view if he were to touch the bronze while reaching for magic? Would we see different ones if we tried again?

Dumond paused his spoon. "So, should the 'rightful owner' possess the Antigonean bronze or not?"

"The rightful owner is not demon tainted," I said, "and he will take care with it. He intends it as a gift for a good and scholarly man, who has been searching for it over many years."

I could not imagine that the grand duc of Riccia carried the taint of magic any more than Sandro did. Perhaps Placidio knew the truth of that. But if Eduardo di Corradini *did* carry magic, perhaps he was exactly the one who *should* own the thing and learn what it meant. Both Sandro and Placidio believed him a good soul. I had met him only once. He'd been polite and not unfriendly, but I had found him water to Sandro's robust vintage. He was very shy. Perhaps he was more interesting than he appeared.

"We proceed with the plan," I said. "The counterfeit goes to the thieves. The true statue goes to its rightful owner. We can solve only the problems that we know, and the dangers of allowing the thieves to win out are too great to ignore. Many lives could be lost. If you need to know more of reasons . . ."

"I'll hold with our bargain," said Dumond, pushing to his feet, "which means I'd best get the mold to the foundry. Wouldn't want to leave my friend Pascal with a pot of molten bronze and naught to pour it into. Once I get to the finishing, I'll leave a small bit of the new work's surface—perhaps the god's manly balls—with a patina that looks and feels the same as the original, but will react to a common solvent I'll provide you. A bare finger's touch will reveal exactly the same as would touching the true statue. But wipe Atladu's balls with the solvent, and the spot will come clean down to the raw metal. Your antiquities dealer has probably done something similar to prove the bronze in the first place, and upon reacquiring it might test again to ensure he's not been fooled. But no man's going to go straight for the balls, is he? And if the fellow knows his business, he's certainly not going to risk washing down the whole thing and destroying the very patina that proves its age. He'll believe it's the same work he thought stolen."

"Good enough," I said, even while acknowledging that no solution was unbreakable. "By the time the false statue is presented, the rightful owner will have the true one in hand."

Dumond kissed his wife's hand with a rueful sigh. "It'll be all night, my *vaiya*."

"Cittina will bring you kailing and tea before she sleeps," she said and bustled him out the door.

I rose to follow him out. "I must be off, too. Thank you for the tisane, dama. It saved my life."

"You're welcome to sit a while, Romy-zha," she said, filling another cup. "It's late to be rushing about, and I've a yearn for company. I'd think it most pleasant to talk with a woman who appreciates *all* of my husband's gifts, so I need not fret my words."

If her *yearn for company* ran as deep as my own, we could talk a very long while.

"Someday I would love to sit down with you," I said. "To learn how you came to meet a most unusual artist from the Costa Drago. To hear if the fantastical stories of your own land are true. But this work I've hired Dumond to do is part of a complicated endeavor, a worthy endeavor that could save many lives and make a better future for all in Cantagna. I'm a juggler trying to control all the pieces to make it work. Tomorrow, I must draw a map, devise a costume to hide me from a man who knows me well, write the script for some playacting, and rehearse it with a man I trust, but scarcely know, knowing that the slightest slip or wrong word could see us both dead."

She did not seem impressed by the list that daunted my spirits.

"Basha says what you've asked him to do is risky. And he didn't fully trust you at first—though clearly that has changed. He never brings anyone untrustworthy into his home."

"I'm glad to hear that. Truly. I'm doing my best to shield him from extra risk."

"All life is a risk. Born with his gifts, he understands that, as do I. Among the Shadhi of Paolin, there are some, called the Enlightened, who deeply reverence the power you and your brother and Basha carry. Our understanding of it is no better than yours. No sorcerers are born in our land. Indeed, Basha found his power much weakened when he lived there. Yet still our leaders spread the fear of magic and quench its fire. But life is hard in Paolin—harder than here—and short, thus in secret the Enlightened teach that we should welcome evidence of realms beyond those we experience every day."

Her story stirred the continuing mystery. Did the First Law have its origin in divine commands or was it some human reasoning that decided extermination was the gods' will? Why were we born in the Costa Drago and nowhere else? Did a monster truly lurk beneath our mountains?

I took off Dumond's cloak, smoothed it, and laid it across Vashti's outstretched arm. "Do your children know what Dumond can do?"

"They've seen many things that they accept as natural—as they are. Cittina knows that certain of those things should not be spoken of carelessly outside our walls. We'll tell the younger ones when the time is right. As for now . . . well, you see, if anyone asks them if their papa can do magic, they would answer *certainly so.* And if they are asked what is his great magic, they would say *why, he can make a bronze bird fly!"*

I laughed and touched his soaring lark. "And who, seeing this, would disagree?"

"What kind of costume are you thinking? As you see, my needle is fine. Also experienced and quick; I clothe four daughters. I've some materials that are unusual. Perhaps I could help with the juggling?"

My hand came off the door latch and I let her lead me back to her cushions and teapot. Eventually, as the night wore on, I told her everything.

16

I shoved a stained chemise, an old black skirt, and a gray bodice I'd found in a rag shop half a year ago into the cloth bag to join the bloodstained green shirt, moth-chewed doublet, and a torn cloak Placidio had delivered a half hour since. I had promised Vashti to deliver what bits and pieces we had before noontide so she could create new garments suitable for a modestly successful scholarly adventurer and his sister.

I had just thrown on my summer cloak when Neri burst into our house like a spooked horse. "It's come!"

The fold of stiff ivory paper he waved stifled my question. Breathing deep, I snatched it and broke the seal—the serpent-coiled pillar of the Sestorale, imprinted in the dark red wax of the Commission on Public Artworks. So much hinged on this message. Justice and enlightenment, or the cruelties, turmoil, death, and destruction of civil war . . . and now this deeper mystery of magic that I could not begin to estimate.

Neri was near splitting his jaque, so I read the missive aloud.

Professoré Vincenzio di Guelfi,

> *The Cantagnan Sestorale Commission on Public Art-works maintains an abiding interest in the display of ar-tistic antiquities of the classical and pre-classical periods of the Costa Drago for the edification of our citizenry. We would be pleased to view your samples and hear your proposal for further exploration.*

"By the Sisters!" A grinning Neri slammed his fist to the door. "We're on!"

"Wait," I said, sinking to my stool, appalled. "Listen."

> *Prior engagements will prevent our commissioners from meeting with you tomorrow evening or the following day as you suggest. Instead, we invite you to appear before this evening in the library of the Palazzo Segnori at the Hour of Gathering—also known in Cantagna as the time of the evening anthem.*

> *With respect,*
> *Beatrice di Mesca, for the Sestorale Commission*
> *on Public Artworks*

"Nine hours from this!" I groaned. "How can we possibly be ready?"

"What's to do?" argued Neri. "You know what to say to people like these, and you said Dumond's wife would fix your disguise. There's plenty of time to do that . . . dress up Placidio . . . talk about what he's to say. He's no dunce."

"It's the statue itself. We're supposed to convince the Shadow Lord that we have the real one and are willing to let him have it. But we can't leave it with him *tonight*. Dumond needs the original at hand every step of the way to make sure he gets the coloring, the marks, the wear, everything as close to perfection as he can. Merchant Boscetti is no dunce either, and he'll be suspicious finding the statue after it's been lost. There is no possibility Dumond can have the work completed in nine hours. To get it done by *tomorrow* evening was already going to be difficult. So how, in the marches of time, are we going to walk out of the Palazzo Segnori tonight still in possession of *il Padroné's* prize?"

"If he takes it, I'll just steal it back."

To explain the myriad ways that could get us dead would use too much precious time. "Find Placidio. He left here not an hour since. Bring him to"—I shoved panic aside—"to the Leguiza Hospice gate at noontide. I'll meet you there. If Dumond and Vashti approve, I'll take him on to their house so Vashti can dress him. We've no time for fittings."

• • •

This time when I arrived at Dumond's workshop, two bronze images of Atladu and Dragonis awaited me. The original stood watching as the metalsmith chiseled the last remnants of the sprues—the bronze that had filled the channels where the molten metal had been poured in and had pushed the air out—from the copy.

"I'll polish away the tool marks," he said, pointing to the few scratches, "and these few other blemishes; still looks like the god has a boil on his bum right here."

But so much else was right. He had already removed the lines where the mold had joined, sharpened details, and tooled the wear marks. Atladu's torso, the beast's haunch, their toes and claws, the god's face . . . all were astonishingly exact, right down to the worn spot where the barb on the lance had been broken off centuries ago, and the more ragged edge where we assumed another entire image had gone missing.

Where the two statues did not match was the color. The new piece, right out of the mold, shone uniformly golden-brown, while the original wore green and black scabs of age. Dumond had no doubts that he would be able to induce similar changes in the finish of the new casting—with the slight exception of the forged Atladu's vulnerable balls. There he would paint on the needed color, so I could easily remove it to prove the forgery.

"I'll need to borrow the original for a few hours and perhaps a few of your natalés or a copper bowl to present as other treasures for sale." I told him of the timing difficulty. "If all goes well, I should have everything back to you by the Hour of Contemplation. Will that set you back too much?"

"Don't go much beyond. This fellow"—he patted his creation—"will need to spend some time in the ovens up to the Asylum Ring along with some compounds I've made, and I've got to mask him proper first. But I'll say I could use a few hours' sleep. The finish might be the better for it. Have you considered . . . if these commissioners and your righteous owner agree that this is the real Antigonean bronze, what's to prevent them keeping it? Then all this is a waste, and you're just as like to be arrested for stealing it from the thieves."

"I'm working on a plan." Which consisted of exactly nothing so far. "I'm sure Vashti told you she offered to help me with disguises. With this shortened schedule, I thought to bring my partner here . . ." I gave him a quick description of Placidio.

Dumond had reservations about admitting another stranger to his home. I couldn't blame him. Vashti had joined us by then, and I told them of our year's relationship with the swordmaster and how Placidio was the only other person in the world I had entrusted with the secret of Neri's talent and mine. I implied that Placidio had entrusted my brother and me with dangerous secrets as well; if Dumond and Vashti drew some conclusion about Placidio's *particular* secret that I had vowed not to reveal, it was unfortunate . . . but inevitable. They ought to know each other, it seemed, two sorcerers embroiled in this strange scheme. If something went wrong, they might need to help each other— or Neri or me.

In the end Dumond left the decision to his wife. She said she knew nowhere other than her own house where she would be comfortable measuring a strange man for breeches. Her daughters would be safely out of the room lest the gentleman be embarrassed to be seen in his netherstocks. "Now come, Romy-zha. Sounds like we must be quick."

"I mustn't stand out," I said as we left Dumond to his work. "The Shadow Lord, the man who owned me, is one of the commissioners. He *must not* recognize me." Only my experiences meeting actors who'd presented plays and mimes in Sandro's house led me to believe such a disguise could work. "I've brought what rouge and eye paint I could find on the way here . . ."

"We shall confound him. Trust me."

I did. I'd never been more certain of anyone after such short acquaintance. Nor had I ever seen such facility with a needle or such an eye for design as that of Vashti Saryali di Paolin. Within an hour she had remade my plain black cotton skirt into a pleasing garment with a scalloped hem, slashed in the front. Behind the slash what appeared to be a full underskirt was a simple panel of apricot-and-gold Paolin silk, woven with an intricate design of cockatoos and their trailing plumes. The scrap of silk came from one of Vashti's own treasured robes brought from a home she was unlikely to see again. Not all of Sandro's silver could repay such a gift.

Her needle transformed other pieces of the silk robe into flowing sleeves. She had marked a matching design on the gray bodice and set Cittina to filling in embroidery, promising to take it up when she was finished with the larger projects. My mostly white shift she threw in a boiling pot with herbs she promised would produce a color to harmonize with the silk. Then, to my dismay, she picked up the blue summer mantle I had worn through the midday shower, cut out the armholes, and reshaped the neckline to make a proper sleeveless gown, the better to show off the new silk sleeves. No seamstress in Sandro's employ could have a devised a more suitable garment for a scholar-adventurer's sister.

She could work no similar wonders with Placidio's breeches, shirt, or cloak until she could see what figure of a man he was. So she gave my most un-nimble fingers a plain hem to stitch—after bathing them in some kind of salts that removed the ground-in stains of a year's writing—and then set to drying the peach-hued shift and gathering it into a modest ruffle to peek out of my bodice. A smaller daughter named Lelah made us jasmine tea, while a pair of tiny dark-eyed twins chased each other in and out of the family sleeping room.

At the first chime of the noontide anthem, I left Vashti finishing up the exquisite embroidery on my bodice and sped down the lane and around the corner to fetch Placidio. He had acquired a flat, brimmed cap that sported a clump of feathers surely plucked from a long dead grouse, and tilted it to mask his facial scar. It looked more like he'd been in a fight at the Duck's Bone.

"So is this seamstress shy of men that you must escort me?" he said, before I could think of what to say first. "Or must her husband be got out of the way?"

"You didn't tell him?" I asked Neri.

"Didn't want to step in the wrong hole," he said. "My sword-master has taught me to watch my ground."

Placidio snorted. "You should be off heaving boulders, boy. No need for you to peep at my netherstocks, no matter what your sister has in mind. Come first day past this business, I'm taking you up the Boar's Teeth with long swords. And you, lady scribe, what didn't he tell me?"

"The commission has agreed to meet with us."

"Good news, then," said Placidio, "but there's more?"

He wasn't going to like the rest.

"You cannot carry weapons before the commission." I nodded at Placidio's belt. "Your sword—our weapons—will have to stay with Neri. He will hide close to the Piazza Livello with the weapons and an escape route ready should we need it."

The duelist bristled like an angry hedge pig. "You said Vincenzio was an adventurer," he snapped. "What adventurer goes around unarmed?"

"One who is asking for a stipend from eight of the richest people in Cantagna," I said. "Many of them nervous people, who have well-armed bodyguards who have never heard of the gentle, scholarly, but bold adventurer di Guelfi."

"Pssh."

"And indeed my seamstress has small children and her husband is our metalsmith and very protective of his wife. Since your costume will not include your weapons, they would prefer you leave them behind when you come."

"Now? You trust the woman?"

"Yes to both. If you please."

Rolling his eyes, Placidio disarmed himself and, muttering, passed his belt to Neri.

Neri belted it on himself and promised to take care, so Placidio would not have to gut him as promised. "I'm off," he said. "I'll be at the Via Mortua gate. If you don't show by the half-even anthem, I'll meet you at Dumond's."

As Placidio glared suspiciously, Neri leaned close and whispered in my ear. "Stay alive, Romy. I've gotten used to you being around."

No words came. I scratched his sprouting chin.

The glare reverted to me. "Now, lady scribe, what else did the lackwit fail to tell me?"

"That the commission agreed to meet with us *tonight*, not tomorrow," I said. "So we've only these few hours to get ready. All the better Neri's got your sword so he can get in place."

"Tonight. So . . ." A slight choking gargle emanated from his throat. "All that preparation you talked of . . . the script and all . . ."

"We'll do what we can between now and the Hour of Gathering."

"Three hours." The time might have marked our appointment with a headsman.

. . .

No two dogs had ever stared each other down more warily than did Placidio di Vasil and Dumond the metalsmith. They did not quite circle each other or sniff in inappropriate places, nor were there audible growls, but the air between them thrummed with suspicion. Only my pledge to each man prevented me blurting out, *We're all sorcerers here. Let's be done with that.* But those were not my secrets to tell.

"Segno Dumond, may I present Placidio di Vasil, a listed duelist and my brother's swordmaster—a friend who has expressed willingness to aid me in this venture. Swordmaster, this artisan Dumond most generously aided Neri and me on a day when we had foolishly put ourselves in danger from the law. I've hired him to make the copy of the antiquity we plan to return to its rightful owner."

Dumond made a stiff, shallow jerk of a bow. "Swordmaster."

"Segn—" Placidio's bow looked to match Dumond's except that Dumond's motion had exposed the two statues standing side by side just behind him. The sight stopped Placidio short. "Fortune's dam," he said softly. "The Antigonean bronze, the relic of Sysaline."

Before I could demand to know how a duelist from the Tibernian fish town of Vasil happened to recognize an ancient artwork, he was at the worktable. "This is the one"—he nodded at the mottled gold-green of the original—"the antiquity you told me of—though you didn't mention it was this particular antiquity. And this other—this is masterful, Segno Dumond. I never imagined . . . I mean, I've seen small things copied. But something so precise. So complicated." He peered at it from every side, even walking around the worktable to see the back. "And you can make it look old? The same?"

"I can." I'd not thought Dumond could scrutinize the duelist any closer. "A careful, side-by-side examination by a knowledgeable person will reveal the difference; details are always lost in a copy. But for this purpose, it should suffice. So you know the piece?"

Dumond snatched the question from my tongue.

Placidio started, as if he'd just waked. "I've seen sketches . . . my dueling clients. A few have tried to hire me to—but I don't do that sort of thing. I only participate in schemes by persons I've taken the measure of at swordpoint. The lady scribe of Lizard's Alley is the first in many years."

I didn't believe him about the clients and sketches.

"Do you have any idea why the grand duc of Riccia desires this particular antiquity so fiercely?" I said. "I don't care where you might have learned it or under what circumstances; those are questions for other days. But the answer might tell us whether we dare proceed at all with this scheme."

He folded his arms across his chest, and for a moment I feared he was done with me and the plan. But his face held more solemn consideration than anger. "Anything I say is naught but repeated rumor, gossip, and guessing. But if this thing has any importance in the world, a person of proven honor and strength of arms should be the one to hold it, I would think. The grand duc is such a person, and evidently he values it."

His guesses might hold more weight than those of others. But I doubted he would answer more, no matter how hard I pressed. This surely trod on the forbidden ground, his knowledge of

Eduardo di Corradini, the grand duc of Riccia. Someday I would know that story.

"This is certain my gentleman who needs his costume altered!" Vashti strolled into the workshop like a calming breath. Her bright gaze took Placidio's measure. "Truly, sir, we must get to work to have you outfitted by the Hour of Gathering. Come."

Placidio trailed off behind her like a giant pup. While Vashti measured and stitched up Placidio, Cittina took me into a stone washing shed warmed by a fire. She said her mam—*naihi*, she called her—had told her to wash my hair.

"She said you want to be different tonight." She dunked my head in a bowl of warm water, scented with lemon and rosemary and more pungent things I didn't know. "*Naihi* guessed that your hair has ever been smooth waves and this earthen dark, so she's put things in the water will change that. She brought them from Paolin for just such cases. She's taught me what to do. You'll be so pretty."

She scrubbed my hair almost dry with a towel and told me not to touch it as I sat by the hot brazier. Vashti came in once to bring me some well-worn linen to sew into palm-sized pouches. "Costuming pillows," she called them. It was welcome occupation, for as the meeting time approached, anxieties fretted inside my belly like hairy moths. To stand in Sandro's presence . . . What kind of fool was I to imagine I could trick him? I had come up with a story, and a possible way of preventing Placidio from having to remember everything, but the scheme seemed ever flimsier as the hours fled past.

When Cittina judged my hair dry enough, she picked at it with an ivory comb rather than drawing the implement through what must be a nest of tangles. I'd cut it off short since starting to train with Placidio, so it was not even to my shoulders. As Cittina worked, I caught sight of a strand here and there.

"Do you have a glass?" I said, choking. "I need to see this."

"First this," said the girl, and clipped something to one side. She stood back to appraise. "*Naihi* will apply your finishing," she said, and snatched the linen pouches and hurried away.

Vashti arrived in moments, her face crinkling in delight.

"You will make a lovely pair." She took my small boxes of rouge and kohl and added her own vials and boxes, dabbing, fussing, and smoothing my face as the mistresses at the Moon House had done. I'd never worn face paint since leaving there. Sandro had said I needed no adornment.

Unseeable divinities! My breath near halted. I would see him today.

"Now," said Vashti, handing me a small round looking glass. "Will he know you?"

"By the Sisters!"

I didn't know me. Red! My hair was a billowing tousle of dark red curls, clipped back on one side by a delicate bronze butterfly. My eyes, lined dark, glistened wide and deep. Flushes of rose colored my lips and cheeks—not garish paint, but shaded so that my cheekbones seemed more prominent, my nose narrower, brow higher. Vashti handed me the peach-dyed chemise, and I donned the garments she'd fashioned out of scraps—colors and fabrics I'd never worn for Sandro.

Placidio stared when I returned into the house, then his mouth quirked up at one corner. "I think we've got him," he said.

And *Placidio*—had I not already seen him barbered, I'd not have recognized him either. Vashti had given up on the worn, ugly doublet. Instead she had turned the green shirt back to front, hiding the permanent bloodstains behind, slit a new V-shaped opening in the collar, and reformed the whole into a knee-length tunic. She had trimmed and sewn the few remaining unfaded, unspoiled pieces of her woven rug into a colorful belt. One of her small silk hangings had become a ruffled neck piece that tucked inside the new front slit of the tunic. The torn black cloak had evolved into a sleeveless gown like mine—scholarly, Vashti said— while one of Dumond's newer leather aprons had been refashioned into the image of a buff jerkin, although, as she cheerfully showed me, there was not enough leather to make a whole one. Lengths of ordinary linen held it together across his broad back, which the scholar's gown hid perfectly well.

The linen pouches had been filled with rags and tucked into his shirt sleeves and the breast of his tunic to mime the current puffed-out fashion. A black silk rosette had replaced the dreadful feathers on his new hat, and dangling ribbons diverted attention from his scar. He looked a new man. He didn't quite believe our admiration.

"Certain I'm one of those jack-willows landsmen put out to scare birds and foxes," he grumbled. "But then none's going to look at me with the fire-haired lady beside."

"Not so, Segno di Guelfi, for you will be carrying these." Dumond had appeared in the doorway. He presented Placidio with my heavy black bag, several linen-wrapped bundles protruding awkwardly. He quirked an eyebrow at me. "Get them back to me soon, yes?"

"Soon." I took Placidio's arm. "Shall we go, Brother Vincenzio?"

17

S how us in without delay," announced Placidio. "We are Vincenzio and Tarenah di Guelfi, expected by the Commission on Public Artworks."

Placidio wore authority with his skin, no matter what garments he threw over it.

The doorward showed no hesitation. He snapped his fingers and a page boy in gilded livery appeared from behind a marble pillar. "Take them to the commission assembly room."

I was grateful and slipped the commission's invitation back into the inner pocket of the gown that had, that morning, been my summer cloak. My shaking hands could have alarmed the guards posted in pairs all around the Palazzo Segnori.

The boy led us up the grand staircase. The entire area of the soaring walls and dome of the atrium was covered with murals depicting Cantagnan history: victories, celebrations, elections, achievements, even scenes of daily life in the city and surrounding countryside.

I knew the padded bench where the boy had been waiting for a summons. On my first visit to the gilded Gentlemen's Palace, Sandro had shooed the waiting pages away and sat with me on that bench while I mastered my nerves, rattled at the prospect of meeting a roomful of his friends and enemies.

He had pointed out noble depictions of his father and grand-father and other storied figures in the grand murals, as well as caricatures of those who had foolishly opposed the Gallanos ascendancy. There was even a tiny portrait of Sandro himself, clothed as a shepherd boy tucked in amongst a feast-day crowd.

"They told me I was to become a shepherd of the people," he'd said, his eyes sparking. "Shall you and I retire to a hayrick after this tedious reception?"

We had not. Not that day.

How could I stand in front of him in this ridiculous disguise—he who could recognize me in the night, who had so easily read my sorrows, my joys, my darkness, and my exaltation? He had accepted what I offered with humility and had given himself generously, despite the irreconcilable positions Lady Fortune had laid on us. Had he loved me? I could not imagine something more or better. Surely to see him, to watch that soulful gaze settle on this awkward deception and recognize me, must shatter my heart.

Yet I could *not* fail. The only way I could possibly get through the next hour was to forget Sandro. To forget Cataline. To forget Romy.

I begged Lady Virtue and the Unseeable divinities to help me lose myself in deception. So many depended on me. Dumond, Vashti, Placidio, Neri, risking their lives on my word that this was a worthy work. Sandro, his honor, his vision, though he must not know, lest he give it all away. Reaching deep, I drew on every smattering of strength I could find inside myself . . .

· *I am Tarenah di Guelfi, a maiden who has traveled the Costa Drago with my scholarly, insightful brother, always reflecting his wisdom and studious nature. His name will be cited in the books of history and discovery, whereas I shall be a footnote at best. In any case, I shall be content. I am insignificant in the world. These people we meet are strangers, unknown men and women of power, who could slay us with a word. And yet our cause . . . our father's legacy . . . is worthy . . .*

My blood heated. Flushed, more certain, I stood a bit straighter as we swept up the stair. I made sure to lavish Vincenzio's noble back with the admiration he deserved. *He displays such assurance, such prowess in his studies, and he bears great admiration for the ideals of the Cantagnan Independency. Alas, that our haste to answer the commission's inquiry pushed us through a sevenday of rain. His cough leaves his voice unreliable. If only the commission had been able to wait the extra day. Yet good Lady Fortune has provided that I, so perfectly of one mind with him, can convey his thoughts clearly.*

The page boy whispered to an usher, who opened a pair of gilded doors, stepped inside, and bowed: "Noble commissioners, I present your expected supplicants, Professoré Vincenzio di Guelfi, and his sister, Damizella Tarenah di Guelfi."

The usher stepped aside to let us pass. Two steps more and Vincenzio bowed, his height lending itself to graceful movements. Such dignity he displayed in his acknowledgment of our modest status while in the presence of such noble persons. Surely it was a good sign that they addressed him as *professoré*—an expert in his field. That meant the recommendation letters in our application had been recognized and approved. I remained a step behind him and curtsied deeply.

A few of the commissioners sat at the polished table, already sighing in the boredom of the very wealthy. Vincenzio and I had sought patronage from every kind of family council, city commission, and scholarly fraternity across three independencies, and many we met had no true heart for history or antiquity.

"Be seated, commissioners," said a wide-browed older woman, gowned soberly in froths of black lace. "We allotted this interview a quarter hour, and Secretary Mardi has set the glass running."

Indeed, a white-haired gentlemen seated at the left end of the table had spun a crystal globe supported in a bright brass ring. The globe now spewed its salts into its companion vessel, as the man dipped his pen and held it poised above a sheet of scraped parchment.

"We welcome you and your sister to Cantagna, Professoré di Guelfi." The woman addressed Vincenzio, as she seated herself in the center of the row of chairs.

The rest of them quickly joined her. Nine of them, not just eight.

"I am Beatrice di Mesca, head of the Commission on Public Artworks. My husband, Piero, here next to me, shares the office. Commissioner Gallanos has brought another guest to join us. Philosophist Rinaldo di Bastianni is a specialist in pre-classical bronze artwork."

The philosophist would be the blur of red at the right end of the table. Manners forbade me stare. The Philosophic Confraternity was very strict in regard to verifying antiquities as legitimate historical artifacts, deserving of public attention. I'd heard that the Academie here in Cantagna disqualified more than they approved, one reason we had solicited recommendations from specialists closer to our home in Varela.

Vincenzio inclined his head to Segna di Mesca. I kept my attention on her, too, as would be expected, not gawking at the rest though I knew that some of the members were very much more important to the Independency of Cantagna than others. One in particular—the true power of the region sat at this table, and we were come to fulfill his commission's desire, hoping to reap a fine future. I'd seen his likeness—who that traveled Cantagna had not? But I would not seek him out and stare.

"Your application was quite clear and well structured," said the bald Piero di Mesca who wore a crimped neck ruff so elaborate and so large that his head looked like an egg perched in a starched nest.

A voice deep inside me laughed and said that the severe Beatrice would approve that head stuck on a platter, as Piero had never met a maidservant he did not bed.

I shoved the mockery aside. Better I pay close attention. Vincenzio wished me to listen and judge the commissioners' reactions to our case, and be prepared to answer questions if his cough became burdensome.

"You are well educated in history, with an interest in antiquities," Piero di Mesca continued. "And you seek funds to support your search for a system of caves on a islet in the Sea of Tears, where some kind of lost treasure awaits recovery. Perhaps you could explain more clearly what evidence prompts you to this venture and how it is you have some, but not all, of the artifacts already."

Vincenzio cleared his throat. Ah, such a terrible cough he's had during our travels.

"Segna and Segnoré di Mesca, and members of the Arts Commission, we thank you for this invitation to present our petition. We welcome Philosphist di Bastianni's addition." His poor voice sounded like crushed glass underfoot. "Our father captained a small fishing vessel. His regular route threaded the Hylides, which as you might be aware is an archipelago of some two hundred rocky islets, most of them uninhabitable. The Mare di Lacrime—the Sea of Tears—is subject to violent storms at the change—"

He suppressed a small coughing spasm. "Pardon, segno—at the change of seasons. After his death two years since, my sister found our father's journal detailing his adventures over the years. The journal describes one of these seasonal storms which drove his boat ashore on a Hylid isle riddled with caves. His crew of three all lost, he explored deep into the caves in a desperate search for fresh water. There he found an iron chest containing scrolls and artifacts of all kinds, items that struck him—a man of limited education—with a sense of great wonder. When the storm eased, he brought home a small bronze depicting the god Atladu, fully intending to find the islet again someday and retrieve the whole chest. But he died too soon."

Vincenzio coughed again, harder, and croaked, "Perhaps my sister might continue, as the raw weather on our hasty travel north has left me something hoarse."

"Damizella?" Segna di Mesca's invitation was cold.

The unwelcome attention did not confound me. I was but Vincenzio's voice and would make sure my speech was properly deferent, but clear and authoritative as befitted an educated woman of Varela.

"When my brother returned from the Philosophic Academie

at Varela, the items we found in Papa's chest intrigued him greatly. An acquaintance at the Academie tested the god statue and assured him it was quite old. We hired a boat and crew to search for the isle, but our funds were limited, and we were forced to discontinue the search. A month ago, our friend at the Academie forwarded this commission's inquiry about a small statue known as the Antigonean bronze. The object of the inquiry precisely fit the description of the statue he'd tested. We brought a few other items from our father's collection, not knowing if some might be from the same trove, as Papa did not list the provenance of each."

Vincenzio drew out several bundles from our bag and unwrapped them on the table: a small galloping horse of bronze chased with pure copper, three finger-sized natalés, and what we believed to be the very Antigonean bronze of this commission's desire.

Some of the commissioners murmured to each other; some leaned back and ignored their fellows, as well as the two of us and our little collection. But the two men at the far right end of the table rose and came round the table to examine the bronzes. The one wearing the crimson toque and matching gold-threaded cloak of the Academie was a very tall, spare man of great dignity. Bastianni, I supposed, an unfamiliar name, though his walk and robed form left me most uneasy.

But like a steel splinter to a lodestone was my observation drawn to the other man, who lifted the sculpted god, ran his long fingers over it lightly, and passed it to the academician. His fine-boned face glowed with appreciation. Deep under dark brows, his steel-gray eyes gleamed with discovery. This was Alessandro di Gallanos, also known as *il Padroné*. Whispers named him the

Shadow Lord. So young for such weighty titles. A tight knot in my breast near stopped my breath, as if I had swallowed a plum whole. I lowered my gaze, unwilling to attract such dread notice.

"'Tis very like the sketches and descriptions, Rinaldo, even to the edge where the flanking figure was broken off," he said, his quiet words ringing clear. "The forgeries I've seen never get that right. Is it possible this is what I've searched for?"

The man in red pocketed a small magnifying lens.

"The weight, the base coloration, the unusual iconography—the design, if you will—all certainly agree with what we know of the Antigonean bronze." The philosophist addressed the whole commission, not just the man beside him. "And though sophisticated for its time, the artistic style is certainly appropriate to what we know of its history. This is no simplistic fakery, at the least. As to whether the commission should invest in this man's story, as yet, I cannot say."

All eyes shifted to Vincenzio, who stood stalwart. Noble, even.

"I make no claims that this is definitely the object of the most honorable gentleman's desire," he said, rasping only a bit. "The possibility has brought me here. Hope, too. Not just for my own fortune, though I do believe this piece is a marvel of another age and that other interesting mysteries remain in the iron chest lost in the Hylides. But I also find hope in the example of Cantagna—your city's interest in exploring our past to ennoble our future."

Well said, Vincenzio! Such eloquence . . . even from one who had always exceeded expectations. We had talked of this.

"What of the other items?" asked a woman in an elaborately curled wig whose face was a landscape raddled by the pox. "Alessandro can decide if the bronze is what he wants. But as a whole do these things merit support? Varela won't like Cantagnan surrogates prowling the Hylides."

Bastianni examined the natalés and quickly tossed them into the pile of linen. "Decent work, but no older than my shoes. This horse is"—he hefted the little sculpture, sniffed it, licked it, whipped out his magnifying lens and inspected it closely—"of Paolin!" he said, astonished. "Old, certainly, though not corresponding to the Antigonean period, if the larger bronze is indeed so ancient. Not a style I'm familiar with, but those who know more of the Land of Smoke and Silk would surely be interested. So might the Varela trade ministry. Damizella, did your father make mention of Paolin in this journal? Perhaps his boat carried more than fish!"

The academician's scorn bit deep, waking the harsh voice inside me. It yelled that we'd been fools to bring the horse. Trade in Paolin goods was strictly regulated.

"N-nay, segnoré." I stuttered, shaken as all eyes turned to me, including the lancet gaze of the Shadow Lord.

"Indeed not, Philosophist!" said Vincenzio. The Shadow Lord's gaze and all others fixed instantly on my brother, shocked at his sharp vehemence. "Our father was no smuggler, but a noble fisherman! He knew the weather and the tides, but nothing of history or the world beyond the sea. Pleasing shapes attracted him. He would not have recognized work of Paolin. I myself was not sure of it."

"Secretary Mardi signals that our time is spent," announced Beatrice di Mesca, as several of the commissioners growled and frowned severely at Vincenzio. "Would you agree, Scholar di Bastianni, that Professoré di Guelfi has sincere reason to believe this bronze sculpture to be the Antigonean bronze?"

"Reason enough, I suppose," said the academician. "Sincerity? Motives are not mine to judge. To confirm true authenticity, I would need to examine it more closely, have a smith confirm the metal's composition, and test the finish to be sure the patina is not recently applied."

"We've brought a sample of the alchemical mixture our Academie used to examine the finish," said Vincenzio. "Tarenah?"

I pulled a ceramic vial of testing solution from our bag.

Bastianni waved it away as he and Gallanos resumed their seats. "Naturally I would use my own."

Segna di Mesca continued briskly. "Segnoré di Gallanos, do you have an opinion on Professoré di Guelfi's application?"

It was not difficult to judge her opinion. Her nostrils had flared at Vincenzio's declaration, as if loyalty to a fisherman was distasteful.

"I do. With all respect to the professoré and his sister," said Gallanos, offering no more than a passing glance our way, "I see too little worth in the project to risk entangling Cantagna with the authorities of Varela. Yet the lost chest produced two artifacts interesting enough that the search might intrigue several collectors in my acquaintance. I can forward the professoré's application to them if he wishes. As to the possibility of this piece being the Antigonean bronze, I would be pleased to pursue the question on my own with no investment of the city's treasury."

"I move to accede to Alessandro's wisdom," said Segna Beatrice. Paying no mind to the mumbles from their companions, she stood. "And so it is declared. Professoré, I commend you on your application and wish you a good day. Please take your artifacts. Segnoré di Gallanos will contact you if and when it is his pleasure."

As by magic, the outer door opened and the usher stepped inside. The commissioners rose, some drawn to the carafes of wine set out on a table to the side, some hurrying toward a private exit behind them. The Shadow Lord and the philosophist strolled toward the open doors.

Reason staved off disappointment; surely Gallanos's interest and offer of recommendation meant success. I began wrapping the bronzes.

Vincenzio murmured in my ear, "What should I do? Do we just go?"

"Leaving too quickly will make our long journey a waste," I whispered. "Surely he'll wish to speak to you. He offered us references."

My brother stared at me oddly, then stepped uncertainly in the direction of the two men, who had paused in the open doorway. He halted at a polite distance and folded his hands at his back, as if he awaited such elevated attention every day.

My heart raced, understanding that this was a moment that would profoundly affect our future.

"I doubt Boscetti ever possessed the true Antigonean bronze," said the Shadow Lord to Bastianni. "He must have concocted his theft story when he realized I'd bring you in to examine it. Or perhaps someone told him of Eduardo's belief that he could identify the bronze inerrantly."

"I tell you again, Alessandro, there exists no inerrant proof of authenticity. The grand duc is lost in a cloud of delusion that masquerades as mysticism. Come walk with me; I worry—"

Vincenzio coughed. Gallanos whirled about, startled.

"Ah, professoré!" Motioning Bastianni to wait in the foyer, Gallanos strode back to Vincenzio. "Thank you for waiting. I get caught up in minutiae and forget my more important business."

Bastianni paused in the doorway. I continued wrapping the natalés, refusing the desire to gawp at their interaction lest the men think me ill-mannered.

"I regret that the commission could not undertake your project, professoré," he said, kinder than I would have imagined such a powerful man could be. "But I shall do as I said and pass your application on to those who might."

"That would be most kind, noble segnoré," said Vincenzio, bowing.

"As a small return for that favor, I would like to borrow this bronze so that Philosophist di Bastianni can verify its antiquity. If it is proved, I'll pay you very well for it. If not, I shall return it undamaged and wish you well in your endeavors."

"You are most— I don't—" Vincenzio burst into a fit of coughing so dire he threw his arms across his face.

The usher drew up a chair and helped him sit. Alarmed, I dropped to my knees at his side. Even when the coughing fit eased, Vincenzio remained bent over, limp and heaving for breath. To my horror, fresh blood wet his sleeve.

"Our regrets, honorable sir," I blurted. "It rained almost every day of our journey from Varela, and we pushed very hard so as to answer your query in a timely manner. Vincenzio was already in weakened health from his winter journey through the Hylides, obsessed as he is with this matter. If I could just get him back to our lodgings. Vincenzio . . ."

Coughs and fevers were at their worst in the spring. Papa had died of typhus only two springs past, yet still Vincenzio refused to take proper care of himself. Where would I find help in this strange city? What would I do without him?

As I tapped my brother's cheek to rouse him, the Shadow Lord ordered the usher to bring a litter. "Take the gentleman wherever the woman says. Fetch an herbalist or physician as she wishes at my expense, of course."

A hand snatched up the statuary bag from the floor beside me. The philosophist held it out to Gallanos. "Best keep hold of this, Alessandro," he said. "Even if it's not the Antigonean work itself, it's accurate enough to confuse the weak-minded. If these two peddle it around, your friend Boscetti might snatch it up and double his fee yet again. If it proves a fake, as I suspect, we can destroy it. Ought to destroy it anyway, as I've told—"

"*Padroné!*" I interrupted, heart pounding at my own audacity. "I'm certain Vincenzio will approve loaning you the bronze. He has such admiration, such respect. But please understand I cannot leave it just now . . . on my own. It is our father's legacy; Vincenzio's future."

His hesitation sent my heart to my throat, but after a moment Gallanos set the bag back where his friend had picked it up.

"Certain, damizella, we will continue this conversation when the professoré is better." Crouching down to put himself on a level with me, he pressed a coin into my gloved hand. "Secure his approval and yield me the bronze by the morning after next and a thousand of these will fund your brother's investigations for a year or more."

"Oh, noble lord." I clasped my hands to my breast and dropped my gaze. "I swear it."

Il Padroné joined the philosophist and hurried from the chamber, leaving us alone for the moment.

As I turned back to my brother, Vincenzio's hand gripped mine and pulled me close. "Night's daughters, Romy, we did it!" he whispered. "A thousand silver solets. He knows the bronze is true."

Romy . . .

In that moment, that touch, the utterance of a name, the world shifted, a sensation as when you descend a stair, stumbling as you discover the steps are twice as deep as you believed. Blinking, I met Placidio di Vasil's grin. As bustling servants arrived with poles, canvas, and blankets, and assembled a sturdy litter, I wrapped my arm about the duelist's shoulders, laid my forehead on his, and grinned back at him.

Smothering elation in mock illness and concern, we allowed Sandro's minions to escort us out of the Palazzo Segnori. When we arrived at the Cambio Gate, Professoré di Guelfi's vigor improved enough to stagger from the litter, and we sent our escorts on their way with a message for *il Padroné*: Professoré di Guelfi and his sister would be pleased to deliver him the Antigonean bronze on the morning after next and submit it to whatever additional testing he wished.

We spoke not a word as we proceeded downward on our own, alert for any followers. Neri, his help not needed, would wait at the Via Mortua gate a little longer as planned, then meet us at Dumond's.

Only as the busy evening traffic closed in around us did I squeeze Placidio's broad shoulder. "What a performance, swordsman! Wherever did you come up with the blood?"

"A duelist always has stitches to break." Slowing his steps, he pulled back and tugged my chin around so he could peer down at my face. "But you, lady scribe, I've never seen such playacting. You had me believing you were Tarenah di Guelfi. I could smell the fish on you!"

I scoffed at his sobriety, even as excitement cooled and sent shivers to tickle my spine, stronger by the moment. Still, Placidio and I laughed at ourselves all the way to Dumond's house, where Vashti's tea waited to warm my weakling nerves.

Dumond soon joined us around Vashti's low table for jasmine tea and a full recounting of our adventure. Neri joined us soon after and we told it all again in more detail. Vashti and Neri tossed questions, and all of us laughed at Placidio's mimicry of the pompous philosophist. Though it had finally occurred to me what made me so uneasy about the man: He was the philosophist who chased Dumond into the Temple of Atladu with a nullifier and his sniffer.

Neri crowed at the duelist's description of my success as a subservient sister. "Teach me how to make her do it!"

I riposted with Placidio's noble defense of his fisherman parent and his attempts at scholarship that kept resulting in coughing fits.

"But he believed," said Dumond, who had been the quiet observer. "The Shadow Lord recognized that the bronze was the true one. A thousand silver solets and he set no condition save the statue itself. No one would pay so much for mere possibility, even a very rich man. Am I right in that, Romy?"

The figures of Atladu and Dragonis sat in the center of our circle, Sandro's silver coin beside it—one with his own likeness on it, stamped by the Gallanos bank.

"He paid Boscetti two *hundred* to find it," I said, "with a contract for two hundred more when the bronze was in his hand. When Boscetti claimed to need more to extract it from Mercediare, he agreed to double that. But he was angry at the petty maneuver, which would not bode well for Boscetti to get paid in any event. *Il Padroné* is generous to those who treat fairly with him, but he's no fool with his money either. So, yes, I think he believes the statue is the true Antigonean bronze."

Neri scowled. "Why did he let it go, then? It was in his hand."

"He didn't want to leave it with us," I said, thinking back to his reluctant return of my bag. "But Alessandro di Gallanos would not like to think of himself as a thief. It might seem a small distinction to those who see him as the Shadow Lord of Cantagna, but not to him."

"I suppose we'll soon know for certain," said Placidio. "Will he respond to our last message with a meeting place or a constable?"

His good humor had vanished, swallowed up as ever by impenetrable shadows. Placidio seemed like two people trapped in one body—the intelligent, skilled man of robust spirit and the bitter twin whose eyes darkened to pitch when others dug too deep or when he let himself enjoy a moment too much. Perhaps that was the curse on those who lived with magic. I hoped Neri would not suffer the same. Dumond seemed more equable, but I had never heard him laugh.

Placidio drained his tea, then nudged the silver coin thoughtfully. "Certain, a thousand silvers would buy a deal of ink."

"Not just ink," I said. "But foundry time . . . or marriage portions for daughters . . . or perhaps a suit of better clothes and an occasional trip to a bathhouse. If we are so fortunate as to pocket such an amount while keeping our heads intact and our bodies out of prison, we would, of course, share equally what's left after our expenses. Would you all agree?"

"I think that calls for more tea," said Vashti.

We spent a cheerful hour proposing increasingly mad collaborations that might yield such a profit. Even Placidio found his lighter side once again. But it was only an hour. We still had work to do. Vashti absconded with our costumes, hoping to improve her patchwork stitching. Dumond returned to the foundry, the Antigonean bronze in hand. A single day's turn and the new statue must be ready for Neri to place in Palazzo Fermi—the most dangerous and uncertain part of our plan.

I left Placidio and Neri at the Duck's Bone, with a mutual vow that none of us would drink anything stronger than cider, and strolled alone through the dark streets to Lizard's Alley. I wasn't sure I had ever experienced such pleasurable satisfaction. To gather with serious-minded people in a worthwhile endeavor—to laugh together while speaking of dread matters—brought back a taste of the life I'd shared with the Shadow Lord. Yet those times and my role in them were entirely entwined with him, a singularity I would always treasure. This venture was rooted in my belief in Sandro and his vision, but I had chosen the course for myself. Yet, still, there was more to my elation . . . to the freedom I felt on this singular night.

I could scarce recall a thought from the commission meeting and its aftermath that was not filtered solely through the eyes, ears, and knowledge of Tarenah di Guelfi. Sandro had looked me full in the face and seen neither Cataline nor Romy. It had been no performance. Rouge, hair dye, and Paolin silk could never manage so impregnable a disguise.

Chills had ghosted across my skin when Placidio uttered my

true name. The same chills I had experienced after my playacting in the street of the coffinmakers—when Neri believed I was truly drunk. The same chills I had experienced after the bronze showed me visions and impossible certainties beyond the world I knew. When fear or anxiety or curiosity forced me to reach deep inside myself, when I chose to set Romy aside and become someone else, whether Tarenah the devoted sister or a drunken harridan, something extraordinary had happened. I had reached for strength and found my magic.

That changed everything I had believed of history and myth . . . of good and evil . . . and of the power that was born in me. For the first time in my life I owned true power that was beholden to no one—something I could work on, shape to my will as Placidio had done, and use for purposes I deemed worthy as Dumond did.

Magic. No one in the world could ever again make me believe it was evil.

18

O n the morning after our venture to the commission, my elation sagged. The risks awaiting Neri at Palazzo Fermi had woken me before dawn and raddled my nerves for every subsequent moment. A step in the alley could be condottieri coming to arrest us. A knock could be a ruse to lure us out. I tried to accomplish some work at the shop, but every time someone used one of the message boxes, the click of the key or the sliding of paper through a slot had me off my stool and checking the box marked 6—the one I'd used for my message to the commission. What would I do if Sandro sent a message that he was no longer interested in the Antigonean bronze?

Neri, on the other hand, slept late. It was midday when he poked his face through the shop door, munching on the cold fish dumplings I'd left him.

I quickly returned my knife to the shelf under my writing table.

"Expecting trouble, Romy?"

"Placidio and I must be with you tonight."

He closed the door behind him and perched on the stool across my writing table. "Told you, I can't take anyone along when I walk with magic."

"Certainly we can't follow you in, but we must be close by in case of trouble. You said walking through walls depleted you; so what if your magic fails while you're inside? What if someone sees you? If you vanish through a wall in front of them, they'll summon sniffers. You would have to fight your way out. You're not going to face such danger alone."

"Good thing you bought me fighting lessons before you decided to send me into a well-defended palazzo to work magic."

He knew his jab would stick me where it hurt. I chose to believe the leer that followed was good-spirited.

"Be serious, Neri! You need to choose a signal to let us know if you're in danger. A hawking whistle or a smoke plume—no, that's ridiculous—but something."

He raised his hands in surrender. "I'm off to meet Placidio at the wool house. Says he needs someone to beat on since he's not dueling today. I'll ask him what might work for a signal. Maybe there's some magical thing."

He stuffed the last of his dumpling in his mouth and leapt to his feet.

"Naught's going ill with your web, lady spider," he said. "I walk into the palazzo, stick the statue in the corner you said, tumble something around that will draw their notice, then get out. Easy."

I wasn't superstitious. So why did I feel the need to weave a wreath of prickly juniper to lay on his bed or spend an hour formulating even more ways the night could go wrong? What if Fermi and Boscetti never found the damnable statue?

My pen yet sat idle when footsteps halted in front of the shop. The rasp of sliding paper brought me to my feet. It surely came from box number six. Though any box could be unlocked from inside the shop, I grabbed my keys and stepped into the street. A flash of mustard yellow darted through the press of Beggars Ring browns and grays. Gallanos livery was the deep green of Cantagna's cypress trees, trimmed in mustard yellow.

It required only moments for the brief note to send me racing down toward the river. I caught Neri just outside the riverside gate. "Tell Placidio that Professoré di Guelfi is asked to deliver his antiquity to the Shadow Lord at his townhouse at mid-morn tomorrow."

Neri clapped me on the shoulder so hard I stumbled over a rock. Happily, he caught me before I rolled down the steep bank into the sluggish river. "Well done, Romy. Well done. Certain the biggest fly is snared in your web!"

DAY 3—NIGHT

A flowing scarf the hue of ripe plums wrapped Vashti's black hair and neck as she drew Neri and me inside two hours before midnight. Tea was already steeping, though something stronger than the jasmine we'd had before. We were the first to arrive for the night's venture.

"Where's Placidio?" asked Neri, who popped back up again the moment he'd sat down. "And the statue's not here yet!"

My brother had grown increasingly jumpy as we made the

long hike around the city from Lizard's Alley. I couldn't blame him.

"I've not seen the *sainye* as yet," said Vashti, "and I sent Cittina to check on her papa. Our little ones are long asleep."

"*Sainye?*" Neri sat again as Vashti pushed a plate of pale white buns his way. "Does that mean *mule* or *battering ram?*"

He'd come home from his practice session with a split cheek, purpling arms, and Placidio's promise that he'd figure out an alarm signal before Neri breached Fermi's walls.

Vashti rounded her arms, raised them high, and swept them all the way to the floor. "It means the supporting things to hold up roofs—tall, big, not breaking. Can be plain or beautiful art, but underneath"—she rapped on the stone floor—"not bending. I always forget the word."

"Pillar," I said, and approved the name for Placidio. I was annoyed he wasn't here yet. Even after most of a year, it was easy to assume the worst. "He didn't stop in at the Duck's Bone this afternoon, did he, Neri?"

"Don't know." He was up again, circling the small room. He'd taken one of Vashti's buns, but left it on the table untasted.

"You have a most commendable bravery, Neri-zhi," said Vashti. "To use your magic in this service does not daunt you?"

"Been waiting my whole life to do something useful. Romy's always serious or yelling at me, but it seems a decent notion to keep her alive."

He paused long enough in his circling to drain the teacup, then moved on.

Concerned creases scored Vashti's brow. "This warring among rich families threatens you particular, Romy-zha?"

Neri interrupted before I could soothe her worry. "The chit

what stole the statue swore to blame Romy for the swipe if Romy didn't put the thing back. She'd have us both lop-limbed or dead for her mistake."

"But preserving and strengthening Cantagna's alliance with Riccia is the important reason for this scheme," I said. "If we manage that, then I'll survive with the rest of the city." Omissions weren't lies—but they could leave you with the same sour feeling. "I'm sorry I didn't explain everything. I didn't want you to think Dumond was risking himself for my safety."

"Were there more circumstances you didn't tell me? When a brave young man ventures a dangerous trial, all must be taken into account."

I thought back to my late-night storytelling with Vashti. I'd told her—and therefore Dumond—of those things I'd hidden from the smith at our first meeting: my history with *il Padroné*, my horror of magic, and how Neri and I had survived the ruination of our family. I'd told her that the thief was the Shadow Lord's wife who had recognized her idea of helping him could be his downfall, but as to my scheme to avert that . . .

"I might have skipped a few details I'd already told Dumond. I suppose I wasn't sure you would be interested."

She gave a sly smile. "It is true I am old enough to be your own *naihi*, young Romy-zha. But I know a great deal more than stitching, just as you know much more than copying the words of others. Basha sometimes forgets that, too."

My cheeks heated.

"Let me see if I am clear," she said. "Tonight your brother uses his magic to put Basha's copy of this statue into the very house where the true-made one was stolen, yes?"

"Yes, and—"

She held up a finger. "Before you explain, first decide if I know of what I speak. It might save you words."

I folded my hands in my lap. Neri actually sat down and did not jump right back up.

"You wish these wicked gentlemen to find the false artwork and believe it is the true-made one never stolen."

"Yes."

"And it is necessary that they find it before the birthday feast tomorrow afternoon. When they bring the false one as a gift to this noble duc, your Shadow Lord will have the true work in hand, and will expose the false one as . . . false."

"All of that, yes. Exactly."

"And the danger to your brother in this adventure has you worried because so much is unknown. This I read in your face every time you look at him, which is quite frequently. Your worry makes his own stomach flutter like moths near flame, which, naturally, makes his risk the greater."

Neri and I glanced at each other and grimaced.

Vashti took that as a spur to continue. "So I will ask, where do you think to place Basha's statue so that all will fall out as you wish?"

We told her about Lucrezia di Fermi's receiving room where Gilliette had thrown her fit and smuggled out the statue, and about the graceless sculpture of the Five Graces that had adorned the chamber the last time I was there.

"Which was how long ago?"

I grimaced again. "Perhaps four years. I was going to have Neri knock over a plant or a stool to expose the statue, as if someone put it there when Gilliette fell ill."

"And what will he say if someone catches him at it? And what will you do if no one visits that room in that very large palazzo tomorrow morning?"

Vashti's brow rose at our silence, and her pointed gaze held steady, speaking all that was needed. Lady Fortune herself would scoff at our error-prone scheme.

"That is not such a *terrible* plan, Romy-zha, but your own doubts prove you hunger for one more certain. I've an idea—more dangerous on its surface, because you are not yet thinking how the talents of your friends mesh. As you found with the *sainye* Placidio last night, a weaving is much stronger than a thread. You each brought your wit and talent to your venture, and so were able to meet the challenges of the unexpected." She interlocked her fingers and pulled, demonstrating the strength of their knot. "And so it could be with tonight's venture. Dumond should join you. He had a *very* fine sleep while you and your swordmaster were having such a success with *il Padroné,* and he will not rest again until this thing is done. But this plan would require him."

Truly I had underestimated Vashti. "What is your idea?"

"Consider. Perhaps the problem is that brave Neri is trying to *replace* the statue, when he should be trying to *steal* it."

"Steal it?" Neri and I echoed in unison.

She tilted her head and poured more tea.

My brother and I turned to each other, our understanding growing in unison. The clarity . . . the simplicity . . . and the danger . . . all made perfect sense. It was much easier to make sure you were seen than to keep yourself hidden.

"Are you willing?" I said.

Neri's handsome face eased into a smile—pleased, while yet mindful of the risk. But this would be a risk that was clear and could be planned for, rather than one lurking in uncertainty. "To get me rescued Dumond and Placidio will have to know each other's secrets," he said. "But if they're willing, I'm game."

THE HOUR OF THE SPIRITS

Placidio and I crouched behind a row of cypress trees. Squinting into the starlit night, I tried to make out the black smudge that would be Neri creeping around the bordering shadows of the grassy lawn. Each motion that set my heart racing proved to be but the interplay of shrub and thyme-scented breeze. He could be anywhere, already in danger. Dread snaked up my limbs.

My companion held motionless, naught but a solid warmth at my side. A stubborn *sainye*, indeed. He had resisted any notion of revealing his magical talents to Dumond and Vashti, until Dumond painted a black circle on the stone floor, infused it with his magic, and jumped through it into his cellar. Placidio had jumped through it, as well, to convince himself it was no illusion. I'd thought Vashti and I would never stop laughing when the swordsman poked his astonished, cobweb-bedecked face back out again, because the ceiling in the rest of the dusty cellar was too low for him.

To get us into the palazzo grounds, Dumond had worked his portal magic on the wall behind this small yard, shielded by the cypresses. Both nerves and muscles were wound tight. I'd not expected we would have to crouch here more than two hours even to begin . . .

In spring, while cool rains and early sunset postponed summer pleasures, most great houses were dark soon after the

Hour of Contemplation. But to our dismay, Palazzo Fermi had blazed with torchlight and music until an hour past midnight.

Shifting slowly, I eased my knee and thigh.

Once a few guests had ridden out, the Fermi watch had made rounds and settled into their guardposts. Last to depart were the matched white horses of the Secchi, and a carriage blazoned with the Malavesi boar—two families of the rebellious old guard. The house itself had taken longer to settle. Neri had made his move just as the last candle gleams were snuffed, no more than half an hour since. We didn't want everyone asleep.

Placidio's hand gripped my bare wrist, loosing a lance of fire into my veins. *Neri's* magic.

Just before Neri left us Placidio had nicked my brother's arm and his own, then pressed the wounds one to the other. Their mingled blood would bind their magic together, he'd told us. The connection would last no more than an hour or two, but during that time he should be able to detect whenever Neri worked magic. With Placidio holding my wrist, I would as well. If he was right, Neri had just walked through a wall.

The palazzo stayed quiet. The fire cooled. Placidio held fast.

A nightingale whistled and trilled over our heads. I whispered my petition its way. *Sweet Virtue, daughter of the Unseeable, show your favor on this fair youth and our enterprise . . .*

Another lancing fire. Then a third and fourth in rapid succession. Another. Another. I imagined my brother dashing across the darkened galleries, up stairs, through the walls of silent public chambers. A longer lapse before the next. That might mean he'd reached the palazzo's great hall . . . or that he'd gotten lost. Unsure of guard schedules and numbers, we had to wait until we were sure Neri wasn't coming back this way before moving farther into the palace grounds.

Another lance. If I interpreted correctly, my brother was almost to his destination, not Lucrezia's receiving room and some artist's dross that might have been discarded over the years, but a landmark that would stand until Palazzo Fermi crumbled—the thrice life-sized bronze of Enzo di Fermi, Rodrigo's grandsire, who with Sandro's own grandsire had laid the foundation of the Cantagnan Independency. Enzo's looming effigy stood on a platform overlooking the great hall of Palazzo Fermi. The location itself wasn't important, only its use as an easy target for Neri's magic, and its proximity to a clear exit. Once he was in position—

"There it is!" Placidio's command accompanied three sharp cracks of explosive power from inside the palazzo. Neri's signal. Not *magical* power, but a smoldering fuse applied to a finger-length roll of parchment packed with nitre powder. A startling noise that could alert the palace to the presence of a thief. And three bursts which meant no emergency, but all going according to plan.

The duelist's hand propelled me to my feet just as shouts rang out. A horn blared the alarm. My blood pounded, though we expected it. Planned it. Now we had to put ourselves in position to aid Neri's escape.

Grateful for the months of running practice, I matched the duelist's stride. We raced through a small gate and onto a graveled path that led through the palazzo gardens, past a fish pond, up a few steps. Neri's magic had led him straight through the honeycombed palace. We would meet him on his way out.

"This way." I motioned Placidio onto a narrower path and

through a fountain court. Sandro and I had once explored these gardens to avoid a tedious entertainment. I knew exactly which paths would lead us to the palazzo's expansive forecourt, sprawled between the outer gates and the grand entry doors.

Torches blazed from the buildings ahead of us. Speed was our first priority; silence and invisibility the next. Black scarves covered our hair, masking all but our eyes, and we'd no weapons drawn, lest reflections give us away.

An arbor led us from another courtyard garden into the grand arcade that circled the forecourt. We headed away from the outer gates toward the entry doors. Disciplined guards held their posts on either side of the wide steps; others—likely more than the two we could see—flanked the outer gates. None must spy our movements. Hugging the elaborately carved wall of the arcade, we darted through the voids where the columns could not mask us.

Sainye. Beneath the mask, I smiled approval at the dark, sturdy form twinned with the pillar behind me. He thought the name silly. I tapped a toe that the way was clear for him to join me.

We slipped forward across another gap. If all went well, we would remain in the shadows and retreat alongside Neri.

My stomach lurched when four or five figures erupted from the palazzo entry doors and spilled onto the broad steps, a single dark figure in the lead. My heart screamed, *Run, Neri!* My mind yelled, *Hold! Not too fast. Let them close, then drop their prize and run like the gods themselves.*

They *must* believe he was reluctant to leave the bronze behind. That he was a thief, not a spy.

They caught him halfway down the steps. He didn't go easy, sending one of his assailants tumbling down to the forecourt where the fellow lay as still and heavy as a sack of grain. In the scramble of lunging bodies, the bundled bronze tumbled out of Neri's hands.

One of the guards posted at the steps yelled, "Get him!"

Neri's fists toppled a second man, who crabbed his way backward to avoid his comrade's fate. Neri kicked him flat and darted down the remaining steps. But two more pursuers shoved him to his knees, twisted his arms behind him, and pressed his shoulders forward as he writhed and wriggled.

The fifth pursuer whistled loudly, then retreated through the doors—carrying news of the thief's capture, no doubt. The two from the guardposts hurried toward the fray. One joined Neri's captors, while one paused to examine the bundle Neri had dropped. Dumond's bronze.

One of the captors yanked Neri's head sharply backward, and the other two grabbed his arms until he could not move. We would have to fight him loose.

"As we planned," whispered Placidio. He detached a bow from his shoulder, nocked an arrow, and let fly. The missile flew swift and silent, until it struck the steps beside Neri and the guardsmen and exploded in a shower of smoke and blue-and-green fireworks—true fireworks, like Neri's signal.

"Now fast," he snapped, discarding the bow in favor of sword and knife.

We sped across the forecourt with the ferocity of a black vulture diving for a nestling swan.

Though sword and knife hung sheathed at my belt, my blade skills were too limited for open combat. But Placidio's weapons flashed with the sparks and torchlight, and without slowing, he slashed one of Neri's captors on his shoulder and drew him away from the others.

"Give it back!" Neri screamed at the guardsman who had just drawn Dumond's statue from the bag. "The Antigonean belongs in a temple!"

I raced up the steps through the smoke and plowed straight into the fellow's back. The bronze clanged on the stone steps. The man stretched out beneath me peered over his shoulder through the smoke and glare to see what had landed on him. Making a fist, I shoved my sharp knuckle into his eye. Then I rolled him over, slammed the heel of my hand under his breastbone, and left him half blind and breathless. We'd no intent to kill anyone.

With his first opponent writhing in pain on the steps, Placidio drew off another of Neri's captors. My eye could not follow the speed of Placidio's arm. I imagined I could feel his magic flowing through my own veins, anticipating the flustered guard's every move. He'd have him in moments.

Not *too* fast, though. This was a battle we must not win. We had to get free, but Fermi must be convinced of our determination to take the statue.

Pinned by the remaining guardsman's firm grip, Neri writhed and twisted, still cursing those who trafficked in "holy works." The smoke had cleared enough to expose me, so I moved in on them slowly, arms extended, knife in my left hand. The guardsman dragged Neri backward, keeping my brother between us. The man's gaze flicked constantly to his comrade and Placidio's clangorous duel.

I drew my sword. One weapon in each hand, I shifted a few steps left, then to the right, ever closer.

"I'll break your thieving friend's neck." The guardsman snarled and jerked Neri backward again. Hard.

Neri choked. His black masking scarf slipped downward. We could not afford to have him identified or for my voice to expose his accomplice as a woman, so I kept silent and halted, arms spread wide.

"On the ground, thief!" said the captor.

I kept one eye on Neri and one on Placidio. The duelist's movements had slowed; he was allowing the guard to drive him back, away from the statue, away from Neri and me.

Arms extended, weapons still firmly in hand, I lowered myself toward the paving.

"Who thinks some scrap of metal is worth trespassing on the Fermi?" growled the burly guard. "I think we'll have these masks off and learn who you are before we chop your hands."

"More coming," yelled Placidio, as he spun and bashed the hilt of his sword into his opponent's head just a few steps above us. "Got to get out!"

I slid the sword, hilt first, toward Neri's feet, then launched my dagger at the brute holding him. It didn't strike the man, but the triple distraction gave Neri a chance to wrench one arm free, reach back, and gouge his captor's eye. Another twisting move and he lunged for the sword, rolled to one side, grabbed the weapon, and slashed at the man's legs.

The guard groaned and crawled up the step. Neri scrambled to his feet, snatched up my dagger, and tossed it back to me.

Eight or ten men surged from the great doors onto the porch and the steps. Two in fluttering cloaks, one red, one white, remained at the top of the steps.

Time to run. Neri and I charged past Placidio's first victim, staying wide of the man I'd laid out who had crawled well away, clutching Neri's bag. I glanced over my shoulder. Placidio stood still as the pillar we named him, staring at the two who were watching the fight play out.

"Call him," I said.

"Run!" Neri bellowed. "Let it go!"

Placidio didn't stir.

"Use Vashti's word."

"*Sainye!* Frog spit! Can't lay a strike on your granny!"

As if Neri had stuck the sword in his buttocks, Placidio whirled and pelted down the stair. The three of us raced straight for the outer gates, where six guards moved into place, ready to block our escape.

"Stay on course," I said. "Just a bit farther. Past the fountain."

One of the gate guards nudged another and pointed at us, as if he'd read my thoughts. The two jogged forward. Faster . . .

"Now," I said, and veered sharply left, taking us toward a span of wall between the fifth and sixth column from the end of the arcade.

The two from the gate saw us as trapped prey and broke into a run. The rest charged after them. We had outstripped the pursuit from the entry steps but they, too, changed direction and bulled after us.

Be ready, Dumond! Sisters grant I'd gotten the placement right. We'd had so little time . . .

The first gate guard reached us. Placidio was ready and left him disarmed and bleeding.

"Go!" he yelled.

Two more arrived as we reached the arcade. I squinted into the deeper darkness. Nothing.

Spirits, Dumond! Where are you?

Swords crashed. Neri and Placidio were both engaged. In moments we would be swarmed.

I held position, knife in hand . . .

An armspan-wide section of the curved wall melted into a solid door and swung away.

"Ready," I screamed, striking at Neri's opponent as the two circled.

Neri took advantage and slashed the guard's legs. We dashed for the doorway, where Dumond stood waving us onward.

But Placidio was caught in a grapple.

"*Sainye!* Now!"

The duelist pulled free, spun the other man, and gave him a great shove, just in time to carom into two of his comrades. Then our most agile pillar launched himself through the doorway after us, while Neri, Dumond, and I slammed it shut.

Palms flat on the thick door, Dumond murmured, "*Sigillaré!*"

As I'd witnessed in the Temple of Atladu, the portal vanished and the section of the Palazzo Fermi wall where Rodrigo di Fermi had once carved his own name above the figure of a lion was its solid self again.

We scooped up Dumond's paint pots in the canvas sheet he'd used to catch the spattered colors and took off through the deserted streets of the Heights. I scarce breathed until we'd stripped off our black scarves, donned the cloaks and hats we'd left waiting, and strolled past the last coffinmaker's shop in the Via Mortua.

"Separate routes, as we planned," said Placidio, "and stay out of sight. Within the hour Fermi will have condottieri rousting every beggar, drunkard, and gate guard." And sniffers, too, if anyone had spied our exit.

Without a word, we scattered, each making our own way to the Beggars Ring through the waning night.

19

My heart didn't slow until I glimpsed the three of them waiting for me in the alley behind the Leguiza Hospice. Words failed. I threw my arms around Neri, not caring if he was embarrassed. I just held him close.

"Are we all clear?" asked Dumond.

"Let Lady Fortune be promoted to goddess this night! I met not a single soul all the way," said Neri, shrugging me away until only our shoulders touched. I smothered a smile.

"I waved at a pair of gate guards in the Asylum Ring," said Dumond. "They were as drunk as Philosophic Confraternity novices on their first visit home. Lest you've never met one, that means very drunk indeed."

Whimsy seized me.

"I had a collier offer to bed me," I said in the same equable tone.

All three men growled and bristled, peering behind me as if the man might have chased me all the way into their protection.

Their concern made it near impossible to maintain my serious mien.

"I told him I'd be happy to do that. I licked his cheek and asked him how he liked his comfort, and if he kept a whip with him, as the client I'd just left enjoyed blood on his back. And by the way, it would cost him fifty coppers. He declined."

Neri bellowed in hilarity. Dumond shook his head and his mouth pursed in a wry amusement. To be sure I'd never seen him smile, save with his eyes at Vashti.

Placidio, whom I'd thought might enjoy the jest most, sat on a stoop expressionless, wiping his blade with a rag. "I saw no one. The north gates are rarely manned at the Hour of Spirits."

"All of you—I think we did well," I said. "If there is any way for this scheme to reach a satisfactory end, this night will be the keystone. How can I possibly repay you?"

"If the end is worthwhile, that's enough," said Dumond. "Like your brother, I've waited my whole life to use magic for something more worthy than avoiding the consequences of using magic. And my lifetime has been more than twice his!"

Placidio rose from the stoop and sheathed his weapon. "We shouldn't be babbling and lying about out of doors."

Only slightly sobered, we made the short walk to Dumond's workshop behind the cooper's yard. But once inside with a lamp lit, Placidio drew us close. "We must lie low tonight. I, or Romy and Neri, should hold the true bronze somewhere well hidden, with one of us awake at all times. And you, Dumond, be especially wary. Rodrigo di Fermi might choose to question anyone who trades in bronze work. His fury will be monstrous."

Common sense suggested caution, but I didn't understand his grim turn. "Why? Yes, thieves invaded his house, a disagreeable matter for any segnoré. He'll likely do what men like him always do—pick out a scapegoat, strip him of rank, give him a flogging. But an incompetent thief"—I elbowed Neri—"has left him Dumond's magnificent counterfeit that he will surely believe is his own prize. I couldn't tell the difference."

"Whatever he may think of the forgery is unimportant," said Placidio, "because he has a guest who's witnessed his humiliation. Armed intruders invading your well-guarded palazzo is one thing. But which is more stupid, to allow the Shadow Lord to steal your prize, or to misplace it and have a thief expose your carelessness in front of a man you hoped to impress?"

As the meaning of his words sank in, I stepped back to lean on one of Dumond's heavy worktables as if its sturdy bulk could prevent the world spinning off course.

"His guest—the man in the white cloak," I said. Fermi colors were red and gray. "White and silver are the colors of Riccia. Eduardo di Corradini was guesting at Palazzo Fermi?"

"Indeed so."

Exhilaration escaped me like wine from a burst skin, leaving my limbs heavy and my mind sagging. "If Fermi has already forged some sort of alliance with Riccia, then gifting the grand duc the true bronze likely won't mend it. And if Fermi and Boscetti get a notion that the bronze they hold is not the one Boscetti brought—that the thieves left a counterfeit—they'll start looking for answers . . ."

Placidio's ferocious gaze stilled my tongue before I could voice another word. The chain of reason yet stood stark against the silence between us. The grand duc had said he could identify the statue inerrantly and might already have told Fermi the statue they had now was false. If they started looking closer, all of our plan could unravel. Which could lead to Gilliette, who would accuse me of stealing it for Sandro. And Neri and I would pay.

"All of this would be for nothing." I could not leave it unsaid.

"Simply exposing Fermi's vulnerability as we just did might weaken such an alliance," said Dumond. "That would be a decent outcome of our night. Yes, Fermi will be furious. But the man's likely furious in any case. Certain, one of those fossils on the Arts Commission has informed him that someone else claims to possess the true Antigonean bronze. He won't know but that Boscetti's lied to him all along."

Dumond glanced from the swordsman to me and back again. Blowing a curt sigh, he scratched the remaining wisps of hair on the back of his head. We were all bone weary. "I suggest we see what comes by morning," he said. "Fermi's fury could fall hard on antiquities merchants. Or traveling professorés."

"None of us should go home tonight, save you, Dumond," said Placidio, "and if you've anywhere to go, you might give a thought to getting your family away till all this settles out. If *any* of them suspect the statue Neri dropped is false, the fury could fall on sculptors and metalsmiths as well."

"I told Romy early on that I refuse to live in fear," said Dumond. "But down in that cellar you visited, there's a door painted on the wall. Do we ever need to leave in a hurry, be sure we can do it, and none'll be able to follow."

Dumond opened the workshop door, then stopped and looked over his shoulder. "Should we expect you two in the morning? Vashti's certain to have your outfits well spruced."

I glared the question at Placidio, who was passing it along to me at the same time.

He spoke first. "Nothing's changed. The Antigonean bronze should go to the one who's paid for it. If the person he thought to gift it to has taken sides against him, that's *his* problem to solve. We'll have done what we can. So I'll deliver *il Padroné* his bronze."

"I agree," I said. "The Shadow Lord is no fool. If he's being played by the grand duc, he'll see it." I hoped.

If Sandro's acuity fell short anywhere, it was in holding too long to a doomed course. He'd clung to boyhood friends like Rodrigo di Fermi and Arrigo di Secchi long after their fathers were plotting against his ascendancy. Once he married Gilliette, his consigliere told him time and again to be rid of the Moon House whore, that nothing but trouble would result. He had clung too long, and sure enough trouble had arrived.

"We'll be to your house at the morning anthem." It came out sharper than I intended. "We cannot be late for our delivery. Placidio and I will decide how to deal with the risks."

Dumond grabbed Neri's sleeve and jerked his head at the door. "Come with me, lad, and I'll give you the prize. Your sister and the swordsman can decide who sleeps with it tonight. Vashti might also have left out a bite and a drink for visiting not-thieves."

Neri followed Dumond into the dark alley that led to his house. I was ready to have a moment alone with Placidio.

He leaned against the doorpost, staring into the night. Maybe having his back to me would help him answer questions he didn't like. At least I wouldn't see his eyes darken when I asked.

"*Il Padroné* believes that Eduardo di Corradini can identify the Antigonean bronze inerrantly. Do you think that's true?"

"If the duc himself has told him that, then yes."

Philosophist di Bastianni said inerrant identification was impossible. Which suggested Eduardo had access to magic. Did the grand duc carry some taint of the blood that allowed him to touch the statue's wonder as Dumond and I had done? Did he own some spelled device that could expose such a mystery? In either case, the grand duc of Riccia would be in violation of the First Law of Creation—a secret so dire it was near impossible to comprehend.

No matter our agreement, I needed to learn what Placidio knew. So I picked my way carefully through his reticence. "The tales I've read claimed the statue was forged by Atladu's own smith who infused it with holiness."

"I don't believe in gods."

But Placidio hadn't touched the statue that first time when he examined it so closely in this workshop, nor had he done so since.

"From what that philosophist said, there is no inerrant—"

"I've no idea how the duc thinks to do that, and I'll make no guesses."

"Then, I suppose the question is: Will the grand duc tell Fermi that his almost stolen statue is a counterfeit?"

"How could I possibly know? You've a better notion of political skullduggery than I can aspire to. But it makes no difference. Dumond is right. Fermi is sure to have a spy on the Arts Commission; he'll be watching for brother and sister di Guelfi. Your Shadow Lord will certainly have heard about this night's doings at Palazzo Fermi, as well. We knew all those things going in. We play our parts and deal with them as they come, or we give up the scheme and you and Neri run to the hinterlands to escape *il Padroné*'s wife."

And so to the next risk. "The grand duc is already in the city, not traveling as we assumed," I said. "What if he arrives at *il*

Padroné's residence early? *Il Padroné* could put us all in a room together to decide who has what statue."

"The birthday feast is in the afternoon," said Placidio. "The grand duc's manners are impeccable. He'll not arrive beforetime and—"

Placidio threw up his hand for silence. Then he slipped sidewise, out of the backlit doorway, hand on his sword. Moments later, footsteps crunched in the alley. No mistaking Neri's unsubtle, determined stride.

Placidio relaxed, and in moments Neri appeared in the doorway with a heavy, canvas-wrapped bundle in hand. "So where do we sleep?"

DAY 4—MID-MORN

Placidio and I hurried through the muddy, crowded streets of the Merchant Ring. Vashti's hair combs and sewing needles had again transformed us into the very model of a scholarly pair, and I carried the Antigonean bronze in a canvas bag under my enveloping cloak.

Every step closer to Sandro's home—my home for nine years, the center of my world and my delight—threatened my concentration. I had considered reaching for Tarenah right away, drowning myself in the subservient sister as a way to lessen the pain of Cataline's memories. But the grand duc's birthday was fraught with far more dangerous possibilities than heartache.

We had spent a drizzly night in the wool house. Placidio and I slept wrapped in blankets we grabbed from Lizard's Alley on our way. Neri had not slept at all, but rather watched over us and the bronze for the few hours of the night that remained. At first light he'd woken us with bread and ale fetched from a tavern just inside the River Gate and the news that every tavern in the Beggars Ring had been scoured by search parties hunting a gang of thieves—in the name of the Shadow Lord.

Dumond had greeted us with more unsettling news. He had visited his friend Pascal's foundry in the Asylum Ring at dawn on the pretext of recovering one of his tools, and returned with reports of constables rousting artisans and antiquities dealers from their beds and assembling lists of slender young men of dubious character who might recognize a sculpture known as the Antigonean bronze.

"I doubt I'd be listed as slender or young, either one," he'd said, assessing his own build, which was very like a bridge piling, and scruffing his almost nonexistent hair. "My friend Pascal would be, the little odd-fish, but none would call his character dubious. Every copper he earns goes to his mam, and he prefers his mam's cabbage juice to wine, and practicing his letters to wedding or whoring. What bothered me most was that those hunting thieves and assembling lists invoked the Shadow Lord's name. Aren't we working to his benefit?"

No longer privy to Sandro's confidences, I could not judge which of myriad possible reasons might induce him to pander to Fermi's grievances, whether or not he expected the true statue to be delivered within hours. Which meant I had no convincing reason to abort the plan.

So Placidio and I prepared ourselves for anything and walked carefully. We avoided both main streets and lonely alleys. We took abrupt turns and flattened our backs to the wall around the corners, ready to pounce on thief-stalkers, constables, or anyone else trailing us. We'd seen naught to explain the spiders crawling up our backs. Not yet.

Despite our roundabout course, and a constant traffic of fish and vegetable carts and vintner's wagons turning into the back lanes that led to the Gallanos kitchens, we arrived before the midmorning bells.

"House, windows, defenses—anything out of order?" Placidio tugged his hat lower over his face as we strolled past the flat, harmonious facade of what Sandro and his family called the Garden House.

The Garden House had begun as a single modest residence in Quartiere dell'Alba of the Merchant Ring—the Sunrise Quarter, a neighborhood of bankers, cloth merchants, and ship and caravan owners. As the Gallanos family prospered, Sandro's grandfather bought a number of neighboring houses, joining them to his with covered bridges, underground passages, and graceful colonnades. The whole was likely twice the size of Palazzo Fermi now, yet conveyed the same image of modesty and gracious hospitality it ever had.

"There should be two house guards just inside the street entry gate," I said, bending over to examine a pot of jewel-colored iris, giving him the opportunity to look. "More than that means the house is on alert. One house archer should be posted at each corner of the main house roof. More than one, or more than one standing post on each of the adjacent roofs, would also be a signal of something brewing."

Placidio settled his hands at his back and surveyed the street, as if bored with his sister's preoccupation. "The numbers are as you say, maybe one or two extra on adjacent rooftops. But the archers are *roaming*, not standing post, and a thick bar is blocking the streetside gate. Maybe precautions for today's birthday feast?"

"Perhaps. A little extra is not alarming." Though Sandro had always insisted his guards be discreet. He believed too obvious defenses made him appear weak.

I took Placidio's arm. We allowed a slow carriage and two parties of horsemen to pass before we ventured the avenue. "They are all house guards, yes? In Gallanos green and yellow?"

"Gate guards in green. Some archers in green; some in scarlet."

My stomach clenched a bit harder. I leaned close. "Captain di Lucci's condottieri wear scarlet tabards. If he's brought in mercenaries, the house is on heightened alert."

Placidio's sinewy arm tightened to steel. "The next person you invent for me to play, lady scribe, must have reason to carry a sword."

"And this time, when we've finished playing Vincenzio and Tarenah, when you're sure it's safe . . . be sure to speak my true name as you did last time. I get a bit lost in my playacting."

There had been no time to try my magic again since we'd visited the Arts Commission. I needed to learn how to keep hold of my own mind—Romy's mind—so I could shake off that other skin and step back into my own when I was ready to. And if I were to use it very often, surely I'd need to rely on my own judgment, my own experiences, my own knowledge of the world to determine my actions. Though the power to sink so deeply into an impersonation was thrilling, having Tarenah—or a drunkard woman—determining my actions made it all a bit terrifying. When there was time, I'd ask Dumond or Placidio for advice.

Placidio stared at me for a moment. "I'll do that. But what—?"

The midmorning anthem rang from the city tower.

The avenue cleared. We crossed to the gate and rang the bell.

"Professoré Vincenzio di Guelfi and his sister to see Segnoré di Gallanos," announced Placidio when a gentleman appeared at the gate. "We have an appointment."

"Fortune's benefice, professoré. Damizella. A moment only."

The gentleman who had answered the gate bell was a gray-haired steward, not the house guard who remained on post just behind him or some condottiere. But straying from Garden House custom, the steward did not welcome us into the small forecourt garden to wait while he dispatched a page for instructions. The gate remained barred. We waited in the street.

I felt exposed. Devoutly wishing I could command the gate be opened as had once been my prerogative, I clutched the heavy bronze under my cloak.

Placidio casually shifted his big body between me and the street. He must have felt the same unease, as he faced outward, pressing his back to mine.

Tucked behind him, I peered through the barred gate into the courtyard garden. The gray-haired steward waited patiently for his instructions at the far end of the gate walk, talking with a second well-armed house guard who wore a captain's badge. Neither were men I knew.

Another armed man ambled through the garden from the house to join them. To my dismay, his red livery was not the solid scarlet of Lucci's mercenaries, but the blue-trimmed red of the Fermi.

"Pardon, sir," I said to the house guard standing just inside the gate, shadowed by the sturdy brick arch. "Can you say how long we must stand out here? My brother has been ill . . ."

He stepped closer—a young man of something like my own age and Dumond's general shape and size. His square jaw sported a beard redder than Vashti's washing could ever produce.

I could not hold a smile. This man I knew very well.

"Excuse the delay, damizella," he said. "'Tis no slight to you. We've firm orders."

A chill draft hit my back as Placidio stepped away. A glance down the avenue revealed a pair of men-at-arms had emerged from a walkway between two of the joined houses. Red and blue livery. Fermi's men.

"You, there!" One of them pointed a menacing finger at us. "What's your name?"

"By whose authority do you challenge me?" Placidio's question boomed with aristocratic offense, a bit severe for Vincenzio di Guelfi.

"By the authority of the Cantagnan Sestorale on behalf of public order and Segnoré Alessandro di Gallanos, the owner of this property."

"I am a guest of the Philosophic Academie of Cantagna, have been welcomed by the Sestorale's Commission on Public Artworks, and have been invited to this house by its master. Yet I am forced to stand idle on a public byway and be questioned by thugs? On what principles do you base your right to interfere with me?"

Placidio blathered at the approaching Fermi soldiers like an experienced Academie debater. I returned my attention to the gate. The red-haired house guard had returned to his post.

"Ssst! Guardsman! Come here. You must open the gate."

"I'm sorry, but I cannot—"

"We are beset by Fermi ruffians. I don't trust them. Can you not help us, Cillian?"

He peered through the barred gate, his freckled face crinkled into a puzzle. "As I said, I've orders. How is it you know my name?"

"A dear friend of mine who once frequented this house told me that Cillian from barbarian Eide, the fierce, handsome guardsman with the red beard, is actually the dearest of young men. She said you have a fancy for sweet wines, and she used to provide them for you in return for your help to move her chairs or fetch flowers to surprise . . . her gentleman."

"Move her chairs . . . You speak of the Damizella Cata—" His cheeks colored a match with his beard. "We're forbid to speak her name since she died so sudden. 'Twas such a sorrow. The most beautiful woman I ever saw and so kind. But you were friends with her?"

"I was."

He tilted his head and peered at me closely. "Indeed, save for your red hair, you're very like."

Fermi's men were but a few steps from Placidio. Placidio bellowed that the Academie would make complaints to the Sestorale about the treatment of traveling academicians. Passersby gathered in the lane.

"Face to the ground, shitheel, or we'll prick that puffed chest and let out your humors."

When one of the soldiers pawed at his arm, Placidio shifted a few steps and swept aside the soldier's hand and his partner's pike that was lowering into a dangerous position.

"Look who he's been hiding!" said the red-faced soldier. "What is a philosophist buffoon doing with a fire-haired doxy? I do believe these are the two we were told—"

I almost fell through the gate when Cillian yanked it open behind me and yelled at the Fermi men-at-arms, "Mind your manners, you two. You're not here to harry *il Padroné*'s guests!"

Grabbing Placidio's cloak, I dragged him through the gate after me, still spouting bombast. "By the Twin Sisters, who are these foul-mouthed fellows to lay hands on scholars?"

Cillian slammed the gate in the faces of the Fermi soldiers, who rattled the iron bars.

"I must inform my captain and Steward Ventoli," said Cillian. Then he swallowed hard and whispered sidewise. "Damizella, are you her kin?"

"What have you done, Cillian?" snapped the gray-haired steward, fury written on his face.

Desperate to protect both kind Cillian and our identities, I laid my hand on the young soldier's cheek and reached for magic. Holding in mind all that I had told him, I whispered the replacement. "It was a righteous deed to protect Damizella di Guelfi and her brother from these Fermi ruffians. You risked all to protect *il Padroné*'s honor as you are sworn to do. They showed you his invitation, and you could never permit his invited guests to be murdered on his doorstep."

I snatched my hand away, as the steward, the guard captain, and their companion in Fermi red joined us.

"Your orders were specific," said the house guard captain.

Cillian stood at attention. "'Twas not righteous to leave *il Padroné*'s honor or his guests at the mercy of those Fermi ruffians, sir . . ."

As the young man gave his testimony, I squeezed Placidio's arm with two sharp bursts. He patted my hand, as any concerned brother might, and laid it on his sleeve. Reassured that he understood, I abandoned Romy and reached for Tarenah.

Our rescuer stood firm in his resolution, offering to assure that we could step no farther than the gate walk until we received *il Padroné*'s permission. It would be dreadful if his kindness got him in trouble with his superiors.

"Vincenzio," I said, "we must put in a good word for this noble young soldier. We could have died out there."

A page boy trotted into the garden. "Steward Ventoli, you are to—"

"—admit my guests at once."

Segnoré di Gallanos himself followed the page boy into the garden and laid a hand on the child's shoulder. "You will be well rewarded for informing me of the altercation outside my gate, Page Tito. Come to me this evening at the Hour of Gathering, when the day's accolades and punishments are handed out. Now off with you."

The boy scampered away.

I clung to Vincenzio. Dread infused everyone in that garden, save my brother and, perhaps, the red-haired guardsman who had protected us.

Gallanos—no, surely the clouds gathered in his visage named him the one of whom people spoke in whispers. The Shadow Lord strolled toward his hirelings. "Did I not pass you the professoré's name, Ventoli?" he asked softly. "And to you, Captain Enzio? Did I not say he and his sister were to be brought to me at the moment they arrived? Explain yourselves."

"We received the names, segnoré," said the guard captain.

"But when we came on duty this morning, Steward Ventoli told us that the exception had been rescinded."

The gray-haired steward lifted his chin bravely, but did not meet his master's gaze. I was not sure that I, wholly innocent, could have met that steel gray gaze.

"Indeed you gave me the names last evening, segnoré," said the steward, his voice not so steady as his chin. "But that was before our other guests arrived and informed us of the attack on Palazzo Fermi."

Captain Enzio chimed in. "They told us that the thieves might be masquerading as an academician called di Guelfi and his red-haired sister. I thought it best to be diligent."

"No orders supercede those issued from my lips, unless they, too, issue from my lips. Captain Enzio, Steward Ventoli, you both are relieved of duty and will appear before me at the Hour of Gathering. Guardsman Cillian, I commend you for preserving my honor—yes, I heard your defense and wholly approve it. You will now hold the gate closed until I send you better comrades."

The red-haired guard saluted crisply and returned to the gate.

The sour-faced man in Fermi red and blue had said nothing throughout. Gallanos had not deigned to notice him. Now he waved the Fermi man after the disgraced steward and guard captain.

"Return to your master, Nesco. We'll have words about thugs in the street later. For now I'll see to my honored guests."

Only when we three were alone did he speak to us. "Professoré, damizella, I cannot fully express my regret at this rude welcome. I have been anticipating your arrival with great pleasure. Are either of you harmed in any way? Should I send for a physician?"

Vincenzio acknowledged his concern with a graceful bow.

"Nay, segnoré. Though unpleasantly surprised at the brutish assault, we never believed the ruffians' prating that it was your will. I feared they were impostors—thieves! But I am left quite unharmed. And you, Tarenah, the same, I think . . ."

"Indeed. The young guardsman's quick work and good service prevented any harm." I revealed the canvas bag under my cloak.

Gallanos's smile infused the garden air. My cheeks heated so fiercely, I dropped my eyes in embarrassment.

"Excellent," he said and extended his hand to a corner of the vine-draped colonnade that circumscribed the fragrant garden. "I have a private study close by. Will you come?"

We followed him into a small, elegant chamber, furnished with a few velvet-cushioned chairs, several shelves filled entirely with books, and a few small artworks. On one wall hung the portrait of a lovely, dark-haired young woman reading while seated in a different garden. It must have been painted when she was not looking, as her expression was so very unaware of anything around her, save the pleasure of her own dreaming.

He stepped to an interior door. "May I offer you some refreshment? Coffee or a refreshing tisane, fruit, pastry?"

"Many thanks, segnoré, but no. We learned that one of my colleagues from the Varela Academie is in Cantagna today and have made plans to dine together. We have hopes—" Vincenzio beamed at me in his brotherly way. "He is a most honorable and intelligent man and admires my sister greatly. I think she takes pleasure in our meetings as well."

Gallanos gave me a small bow. "Never would I think to interfere with a young woman's pleasurable engagements," he said. "We should be able to conclude our business quickly."

He offered us a seat, then excused himself and stepped through the interior doorway to speak to someone just beyond.

Vincenzio remained standing, tugging on his hat, brushing his lip with his hand. I supposed it was the assault outside the gate had left him so nervous about this dealing. If Gallanos decided that the bronze was not what he wanted, it would be hard, but seeing my dear brother so ill as he had been, and in such danger as on this day, had made me reassess our venture. Money or not, validation of our work or not, I would be satisfied, as long as he was safe and well.

"We should set it out," he said softly. "Keep his attention on the bronze."

I unwrapped the statue and Vincenzio set it on the low table that centered the chairs. I followed his lead and remained standing.

When Gallanos returned, he caught his breath and paused in the doorway. "It is lovely, is it not, professoré? The moment I saw it I believed it to be a work crafted with divine inspiration. Twenty imitations have I examined over the years, and not one got the wings right. But this . . . so graceful . . . so fluid . . . as if the artist had sculpted the wind itself. I've only one test of any meaning still to do."

A gentleman had come up behind him in the open doorway. He was taller than *il Padroné* and slimmer than Vincenzio, but equally imposing. His white doublet was embroidered in silver, the collar enclosing his long neck encrusted with pearls. A diamond fibula pinned a short satin cloak at one shoulder. A long nose and wide brow shaped an intelligent and well-proportioned face, if not one ravishingly handsome. Yet his visage glowed with purest wonder.

"Ah, Segnoré di Gallanos, I didn't imagine I'd see another work so superbly crafted so soon after the other."

Gallanos held back as the man in white knelt beside the marble-topped table and reached out a slender hand, ringed with a band of rubies. Closing his eyes, he drew those well-manicured fingers along Atladu's back and Dragonis's wing and held for a breathless moment. Even before opening his eyes again, his smile illuminated the room.

"After last night's disappointment, I dared not believe you. The other *looked* so fine. The merchant had convinced Fermi and me of its provenance with his tale of dodging Mercediare officials, outwitting smugglers, bribing caravans, but when I examined it closely . . . As I've said before, there are subtleties in design and crafting that uniquely identify the work of Antigoneas of Sysaline that are telltale to the fingers even more than the eye."

Laughing in pure delight, he rose, turning the statue, weighing it, lifting it to the light while examining every surface, every flaw. "Glorious. Everything I imagined. Ah, Alessandro, someday this could change our understanding of the world."

Reflecting his guest's pleasure, *il Padroné* extended his hand to Vincenzio and me. "These two are your benefactors, Your Grace. Professoré di Guelfi and his sister, Damizella Tarenah. Professoré, it is my privilege to introduce His Grace Eduardo di Corradini, grand duc of Riccia-by-the-sea."

I curtseyed deep and held position. Vincenzio had already dropped to one knee. He properly kept his head bowed, while I found it impossible to draw my gaze from the elegant young duc.

"It is our honor, Your Grace and Segnoré di Gallanos," said Vincenzio, so soft and hoarse I could almost not hear him.

The duc offered each of us a hand. As I kissed his jeweled ring, he said, "Professoré and my young lady, I am most grateful for your efforts to get this to my good friend Gallanos. I grieve with you for the loss of your father who recognized the virtue of this work, a treasure I've sought since my youth. You have my word that I will care for it, preserve it, value it, a wish *il Padroné* tells me you share. May you have great success in your future endeavors.

"And Alessandro"—when he turned to *il Padroné*, a great weight lifted from my shoulders—"such a gift for my birthday, a day that has never been of much pleasure to me. I am forever in your debt."

"It is my sincere delight, Your Grace."

The grand duc wrapped the bronze in its silk covering and nodded to the door. "Shall we show it to Fermi, *Padroné*? We can honor his diligence at searching for it, while laughing with him at those pitiful thieves who risked their lives to steal a counterfeit. You must be more discreet when offering a bounty for a work of art. Everyone knows that your purse is very well stocked and your generosity unmatched."

"As you wish, Your Grace."

Gallanos paused a moment as they turned to leave the room. "My man will be with you shortly to express my thanks more fully, professoré, damizella," he said. "As we agreed."

Then he took the grand duc's arm and strolled through the open doorway. "I'm afraid Boscetti is the one who comes out worst in this matter. That does not break my heart . . ."

In moments, a very large man of striking appearance joined us. Though his weathered face indicated he was no older than Vincenzio, his bristle of hair was purest white. Well armed and clad in expensive leathers, he closed the door and offered me a hand up.

Vincenzio remained on his knee, unmoving, as if lost in meditation. I nudged him, for the man held out a sizeable leather purse that clinked gloriously. "Attention, brother."

Vincenzio shook off his thoughts and leapt to his feet, startling the man when he overtopped his height.

"*Il Padroné*'s payment, as agreed." The man passed the purse to Vincenzio. "He thanks you for your efforts and believes your dealings are now concluded. As this bag is heavy and we've rogues in the neighborhood, I'd be pleased to offer you an escort to wherever you wish."

"We shall do very well on our own," said my brother, his customary assurance recovered, "though I thank you and offer my gratitude to *il Padroné*."

"At the least I'll show you out by a more discreet way than you arrived."

He guided us through a long passage of storage rooms and servants' quarters, past a kitchen courtyard to the gate where wagons and carts were lined up to be emptied by an army of servants.

"This exit is not meant as a slight, professoré, but a measure for your safety."

"We appreciate your care," said Vincenzio, offering his hand. "What is your name, sir?"

"Gigo, professoré. Segnoré di Gallanos's bodyguard."

"I am honored, Gigo. Good day, sir."

We left through the delivery gate and hiked briskly through the city. We were approaching the Cambio Gate when I finally broke the silence. "Vincenzio, were we not supposed to go up to the Academie to meet Laurent for lunch?"

My brother turned his face to the blue sky and bleated a laugh that sounded very like our mother's ram. "By the Sisters, you do get lost, don't you?"

He laid his hand on my cheek. "Ah, Scribe Romy, be careful what you ask me to do next time. If I'd run off to leap into the river as I would have preferred, I might have left you as Tarenah di Guelfi forever. And here we are rich, with our partners and your brother surely frantic by now!"

My steps faltered as the screen of Tarenah's perceptions was ripped away and the morning's events exploded in my memory with perfect clarity. Every image, every terror, every emotion, every question. *Romy's* perceptions and reactions had been waiting like a dammed river. The scent of leather-bound books. The coffee and pine bark smell of the man who had shaped my life. The powerful grace of Eduardo di Corradini's presence; the gleam of the ancient ring I had kissed—a modest silver band of rubies on his warm, elegant hand. The husky quiet of the duelist beside me as he knelt to Eduardo. The abiding question: How did the grand duc know the bronze was true?

I glanced up at the man holding me upright. The grief writ on him so clearly made it impossible to ask him the questions I ought. Like whether it was possible the grand duc of Riccia was a sorcerer. Like why our meeting with that same grand duc made him want to drown himself. Mercifully, he did not ask how it felt to see my portrait yet hanging in the Shadow Lord's private library. Sandro . . .

"I think we should buy some wine on our way back," I said.

"I support that entirely. A great deal of it."

And that we did.

20

Not only wine, but a plump goose, a wheel of Kairys cheese, fresh lettuces, and a pastry of green plums and raspberries arrived at Dumond's house with us. After an hour of feasting, toasts, and the tale of our morning, I emptied the purse in the middle of Vashti's table.

First, we dispersed repayment for the cost of our costumes, Placidio's discarded bow, and Dumond's expenses for metal, alchemical salts, and bribes. Vashti insisted on taking her customary payment for her needlework, rather than a share of the remainder.

"We couldn't have done it without you," I protested. "You certainly bore a share of the risk, as well offering us your wisdom and opening your larder." I poked at Neri, who had finished the last of the pastry and was returning to the half-devoured wheel of cheese.

Vashti was adamant. "My provision and my wisdom are available to any who enter my home. My small risk is my eternal pledge to Basha, which has no price. The four of you, though—your pledge to each other is your blood. It is that pledge must reap the prize of your deeds."

Her insistence imparted a proper solemnity as we counted out the four shares. How could we not sober when considering the dangers we'd faced and could still face?

What if Fermi brought in sniffers to investigate our escape from his palazzo? How long did traces of magic remain?

What would become of the counterfeit bronze? Dumond had destroyed the molds for the counterfeit, and believed the heat of the firing ovens would have destroyed any trace of magic on the false statue itself. But Boscetti would be enraged at the upending of his bargain with the Shadow Lord. Would he recognize some detail in the counterfeit that proved different from the statue he'd brought from Mercediare? What if he probed too deep?

And there was still Gilliette, a vicious, unpredictable child.

Vashti dropped four empty canvas bags on the table as I shoved equal stacks of coins to Placidio, Dumond, and Neri.

"We must be careful spending our pay." Vashti nudged a thoughtful Dumond.

"Indeed," he said, brightening as always when he looked at her, "but 'tis a certain boon to have a bit to put away for the girls."

Neri rolled his eyes when I raised a brow at him. "Yes, yes. I know. Extra silver spread around breeds curiosity. But what an adventure, right? Even without the coin? Racing down those steps, knowing you two were there hidden and Dumond ready to work us an escape, and that those *stronzi* couldn't possibly imagine how I could get away. By the Sisters, I'd do it again in an eyeblink!"

A shower of groans followed this pronouncement, and a mock strangling from Placidio that exposed wicked bruises about Neri's neck from his struggles with the Fermi guard. We filled our cups again.

Vashti tilted her head and fixed her gaze on Dumond.

"You'd work another scheme, Basha, wouldn't you, if another *worthy* matter rose? I've not seen you so lively since we birthed Aria and Enia."

"Pssh. I've a full tenday ahead of me, getting out work I've promised and delayed. Ask me after."

Which was not a *no*. My answer would not be *no*, either. After such an adventure, returning to a life of copying others' words held no particular charm.

"What of you, swordmaster?" I said. "If we were to come across another problem needed solving, one that our talents might address—a *worthy* matter, as wise Vashti says—would you be willing?"

"Only on conditions." Placidio drained his cup and leaned forward to wag a finger at my brother. "Observing Neri in a real fight tells me we've a deal of work to do. And you, lady scribe"— the finger shifted my way—"I'm guessing Dumond's daughters could place a thrown dagger better. So I would require you continue your lessons. Beyond that: I don't promise ever to dress up again, but my sword can always be had. Cheap."

He flashed his ever-brilliant grin, and smothered it again almost before one could note it.

"We're more like to see dangers from this scheme we've just worked than any future ones," Placidio continued. "Your message drop served us well. I was thinking to hire a box for myself to collect dueling solicitations. If Dumond did the same—and checked it regularly—we could keep each other apprised of rumor or inquiries, and ensure we're not seen in company more often than our professional relationships require."

"A fine suggestion," said Vashti and Dumond together. "How much to rent?"

Pleased, I shoved their offered coins away and drew a ring of small keys from the bag I'd brought from Lizard's Alley the previous day. "For you, no charge."

I pulled two keys from the ring and passed them on. "Number twelve for Placidio. Eighteen for Dumond and Vashti. Number six will remain my own. Anything else you *ever* need, anything within my power, you'll have it. Your help has saved my life and Neri's and likely many others'."

One more toast and Dumond left to fetch the children from one of Vashti's regular customers. Placidio collected his weapons from Dumond's shop and returned to don his own shabby cloak and scuffed cap, the black silk rose replaced by the scraggly grouse feathers. Neri helped Vashti wash cups, while I cleaned the paint from my face, washed the curls from my hair in one of Vashti's dye pots, and scrubbed in the blacking she said would keep my hair dark again until it grew out to its natural color.

Placidio, Neri, and I soon bade Vashti farewell and walked out together on the Ring Road. The bright afternoon had been devoured by thick gray clouds. Whether it was the oncoming night, the threatening rain, or a natural reaction to the afternoon's exuberance, we talked very little as we rounded the Beggars Ring.

My mind refused to relinquish the recent days' strange events. The bizarre visions when I touched the Antigonean bronze returned with shivering clarity. Knowing that I had been subsumed so deeply in Tarenah di Guelfi's invented mind that I needed a third hand to bring me out made my breath come short.

"Fesci's expecting me tonight." Neri broke our quiet as we neared the river. "Suppose I'd best give you this."

He chunked his heavy little bag in my hands.

"Who'd have thought I'd ever have my own stash?" He patted it fondly as I tucked it under the cloak Vashti had lent me. "And earned by doing what was forbid so long. *And* Romy the harridan approving it."

His spark illuminated the gloomy evening.

Placidio grunted. "It's still forbidden, cockwit."

"I know; I know."

"I've not told you two what's happened with my magic," I said.

"You forget, Romy-zha"—Placidio leaned his head down confidentially as we walked—"I was touching your face both times I spoke your name."

His face was exasperatingly impossible to see in the deepening gloom.

"What touching?" Bristling like a very young wolf, Neri stepped round in front of Placidio and me, blocking the path, his hand perilously close to his sword hilt.

"Don't be ridiculous, Neri." What made male creatures start preening their feathers around women—even their elder sisters—the moment they learned to fight?

"A magical touch . . . all as a part of the lady's plan, of course," said Placidio with a lustful growl. "Be off to your work, boy. I'll see she gets home safely with your *provisions*."

"Not until you tell me exactly what you mean. Romy?"

"Ignore the baiting, idiot-child," I said. "He's talking about our brother-sister playacting. I'll tell you everything when you get home. *Not* that my behavior is any of your business."

"And keep your fool hand away from that weapon when someone picks a scab," snapped Placidio. "Keep your mind engaged. Can either of you tell me how many beggars were sleeping in the alley we just passed? One could have been a thief and noticed that purse you passed. You each put the other at risk. *Two* climbs up the Boar's Teeth tomorrow. And for her on the next day."

"Always training," I said, once Neri had swallowed his humiliation and taken himself off.

"Don't want him cocky. It happens easy when you're coming down from your first combat—whatever kind it is. The fight doesn't stop. You feel invincible."

"I don't," I said. Our pace slowed as I explained how it had felt being Tarenah—and the strangeness after. "Magic is the only explanation," I said, "a deeper form of the story lies I've told. I need to understand how to control it, so if a friend's hand is not there, I can find myself again."

"It's no doubt you triggered magic. Both times I felt the clear relinquishing. 'Twasn't shocking or huge or ungainly either time. Fine, though. Can't say I've experienced much of anyone else's power, but I'm guessing you've still used only a part of what you've got."

"Not sure I want more."

"Certain, you do. You want to know all the aspects of your particular gift, as well as whatever else your body can make from the magic that lives in you—light, fire, healing maybe. Then you make the choice to use it or not. Control is the keystone. We'll talk more at your next lesson . . . after the fighting, of course. Get Neri to work with you. It'll make him think about such things without me beating on him about it. He's a good lad, but reckless. That'll kill him surer than any blade."

I might have been poised at the border of two worlds, speaking of such dread matters—of intentionally violating the First Law of Creation, while lamplight and the raucous music of pipes and tabors spilled from the Duck's Bone just up the Ring Road. My mundane scrivener's shop and the turning to Lizard's Alley lay just beyond the light.

"You've been good for Neri. Exactly what I'd hoped." I extended my hand. "Fortune's benefice, Professoré di Vasil. I can find my way home from here."

He refused my hand and made his mocking bow. "By Virtue's children, damizella, I shall not leave you before making sure no threat awaits—with all respect to your improving skills. This is a fraught night."

I wanted to kick him. But my determination to make my own way in the world must not make me stupid. Talking about risks did not dissolve them. "As you will."

The clouds had finally relinquished their burden and produced a steady rain. We strolled companionably down the Ring Road past the tavern and the dark shop. Placidio scouted the alley and the vicinity of the house, finding nothing suspicious. Once inside he waited, politely turning his back while I lit a lamp and stashed my money bag and Neri's.

"Now I'll take my leave," he said, once I'd told him all was well. "Seems I've an early call tomorrow."

"Peaceful night, swordmaster. Fortune's benefice."

"And Virtue's hand."

He retraced our path down the alley. I'd have sworn his dark shape grew larger with the distance. Such an odd man. So variable. So secretive. Perhaps a friend, I thought, which surprised me, as I'd never had one, nor imagined I ever would. Sandro, of course, had been something else, though I had always imagined friendship to be part of it. So sheltered, I had been. So naive, despite my harsh beginnings. I closed the door on the night.

As I unpacked my clothing bag, my keys fell out. Two days since I'd checked message box number one, which I used for common business. I'd given the number to several of my regular customers. I ought to look before I slept.

So I threw on my wet cape and whisked up the alley and around the corner. The cloudburst had ended as quickly as it had begun. Not bothering to open up the shop, I unlocked the box from the outside. No messages waited. As long as I was there, I opened number six, as well, not that anyone outside my circle knew of it, save the Commission on Public Artworks and its most prominent member.

A scrap of folded paper sat in the dark box. A shiver rushed down my back.

The outreach of light from the Duck's Bone revealed that there was nothing written on the scrap. It happened frequently that children stuck things in the slots, curious at the use of the row of boxes. But this paper was fine and clean.

Nerves aflame, I stared at the blank page as if it might speak.

"I couldn't decide what words to write. Not until I was sure."

I whirled about—voice useless, spirit shredded at his first intonation.

"Cataline, my glorious chimera."

21

He stepped from the deepest shadow, cloaked and hooded. But I didn't need to see his face to know him.

Sandro. In the moment of my mind's utterance, I knew I could not speak that name aloud. Not because he had forbidden it, but because doing so with him so near would be my undoing. No magical shield protected me either from his recognition or from the maelstrom that rose in my spirit—a storm of hatred, longing, lust, devotion, fury, hope, grief, betrayal. Was he testing me?

"There is no one here named Cataline, segnoré."

He closed the distance between us, until the scent of the coffee he so relished had my heart racing. "Had half a century passed since I saw you last, I would know you."

I blessed Vashti's insistence that I wash the red and the curls from my hair, and my Moon House tutors for teaching me outward composure despite terror wreaking havoc within. Sandro had certainly *not* recognized me when Tarenah di Guelfi walked into his house. I would have seen it. But had he learned something since?

"A year can bring many changes. I cannot imagine what half a century would do."

"Let's not spar," he said. "Not tonight."

Reason commanded I stay silent until I could set my mind to this moment. I dared not fail to consider every word, every implication. This man would condemn my brother, my friends, and even Dumond and Vashti's daughters to the Executioner of the Demon Tainted if he believed it necessary. He would take no pleasure in it, but he'd do it. He had let Neri live, but had given me fair warning. The message boxes had always been a risk.

He tipped his head to one side. His examination buzzed my skin like scurrying ants. "Will you walk with me? I know this is not easy."

He would not permit a refusal. Years of listening behind the painted screen had taught me every nuance of his speech, and certainly he could read me just as well. No matter what had brought him to this meeting, I had to control its progress and its outcome.

"Perhaps we could sit inside, *Padroné*. I've been out for a walk. My feet are tired and I'm chilled from the rain."

"Certainly, I've no wish to make you uncomfortable." Coolness had crept in. Good. Had he expected me to fall at his feet weeping? Waiting at the message boxes, he'd not likely seen me walking with Placidio.

I unlocked the shop and lit a small lamp on my writing table. If Neri walked past, he'd notice I had a visitor and, I hoped, stay at a discreet distance. No doubt the Shadow Lord's bodyguards, Gigo and Ettore, lurked nearby.

While I hung my sodden cape and scarf on a hook by the door and took Sandro's dripping cloak to hang beside it, he took quick inventory of the room: shelves laden with stacks of parchment, the jumble of uncleaned pens, empty flasks, half-eaten cheese, and half-written pages—the detritus of three hectic days.

"So this is your house?"

My hand offered one of the two stools.

"I work here," I said, taking the stool across the table from him. "Writing work for lawyers and private citizens. Even some for you."

I slid my copy of the city's latest regulations for fire buckets and sand reserves across the desk. "It's something of a family business."

It pleased me that neither anger nor bitterness tainted my reminder of the occasion that had changed everything. But the lamplight caught the recognition in his eye. As I expected, he reflected no discomfort. His judgment had been more than fair, considering the law, and that particular law was not in his power to change even if he wanted. Not yet.

"The occupation is useful and satisfying," I said.

"Evidently it suits. You look well. I'm glad for that."

The moment stretched uncomfortably.

"What brings you here, *Padroné*, if I'm permitted to ask?" It was not to review my health. "Are you considering a message box system for the rest of the city?"

No use avoiding the subject. Though perhaps we should have stayed outdoors. The weight of his presence in the small room was suffocating.

"Tarenah and Vincenzio di Guelfi. Are they friends of yours?"

No subterfuge in the question—no sarcasm. An encouraging

sign. But certainly a deep curiosity and a determination to satisfy it. That was the dangerous part. Distraction or subterfuge wouldn't work.

"They are recent customers of the shop who rented a box here—as you clearly know. Number six. I was checking to ensure they'd not received any stray messages, as they returned their key and left the city this afternoon. They told me they had completed their business with *very important people*. So that was *you?*"

He propped his arms on the table, hands folded, and leaned forward with easy intimacy. "They brought me the Antigonean bronze."

He had fooled many people with that ease.

"Truly?" I said. "After your long search? You must be very pleased. I'm happy for you and pray it serves as you hoped."

A slight hesitation in his breath.

Had I misstepped? Too quick to recall a matter we'd spoken of only a few times? Too familiar, speaking about his designs, caring about his hopes? Had he expected me to curse him?

"I do not wish you ill, *Padroné*. Many who have been privileged to hear of your vision for Cantagna pray for its fulfillment, no matter our personal circumstances."

"That is . . . gratifying." The slight rise of his brows signaled irony—the kind he often directed at himself. "So do you know where the brother and sister di Guelfi might be found? I've a question for them about the bronze."

"They had no plans to remain in the city. I know that. Nor to return here, I believe. They asked me to forward any messages to the Philosophic Academie in Varela." More than anything at that moment, I desired to ask what was his question, but I dared not demonstrate too much interest. "A question so urgent as to bring *il Padroné* into the Beggars Ring on a rainy night sounds worthy of a post messenger. You still have a few, I presume."

He smiled. Only a vision of my father's chopped hand and Neri's wrists tied to a stake in my house prevented it melting the desk between us.

"I'm here because I need answers from you, Romy of Lizard's Alley."

The world slipped nauseatingly askew at hearing that once beloved voice pronounce that once despised name. I stayed silent lest I spew out the remains of our victory feast, but I opened my hand in invitation for him to continue.

"I needed to see whose hand held the key to the message box numbered six. Until you opened it, I could not reconcile what I knew with what I've experienced, with what I've been told. With what I never in the least could have imagined until I started thinking about it. Once I allowed the possibilities . . ."

He settled back in the chair as if it were lined with velvet cushions. One hand cupped his chin, a long finger tapping his jaw, as ever when he was working out a complex problem. "The circumstances surrounding the statue have been curious. You may recall Merchant Boscetti, the antiquities dealer, who claimed to know its location?"

He waited for my nod before continuing.

"Boscetti chose to allow Rodrigo di Fermi's bid for the bronze to outweigh my multiple donations to his coffers. Rodrigo believed that the bronze would open the grand duc's ear to his grievances, especially those with me. I like to think Eduardo is a better man than to be swayed by a small-minded swindler, but Rodrigo can be very persuasive."

"But then . . . you said the *di Guelfis* brought you the bronze."

"Indeed. The strangeness began four days ago when the statue Fermi bought from Boscetti disappeared on the very same day my wife visited the Fermi house. Gigo and your Micola were accused of stealing it."

"They would never! No house could ask for two more loyal and honest servants."

Though I knew of the charge already, my horror was unfeigned. Had they been employed by a different segnoré, they could have died for such an accusation, no matter that the law required a magistrate to hear the case.

"My response was the same," Sandro said. "They both remain securely in my employ."

"I'm very glad to hear that." Especially for Micola. Gigo had been Sandro's servant since they were boys, and his bodyguard and indispensible right arm since they had come to manhood. No other servant, no matter how faithful and competent, would ever own the same regard.

"Matters grew stranger yet. Two days after the statue went missing, Professoré di Guelfi and his sister, bearing the most reputable credentials, brought several treasures before the Public Arts Commission, including a statue they believed to be the Antigonean bronze. Ah, it was gloriously beautiful! Dragonis's wings, Atladu's musculature . . . you could feel the life in them. And it was most certainly of the proper antiquity, if not the original, then perhaps a copy by the same sculptor."

I resisted the urge to either overdo my reactions in response to his or remain entirely reticent. Cataline had always been curious. "Strange indeed. Did they steal it from Fermi?"

"I was tempted to have them questioned, but the professoré was ill, and the sister . . ."

A long pause rattled my bones with cold shivers that had naught to do with damp hair or sodden shoes.

". . . she was so worried about her brother, so modest and yet so forthright in her admiration of him and her concern for her family's legacy."

He shook his head and laughed off his own bemusement. "You'll think I've tumbled into the swamps of sentiment! I offered to let her bring the statue to me when the brother was fit again."

By the Unseeable . . . the magic had truly hidden me from him. He had believed. Why did that realization draw tears from these eyes that had abjured them for so long? Fortunately Sandro was lost in his own thoughts long enough for me to blink them away.

"Certainly a risky choice to let it out of your sight," I ventured. "But, then, you're not easily duped."

"Mmm."

Despite the noncommittal response, his hands dropped to his lap, and he focused on me again, more settled in mind.

"The next curiosity occurred the following day when I had sunset coffee with Gilliette. She had taken to her bed since her outing to the Fermi house and the accusations that followed. Before I could tell her I was happy she felt well enough to join me, she blurted out that Paola di Boscetti had visited her that afternoon and reported that several of Paola's servants and neighbors would swear they had seen *you* lurking about Palazzo Fermi on the day of Gilliette's visit, the day the statue went missing."

"Me?"

"You and a younger man who resembled you closely."

My spine straightened as if I stood in a witness box before a judiciar of the Philosophic Confraternity. "And this would be four days ago from today, you said?"

"Yes."

"Would you like an account of the clients I visited on that day, *Padroné*, or those who visited me?" I erased every coloring of emotion save indignation from my voice. "I keep meticulous entries in my journal. And if the implication is that the 'young man' was my brother—who has been scrupulous in his adherence to your parole over the past year—and that somehow *we* were involved in the loss of this statue, you may query his employer at the Duck's Bone tavern as to his work hours on that day and evening. I'm not sure which is more insulting—the implication that Neri and I would violate our parole for *any* reason, or that we would be stupid enough to hand over the spoils of that violation to strangers so they could present them to the very man who holds our lives in his hand."

I was tempted to rise and offer him the door, but decided against, lest my jellied knees give way. *Stupid, stupid little wife.*

Sandro did not stir, nor did my cold fury rouse any hint of embarrassment in him. He had come down here in the middle of a rain shower. He'd no reason to believe I had stolen the statue. But he suspected something.

A twitch of his hand displayed unconcern. "There's no need for me to investigate your whereabouts on the word of Boscetti's wife. And I have never, nor will I ever, accuse you of stupidity. Or ill intent."

He paused just long enough for those last three words to make me blink.

"I told my wife that I did not heed rumors from the wives of those who attempt to cheat me *or* rumors that grow from . . . needless, childish frets. But then the story takes yet another turn. On that very night a group of—what shall I call them? Thieves or mercenaries, perhaps?—breached the walls of Palazzo Fermi and attempted to steal the *very* statue which had been reported lost! Though unsuccessful at removing it from the palazzo, they battled fiercely and escaped. Curiously, not one witness to that battle or that escape—not even Rodrigo di Fermi or the grand duc of Riccia-by-the-sea who observed the entire encounter—can tell me how those four got inside the walls or how they got out, unless it was by the personal intervention of Lady Fortune . . ."

Or by magic, he did *not* say, though the words hung in the air between us.

"So the bronze was at Palazzo Fermi all along," I said, discipline staving off dread. "Truly a cautionary against hasty judgments!"

His hands opened in acknowledgment. "Certainly someone inside Fermi's house could have taken it on the day of my wife's visit and hidden it away for these conspirators to fetch later, perhaps in hopes of forcing me into regrettable actions. I've given the whole business a great deal of thought since this morning— the strangest day of the four. At dawn my wife burst into my bedchamber full of apologies, insisting that the rumors of Mistress Cataline's presence had been disproven and that she prayed no harm had come of her reporting them and that she would absolutely never, ever let childish frets rule her judgment again. At mid-morn the di Guelfis returned as promised with their Antigonean bronze. Not an hour after that, Fermi and Boscetti arrived, preening, with *their* Antigonean bronze."

"A second one! And after all that, which statue was the true one?" The grand duc had been so certain, yet dread thundered so loud in my ears, I could scarce hear my own question.

"The two were very like. To this moment I could not pick out one from the other. But—as I began this tale—Professoré di Guelfi and his sister had brought the true one. Eduardo had insisted all these years that he would know it inerrantly, and so he did."

He leaned forward and widened his eyes in good humor, as if to tell me the latest story from his old groom Alfi—the silliest man I'd ever encountered. "I tested him three times, switching them around, and he always knew. Something about the curvature of the wings, he said, or the position of the god's feet—one of the characteristics of artworks attributed to Sysaline, which, as you know, I've always considered so subtle as to be suspect."

Was it possible Eduardo di Corradini didn't know what the touch of magic evoked from the statue? That was difficult to believe. But then, even the grand duc of Riccia-by-the-sea was subject to the First Law of Creation.

"Fermi must have been livid," I said. "And Boscetti . . ."

"Boscetti will not be plying his trade in Cantagna for at least fifty years, nor will he be able to grasp his artworks or his money to his satisfaction. Both his market license and his thumbs have been revoked."

"According to the law," I said, revolted at another reminder of bloody axes and mutilated flesh.

"According to the law. All else seems to have fallen out exceedingly well. My wife has promised to perfect her judgment. Rodrigo di Fermi insists that he was suspicious of any merchant who offered to violate a contract and was planning to serve Boscetti up to me once we had proper identification of the statue, and by the way, could he offer his support for the new theater I've been badgering the Sestorale to approve at their next meeting. And Eduardo will ride out tomorrow with a treasure he has yearned for since he was a young boy."

"Why is the grand duc so fixed on that particular artwork?" I said. "I know he is a scholarly man, but of all things, why that?"

It was likely not the proper time to satisfy my own curiosity, but somehow the quiet night . . . the pool of soft light . . . this wandering conversation that could be a dream for all its likelihood . . . put us outside of time. When would such a chance come again?

"A sad bit of history. I likely mentioned that the sculptor Antigoneas was said to create his art in the drowned kingdom . . ."

"At Atladu's forge in Sysaline. Yes."

"When Eduardo was a boy, his elder brother—a beloved elder brother—leapt to his death from the walls of their father's castle into the sea. From that night, Eduardo says, he has prayed for Sysaline to be real, thinking that perhaps his brother found his way to the city under the waves, rather than plummeting into the Great Abyss."

The Great Abyss where suicides and the unvirtuous were tormented by demons left from the Wars of Creation . . . or perhaps to a lonely abyss of the spirit torn by demons he could never quite escape.

"Very sad, indeed," I said, tucking away the story I had no right to know. "Thus, a satisfactory resolution for the grand duc and for you. Yet something nags at you."

Foolish to pry, perhaps, but he'd not have come here simply to tell me this story, as he would have in the days I awaited him on the far side of his closet. As if he had never declared me dead.

Alessandro di Gallanos, *il Padroné*, did not exempt himself from the consequences of his judgments.

"A number of things nag at me. Certainly the startling coincidence that the young professoré and his sister rented a message box from one Romy of Lizard's Alley. Most definitely the mystery of the thieves who invaded Palazzo Fermi so efficiently, fought bravely—and yet abandoned their prize so easily, while escaping in such inexplicable fashion. And then there is the incontrovertible fact that the false statue was made—or at least finished—*after* the di Guelfis appeared before the Commission on Public Artworks."

"How was that possible?" I blurted the question without thinking how bald it sounded. As if I'd been thinking about the matter for days. "I mean if it was hidden at Palazzo Fermi all along . . ."

"Have you something to drink, Mistress Romy? All this talking."

Something to drink? *Mother Gione come rescue me!*

"I have wine. Not the quality—"

"I care naught for the quality, only its existence."

Indeed his eyes sparked with the kind of excitement that made everything taste, feel, or sound brilliant. He was enjoying this conversation, which was not at all righteous.

Thank the Sisters I had a clean cup and a flask of the Duck's Bone's best. I poured him a swallow that emptied the flask and slammed the cup to the table in front of him, annoyed that he could be amused while I feared for my life.

He drank, and as distraction is wont to do, the activity revealed something more. As he focused on his cup, a trace of sadness doused the spark in his eyes, as sure as the lees followed the pungent liquid. Was it that I had displayed the same pique a thousand times in response to his teasing?

I dropped my gaze, unwilling to see more. "Go on, then."

"On the night I first met the di Guelfis I did something that would be unforgiveable in the eyes of an antiquarian," he said once I was seated again. "I wanted to ensure they brought back the exact statue I'd seen, so I marked it—a subtle scratch in the patina under Dragonis's wing—not deep enough to show bare metal, just enough I could identify it. And indeed the statue they brought that last morning—the bronze that the grand duc identified as authentic—bore that same scratch. But what challenged my imagining was that the forgery Fermi brought me—the one abandoned by the purported thief at Palazzo Fermi—displayed an identical scratch."

An added mark! I'd never even considered he'd do such a thing. And Dumond had not had time to catalogue the bronze's every detail before I whisked it out of his hands for our meeting with the Arts Commission, so he dutifully made sure that his forgery included every mark on the original. The forgery had to have been finished between the meeting of the Arts Commission and the "theft" at Palazzo Fermi. As it had been.

Every response that leapt to mind immediately declared itself false. Feigned. Unnatural.

The lamp sputtered and I busied my hands in feeding it. Even when that was done, I could not sit or speak. Perhaps keeping a distance from the light would prevent him observing my dismay at our mistake.

Sandro did not wait long to go on. "That forced me to give thought to the sequence of events. The only explanation that made sense was that our thieves did not go to Fermi's house to steal the statue, but to place the false one there. As neither Fermi nor Boscetti is subtle enough or inventive enough to arrange such an elaborate and fascinating invasion, and there were plenty of bloodied witnesses to demonstrate that the fighting was authentic, I am left with the question of who might actually be so subtle and inventive as to create such a scheme—and why."

I felt frozen in place. Sandro appeared not to notice, staring into the air, his brow creased as if he were only now worrying at the puzzle.

"Only a very few people in the world would understand what gifting the statue to Eduardo meant to me. Only a few would know what authenticating witnesses would be needed to place the true statue in a stranger's hand rather than in my house— where I had shouted my sworn word it was not. Only a few would know what sources I would trust for recommendations of a young professoré of history. And only one among all of those might have the . . . resources . . . to create a miraculous breach in Palazzo Fermi to deposit so exact a replica, ensuring that those trying to destroy me gained no benefit from their treachery. That's why I had to see who held the key to the di Guelfis' message drop in the Beggars Ring."

After such clear indictment, I should have been trembling with fear, but all I felt was the anger of a cat who had chased the dangling string too many times.

"A very pretty explanation you've devised, *Padroné*. But how could I possibly know anything of Boscetti's treachery or Fermi's weaseling? How could I know that simple possession of the statue could compromise your sworn word?" I spread my arms to encompass my little shop in the heart of the Beggars Ring. "Do you recall that I am no longer in your confidence?"

"Certainly there is no forgetting where Lady Fortune has taken us."

All jest, all excitement fled for that moment. Then with a subtle movement of neck and shoulder, as if adjusting the weight of a heavy cloak, he shook it off and blew an exasperated breath.

"Thus, some few hours ago, I put those very questions to my young wife, telling her that she should consider her suite as her prison cell until she told me a story I would believe about the day she lunched at Palazzo Fermi. My demand reaped much fuss and much crying and much pouting, countered by some severe words, some absence, and interminable reassurance, but eventually she confessed her sin. She even convinced me that she took the statue in hopes of doing me a service! That, and the fact she recognized on her own that contradiction of my sworn word was not only a serious, but a dangerous matter for the both of us, kept me from sending her back to her father. Certain parts of her actions—the threats to my servants and to a person I had made very clear was forever beyond her reach—are difficult to forgive, but overall I think we shall have a far better understanding in the future."

I was mute, in retreat, my back flattened to the wall. He had figured out everything, save who my *resources* were. And how difficult would it be for him to track them down?

"You could sit." It was a suggestion, kindly spoken. "If I planned to arrest you, we would not be here. If I wished to slay you, you would be dead."

"Then why?" My constricted throat scarce yielded the question.

"First, to inform you that on the next Quarter Day, you will be notified that your brother's parole is satisfied. Second, to express my gratitude and my awe. Not one person I spoke to had an inkling of what actually transpired these few days. Nor would I, save for the natural mistrust that made me mark the di Guelfis' statue. Those two—I don't know where you found them, but they were so very convincing, I doubted my own suspicions. Beatrice wants me to invite them back next year to tell us what antiquities they've discovered in the Hylides."

"Gratitude," I repeated, stupidly. "Awe." And Neri free. I needed to slap the exhaustion from my cheeks. He had not spoken the word *sorcery,* but he knew.

"You have opened my eyes," he said, as serious now as on the night he declared me dead. "I know you as well as I know anyone who walks this earth. I know you are entirely human and no spawn of monsters. So I come to my third reason for being here. Last evening up in our northern territories—entirely unrelated to bronze statues and the aspirations of a sometimes-wise-sometimes-foolish banker—servants of the Mercediaran Protector Vizio accused one of their countrymen of being an infamous spy who goes by the name *Cinque.* Our authorities in the region were required by treaty to arrest the man. That same treaty requires that we turn the spy over to the Mercediaran ambassador here in Cantagna within twenty days."

Over the next quarter hour, Sandro told me of the impossible situation surrounding the spy's arrest. He spoke of unbreakable treaties, unbreachable prisons, the straitlaced Mercediaran ambassador, and a certain document he believed this Cinque possessed that the ambassador would certainly wrest from him. When he finished the tale, he sat back and waited for me to answer.

Breathless with the import of his acknowledgment, I could not ignore the significance of his telling me of his dilemma. Even so, even alone with him, I was not ready to lay bare my secrets.

"So you wish those who worked this scheme to get the Antigonean bronze to its proper owner to ensure the spy's information never falls into the hands of the Protector of Mercediare?" The ambassador's thuggish employer was Cantagna's most dangerous enemy.

"I cannot ask, command, or coerce anyone to devise such a plan," he said, "nor could I come to the defense of anyone caught doing so. Mercediare would deem the slightest hint of my involvement an invitation to destroy Cantagna."

His own distancing proved my instincts right. Sorcery was and would ever be a barrier between us. Yet my head spun at such a reversal of expectation—that he would ask for help and believe I could provide it. And to my astonishment . . . and relish . . . ideas for how to accomplish the deed sprouted like blades of grass in spring. The others had said they were willing to go again for the right cause. This was just so much sooner than we had imagined.

"The information this man Cinque carries is truly dangerous?"

"I've never met Cinque, but I've had dealings with him. If the Protector gets hold of this document, her campaign of vengeance and assassination would fall directly on Cantagna, Cuarona, and Varela. The only way Cantagna could survive would be to summon Eduardo to honor our alliance, plunging the whole of the Costa Drago into war for a generation."

A generation of war would send Cantagna back to the ages of poverty and corruption that had followed the plague years. Thousands would die, along with all our dreams of enlightenment.

"Those involved would be paid, of course," he continued, "certainly not enough to offset the value of their service or their risks, which are incalculable, but at a rate on par with that of retrieving the Antigonean bronze. What do you think?"

Courtesans are educated in many arts, trained in scheming, dissembling, and disguise, and they are nourished with tales of intrigue and the satisfactions of playing a part well. It was made clear that personal happiness had no role in their future. I had been gifted with far more personal happiness than I could have expected, but a different future awaited me now—a future of my own devising—a freedom I relished.

I had already chosen to accept the risks of using magic for good purpose. But I knew the price if I was to accept those risks directly from the Shadow Lord. Whatever embers this meeting might revive in either of us could never be allowed to take fire. Our break had to be complete and permanent. The sooner, the better.

"I, of course, have no interest in political matters." I rose from the chair and fetched his cloak. "How could I—the daughter of a thief, a onetime Moon House pleasure girl who scrapes out a living copying other people's words? But message box number six has been claimed only this evening by someone who expressed interest in providing discreet services. I'll pass on what you've said and advise the renter to notify you directly—and discreetly—of interest in your offer. I would advise you to settle on a safe, easily accessible cache where the renter can leave messages for *you*. From that point, of course, my involvement is at an end, as long as my new renter pays my fee."

"No one should contact me. Ever. But a discreet message could be directed to a trusted advisor—my consigliere. You know Mantegna and how he works. You could pass that information on to your customers."

"Indeed so."

Long graceful fingers accepted his cloak. My gaze lingered on them, devouring them.

"I appreciate your aid in passing on the mention of my need. Of course, no blame shall be laid to *any* party, if that need cannot be satisfied. It is a thorny problem."

A swirl of black cloak and hood enveloped my visitor, so I could raise my eyes again without looking on his face.

"Tell me, mistress, how will Mantegna know that a communication is from the renter of box number six?"

"It will be marked with the name . . . Chimera," I said. What better name than the impossible made flesh?

"Very well." Words as cool as autumn midnight, but even through the enveloping cloak, I felt the warmth of his pleasure. "Chimera it is."

I shuttered the lamp and pulled open the door. There were no lights anywhere. Even the Duck's Bone torches were doused.

He paused at the threshold. "Goodbye, Mistress Romy of Lizard's Alley. Fare thee well in *all* thy future endeavors."

I dipped my knee, as was proper. "Blessings of the Twin Sisters, *Padroné*. May your dreams of enlightenment bring glory to your city."

The rainy night swallowed him, and with him, the life that

had never truly belonged to me. For better or worse, I was free. And his last gift was an open door.

After a few quiet moments, I called softly, "Safe to come in."

A cold, soggy, slim body squeezed past me, and as the rainy night deepened, Neri and I gave thought to spies and secrets and unbreachable prisons.

Acknowledgments

Many thanks to hand out. To the word posse that keeps me honest: Susan, Satchyn, Courtney, Curt, Brian-1, and Brian-2. To the Writers of the Hand for focus, friendship, laughs, and don't forget the wine and chocolate. To Mike and the other staff of the Hand for providing a writing home away from home. To Brenda, always and ever sharing beauty with those fortunate enough to be in her orbit. To Lucienne for believing. To Lindsey for deep reading. And most especially to the Exceptional Spouse for his infinite patience and everything else.

About the Author

Cate Glass is a writer of fantasy adventure novels. She also dabbles from time to time in epic fantasy and short fiction. For more information, check out categlass.com or follow her on Twitter @Cbergwriter.